CHAOS BETWEEN

BOOK ONE

MERCY

AND

MALICE

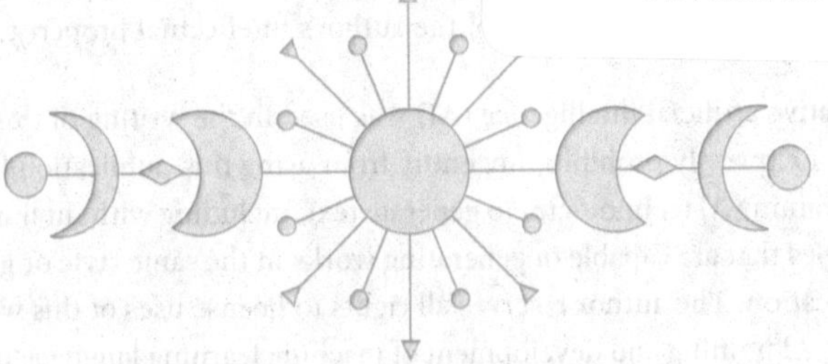

TAYLOR GOODE

Book Garden
PUBLISHING

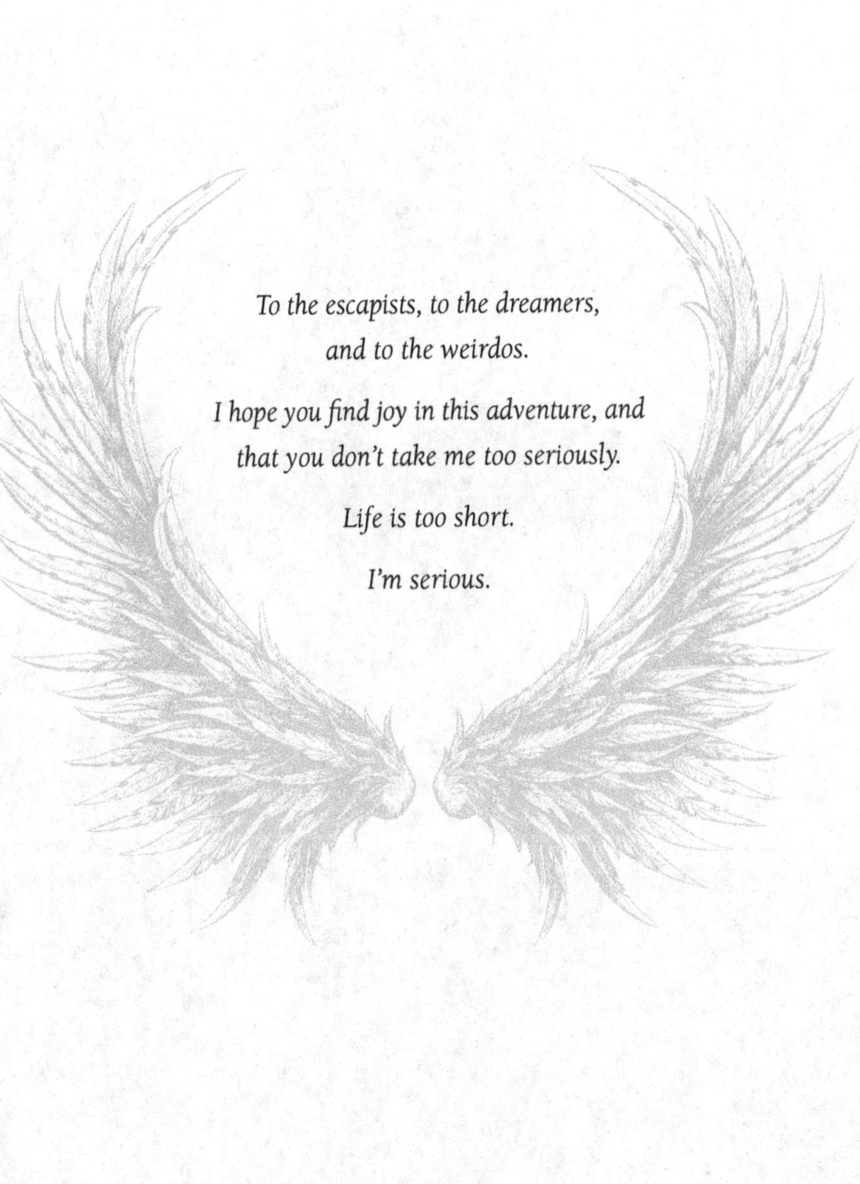

To the escapists, to the dreamers,
and to the weirdos.

I hope you find joy in this adventure, and
that you don't take me too seriously.

Life is too short.

I'm serious.

1

All I'd wanted was my first kiss.

Instead, I almost killed the poor bastard.

Attending my first party. Socializing with strangers. Those all seemed like simple enough tasks. Typical even for a Saturday night in Haverwick, where not much else happened. Peter, the cute guy in the graphic-tee that fit above his belt at an awkward length, was the one who invited me. I barely knew him but from what little I did, he might've been a doormat.

His guests—or *friends*—treated his house with shockingly little regard. Empty cans had accumulated on the floor, avoiding the trash's convenient functions. Some smoked in carpeted rooms as if it were their own, leaving pungent trails there as well.

I was beginning to think I hadn't missed much in my years of solitude.

Not when humans were so… *ick*.

Aside from their blatant rudeness, everyone seemed to love Peter's company; shouting his name as he passed, grabbing his hand or shoulder in boisterous greetings. I wasn't surprised, though. His friendly personality had drawn me in too. I still don't know why he'd asked me—the friendless weirdo working at a potions shop—to come.

My stomach tightened when I remembered the stupid note I'd left for my aunt. I kept telling myself there was no reason to feel guilty. What twenty-year-old had to sneak out?

Twenty-*one*. It was my birthday after all.

"Want something to drink?"

Peter had been bombarded since I arrived, so his sudden attention caught me off-guard. I did my best to not appear anxious and forced a confused smile.

He leaned in close to repeat himself over the noise. "A drink! Want one?"

His shirt smelled like it had just left the men's department store with all the suits and leather. Did every cute guy smell as good or was Peter's cologne godsent?

Oh, shit. I forgot he'd asked me a question.

"Water?" I said, forgetting what other beverages existed.

Peter grinned, and my heart fluttered like it had sprouted wings. That, or I was dying.

I followed him into the kitchen. After the third bump of my shoulder, I forced my arms down to my sides. *Don't panic.* There had to be some open space, somewhere. I questioned the legality of having that many people together in one room. Perspiration glittered on their brows from dancing and their heat fogged up the windows.

Again. *Ick.*

Peter avoided the long table of various bottles and cans in his kitchen to grab water from the fridge. A couple of girls with red cups giggled in our direction. Should I have just accepted the drinks everyone else had?

"I feel bad," Peter said, "You look uncomfortable."

Just worried about getting everyone killed.

I shook my head. "It's just loud."

"What's a normal Saturday night for you?" he asked.

"Pouring wax," I said, cringing a little, "Sometimes watching really old sitcoms. There's usually food."

"Wax, huh?" Peter snorted, which turned into a genuine laugh, and he pointed to the black material that molded around my fingers. "Is that what the gloves are for?"

I wore gloves to prevent the *bad* things from happening.

As long as I didn't touch anyone with my bare hands, everything was fine. I only had a vague memory of it ever happening, but the stranger's face, blue and twisting in shock, left an imprint in my mind. A repressed memory from my childhood.

I didn't tell him any of that. "Ah, no. I just have cold hands."

A lie but no one questioned me about it when I gave them that answer.

"Candles and brews…" He paused, tapping his chin as if deep in thought. "I'm starting to think the rumors about you two being witches are true."

"That's just my aunt."

Peter laughed again, but I was serious.

"She's protective of you, huh? Homeschooled?" he asked.

I nodded. "Sometimes it's nice, but I'll always wonder what it could've been like with—"

Friends.

"—more."

"I get that. We make the best with what we got, right? So, what would you like to do with your freedom tonight?"

Honestly, I could've kept talking with Peter, but I feigned interest in meeting his friends. Some of them I recognized from the shop. I couldn't remember their names, even seconds after getting introduced. There had to be at least three Joshes, and after that, I gave up.

I didn't want to assume but I felt weird looks from all of them. Their eyes lingered everywhere *but* my face. I didn't think I'd dressed too outlandish, just jeans and a top like most people, but apparently it was all wrong. Girls stared too like I'd deeply offended them by breathing the same air.

There was no way they knew what I was…

Right?

After an hour, or maybe twenty minutes, I felt fatigued. Mentally. How could anyone handle gatherings of that magnitude for long? No one in that house possessed any supernatural genes that spared them from needing regular rest. I was in a room full of mortal masochists.

Peter's hand suddenly rested on my hip and my eyes widened.

"Need a break?" he asked. "My room's quiet. I-I promise I'm not suggesting anything else."

My blood felt hot. He'd been a gentleman so far but if he stole a kiss, I wouldn't have minded. Hell, I would've given it to him. That "first" milestone had sat pending for too long and was becoming a real burden.

We did our best not to catch anyone's attention as we headed upstairs. He sped up when someone said his name, dragging me along by my gloved hand. Seeing him so comfortable with the smallest touches made me feel good. Adored even.

Normal.

Peter welcomed me into his room. Considering the exciting life he had, his room left little to the imagination. Dark walls, a bookshelf, solid colored bedding, and a drawer with an unfolded shirt sitting on top.

"We're safe," he said, "Sorry, I didn't clean today."

"It's cleaner than my whole apartment," I said. With nowhere else to sit, I hovered over the edge of his bed. "Thanks. This has been fun."

"Don't lie." He plopped down next to me with minimal hesitation. "I should've asked you to dinner, not thrown you into the lion's den."

I covered my warm cheeks with my hands. Blushing? Seriously? As if I needed to appear *more* sheltered and awkward. A few sweet words and my body went into a panic. "It's okay. You don't really know me."

Peter gave me a crooked smile. "The first time my friends and I saw you, we thought you were really cute. They dared me over and over to get your number. I finally did after I quit being a chicken."

"You? You're so natural around people."

He shrugged and webbed his fingers together. "Don't tell anyone, but I'd rather be home alone with a pizza and maybe a movie. Your nights sound nicer than mine."

I didn't believe that for a second, but then I saw tiredness weighing down on his eyes.

"I wish I could invite you over some time, but my aunt…" I stopped and chewed my lip. Any excuse I came up with would sound lame.

"What's up with that anyway? Are you secretly a celebrity? A criminal?" He emphasized that last bit as a tease.

Haha.

"She doesn't like people," I said.

"What about you?"

"Me?"

"Yeah. Is living with her what you want?" he asked, "Or would you rather see what else is out there?"

I felt him turning to face me better. His arm positioned itself behind my back, hand pressing into the mattress. We were so close. Normally, I would've freaked out, knowing I needed to keep my distance, but I didn't want to. I liked being near him.

"I don't know if I should," I said.

"What's that mean?"

"I don't know."

When I chuckled, he laughed too. Peter's eyes took a slow tour about my face. "This is a dumb question, but you're aware of how pretty you are, right? Like, way out of my league."

"League?" I asked.

"It's the hotness hierarchy."

"Oh. That's stupid."

Stupid and totally human. I didn't mind the compliments, though. It made the butterflies in my chest speed up and hit the walls. My aunt never belittled me but rarely commented on my appearance in any way. So, this was nice.

"It's stupid, but it's real," he said, "Look. I'm nervous around you."

Peter lifted his shaking hand for me to see. I couldn't help but snort at his demonstration, adorable as it was. "Now you're really being silly," I said.

"Damn. Maybe you'll believe me one day." The way he said that like we'd see each other again made the mood melancholy. For me, anyway; knowing that might never happen.

"Maybe one day," I repeated.

"Thanks for braving tonight," he said, "It's cool finally hanging out with the mystery girl."

"Is that my big selling point?"

His eyes dropped to my lips, and my heart stopped. "One of them. What do you think of *me* after meeting my friends?"

"They're… pleasant." I couldn't focus on anything with his face getting closer with every breath. "Especially the one with the third nipple. He told me many times."

"Yeah, Josh is pretty proud of that."

What would Peter think if he found out my only friend was my aunt? And the cats. They were technically strays that ate at our house, but they were the only company she allowed.

"I think you're a nice person," I said, and avoided bringing up the cats.

Peter sat quietly for a moment. Something about the seconds of promise ticking by thrilled me. His eyelids dropped about halfway as he examined my face some more. The fateful moment had arrived.

What the hell was I supposed to do next?

I didn't know if relationships were even realistic for me. Any semblance of a dating life would have to take place after my aunt fell asleep. Peter might not enjoy that. He could find a normal girl with parents who'd adore him. But I wanted to be selfish.

That's what demons were good at, after all.

Just once, I wanted to give in to my inherited sin. People sinned all the time. What was the worst that could happen? I turned my head, hoping to give him some sort of signal. Would he hate kissing me since I wasn't experienced? My bravery took a backseat and I could hear Hell roaring with laughter.

Everything changed when Peter brought himself in. He kept our lips from touching, just barely. I stopped breathing but forced myself to close the half inch from him. His lips were soft and warm, like sweet tea on a sunny day.

I migrated deeper into him, pushing against his face to feel more of his lips. Peter responded by sliding his hand up my thigh and stopping at my hip again. *Holy crap.* My skin begged for attention too with pestering little tingles. I didn't even know how or what to ask for. Asking for anything sounded too stressful, but Peter acted like he understood what I wanted better than I did.

The hem of my shirt lifted, and he explored my flesh with all five fingertips. The tickling should've had me kicking like a rabbit, but I endured the pleasant torture. Peter's next kiss delivered a hunger less timid than the last. To avoid breaking my neck backward from the force, I held his shoulders with my, still gloved, hands.

I couldn't tell if my lips moved correctly, or if they had at all. When his wet tongue glided across my mouth, my eyes popped open. I knew people kissed that way but… *holy.* His mouth tasted like the peppermint candies we'd eat during the holidays.

Peter grew more aggressive with each following kiss. The heat I felt building from his core warmed my toes and numbed my brain. We kept going until my lips felt raw. When I pulled away, gasping for air, he dove back in like fish deprived of water.

Should it have been that intense with someone I barely knew?

The thrill of the moment turned my concerns fuzzy, but didn't dispel them completely. Somehow, I ended up on top of him. He pulled me down against his chest with all his human strength. His tantalizing hands felt for my shirt again and lifted higher that time in some urgent race.

A wave of unease crept to the shore, and I almost stopped everything. The idea of being in only a bra made me want to hide, but Peter's feverish desires pushed the insecurities away. Everywhere he gripped, more sparks blossomed. Maybe my hesitations came from trying something new? I let him pull the fabric off and toss it to the side.

It was incredible, like finally being bold enough to bite the forbidden fruit. The longer we kissed, the more energized I felt, which seemed backward considering how much we were moving. All awkwardness from the party be damned. I could've taken on a hundred parties with hundreds more people. Maybe, I'd even go home that night and tell Naomi I wanted to change my life.

Why had I waited so long to *feel* someone?

That answer reared its ugly head when Peter's sudden cough shook me from my fantasy.

"Is this too much?" I asked, raising myself away from him, "Peter?"

His eyes were wide. I felt him going rigid beneath me. His hands curled into fists, no longer touching me. My insides turned to ice. The heat of the moment frosted over in seconds.

"Peter?" I waited for a response.

None came.

I removed myself and dropped my ear to his lips. No airflow. I pushed hard on his chest with both hands. "Peter? Come on..."

Had he been deathly allergic to something? Cats? I had no degree in romance but *dying* didn't seem like a normal response to intimacy.

This was my fault.

Had to be.

But my gloves never came off. I took my stupid medicine, that tastes like dirt and hot dog water, like I did everyday. Everything I could do to prevent myself from harming him, or anyone, I did!

Naomi warned me about being close to humans.

Demons hurt people. I was stronger in ways I didn't fully understand. All she ever said was "no." Don't seek it. Don't acknowledge it. Don't act on it. But accidents were common, especially for a half-demon who grew up with a witch mother.

Only half, but apparently it was just enough damnation to require my own set of rules. Wear gloves, take medicine, and stay a safe distance from others. That was all I had to do, and still I'd screwed up. Big time.

My crimes wouldn't be taken lightly by our angel-run government. Even if Peter survived. That was why my aunt had chosen Haverwick as our hiding spot and tried living as *humanly* as possible. I was in deep, stinking *shi—*

Peter's sudden sharp gasp flooded me with relief.

"Peter! Thank gods," I laugh-cried, looking more manic by the second. His blue eyes shut halfway, still unable to focus on me. I frantically searched the room for my phone. *Shit.* Of course, it died. I chucked the blank screen away. Where had Peter put his phone? I felt his pockets and searched his dresser. Nothing.

The house had been filled with guests but when I shouted for help, no one came. Music still played from the living room below. Someone had to be around.

I rolled Peter onto his side. "Wait here and don't you dare die!"

Peter responded by twitching like a fish on dry land. Still in a bra, I snatched a flannel that hung from the doorknob before bolting out of the room.

How long did I have until a reaper showed up?

Peter was alive so I hoped they wouldn't come, but I'd heard that reapers worked efficiently. Something about making a swift end to our suffering. Very few encounters had ever been reported involving reapers. They appeared silently, like smoke through the cracks in your door, wore masks of bone, and carried their signature scythe.

I don't know who decided a scythe through the chest was merciful, but I guess it beat living inside a rotting corpse, trapped in a skeletal prison of torment forever.

Gods… The morbid thoughts rushed through my brain as I scrambled down the stairs. Peter's flannel that I had stolen remained unbuttoned all the way down. I didn't care. All of his friends had phones. I witnessed plenty of them taking videos of themselves earlier.

My heart pounded in my ears. Had the party gone eerily silent? Would they assume I'd hurt Peter on purpose? I managed to get one of the buttons of the shirt closed after reaching the last step. The lack of bodies in the living room did nothing for my nerves or Peter's mortality.

"Someone?" I tried again. "We need to call an ambulance!"

Where the hell had they gone?

Tipped-over beer cans and soda bottles still littered the floor. I crunched pretzel crumbs beneath my shoes, amongst other snack residues. Some of the furniture had been knocked over and books were thrown from their perches. But no guests. Had I scared them away with my yelling?

Some friends, Peter. Not like I had any to compare to.

Then, faint screams came from the front yard. No one should've been shrieking in terror at a party. However, a full moon had taken over the sky. A lot of weirdness happened during full moons. Could a rogue werewolf have crashed? Possible. Technically, a demon—*me*—had crashed the party too.

The front door creaked, hanging partly ajar. Blood painted the white porch in red streaks. Had some drunken idiot cut himself or had my werewolf theory been correct? Half scared, and half annoyed, I stormed out to find someone.

A looming shadow made from thick clouds cast itself over the little town of Haverwick. Still, I spotted Peter's many guests. All of them either stumbled in the dark or ran down the street like their lives depended on it.

It took me a second to locate the source of everyone's distress. A large figure hunched over the curb, making sharp, jerking movements as it struggled to stand. Even from the poor angle I had from where I stood, I could see inhuman features about it.

Then, I smelled it. The heavy mixture of burning stone, iron, and rotting meat.

Magic and death.

When the enigmatic mass lifted its head I gasped at what hid beneath the mop of peppery hair. It wasn't human but… humans. Three faces melded into one enormous head. Limbs were scattered about its body like a spider manifested from a nightmare. A fat jade ring rested on a single pale finger that stood out from the fleshy masses.

Its swollen head hung heavily from its shoulders, barely able to lift in my direction. Each of its six eyes emitted a haunting, white glow. Gargled growls escaped through its many mouths. Blood had already stained its teeth. Whose blood?

My jaw snapped shut when I found one of the Joshes I'd met earlier. Not all of him, though, only pieces, and a red smear on the sidewalk.

2

The monster pushed itself off the ground and rammed into a parked car. An alarm wailed upon impact and drowned the distressed shrieks that ran further away from the house. It bounded after the straggler, each powerful step clumsy from dragging every limb at once.

Two of Peter's friends hid behind a parked truck instead of running. They taunted the thing with some flimsy wood planks they found in the truck's bed. Idiots. I'd already planned my return to the house, with weighty furniture pieces to barricade the door.

Then I heard the monster reach their car.

The boys hollered like they were watching a sporting event. With one swoop of its arm, the monster rolled the truck. It crushed the car next to it and exposed the guys hiding beneath it.

Time slowed as their impending doom played before my eyes. If I did anything inhuman to stop the monster, someone could report me. I hoped they wouldn't since I rescued them, but it was still a risk. My aunt's efforts to keep us hidden would go up in smoke. I'd only met Peter the other day. He could want to report me too. All it took was one human witness against a demon.

I should've run and never looked back.

"Hey!"

But I'm an idiot too.

The monster turned at my voice. *Oh, gods.* So much regret. It all seemed so heroic in my head, but now? Dead. I was dead. If I could hold it off until help arrived, I could save Peter's obnoxious friends. Hopefully, that didn't mean giving up my life.

Even as a demon, I couldn't predict my chances against that thing. I'd never fought anything like it in my life. The dummies in our apartment that my aunt practiced on, or the one time I had to fend off a curious vampire, hardly counted.

The monster's neck looked too thick for decapitation. Not like I had a weapon, or stomach, to do so. Barbaric, I know, but head removals worked as a universal method of killing. I didn't make the rules. Life and Death seemed to enjoy brutality.

The boys in the truck began shouting and banging on the turned over car. If they were surprised by my boldness, I felt the same. Their attempt at a distraction worked for maybe a second, but the human spider-monster came at me at a speed I hadn't expected.

I fled toward the black asphalt just as four of its six arms came down hard. Before I got pounded into wine, I dove to the side. My gloves saved me from shredding my palms. It stumbled around like a toddler before but seemed to have gotten faster.

Small craters imprinted the ground where I'd been standing.

"Call for help!" I snapped at boys and ran.

The monster followed. I could feel its heavy stomps shaking us like an earthquake. *Too close.* Something hard came swinging at my side. My body flew into someone's car, and my back cracked their windshield.

"*Fuck...*" I rolled off the hood, catching myself before face-planting on the cement. A crippling pain spread around the area of my tailbone. Something cold and wet clung to Peter's flannel. I must've been bleeding.

I needed to heal. *Soon*. Real soon.

Most supernaturals could cure themselves rapidly, but I'd never endured such injuries before. Only minor cuts and bruises. I had no timeline for reference.

When I stood, a colossal shadow fell over me. The thing gnashed its teeth while strings of drool dripped through the crevices of its chapped lips. It took a wide swipe at me with one of its beefy arms.

The mass hit like a bus. I caught the moving limb with my hands, but my body screamed in pain. My knees buckled under the weight. Using all my strength, I restrained its meaty hand from pulling back for another blow. Sadly, he had more limbs to go around.

It brought up two more, and I just watched. I imagined the pain of broken bones and a crushed skull. Supernatural healing didn't mean anything if I had no functioning brain left. If reapers were watching, I prayed they'd take my soul quickly so I could avoid the agony.

But I doubted they would take an undying person. So I called internally to any deity that would hear me out. Good or bad.

Something answered.

My blood boiled like I'd summoned Hell in my veins. I looked up into the creature's gnashing teeth and a second later, a black shroud bursting with golden fire covered me. Each flame tore free from the mass, consuming my vision and eating away at the monster. With no clue where it came from or what, I knew I had to release the erratic power before it consumed me too.

Shrieks, like nails on a chalkboard, scratched my ears, but I couldn't see beyond the darkness. I blacked out, only for a second, before waking up flat on the cold gravel. Long strands of copper hair spilled across my throbbing head like rivers of blood. Every one of my bones creaked as I sat up.

I had done some strange things in the past, but *that*?

That was new.

Had it actually been me? Someone could have cast a spell somewhere nearby. The ghostly, black mist returned to my body, disappearing through my pores. My arms burned red before softening again, taking the heat and chaos with it. Even more concerning were my veins that glowed white beneath the fleshy surface.

When I saw my three-headed attacker at my feet, I gasped.

It didn't move. Streaks of glowing lights etched a spiderweb into its charred skin. I lifted my ankle and nudged it with the tip of my shoe. One of the three faces crumbled into a dust pile of bones and teeth. I trembled and covered my mouth to avoid inhaling the ash.

What had I done?

I searched for any remnants of the mysterious power. It saved my life, but if it happened again, would *I* turn into a crisp? The monster had been barbecued. Why had it been there in the first place? Something that hideous had to have a demon or witch nearby calling the shots.

The creature stirred.

My breathing became strangled. The remaining half that hadn't disintegrated fought to piece itself back together, like two worms wriggling through dirt, except the dirt was ash of its own flesh.

Another set of eyes watched me from across the street. Someone stood in a dark hooded jacket that tapered out like a cloak. He was still, not racing in desperation to get help. Instead, he lifted a pale hand. A black knife extended his reach. He rotated his wrist like opening an invisible door and twisted his weapon into it.

Broken body parts from the creatures reacted to his movements. Its two remaining mouths hissed and groaned as its faces were dragged back toward the stranger's feet by an invisible force.

My ass remained cemented to the spot while I shook like a leaf. The smell of magic in the air became unbearable.

I kept my eyes on the hooded man and slid backward on my palms. His head jerked upward, revealing a pair of eyes that reminded me of orange and red fire. They refused to blink, unsettling me further.

His first steps toward me started slow but when I flipped myself over, the sound of his heavy boots picked up into a sprint across the road. I grasped the side of the car, prepared to use it as a shield. The pain in my side made me think I had a cracked rib, or two, adding to my negative odds.

Was he a powerful sorcerer? A demon? Cultist?

I couldn't think of a reason why he needed to get to me, except to finish what the monster started. Maybe he didn't like witnesses. I clutched my side, feeling the soreness of my body trying to heal while I pushed myself forward. Could my power save me a second time? If I even knew how to conjure it again.

The stranger's hasty movements came to an abrupt halt. I dared to look back, confused by the silence, but he'd vanished. The monster pile had gone as well. I let out a breath that stabbed my lungs. Flashing lights and loud sirens approached from down the street, along with black cars marked with a halo that encapsulated a single angel wing.

Help had finally arrived.

Peacekeepers.

3

They parked hastily in all directions, blocking my escape. Normal cops I could probably outrun, even with an injury, but peacekeepers? They were bigger and badder than humans. A bit like me, except worse because they were actually trained and consisted of vampires, werewolves, and, most iconically…

Angels.

I looked up at the sky, seeing what appeared to be shooting stars fresh from Heaven. Not one, but two angels dropped down onto the scene. Their wings billowed like white flames made of starlight, burning lines in the sky that extinguished as soon as they landed.

One of them turned to me. Bile crept up my throat. I'd only seen an angel in person one other time, as my aunt and I made an effort to avoid them. His golden eyes scanned me and then the area around us.

I pressed my lips firmly together. Surely, he was calculating if I was the threat. Assuming the rumors were true, angels were very perceptive of people. Able to see the good and evil in others, and all that. Basically, I'd escaped death for nothing.

"Are you injured?" he asked, "What happened here?"

My bravery slipped as I gracelessly fumbled on my words. "P-Please. There's a boy in that house, Peter, and he's—"

I faltered, suddenly feeling lightheaded. Their car lights continued to blind me. Squinting made my headache worse. Voices shouted all around me, but I couldn't make out what anyone said.

The second angel came forward and caught me by the arm. I hadn't realized I'd been wobbling in place. A surge of warmth overtook me. And panic.

He *touched* me.

The hand clasping my elbow grew hotter by the second. My sleeve kept him safe. Or was it keeping me safe? His face became a blur, but I continued to suffer from his comforting aura. Collapsing in his celestial prison would almost be a welcomed outcome, but I couldn't fall for the enticing trap.

"You okay, there?" he asked, "What's your name?"

Don't answer.

"Jess…"

Idiot!

"You don't look so good, Jess. Can you tell me what happened?" He kept asking questions but I feared giving away vital information by accident. I'd already given him my name. Not all of it, but enough that Naomi would have my head.

I had to get away from him as soon as possible.

A peacekeeper came over in his all-black suit. Others scattered around the scene. I eyed his curious material, both padded but thin around the joints, almost like spandex. Two arm cuffs made of heavy metal swung by his hip.

"…license?"

I shook my head, missing half of what he said.

"Your *license*." The peacekeeper repeated more gruffly. "If you're human, a driver's license." But the cold scan I received from him told me he already sensed that I was otherwise. "Are you under the influence of drugs or alcohol, natural or otherwise?"

"What… No! Get Peter, he could be *dying*." I needed them to grasp my sense of urgency without making myself look like a lunatic, so I did my best to stop swaying. Peter had been breathing when I left him, but barely.

The peacekeeper said something to the angel still supporting me. They sounded tense. My focus still sucked. If they weren't going to mention Peter, it wasn't important. Could I make a run for it? My ribs hurt less than my pulsing head.

As if hearing my thoughts, the angel's grip tightened. I jerked back, realizing the danger, but he whispered in my ear. "Just do what he says. I'll look for your friend."

It hurt my pride to hear myself plea. "But I didn't do anything wrong. What's happening?"

Had they figured it out? Was my cover blown?

The angel handed me off to the peacekeeper who'd asked for my license. He wasted no time in ushering me toward one of the black cars. His hands felt tougher than iron. I searched over my shoulder for the angel and found a handsome man with wavy hair entering Peter's home.

Good… Peter is safe.

Unlike me.

"Please, wait—" I attempted to stall but the peacekeeper shoved me forward. My wrists were held down at my lower back. Cool metal bit at my wrist.

If they took me in, my aunt and I were screwed.

With a deep inhale, and enough strength to potentially re-break my ribs, I twisted myself free of the peacekeeper. I succeeded in catching him by surprise. He fumbled just enough for me to jump away. To seal my coffin, I shoved my foot into the middle of his back. Nothing for a big guy like him but, technically, still assault.

He toppled right over and my window of opportunity flew open.

The wind licked at my face as I ran. A burning pain still throbbed in my side. He'd managed to cuff one hand, and the chain, along with the empty hoop, kept threatening to whack me as I pumped my arms.

Voices rang from behind me.

And then, sirens.

* * *

Crap.

Crap.

Shit.

Crap.

The peacekeeper I evaded let out an earth-shaking roar, only adding fuel to my hastening legs. I didn't know who else followed. Sprinting off made me look as innocent as attacking him did, but what other choice did I have? They tried arresting me and hadn't even seen what happened.

I used the city to my advantage, dangerously running through traffic and leaping over oncoming cars. Their headlights praised me while the drivers cursed my existence. I made it across, but behind me, I saw the same peacekeeper having no difficulty using maneuvers similar to mine.

He landed a bit heavier after each pounce, causing cars to swerve around him instead. There were no significant indicators as to what supernatural he was, but he ran hunched forward like he'd go on all fours any second.

He was fast. Too fast.

Just then, I heard a guttural growl and looked again. My pursuer made a half transformation, keeping most of his facial features the same, except for larger teeth and hair around his neckline. He used his larger arms and legs to increase his pace and push him forward.

Oh, *gods.* Just my luck.

He was a werewolf.

Black claws sprouted where his fingers used to be. I had to mess with his senses somehow; find somewhere loud and congested with plenty of smells to go around. I spotted a crowd of people lingering outside of an old movie theater. If only Haverwick had more citizens to disappear into.

Several pedestrians grumbled at my rudeness as I rushed through them, bumping shoulders and chests.

"Out of the way!" A deeper and darker voice commanded from behind me and the mob scattered nervously. My heart pounded even louder, realizing the peacekeeper sounded different now. Scarier. Closer.

A woman squealed behind me. People avoided me, ruining my sensory shield. The situation probably became clear to them. The excitement that numbed my injuries faded. My poor rib kept attempting to repair itself only to get jiggled free, reawakening the shooting pain in my side again. I needed one more street— one *last* distraction—to evade the peacekeeper's vision.

A city bus pulled up to a stop. I could hear the peacekeeper's ragged breathing closing in. Turning around would slow me down, so I didn't dare check if he had made a complete transformation.

He followed me across the street again. Peter's flannel had splotches of my own blood scattered all over. Fresh blood. I'd never lose the peacekeeper with it on. I gripped the top button of the shirt and yanked. One down. Two…

More oncoming traffic. Even out of range, the cars swerved and honked angrily at me. The bus lights blinked, indicating departure, and the doors hissed. I ran to the first double doors I could reach with my flannel wide open and one arm already free. With a final pull, I chucked the soiled shirt into the closing doors.

Blood should be too tantalizing for a werewolf to ignore. If that didn't work, it was over. I couldn't run anymore without healing. Using one hand to hold my ribs together, I dove behind the nearest building next to a potent dumpster.

The bus rolled away, but then, the peacekeeper jumped on top of it.

It clanked and teetered from his weight. I threw a hand over my mouth to stifle my alarm. Hair covered his body now; teeth bared and dripping with saliva. His uniform ripped to make room for his widening beast form.

With a harsh screech, the bus stopped. Doors were flung open and a man stomped out looking red in the face. He exchanged some choice words with the peacekeeper, bravely I might add, who responded in growls. More importantly…

He'd taken the bait.

The peacekeeper's claws scraped the metal roof while he prepared to dismount. He sniffed loudly and I cowered deeper into my hiding spot. After the sickening sound of cracking bones, he shrank back down into a man. The transition didn't seem to bother him, but I shared the same stricken expression as the driver, whose flustered face turned a shade of green.

I waited until the peacekeeper entered the bus before making my move. My throat felt shredded and dry. I didn't have anything to cover my bra, but I kept going down the dark alley and then another. People had seen weirder shit, right?

I crossed my arms and regretted having worn the lace.

When I had a moment, I leaned against a cold, brick wall and tried mapping out the area. I took every narrow alley available in a smaller town, avoiding strangers and car sirens. My aunt said that if I were ever compromised to call her immediately but as fate would have it—assisted by my own stupidity—my phone was still at Peter's.

Borrowing a stranger's phone while cuffed and bleeding didn't sound promising either. Someone could get the wrong idea about my intentions with so little clothing on, especially at that time of night.

I walked in more circles until I found the path toward home, crossing my fingers that I hadn't been followed. Eyes were everywhere, and you never knew whose. Good guys, bad guys; a thin line depending on who you asked.

Not a peep on our street. *Good.* Most everyone closed their stores and went to bed. I made it through the back entrance of our potion shop with my key, plus a wordy enchantment Naomi forced me to memorize. It was worse than a network password, mainly for the repeating phrases.

We lived just one floor above in a small apartment. I pounded on our front door with both hands and heard the deadbolt sliding out of place.

"Eggs or flour?" Her muffled voice asked from behind the wood barrier.

I rolled my eyes. We had a code to be sure neither of us was a shifter in disguise. "Just a pinch of salt…"

Once it opened, Naomi's wild, dark, and curly hair blocked the vision of our living room. The heavy scent of lavender and patchouli wafted in my face. My aunt looked me up and down. "What the hell happened to you? You're *naked.*"

"I could've been followed," I said, hoping that would get me through the door faster.

"Gods of Terra." On occasion, when something really incredible occurred, she would acknowledge the ethereal entities; whichever came to her mind. Naomi made a quick scan of my face. "Are you hurt? Where were—*never mind!* Get inside."

She ushered me in and slammed the door. Not that a deadbolt would do much against peacekeepers.

"What do we do?" I asked, "Naomi, I'm sorry—"

"I found your little note letting me know that I 'didn't need to worry.' Wanna run that by me again?" Naomi snapped at me as she threw open cabinets, grabbed miscellaneous jars, and shoved them into a bag. "Where is your shirt?"

"Oh. It's uh—" But there didn't seem to be enough time for me to answer anything.

"Change into something else and pack a bag. *Gods*, Jess. I've done everything possible to give you a normal life and you threw it away for what?"

I didn't want to unload on her right then about how I'd been feeling. Suffocated. Stagnant. Bored. Depressed at times. I could only make so many candles and soaps at work with her before descending into madness.

When I opened my mouth, she cut me off, "Talk while you pack."

Huffing, I hurried to my room and grabbed a duffle bag. "I wanted to *feel* normal. I'm almost twenty and I've never kissed anyone. Peter was nice—"

"You *kissed* him?"

We shouted at each other from across the apartment. I pulled on an old hoodie that I'd left on my bed. "Yes, I kissed a boy, Aunty. Don't act so surprised."

She barked a laugh. Her short little body bumped into mine on her way to my closet. "You knew what would happen. You know it's dangerous."

"I had gloves," I said.

"*Really*, Jess?"

"It's not like you and I ever talk about it! So, what, I can't have a relationship with anyone? I can't…"

"Kissing is worse!" She shoved a sweater into my chest but the anger melted from her face. Her voice came out much softer. "I know. I know. We'll have a real talk after we get the hell out of here. Okay?"

I nodded but my earnest packing fizzled. Did that mean I could never be with someone?

"I hurt him," I muttered.

"What?"

"At the party, I think I really hurt him… I also blew up this giant monster thing with three heads."

"What were you doing at a party?" she asked.

"*That's* your concern?"

She threw her hands up and her curls bounced aggressively. "It's why any of this is happening in the first place."

I felt my own temperature rising. "*Why* is this happening, Naomi? Why do we have to run? Why couldn't we just register like everyone else? *Look* at me. Do I look like something that wants to go crazy in a town of helpless citizens? But that idea's fudged now because I already look guilty as hell."

"Register you?" She spat. "So EXO can take you in as one of their little soldiers?"

"Speaking of, a peacekeeper followed me. A wolf. I lost him in town." I paused, knowing I should add the rest, "They had angels, too."

Her face paled and she stared at the floor with wide, brown eyes. The longer she took to respond the more sickness I felt sitting in my guts.

"As I said, we'll discuss all that later." She took a breath. "We *have* to go."

We returned to our efforts in silence until we both had stuffed backpacks with popping zippers. An emergency evacuation happened once before. That involved a group of zealots and I'd only been six, maybe. I couldn't remember much, only the fear coming from my aunt, but Naomi brought it up any time I was feeling extra rebellious.

We were uprooting our lives. Again. We hadn't gotten close to anyone local, but I enjoyed Haverwick. I liked how the leaves turned red instead of yellow. My favorite hiking trail had a great view of the mountains. The memories of Peter would fade from a childish dream and into a distant nightmare.

I assisted Naomi in pushing the couch against the wall and sliding the coffee table out of the way. Not sure why, she just started doing so. She grabbed a black broomstick—that I didn't know we had—and set it down in the middle of the floor.

My concern grew when she sprinkled dark powder in a circle around it.

"Naomi?" I asked cautiously, "This doesn't look like white magic."

"It's not."

I felt the hairs on my arms rising. The scent of charcoal made the back of my tongue taste bitter. Whether I wanted to acknowledge it or not, we were both creatures of darkness, but seeing her work so efficiently to make her witch circle gave me chills.

Naomi spun the broom once, like a bottle, but it continued to move on its own long after it should have stopped. Its speed increased until the dark circle she created started to fume. She chanted something under her breath and I could feel the power in her words like static in the air.

"What exactly are we supposed to do with that?" I asked.

"You're going to take my hand and we're going to jump."

"Come again?"

She sighed. "It's going to take us to a secret location. Far enough away that no one here should follow. It requires a lot of energy and expensive materials so let's not waste it."

I swallowed, watching the moving broom become a blur. It sucked in the air around us. My hair pulled forward, wanting to get swallowed by the black hole. "You sure about this?" I clutched at my billowing shirt. "We can't just take the bus?"

"Hold my hand," she said.

I did as she asked, feeling her pointed, violet nails digging into my skin. Naomi took a step forward, bringing me along. "You can close your eyes if you want. But do not let go. Understand?"

"I guess…"

"It's going to feel like you have to pee. Just ignore it."

"Wait, what?"

"One." She started the countdown. "Two…"

I definitely shut my eyes. Not the worst thing to happen that night, but jumping down a hole made by her *broomstick?* The spell had given me zero hints about our next location.

I thought I heard her say "three," but our door burst open at the same exact moment.

The room turned icy like Naomi's spell had unleashed a blizzard instead. My aunt's dark eyes flared but she never lost her focus.

I on the other hand couldn't resist and looked at the intruder.

A messenger of Death stood in our doorway.

Ashen bone took the place of his face. A shadowy mist acted as the glue, replacing muscle and cartilage to keep the skeleton intact. The reaper didn't wear black robes like I imagined, just a gray hoodie and jeans like some average guy but without flesh.

He did, however, bring his scythe.

Naomi tugged me forward. She took her leap, but my feet hadn't moved. I couldn't. My eyes were locked on his weapon. The handle, along with the curved metal, were both solid black, making it appear as all one, fluid tool.

I expected the peacekeeper again, or maybe the angel. Why a reaper?

Naomi's hand tightened and I fell forward toward our dark portal. If a reaper came, did that mean we were about to die? Naomi's broom could've been faulty or laced with black magic.

I fell in after my aunt but something yanked me back out.

"Naomi!" My grip on Naomi broke. I watched in horror as she disappeared. She continued through the portal while my hand closed around empty air several times in an attempt to reach her. I was stuck, like a worm on a hook.

When I looked back, the curved end of a scythe caught the back of my sweater. I choked from the fabric pulling up against my throat. My stomach dropped when I thought I noticed Death's lipless smile.

The reaper swung his scythe across his body, vaulting me away from the dark circle. I rolled to the floor and caught myself on the edge of the coffee table. In a daze, I crawled back to where Naomi vanished, but the darkness snapped shut.

"No…" I smacked the wood surface but only a few sprinkles of the black dust remained.

She was gone. I'd been left behind.

The icy chill grew and swallowed all remaining magic in the room. Heavy footsteps took their time reaching me. When a pair of black shoes stopped inches from my hands, I brought my head up. No longer using the fleshless face of Death, the reaper appeared to me as a young, human man.

The hood over his hair shadowed his face. Still less intimidating than his earlier appearance. Silver eyes shone through, and I felt my soul freeze by his gaze. I prepared myself to fight or run, while the reaper seemed relaxed.

His shoulders slumped over as he studied me. His deep voice startled me, but nothing cruel emitted from his tone. "You're in trouble, you know."

I shuddered. "Am I… dead?"

Why else would he have come?

His lips curled. "Obviously not."

"Why did you—" I started to ask but stopped when the man lifted a pale hand toward my face.

His cool finger touched my forehead and I immediately felt drowsy. Everything became numb and I succumbed to the comforting arms of gray fog.

Cold.

The new t-shirt, gifted to me by the guards, did little to protect me from the freezing room I was being held in. Waiting. Just waiting.

I wrapped my arms around my body and kept my palms tightly shut. No gloves either. I couldn't remember all that happened. When I came to, peacekeepers were escorting me from a car and into the station. After a brief medical exam, basically ensuring I wasn't broken or bleeding, I was brought to the pod. A captured criminal.

My company consisted of harsh faces. We all wore the same plain white shirts. The humans occupying the room next to us wore gray. Which meant, they already knew I wasn't human.

Fucking great.

My aunt and I discussed a fail-safe in the event that I was ever captured but it usually ended with her getting frustrated, admitting failure, and insisting that I needed to never let it happen.

Oops.

I had no idea when she'd come back for me.

If she came for me, but I didn't want to think about that. She always had her secrets but she cared about me. We were family. Naomi always wanted to protect me. She'd come back…

I kept to myself at a table in the back corner. Not everyone in the pod looked hostile. Some eyed me cautiously while others hissed or gazed into oblivion, distracted by their various narcotics.

Also upon waking up, I noticed a mild surge cycling through my body. Everything that hurt before had healed up, but something new awakened inside me. The scattered, destructive chaos. It cooked that monster right in front of me and continued to taunt me with a soft drumming, like a second beating heart.

I had no clue what to do about it or when it would strike again. Had the power been my own, something all demons had? I doubted anyone in my current vicinity had the answers.

Guards brought in a half-turned werewolf next, frothing at the mouth and jerking at his restraints. One of the guards jammed something in his arm. A loud yelp pierced the room and he reverted back into a human. They assisted him into a chair, docile thanks to whatever drug the guards were equipped with.

I wanted to avoid attention completely. Especially getting poked by anything. So, I kept to my corner. The room filled with more bodies that reeked of sour booze, sweat, blood, and wet dog. Guards would take people outside and never bring them back. I assumed they received their new, permanent cells.

It wasn't the fear of death that seized me but being locked in a cage for eternity. Naomi said, while not immortal on Terra's plane, demons still had superior lifespans to humans. Imagine, multiple life sentences. At what point would I wish for death?

I fought the urge to cry; not wanting to appear weak. Twenty-one and unregistered wasn't a good look for me. Anyone with mixed DNA had to put themselves into the supernatural database, which Naomi obviously refused to do. While the world slowly accepted supernaturals, it still underwent social growing pains. Cults and political parties still fought against coexistence, with violence or shackles enforced by words. I'd have a better chance as a werewolf or vampire…

Doomed. I was doomed.

The security door buzzed, allowing a guard and another newcomer through. He waltzed in, no break in his stride as if he owned the place. His black hair looked windblown with traces of something colorful. Glitter?

"Mouth shut, Aiden, or I'll grab the muzzle." The guard escorting him spoke like they knew each other. Aiden jerked his head in my direction, as if I'd shouted at him. I hadn't. But I *was* staring.

Red eyes were the dead giveaway for any vampire. They only varied in shades of crimson, sometimes turning as light as amber. His eyes were bright as rubies.

"Muzzle?" he chuckled, hoarsely, "Sounds kinky."

The guard shoved him hard once, forcing him onto a bench.

"I'm *kidding*. I'm not hungry, anyway."

I let out a breath, mentally thanking the guard for not sitting him next to me. The gratitude was short-lived, however.

"Hey, Cupcake," Aiden rasped like he smoked regularly.

I kept my head facing the door. There were dozens of us in there, surely he'd addressed one of them as a tiny dessert? When no one responded to him, I did the stupid thing and peered over my shoulder. Aiden leaned forward, eyes glowing.

"Cupcake?" I asked.

"Well, I don't know your name and you look too sweet to be here." He rested his elbows on his knees and gave my throat a scan. I faced back around, using my hair as a neck shield, but that didn't stop him from chatting.

"What curious thing are you? A shifter?" he asked.

Others in our company had given me puzzled looks when I first arrived. I knew why. On the outside, I *looked* human. Pretty average as far as I could tell. I didn't have any outstanding features. No fangs, horns, or wings. My aunt even dressed me down, hiding my body beneath heavy clothing and sunglasses in public.

She told me the angels would come for me if they ever find out. For a demon, that basically meant death.

Aiden hadn't been the first supernatural to inquire, given their keen senses. If it wasn't my scent, something else triggered their nosy tendencies. But my identity, *my* business. I ignored him again, hoping he'd grow bored of me.

He scoffed. "Fine, then what brings you here?"

"*Parking ticket*," I said, barely glancing back and crossing my arms, "You?"

Aiden waited until I looked at him again to answer. He licked the corner of his lips where a maroon stain still lingered. A metal ball glimmered in the center of his candy-red tongue.

"Just a bit of bad luck. She promised she wasn't a screamer."

I ducked my head into my chest. Why was he boasting about his donor screaming? In what context? I didn't want to know, actually.

I knew what vampires had to do in order to feed. What I'd done to Peter hadn't been so different. I could be just as scary as anyone in that room and yet, they could all probably hear my rapidly beating heart.

I made a mental list of apologies to my aunt, and to several gods, for any petty things I'd been upset about; meeting some repentance quota. Just in case I got eaten before being sentenced.

"Winters."

My head shot up. The guard at the front waved me forward. I rose with a tremble. The walk felt impossibly slow but I made it to the guard before I knew it.

I heard Aiden chuckle behind me.

"Later, Cupcake."

* * *

The guard left me in a new and empty room. Not much for decoration save for a rectangular mirror on the wall and a table with four metal chairs. A fluorescent light shone high above me, irritating my eyes.

"Wait here." The guard left me to stand awkwardly. Chairs were available but I remained standing. What would they ask me? I didn't know how I came into existence. My aunt said she saved me after a coven of witches abandoned me. At the time, I'd been an infant, so no memories there.

Then she drugged me into suppression and raised me like a normal human. To her best efforts.

A soft knock made my stomach lurch. I moved away from the door and a man of rich, dark complexion wearing a suit walked in. He gave me an inquisitive glance before gesturing to one of the chairs. "Please, have a seat, Miss Winters."

Peace flooded the room, which didn't make a lick of sense. I'd been sweating and chewing my nails off but as soon as he walked in, a spell wrapped an invisible, warm blanket over my shoulders. Ironically, it made my anxiety worse. I didn't trust the new feeling imposed on me.

The man sat across the table from me and I noted more of his appealing features. There was something beyond artistic about his perfection, like his creator took greater care with his design. The lack of blemishes on his even skin tone, his impeccable posture, and defined chin. All beautiful. Also, not human.

He dropped a thin file on the metal surface, keeping the scarce amount of paper on the inside from slipping out. I wiggled in my chair, wondering what he would say first. His yellow eyes had a crystalline reflection to them like looking at the inside of a diamond.

Vampires weren't the only ones with distinguishing peepers.

My interrogator was an angel.

I did my best to hide the fright from my face as my insides crumbled. Angels had powerful effects on people; just another attribute that singled them out from the rest of the world. That and being so damn pretty, but the same could be said about most demons.

He cleared his throat. "Call me Jarmiel. Do you know why you're here?"

What a loaded question.

"No," I said, "Is Peter okay?"

"He's alive," he said rather dismissively, "Could you elaborate, Miss Winters?"

I sank into my chair, feeling the weight lift from my shoulders. Peter was alive…

Thank the gods.

"Miss Winters?" he repeated.

"I didn't kill anyone," I said, remembering the brutally dismembered person in Peter's driveway, "There was a monster rampaging around."

"We know."

"Oh." I frowned, unsure of where our conversation was headed. "Then, I don't know why I'm here."

Jarmiel laughed once under his breath. "For someone who assaulted a peacekeeper and ran, you're taking a very coy approach."

I held my tongue.

"You're in our system as a human," he continued, "Someone with your *abilities*, and at your age, should be classified differently. Can you explain why you haven't been registered properly, Miss Winters?"

There. The real reason they'd brought me in.

I swallowed my rising scoff. If they didn't have proof, then I was innocent. "I'm registered correctly, sir."

Jarmiel flipped through the minimal pages of my file with an unreadable expression on his face. He moved on, "Can you tell me where you were at around ten p.m. last night?"

"Peter's house," I said, "Shouldn't I have a lawyer?"

"And what were the two of you up to?"

My brow raised. They wanted to know how Peter got in his condition. Understandable.

But what if he'd already come-to and told his side of the story? Which was what, exactly? Did he even remember? He could've said something damning without understanding the consequences.

I had to do my best to keep the story believable. "We were just talking."

"What about later that evening? Any changes?" Jarmiel asked.

"We cuddled, I guess, and… this is kind of awkward, isn't it?"

"It's not. It's important," he said, "So, you were engaging in sexual activities?"

I choked on air.

"T-Technically? I guess we were getting to that point."

Jarmiel proceeded, unbothered, "And after that?"

"He had an asthma attack or something," I said, "I don't know. I made sure he was breathing before finding help."

An easy lie considering most of it was true. I didn't even fully understand what I'd done to Peter. Away from the trauma, I could think more clearly. I *did* remember a weird sensation while we kissed. Peter's lips tickled mine like we were making tiny sparks of electricity.

Stupid.

I knew my touch could hurt people and I kissed him anyway. Why had I thought he'd be the exception? It wasn't like I killed people just from bumping into them on the street, so the duration of the touch could be a determining factor. But Naomi's way of "dealing" with things was to ignore it; bury it and bury it some more. I never learned my limits.

Jarmiel interlaced his fingers and set his hands on the table, "The hospital told us he had no external or internal wounds, and yet, his body shut down."

He was baiting me again.

"Not sure what that means," I said. Demons were known for terrorizing humans in several ways; deception and murder being the most infamous, but also stealing souls and possessing bodies. Some even ate humans whole.

Not my thing, for which I was grateful.

If what Jarmiel said was true, I had to guess that "energy" dealt with the soul. The medicine Naomi gave me every morning supposedly suppressed my demon-related urges. Another concern of mine to add to the pile, especially with her gone. I'd always had it. Always had her. I didn't know anything different.

"Will Peter be back to normal soon?" I asked.

"You care about the boy?" Jarmiel watched me intently but I sat there doing the same. "He will be. I'll ask again, were you aware of what was happening to him and your part in it?"

"You mean when I gave him CPR?"

He laughed once. "You had no magic, no weapon, but somehow you were able to thwart a creature much larger than yourself. And I'm to believe you had nothing at *all* to do with Mr. Calder?"

Calder.

Must've been Peter's last name.

I squeezed my hands together underneath the table, wishing the interrogation would end. How the hell did he know about my fight with the monster if he hadn't seen it? "I don't know what you're talking about."

"Registration is important to prevent these kinds of accidents. The council is going to request your cooperation for an examination. So, we can get to the bottom of this now, or later."

I shook my head. "My aunt is human. I'm human."

"Naomi Winters, yes. We tried reaching her. Do you know her whereabouts?" Jarmiel asked.

"No. I don't."

Somehow, he seemed to believe that. I didn't receive any deep sighs or death stares from that. "We did a little digging, hoping to gain a better understanding without her assistance," he said, "There doesn't seem to be much information about you or your parents."

"They're dead," I said, "Naomi said they weren't close and I don't have anyone else."

"I'm sorry to hear that. It would've helped clear some things up. Your parents, on record, were humans. But what's more…" He flipped one piece of paper over, "They also didn't appear to have any children."

I felt an unsettling pit in my stomach. How had they found that information so fast, anyway? Naomi said she had my back-story airtight but it seemed the angel found all the holes.

Wondering if he could sense my panic made me panic even more. "I don't know what to tell you."

"Is Naomi Winters related to you by blood?"

I knew why he asked. Naomi had dark eyes and dark, curly hair while mine lay flat and copper, like strands woven out of coins. My height surpassed hers by a head, and we always joked that I was a warrior beside a wicked pixie.

Still, I shrugged.

Jarmiel's thin eyebrows pulled together causing wrinkles to appear on his forehead. "Tell me, Miss Winters, or do you prefer Jessebel?"

"*Jess*, please," I said.

His already piercing, golden stare magnified his frustration. "Jess. Do you mind if I show you a video?"

"Sure." What video?

Jarmiel leaned across the table with his wide-screen phone and started playing a clip. It looked like an amateur recording from someone else's phone. I could hear the deep voices cracking in octaves as they freaked out, like they were…

the drunk idiots from the party!

They'd recorded me.

In the video, I'd already splintered the car windshield after getting backhanded by the creature. Its unearthly racket drowned out the screaming guys who still held their phones for some reason.

As I continued to watch the screen, I noticed the dark, wispy aura building around me. Crackling sparks of gold channeled through the cloud-like fireworks. My face transformed until I seemed possessed.

The video stopped.

"We found you soon after, almost delirious. Before you ran off, that is. The Ghoul was nowhere to be seen," Jarmiel said, rewinding to the screen with my face clearly visible. "That is *you*, correct."

"I swear to the gods—"

"Don't."

"R-Right." I stammered, "I mean, kids do crazy things with videos these days. The filters these tech companies are coming up with are insane."

He slammed the phone face down on the table and lowered himself back in his chair. How could someone so pretty also be so terrifying? "Miss Winters, do you know how many trained hunters, peacekeepers, and purifiers *die* every day to something that size? You expect me to believe you have no idea how you defeated it?"

"Yes. Because I didn't," I said.

Truth. It lived. Sort of.

"Do you know what you conjured in order to protect yourself?" he asked.

"You mean the filter?"

The angel looked ready to blow a fuse when the door opened. A much calmer and younger man stepped in. A chaotic mess of caramel hair sat atop his head; a hot and cold difference from this other angel who kept his hair cut short.

"Hey, guys." He waved, "Sounds like we are getting nowhere, huh, Jare-bear?"

5

J*are-bear?*

Jarmiel's face dropped. "Don't call me that."

"Jarmiel's such a grump, huh?" The new guy asked me. He maneuvered around the table and got on his knees, as no chair was presented to him. A casual smile graced his face as he crossed his arms on the silver slate.

I looked between him and Jarmiel, or Jare-bear, wondering what their dynamic was. Even what he wore didn't complement his partner in any way. Jarmiel's had tight, wrinkle-free clothes, while the second angel had a loosened red tie and brown jacket hanging open. A brass, circular pin with a wing inside, sat proudly above his chest pocket.

"You look childish," Jarmiel muttered.

The other angel tilted his head further into his forearm, still gazing at me. "My name's Zakiel, but everyone calls me Zak. Nice to meet you again, Jess."

He used my name correctly as well, even though he hadn't been present when I'd corrected Jarmiel. How many others were watching our conversation?

His angelic eyes had a more familiar, human, subtleness to them; warm and a deep shade of brown. As if to reaffirm he was an angel, he showed off his wings. They exited the back of his shirt like lightning bolts frozen in time. The glowing element flickered and danced like fire. I expected to burn the closer they got, but the heat they gave was nothing more than a summer's breeze.

"You were there," I said, finally remembering, "You found Peter."

"That's me," he said, "I couldn't help overhearing Jarmiel butcher this interview. Look, she's scared. This was a weird, one-time occurrence and you didn't know what you were doin'. Do I have that right?"

I fidgeted, reminding myself not to slip up just because he was attractive. All angels were, but something about Zak messed with my mind. It could've been his wavy hair that made him look like a marble statue come to life, but that seemed too shallow a reason for the sudden desire in telling him all of my dark secrets.

"I've seen monsters before, but nothing like that," I said, "And I've never…"

"So, you've dealt with this kind of thing before?" His face and his tone perked up. "You're still pretty young."

"She's twenty-one," Jarmiel said under his breath.

"I thought she was twenty—ah," Zak snapped his fingers together, "Happy birthday!"

"Thanks…" I said, "I know I'm not a child but I haven't experienced this before. I *have* seen what your peacekeepers can do."

Peacekeepers, at least according to the humans, were "unholy" servants to the angels. Supernatural soldiers that defended the New Peace order in an effort to obtain salvation.

At the conclusion of the war, humans were lost. The fear of demon's returning turned many into demons themselves. Sure, Hell had been defeated, but Heaven and Hell could never truly die. Terra was without order, so the angels accepted responsibility for "healing" humanity. The New Peace. And EXO kept us out of a war with ourselves.

Peacekeepers and purifiers became the new law enforcement project, hunting unlawful beings that surpassed human control. Purifiers are human but gifted with light magic. *Blessed,* as they say.

EXO was, at its basic principles, a fight of fire with fire. Not to mention, a controversial nightmare. All parties had issues with weaponizing the supernaturals, either wanting more control or no affiliation whatsoever.

"I'm sorry," Zak said, "It must have been scary for you."

His crystal eyes could blink at me all they liked. I stared right back and nodded. In a world with demons and angels, charisma became a dangerous tool. Zak's smile never wavered. If anything, his lips reached higher up his face.

His volume made me jump. "*Still!* You saved your friends back there. That's pretty cool. How'd you do it? That's all we want to know. We can find out for ourselves, but I'd rather you just tell us."

Damn. He sounded so kind but that threat was a block of ice.

"I think I'd like my phone call," I said, "You do that, right?"

"Am I making you uncomfortable?" Zak asked.

"Not at all." I decided to be just as sly. One of my aunt's many talents was distrusting everyone, and how to tell if you were being schmoozed. Zak cloaked his cunning with dazzling light but I could still tell. He wasn't someone to take lightly.

While Jarmiel sighed and rubbed his temples, Zak kept grinning at me like we were in the thick of a chess match.

"Let's take her in," he said suddenly.

Both Jarmiel and I expressed our confusion in unison with pinched brows. Zak chuckled at his partner's bewilderment. "The council said we could recruit 'special cases', right?"

The vein in Jarmiel's forehead returned with a vengeance. "Zakiel… no."

"Come on. Show some *mercy*. She has a good heart, you can see."

Jarmiel shook his head.

"Jarry…" Zak taunted.

"Even *if* I agreed, there's paperwork and divine counseling, not to mention *the law*," he snapped, "You can't keep—"

"Hey, hey, calm down." Zak fanned his hands, calming Jarmiel's emotional flames. "I have a good feeling about this one. We'll go over all the paperwork together. It'll be fun."

I interrupted, "Sorry but what are you talking about?"

Jarmiel clenched his hand into a fist. After he simmered down, his piercing stare fell on me again. "You may have your phone call while I have a word with my partner."

* * *

Just as he said, Jarmiel gave me a phone while they stepped out. I didn't trust that they wouldn't be eavesdropping or recording everything but I *needed* to speak to my aunt.

I tried the safe number first.

"The number you have reached is out of service, ple—"

I hung up. Naomi wouldn't have abandoned me. She had to have a plan of some kind. We'd gone over several scenarios, but not many of them involved me in jail.

I'd just have to be patient and look for signs.

After a stunned few minutes of me suffering an internal panic, Jarmiel walked through the door and flattened his tie to his chest, not making eye contact with his beach-haired companion.

Zak stepped the rest of the way inside and shut the door behind him. "No luck?"

Like he didn't know. Something about his casual tone rubbed me wrong. Yet, I didn't get the vibe that he wanted to destroy me. Jarmiel on the other hand hadn't made an effort to speak. He sat stiffly in his spot at the table and I heard his nostrils flaring. Somehow, he was still impossibly beautiful.

I glowered and slid the phone back over to them.

"Sorry, Jess. We ran into the same issue trying to reach your aunt," Zak said, "I'm sure she'll find a way to contact you eventually. For now, I'd love to find the best and most fair solution, but we need to be a little more honest with each other first."

"You want honesty?" I asked, "I think you're trying to intimidate me into a false confession, which I don't think is very *angelic*."

His wings faded away in an instant, like he had an on-and-off switch.

"Intimidation wasn't my intent," he said, "I can't tell you what to do *but*, you should know that we already have a good idea of what you are. You're not leaving here, Jess."

I bit my tongue until it bled. Was I headed for prison? Helping Peter and his friends was the wrong choice.

Zak raised a finger. "Unless you'll hear me out?"

"About your special cases?" I asked.

"Uh-huh. Could I see your hand for a moment?"

Oh no.

Could I just refuse? What would happen to an angel if I touched them?

"I'm just making an observation," Zak said with a tilt of his head, "Nothing more."

He reached over the table and I instantly felt dizzy. I didn't move; a silent confession. A single tear slid down my cheek, further signifying my guilt. I tried to be a decent person. Never stole anything… *Hell*, I was a freaking virgin!

Zak waited. His inviting fingers looked like a guillotine. I met his eyes and the air caught in my throat. I didn't see a valiant warrior anxious to purge me from the face of the earth.

I saw a man who pitied me.

My heart threatened to explode. His brows pulled slightly inward as he watched me suppress more tears. If they knew everything, there shouldn't have been pity to give. Not to a de-mon. I carefully brought my hand forward.

His fingers closed around my skin and I shut my eyes, afraid to see what came next. Would he be in pain? Get angry? A rush of heat and adrenaline flew into my chest and shot to my brain. It wasn't fear I felt, but bliss. Pure, light, and serene.

And then, fear.

When I tried to pull back, his thumb pressed into my palm. He kept his grip without being too harsh. A new wave hit me; like the gust of a warm summer's breeze. I almost cried a second time and not from the tense situation. Somehow, I just knew. I'd tasted something vital for the first time.

Peter hadn't given me that rush.

"There." Zak's laugh slapped me out of my trance. "Was that so hard?"

I gaped at him. An angel being a callous bastard? Was that even legal?

I waited for him to retract and look at me in disgust. He did neither. Instead, he turned my hand around to examine my knuck-les. "You're an interesting person, Jess. Do you feel threatened by me?"

That earned a long pause with more of him studying the creases in my wrist. My fingers were on fire now, still taking in whatever that man was made of. Even Jarmiel's interest peaked. He made an expectant turn to his partner, awaiting further report.

"Yes," I said. That, and I was in complete awe of what he'd made me feel. A tiny knot formed in my stomach, filled with a new and terrible wanting. It was nothing more than a spec but if that yearning or hunger grew…

I gulped, looking back down at Zak's hand.

"If it were possible, would you harm me in order to escape?" he asked.

"If I had the choice, I'd get to go home without anyone get-ting hurt."

"Good answer." Zak lifted his handsome face. "Unfortunately, I'm not sure that's going to happen. I can, however, make you an offer. Come with me to EXO. Become a peacekeeper."

I thought I misheard him at first. EXO, the headquarters for peacekeepers and purifiers, was what Naomi wanted to protect me from. That and the rest of the world. "You actually want me?" I asked.

"You clearly have some untapped potential," he said, "This offer includes letting us study you, but I think you'll find it beneficial to you as well."

He finally let go of my hand which I greedily stuffed back into my lap. Heavy disappointment followed. I already wanted to feel his comforting sensation again.

Jarmiel, who'd barely said a word, entered the conversation. "In some cases, The Council will grant pardon in exchange for service. You will also learn how to use your strengths more responsibly."

"As opposed to diluting yourself with various… potions." Zak turned his head down but his eyes remained up. He revealed a velvet pouch from his jacket, only a few centimeters deep, pulled the ties apart, and dipped a finger into its contents. "This was in your house. *Lots* of it. I mean, it's pretty advanced alchemy but I doubt it's doing anything other than poisoning you."

Sharp words sat behind my clenched teeth.

Naomi wouldn't *poison* me.

Zak brought his coated finger out to examine, "Might make a decent dry rub. Is there rosemary in this?"

"Is EXO my only option?" I asked, my jaw still tight.

"I think it's a pretty good one, considering your lack of alternatives. I mean, if you have the power to help people, why not try?"

The "potential" he wanted me to tap into could be ugly. Demons were violent and ravenous, but aside from my deadly touch, I never felt like one. I didn't *want* to bring anyone harm.

Although, my touch hadn't had much of an effect on Zak. If anything, I felt more than he had.

He flattened his elbows against the table and leaned forward. "Look. This is the best I can come up with. Running got you a few months in jail at least, and, to be honest, I think you'll enjoy EXO a lot more."

I blushed, feeling embarrassed about my escape for some reason. "What'll happen to me? Where is EXO even located?"

Zak beamed at me with a ray of heavenly light. "We'd head to Volhold. EXO has a facility for trainees in the central city. You'd have a room and everything."

"I would *live* there?"

"Yes."

Cold nervousness filled my chest.

Volhold… Central yes, but not only that. The big capital city where the majority of the angels resided and not a short drive from home.

"Is living with demon hunters a bit… moronic?" I asked.

"Not if you're on our side," Zak flashed a brilliant smile. "Big decision, I know, but we don't have lots of time to think it over."

Jarmiel scoffed, seeming to know something I didn't. I'd only been told the bad about EXO; angels using supernaturals to even the playing field. Naomi said they were forced into it, like me; given a choice between a rock and a hard place. We sign our lives away to the angels in their hopes that all evil will be destroyed, and us along with it.

On the one hand, EXO could help me learn to control my abilities. Something Naomi never offered to do, or maybe she hadn't known how. *Maybe,* I could have the freedom I'd been longing for. At the very least, freedom from the constant worry of killing others.

Naomi wasn't there to save me, anyway. And if she had a plan, that plan could work better without me behind bars.

"Okay," I said.

Angels wasted no time.

It hadn't even been a full twenty-four hours since the incident and we were already piling into a car, on our way to EXO. As we left the station, Zak reassured me that the handcuffs around my wrists were just for show at that time. Jarmiel followed us quickly, and I couldn't shake the feeling that we were all doing something we weren't supposed to.

We made it out, only receiving simple nods from the guards. Zak shielded me with his body from most onlookers which I found both comforting and confusing. He kept things that way until we reached a black van parked by the curb.

Jarmiel opened its sleek doors. Going to Volhold meant I was leaving home, and a way for Naomi to reach me, behind. If we wanted to see each other again, we'd have to go through EXO. There was so much I needed to ask her. Was there anything from my past that Naomi knew about and hadn't told me?

Like my *real* parents?

I hesitated by the car door. Jarmiel glanced down at his watch, trying to do so subtly but I still noticed. Even if the angels were anxious to leave, they were being respectfully silent about it.

When Zak offered to remove my handcuffs, my fingers trembled something terrible. He chuckled. "Deep breaths, Jess. We don't need you passing out before we even get there."

He held his thumb over a smooth metal square connecting the cuffs. A light flickered, followed by a high-pitched beeping, and both bracelets popped open. His hand grazed mine and the spark of heat returned. "I won't put them back on so long as you don't try and run again, deal?"

"Sure..."

I slid into the back seat, expecting Zak to do the same, but he never got in the car. Jarmiel, however, did and closed off our row. I looked through the filter of glass at the station and gave Haverwick a silent goodbye.

Zak rapped his knuckles on the driver's side, and the chauffeur rolled the glass down.

"I'll see you guys there. If you need me…" He pointed upward with a knowing smile and then left.

"What's that about?" I asked.

Jarmiel answered with a slight shake of his head. "He doesn't like small, enclosed spaces."

Zak unfurled the alien lights from his back, creating wings that were double his arm span out of blazing energy. He pushed off from the ground, disappearing from sight.

Our driver shifted gears and we began rolling away. I held back more tears, missing my aunt and crumbling internally about the future. If Namoi were with me, she'd probably say something like "Stay strong." "Stay in control." "Don't be stupid." "Stay alive."

I planned on doing just that.

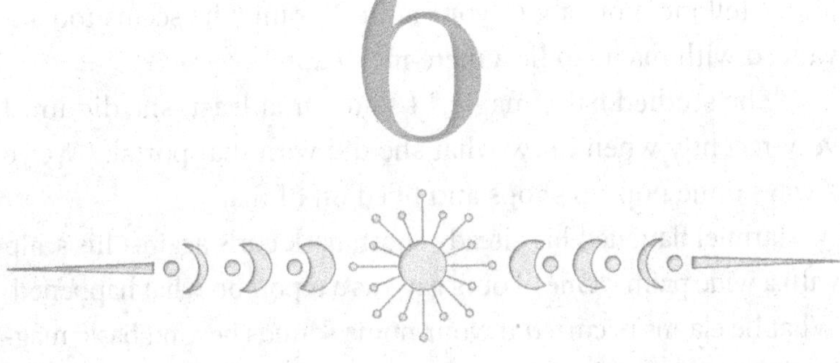

The drive had been quiet.

Jarmiel kept a watchful eye outside. Something seemed to put him on edge but that could just be his personality at this point. Volhold wouldn't be much farther. It had taken hours. I thought boredom would knock me out for most of it, but the scenery preoccupied my focus. We drove through parts of our small world I'd never seen before.

The buildings, parks, and gardens were shown with more care. Not littered with gum or crumpled wrappers. Based on my shallow observation, it didn't appear that anyone struggled financially. No homeless either.

"So… What should I expect when we get to EXO?" I asked.

"You sign a contract. The standard two years of service that you can renew for a longer term," he said, "Zakiel will give you a tour of the facilities upon our arrival. Then, you'll join the others for training in the morning."

Two years? Would I even live for that long if I hunted monsters every night?

Jarmiel's words were clear but slowly spoken. It had been a long twelve hours for me too. He stopped to run a hand over his face. "Tell me more about your aunt, Naomi. She seems too advanced with magic to be a mere merchant."

"She studied basic magic," I said. Or at least, she did until very recently when I saw what she did with that portal. "We've always done pop-up shops and lived off of that."

Jarmiel flattened his already short, dark curls against his scalp with a wide palm. "One of ours gave us a report on what happened. What he claims occurred in your home sounds beyond basic magic. You two were planning to disappear, but only she got away."

So he already knew the answer. I thought he'd left the baited questions back in the interrogation room.

"That's what happened, yeah," I said, "Is there a reason Zak wants me at EXO? Does he just collect who he can?"

"Zakiel has his reasons…" Jarmiel opened his mouth like he had more to say, but shut it again. I didn't expect a warm welcome to a demon-hunting corporation but at least I wouldn't be alone.

"Are there others like me?" I asked, truly ignorant of the existence of other, well-mannered half-demons. Most supernaturals were treated like demons anyway.

"Miss Winters, I must confess, we're not entirely sure what you are."

Stunned, I turned my whole body in my seat. "You were bluffing?"

His golden eyes seemed to glow in the dim, evening light. "I've met many hell-beings in my time. Your aura doesn't match. Very strange."

"Why is it strange?" I asked. Wouldn't that have been a good thing?

"Lesser demons are bound to a master or a painful hunger; both of which govern most of their existence. That's why when tasked with hunting demons, it usually ends in their death."

It would make sense as to why demon attacks ended so violently. My choices only ever felt restricted because I had to hide, not because a devil told me what to do. Naomi didn't count.

"Demons also can't stand the presence of angels," Jarmiel continued. He drew out each word, watching for my reaction. I saw the driver's eyes through his rearview mirror.

"Strange," I said just as carefully.

"Indeed."

More silence, until I caved. "What does that mean, exactly?"

"I'm not sure. It could be that whoever your second parent was, or *is*, has rather resilient DNA that counters your demonic traits. Or, that medicine your aunt concocted is stronger than we realize. This is something we could explore with a few blood tests."

I pressed my back into my seat and sighed. *Needles. Fantastic.*

We passed the same billboard advertising a new pharmaceutical movement at least twice. I pressed my nose to the window to read it in its entirety. It claimed that they'd found a cure-all for humanity. The black and silver logo of an R and B posed just as striking as the man beside it. Roman Blaxill.

The poster made him look like a giant; broad and chiseled. Every edge of him seemed sharp from his chin to his shoulder pads. His red eyes met any onlooker no matter the direction. The fact that he'd gotten a board in Volhold at all should be impressive.

My aunt would make comments about vampire-made drugs as a scam to get people addicted. Something about it creates codependency between humans and them. Blood and drugs. She could be right, but humans ran plenty of scams and were already addicted before vampires came to light.

The driver spoke up. "It's slower up ahead. Sorry, Jarmiel."

Cars honked at one another, desperate to get around whatever clogged up the streets. I scoped out the scene through our windshield and saw multitudes of people around a crosswalk. Behind them, was a squatty building shaped like a white, mountain plateau. And behind that, towers of equal elegance and silver, pearly window frames.

"Is that..?" I started.

"The court halls," Jarmiel said, before motioning to the driver, "Take us around, please."

"Yes, sir."

Court halls were established in many major cities quickly following the conclusion of the war. I'd never seen one up close. They replaced our court systems from years past. The Angel Council, who all but claimed rulership, used the halls to conduct their New Peace order and properly punish the guilty.

If Zak and Jarmiel hadn't swept me away, I might've had to stand in a room of angels and await their holy judgment. Not everyone loved the system, but following blindly came easy when another war with Hell frightened so many. Call me a hypocrite or a traitor but I didn't like demons much either.

The falling sun reflected off of the building's pearly exterior. I had to squint to see the painted symbol on the entrance. A handsome, winged angel thrust a fiery sword into the chest of a monstrous demon. A cheery welcome to all visitors.

Just below, marking the grass, were elegant, gold-plated tombstones. A monument from the war. Each plate listed the names of those who died. You'd think that grounds solemn in nature would be trodden on with care, but I couldn't find reverence anywhere.

Protesters held up their signs, chanting something I couldn't quite make out. I pinched the fabric of my pants and migrated toward the middle seat. Our driver managed to turn down another street and avoided the hungry mob, but we passed a few newcomers with signs that read, *"medicine worshiping devils"* and *"vampires tainting the health of citizens."*

"You're frightened," Jarmiel said.

I saw how close I'd gotten to his side of the car and scooted back over to mine. "It's true, then? Angels can read people."

"It doesn't take more than a pair of eyes to see how troubled you are and the readings aren't always clear."

"Is that what Zak was trying to do before?" I held up my hand, still uncomfortable not wearing my gloves. "Do you also have to touch people?"

Jarmiel eyed my palm like an opened diary he fought to not read. "It helps. It would be like asking you to look through a window and tell me the scene. Standing too far back makes it difficult to see. Dirty smudges on the glass might distort or hide the details. If you're close enough to touch, however, the picture becomes clearer… No, I can't read your mind."

I lifted a brow. "Then how did you do that just now?"

"I was guessing."

The possibility still made my heart quicken, but we soon pulled into a gated area hidden in the forest of tall buildings. A single building sat guarded inside, mirroring the clean city that surrounded it. Its purpose confused me at first; business or religion? The formal finish at the bottom didn't quite compliment the stained-glass window at the top. A mural had been painted of the angels at war like it had been a place of worship. A church? The barrier of iron bars gave it a sense of great importance. Or a warning.

Guards, more peacekeepers, ushered our car in. My back stiffened at the sound of the gates clanging shut behind us. I felt sick. The adrenaline finally wore from my body and let me feel the full extent of my fear, like dreams after the sensation of falling.

Jarmiel's hand on my shoulder kept me grounded. "We're here."

That seemed obvious but I hadn't made the effort to move. How long had we been parked? I stepped out after him and took a good look at my new "home." Too cold and polished. Even the groomed greenery, planted in uniform lines, hurt my eyes from their vibrant leaves. The only personality came through the mural, and even then, you had to look up to see it.

Zak returned, dropping down on us from the sky. His wings sounded like sails blowing in the wind, which followed him in step and tousled my hair. "*Whoops*. My bad."

He chuckled while I fixed my face. "Welcome to EXO, Jess. Our largest facility," he said, "Volhold is a popular place but unfortunately, that includes crime. After you're officially a peace-keeper, you'll get to explore several cities, depending on where your mission sends you."

He made it sound like we were on vacation.

Peacekeepers greeted us, all of them darkly clad in their com-bat uniforms and with the same brass badge as Zak's. I watched them like a hawk. Even if I'd arrived as one of them, their ap-pearance triggered my need to flee. It shook me when they broke out of their stony character to make jokes with Zak.

"New recruit?" one of them asked and his lip twitched. I must've looked entirely out of my element, walking around with stiff legs and shifty eyes. He stared a moment too long and I crossed my arms, sensing his eyes traveling downward.

Not to make assumptions but that had been weird... *right*? Was everyone going to be that brazen? It reminded me of Peter's friends and how they'd greeted me. Never hostile exchanges but certainly bewildering.

Zak's golden-brown head rotated to me, and he winked. "Yup. You remember your first day here. Be kind."

They nodded and extended a polite enough welcome. I held my breath when I thought they would try shaking my hand, but thankfully, no one released them from their belts.

It came as no surprise that Zak was popular. I watched him get along with every single person we passed, reminding me a bit of Peter that time at his house party. People were just drawn to them. Although Peter was human and Zak had an other-worldly level of charisma.

All the angels were gorgeous but Zak stood out like a sun-flower in a bed of roses...

Okay. So, he's hot.

So was every other angel. What wasn't there to like about a flawless, handsome face or a blindingly bright personality? The goldish brown crystals of his eyes promised more summer heat that my body suddenly craved. Beauty like that had to be dangerous, like the pull from a siren's song. I shouldn't trust him right away.

As we traveled further from the entrance, my skin buzzed like we were passing through an unseen force field. Zak noticed my frazzled state. "Our security system can detect when abnormalities pass the barriers, big or small. Or invisible. Can't be too careful."

"Do people often break in?" I asked.

Did that mean Naomi could get me out?

His eyes narrowed for a split second like he heard the question I'd kept to myself. "Not often. Under normal circumstances, you'll go as you please, so long as we don't have you on a job. Since your circumstance is *special*, plan on sticking around. We need to earn each other's trust first."

Zak continued to stare at me over his shoulder but after a moment of me not budging, he smirked. Was he messing with me? How cheeky, for an angel.

A small courtyard connected the mural building to two smaller ones; one flat and rectangular, and the other made with bricks and reached three floors. They formed an uneven triangle with grass and cement path down the middle. Behind the squatty building was an extended path that led to a track. Freshly raked lines had been dragged through the dirt.

It wasn't "jail" but still felt like a prison. Albeit a nice one. I took in as much as I could but Jarmiel and Zak kept a steady pace. Just to be sure that neither could actually read my mind, I shouted some choice profanities in my head and watched the back of their heads.

Nope. No jerking of alertness. Words in my head were safe.

Zak's walk changed into something more loose and jovial. For someone who preferred flying over driving, I hadn't expected him to feel content in a cage. I felt something off while watching him. Jealousy, maybe? How could he be so annoyingly happy all the time?

"Let's get that pesky paperwork out of the way first," Zak said, "We have an educational video for you too. Apologies ahead of time. Everyone has to watch it."

He chose the main building for that, opening a pair of glass doors for Jarmiel and me to walk through. I would meet the commander of EXO. Or one of them. What would he, or she, be like? I imagined a godlike being ready to strike me down after sensing me in the hallway.

We ascended to the second floor on steel staircases, bumping into a few more faces Zak knew. They either halted completely like statues or inquired about our day. Even with Zak at my side, I could feel the peacekeepers studying me.

I knew what I looked like and still worried they'd notice something strange. My eyes were a shade of blue and green, not black like the demon's of Hell. My dirty-red hair desperately needed a trim. The essence from my summer tan still clung to my skin. All human-like camouflage.

For a while, I thought Naomi hated how I looked or secretly hated me and did everything while holding a grudge. My appearance had been a recurring argument between my aunt and me. She discouraged anything flattering, especially when I worked in the shop. Nothing could hug my curves, of which I had much. No makeup beyond tinted balms, until I turned about fifteen and demanded mascara. I figured her choice in my bizarre style helped to disguise me, although I could argue that it had the opposite effect.

In a single day, I'd felt more eyes on me than I had in my lifetime. I wanted to crawl inside my shirt and hide, except that it actually fit me correctly and left little room for such cowardice.

Zak stopped at a door and knocked, but didn't wait for a response before swinging it open. "Here we are. Your great leader... Me!"

He spun on his heel with his hands tight behind his back. I leaned around him to see if he was kidding. He wasn't.

The walls were bare and hardly anything decorated his oak desk, save for a few loose papers, clips, and an old foam cup that had to be days old. I had a feeling he spent little time there.

"Wait, really?" I asked.

Zak held his pose a while longer. "What? What's wrong?"

"I just thought it would've been Jarmiel..." I heard a snort from behind me and Zak's smile deflated. "I-I just meant he seems older?"

Older, serious, and mature.

Jarmiel stepped around me. A new glow emitted from his face. "Perhaps, if you behaved accordingly, Zakiel, no one would question your authority."

"She said you look *old*," Zak said, sounding like a sassy child, "Ancient. Wise."

Jarmiel sifted through a filing cabinet behind the desk and removed a large folder. From within, he drew out a white sheet of paper with gold lettering. "Let's get this over with. Bring up the video."

"Right." Zak swooped around his desk and retrieved a silver laptop from a drawer. He flipped it open without having to do much clicking on the keypad.

When he faced the screen at me, I prepared to be brainwashed as well as informed. As soon as the music started, I recognized it right away. The same video was released to the public ages ago to give everyone the rundown about the war.

We called it the Unhallowed War.

"How can a world drowning in so much darkness ever find peace?" The narrator begged the question as images of Terra fifty years ago faded in and out of sight. Everything went black when the voice revealed that our previous leaders had been guilty of blood rituals. "In exchange for their leadership positions and riches, the demons demanded more blood until they eventually harvested innocent souls. The pure…"

I averted my eyes to a blurry photo of a body left on a stone altar. They didn't reveal a face, but my chest burned with hate and pity for the human I never would've known. Only demons could be so cruel to ask, but were humans any better to deliver..?

Understandably, the crimes caused an uprising, but by then, it was too late. The demon had enough power to break the barriers between realms and invade Terra.

"Then began the fall of human civilization…" The narrator kept a solemn tune. Much of the calamity was captured on video too. Earthquakes tore down buildings and temples across the world. Monsters escaped the shadowy depths and ravaged anyone and anything in sight. The greater beings, demons of higher regard, rode in on their chariots of blood or captured the skies with wings from their backs. It would've been a spectacle if not so terrifyingly horrid.

The video didn't reveal anything too violent. Just enough to make a point. Demons devastated the human armies. Countries were seized and cities were demolished. Humans still had their numbers but they quickly dwindled.

"Hope was lost," the narrator said, "Until, a spark was lit."

The heroic act from Heaven. Angels heard the mortals cry for help and sent their soldiers to Terra. Their numbers didn't match the Demons so they took to natural means to repopulate the earth with angel children. More soldiers. That began the tragic period of demons, and even humans, hunting the children.

"A brave group, later given the name Hallowed Saints, preserved as many angels as they could to stand against the demons. Years of chaos, starvation, enslavement, torture, and death were finally brought to an end." The screen got so bright that I had to squint. Angels flew from the skies, descending on Hell's leaders.

Their angelic light broke through the dark that tainted the land. It still took a year to achieve victory.

The original video usually ended there but that time, the narrator introduced the supernaturals also involved in rescuing the world. "Vampires, werewolves, people of the sea and of the woods, fairies, and beings beyond human imagination also wanted demons banished from Terra."

No one had believed that the supernaturals would side with the humans. Before the war, no one could even agree that they existed, labeling them as myths and legends. Human history didn't exactly glow with records of peace and acceptance.

I leaned in closer, listening to the words I'd never heard before.

"Theodore Blaxill, leader of a militant group of vampires, single-handedly rescued an entire underground group of humans and angel children. He's remembered for his thirst for justice."

Why would they remove any of this from the original video? Wouldn't it help humans appreciate supernaturals better? I was about to ask but then, an angel captured the screen. "The answer is yes. Terra can overcome and find peace again. New Peace."

I noted the casual name-drop of the angel's recovery movement. The man's black hair reached past his shoulders, not a single strand separating from the other. His complexion was bright like white sand on a beach, but with a groomed beard that framed his lips and chin. With one slight tilt of his head, I caught the glistening of jewels from his ebony eyes.

I don't even know why I thought it, but I knew I *never* wanted to meet that man.

"The only way to achieve New Peace is to strive for the light as one. I am Uriah. Welcome to EXO," he spoke and my ears tingled. The EXO logo of the angel wing inside a circle spun around in the middle of the screen. "Peacekeepers can be today's Hallowed Saints. Demons have lost the war but the threat of Hell is never truly gone. We will defend the souls of Terra forever—"

Zak slowly closed the laptop before Uriah could finish his last thoughts.

"Wasn't that lovely?" He removed it from the table, leaving me to question why he'd made me watch it in the first place. I watched him fiddle with a few pens from a jar while Jarmiel slid the paper across his desk. My eyes could barely process any of the words I looked at.

"This contract is binding, Miss Winters," Jarmiel said, "Two years with the title of peacekeeper, under the command of Za-kiel, The Angel of Mercy. This includes the three-month training period until your rank is achieved."

I felt like a heavy stone dropped into my stomach. An angel's full title was rarely shared; something to do with their own humility, I think. It all made sense why Zak had recruited me. He'd shown me *mercy*.

Zak used his pointer finger to push a gold pen as close to me as he could before the thing could roll off. "Having second thoughts?"

I bit the inside of my cheek, filtering a few of my original, shrewd comments in my head. He knew perfectly well that I didn't have other options. I picked up the cool metal with my, now sweating, palm. "Why me? You guys don't know anything about me or if I'm even qualified for this."

Zak finally lowered himself into his seat. "You mind if I have a moment with Jess?"

"Yes." His colleague answered.

"Will you allow it anyway?" Zak asked.

Jarmiel didn't bother. He took his leave. Zak leaned back in his chair, only to stand right back up again. He sidestepped around his desk, gliding like in a dance. "How do you feel towards humans, Jess?"

"Humans? They're fine. I sort of envy them."

"Really? They're weak compared to someone like you."

I flinched. "I don't know. A simple life sounds like a peaceful one."

"How do you feel about yourself then?"

I refrained from answering too hastily. There was distrust and loathing between demons and humans and for good reason. I didn't love that I had demon blood, or the blood of anything that thrived off of the sufferings of others, in me. Aside from my irritating inability to touch others without causing them pain, I couldn't understand what made me anything like them. "I wish I wasn't what I am," I said.

"You hate demons?"

"Don't you?"

Zak rapped his fingers on his jawline but didn't answer. "What about vampires?"

"They creep me out a little. I'm sure some are perfectly pleasant."

My aunt and I had a hard time with vampires and shifters in the past. Their keen sense of smell along with my scent attracted a lot of attention; yet another reason we chose a boring, human-populated city.

"And what about me?" Zak asked. He stopped his ceaseless wandering and planted both feet in my direction.

"You? You're… I just don't see you as someone I could relate with." I gestured to his entire frame. *Flawless. A beacon of light.* Definitely not related to demons.

Zak found a spot on the wall to lean against. His luscious head of hair fanned against the white paint. "Angels relinquish half their power when they live on Terra. Did you know that? The same goes for demons. This seems to be the only realm where light and dark can survive at the same time, unlike heaven which is primarily light. I was excited to live in humanity. In imperfection. How else do we better understand something than to experience it?"

He paused. "I was ignorant at the time. I thought I was already perfect and above humans. After living another twenty-four mortal years, I realized that was never the case."

Zak's young face aged the more I heard him speak. The veil to his wisdom and pain lifted and I saw a spirit well beyond his years, which I guess was accurate.

He snapped back to his happy self. "I don't think I'm better than anyone, just as I believe you're not a lost cause. A demon with a heart like yours… that could change things."

He finally said it out loud.

Demon.

I felt my brow pinch. "Change things how?"

He withheld his next words by pressing his lips together. It took another moment for him to release them. "I'd like to see the dawn of *real* peace, and that may look differently to so many species all living together. Your existence alone is enough to convince me it's possible. I know we discussed demon magic but *light* comes from you too…"

"Light?" How could that be? Had that been what the golden sparks were in the dark cloud? My gaze dropped. I didn't want to get my hopes up just to be crushed when I remained a monster. "I don't understand."

"I don't either but we have time to figure it out," he said, "Of course, achieving peace could take several lifetimes, but it can begin now. With you."

"Is this the pep-talk you give all your recruits?"

Zak shook his head slightly. He returned to his desk where the contract still lay on display and set his fingers on the header. The gold pen had made a home in my palm but I finally lifted my hand to meet the parchment.

"I'm asking a lot of you to be here, but I promise to help you in return. You don't have to live in fear of yourself." He spoke so softly and out of character that I had to look up and see if it was still him. I felt the world slow under his gaze. "Can you trust me?" he asked.

"I can't promise anything like peace…" I said, wanting to see if that would change his mind. "I'm not exactly a hero."

"The best heroes are the ones who don't want to be."

"What does that mean?"

Zak shrugged. "The ones who don't want the responsibility are the ones who understand the weight of it. I know you saved those kids from the party at the expense of exposing yourself or losing your own life. Give yourself more credit."

I scoffed. I *would* do my best; my best to avoid jail or a death sentence.

The pen moved slowly across the line at the bottom of the page until my name was printed in swirls of black ink. Zak's smile grew until it felt like we were sitting in proximity to the sun. "Welcome to EXO, Jess Winters."

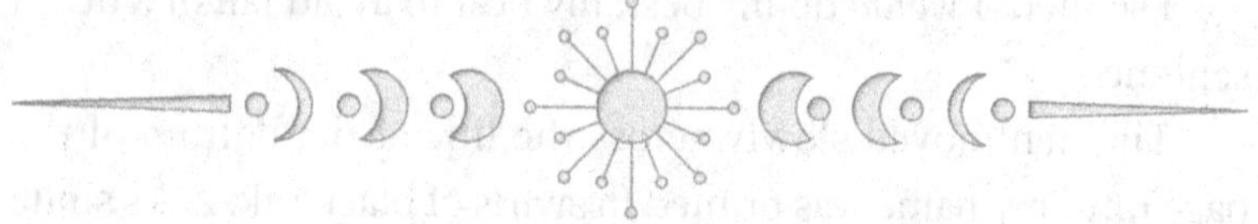

I was a dog on a leash.

The invisible chain, conjured from my own imagination, tugged me along as I followed after Zak. Either my subconscious took our binding contract too literally or something else.

I'd signed my life away for two years. Not too awful. Although, I wondered how long jail time would have been in comparison. At least I wasn't sharing a cell with a roommate who wanted to eat me.

Jarmiel hadn't waited for us so Zak and I were alone again. I didn't know how to feel about his friendliness. He kept the small talk going while we descended the building again, like my life hadn't dramatically changed. The elevators opened at the bottom where a mini-mall happened to be.

More people in peacekeeper gear waved as they walked by. Immediately, my chest constricted, feeling the attention growing around us. Everyone knew Zak and he, being so polite, introduced me as well. So different than when my aunt and I were in public.

Zak entered the first store to the right. Shelves neatly stacked with goods fanned out in the semi-circle-shaped room. "Grab whatever you need. Clothes, snacks, whatever you want in your room."

My room. I felt my make-believe leash loosen as I wandered through the aisles. What do I even get? Food sounded good. *Really* good. When was the last time I ate?

I picked out some bathroom essentials like soap, toothbrushes, deodorant, and a towel; stuff that I hadn't been able to take from home. My clothes were still there as well, so I picked a few outfits to at least get me a couple of days' use.

From the weight of my haul, I worried about the expense but when I checked the tag on some stretchy pants, my jaw dropped. So cheap! Cheap compared to how much I'd seen similar ones go for online.

I grabbed three more in different colors before finding the food. The junk was conveniently stationed next to the aisle with synthetic blood for vampires. The dark, ruby contents of the glass bottles reminded me of barbeque sauce and I gagged a little.

When I returned to the register, Zak eyed my armful of chocolates and clothes and laughed. "I think we should grab some dinner."

"Sounds good." My voice had a scratch to it. The day went by so fast without food or drink. I popped open one of my water bottles before I even checked out. "I can pay for this, Zak."

He already slid a card to the woman at the checkout. "Allow me. You can come back once we set you up with a card."

I blushed, feeling like an idiot. No shit, I didn't even have my wallet on me. "I can put the pretzels back… What do you mean, set me up with a card?"

"Keep the pretzels! The cafeteria is great but so is having your own stash. We'll get you a new license and a currency card. Works like any old card."

"I'm getting paid?" I asked, feeling like a child with a million questions, "I thought this was, like, punishment."

"Are we not having fun?" Zak clutched his chest, letting out a dramatic wheeze. "I'm kidding, sort of. Peacekeepers get paid per job, along with a monthly stipend. The stipend is enough to get you by, so don't go nuts with it."

"That's really cool, actually," I said, "Um. Thanks for the clothes. And pretzels."

"Anytime."

Were the angels using tax dollars to pay EXO's members? The war couldn't destroy *everything* and as godly as angels were, they couldn't create gold, nor come up with another incentive for the humans to cooperate.

I glanced down at my selection of gym clothes. "Do I need to buy a uniform?"

"We'll provide that later," he said, "All you need to worry about right now is getting in shape for the exams."

Our next location took us up one flight of stairs. An assortment of smells, baked bread and the cozy bitterness of coffee, hit my deprived stomach, making it growl in protest. "This is the cafeteria," Zak said, "You can come here between six AM and nine PM. They have pizza today, excellent."

Three of the four stations offered human-friendly menus and the last, a beverage station where the coffee smell was coming from. The closer we got, I picked up on another, more metallic scent. Jars lined on the shelves, disguised with decorative calligraphy, containing synthetic blood; a vampire bar. They also offered coffee, tea, and smoothies.

Zak offered to buy my pizza too. I didn't want to loot him for all he had but he kept insisting and my stomach kept grumbling. "Once you have money, you can buy me dinner," he said, "How's that?"

Watching him put away pizza was an event. He bought three slices for himself and inhaled them in three bites each, somehow keeping grease from his lips and the vulnerable, white shirt he wore. Did he have to be perfect at *everything*?

He pinched his fingers together and sprinkled the crumbs onto his plate. "I know we just got here but what do you think?"

"This is *really* nice compared to jail," I said.

To be honest, I felt like I was being tricked.

He winked. "I think so too."

"You must get a lot of funding?"

"We didn't use to. Heaven's law states that we shouldn't seek income of any kind but Terra is different from Heaven, though."

"How else do you live?" I asked.

"With love, of course."

I took another bite of pizza and mulled it over. That sounded cheesy as hell.

A small TV hanging out of the kitchen where we got our food had a story about a recent citizen's death; some hot, young socialite who recently married a brooding artist with a taste for blood. But the groom got hungry on their honeymoon.

The table next to us had a couple of female peacekeepers snickering over it. I ignored them at first, but their excited voices stole my attention.

"Not sure why humans keep trying to marry vampires. Don't bring things into your bed that wanna eat you."

Her friend giggled. "Funny. That's exactly why I let people in my bed."

The two women caught me staring and waved. I politely returned the gesture before dying of embarrassment.

"Zak?" I blurted out, unsure of what I wanted to say yet, "I'd feel better with gloves on. I didn't see any at the store but could we go back?"

Zak's smiles should be bottled and sold as antidepressants. He didn't even have to say anything and I felt safer.

"Here." He reached into his brown jacket and handed me some basic, black gloves. When had he gotten them? My routine kicked in and I slid them over my fingers in record time before letting out a breath.

"I didn't hurt you back at the station?" I asked. He had been pretty careless around me so far but I didn't want another accident, like with Peter. The news story about the vampire could have been about the two of us; "local boy killed by demon girl at a house party."

"*Ah*, don't worry about me." Zak scooped up my trash and tossed everything before I could offer to do it myself. " I don't think you could kill anyone here so easily with a single touch."

"You don't"

"Most of the people here are trained to handle, well, people like you and me. So, we're more equipped should you lose control, which *won't* happen because we're going to teach you too!"

What was it I felt? Relief? While being lumped in with other demons stung, the realization that EXO wasn't helpless to my abilities reassured me.

"Ready to see where you'll be staying?" he asked.

My stomach knotted up. Nerves? I *knew* I couldn't be hungry after that, but an annoying itch lingered that pizza couldn't scratch. Water hadn't helped either. The headache I felt a while back returned. Funny, I hadn't been one for migraines.

I followed Zak back outside while massaging my temples. It could've been the stress; a lot had happened. My aunt spirited off somewhere and I hadn't exactly had a moment to stop worrying. We ventured back outside to the courtyard when I heard Zak trying to get my attention. "You okay?"

"Yeah," I said, "Just my head."

Something seemed to click in his mind and he snapped his fingers together. "That stuff your aunt gave you, you've been taking it for a while, right?"

"All my life." Brewing her powder into a tea had always been the easiest way to get it down. Add a little honey and I could ignore the sharp or bitter flavors.

"Let's clear it out of your system. The less dependent you are, the easier self-control will be."

I figured he'd bring that up. It wouldn't be the first time I tried skipping days out of spite or curiosity. The headaches had never been a consequence before, but "that stuff" kept me more human than a demon, according to Naomi. Without it, I didn't know what I would turn into.

"You think I'm having withdrawals?" I asked. Naomi claimed nothing addictive had been added to it. Just herbs and a spell or two.

"After almost twenty years of repression?" Zak shuddered. "You'll definitely have withdrawals. I'm surprised you're not in worse shape."

"What if…" I licked my lips. The question felt stuck to my tongue.

What if I did have a hideous demon form and the drugs kept me human?

What if I quit the drug and grew horns overnight?

He smiled. "Whatever it holds back, it's nothing you can't handle."

Again with his unreasonable amount of confidence in me. What exactly had been in those supplements? I thought long and hard about the taste of my pills or tea. Dirt. Always dirt. What ungodly food groups helped a demon thrive, the blood of virgins? *Gods, I hope not.*

Had Naomi even been capable of obtaining human essence? Stealing a lock of someone's hair worked for charms and curses. What would a potion of suppression require? I had an idea, although I hoped Naomi hadn't been familiar with it. A darker circle existed in our world that advertised the forbidden; a black market. They had anything you could think of or *wouldn't* think of. Humans, supernaturals—yes, the living and breathing kind—drugs, weapons, magic, and various dangerous artifacts.

I pushed the thoughts away. My aunt's paranoia would've kept her far away from something sketchy like that. But then,

I remembered what she said about her teleporting broomstick and how "expensive" it had been.

While I endured my third mental crisis of the day, we came upon the brick building. A spacious common area waited beyond the doors. The warm brown and orange tones felt much cozier from the cold exterior of the other building. Couches had been staged with plenty of pillows. A medium-sized flatscreen hung on the wall, still humming from someone forgetting to shut it all the way off. Vending machines sat available next to a communal kitchen where the essence of someone's burnt popcorn still clung to the air.

"Here we are," Zak said, "You'll find more peacekeepers in training here. Many of them are in similar situations as you and just need a place to stay."

"Am I the youngest recruit?" I asked.

"Nope. Eighteen is the volunteer age and most new recruits we try to keep under thirty."

"You mentioned earth years. How old are you, exactly?" *Am I allowed to think about what his thick hair or muscly shoulders feel like, if he's a billion years old,* was my real question.

Zak's cheeks puffed up like I'd insulted a squirrel, not an angel. "Isn't that a rude question?"

"It's just that you don't look much older."

"Relax, I'm joking," he said, "I'm twenty-five earth years, I think."

"You think?"

"Eternity does a good job at ruining birthdays."

While I silenced the obnoxious butterflies in my stomach, someone made their way down the set of stairs and into the room with us. Mousy hair dressed the stranger's head in a tousled mess as if he'd just woken from a nap. His face appeared sunken with deep, dark rims around his eyes. He looked like a walking corpse. My eyes gravitated to the plaid pants hanging from his hips.

His casual appearance caught me off guard and I was surprised further by his deep, drawled voice. "Oh, you're back."

"Look at you, sunshine," Zak said, "Come say hello."

Upon first glance, he struck me as someone who stayed in on weekends with a pizza and maybe his pet cat. Not keen on social gatherings. However, he approached us without a lick of nervousness. "Call me Guy. What poor soul did Zak recruit this time?"

A guy named Guy? Easy enough to remember. If he'd intended on being humorous with the indifferent expression on his face, I couldn't tell. The low vibrations he spoke could lull me into a deep, dark sleep.

He sounded oddly familiar.

"Have I…" I analyzed his face for a second too long. My voice struck a high note to compensate for being rude. "I'm Jess. Nice to meet you."

A tiny smirk formed on Guy's lips. "Zak treating you alright? He can be a bit abrasive."

He watched us with cool, gray eyes and I noticed something interesting. With a little trick of the light, I could see soft, crystalized lines in his irises but he didn't possess the same warmth as Zak or Jarmiel. Could he really be an angel too?

"That's not very nice," Zak said, "I bought her yoga pants."

"*And* intrusive." Guy shrugged. "Glad to see you ended up here. Probably your best outcome."

I felt my brows inching closer together. He spoke as if he knew about my arrest already.

Zak proceeded to ask Guy how things went during his absence. From the lack of sparkle in his eye, it appeared Zak actually knew how to be serious when need be. "Thanks for holding down the fort. We can chat more later."

He turned to me. "You're on the third floor, Jess. I can show you."

Before I could follow after him toward the stairs, Guy extended one, pale hand from his pockets. "I'll be seeing you around, then?"

There shouldn't have been a concern since I had gloves again but before our fingertips even touched, a chill prickled down my neck. Taking his hand was like grasping an icicle, even with fabric covering my flesh. The cold traveled all the way up my arm and spread into my chest.

I looked up and saw *him*. Again.

The face of Death.

His bony complexion had two bottomless pits staring back at me. How did he do that? An illusion or was the human flesh he wore the actual facade? I took my hand back with a sharp gasp. As soon as I did, the mirage faded, and Guy's image returned. He sported a cheeky grin while I calmed my beating heart. "Goodnight," he said.

The warmth came flooding back almost immediately after Guy stepped away. He took a bottle of water from the fridge and I scurried off to find Zak. I thought we'd take the stairs but he stood in front of metal doors to another elevator.

My eyes remained glued to my hand for a while until I heard Zak suppressing a snort. "Sorry if he startled you."

"Was he the one at my apartment?" I asked a little hotly, not enjoying his humored reaction.

"Yes," Zak said, "You gave Max some trouble, so I called reinforcements."

My spine stiffened. *Don't tell me…*

The werewolf who chased me down. A new chilling sensation danced down my back, quickly followed by dread. Of course, everyone I'd evaded would be there.

It really had been Death, then. I touched a reaper. *And he wears pajamas!*

"How did you get reapers to work for you?" I asked.

"Just the one and he chose to," he answered simply, but there had to be more to it, "Hey, let's get you settled. I'm sure you're tired."

Like I would fall asleep anytime soon.

The elevator doors opened to a maroon, carpeted floor, and we rode upward until the lit-up numbers hit three. Once out, we stopped at the first door to our right. "We just got new mattresses, so no need to worry about the cleanliness of the previous tenant," he said, "Not bad, huh?"

He pushed the door in and allowed me to step inside. I expected a cot, metal bunk beds, a roommate, or the width of a walk-in closet. But no. It had a single bed with a blanket and pillow folded at the end. An empty desk sat by a window where I could watch the city from a distance. My own room back home felt cramped in comparison.

"Not bad?" I laughed, "Is this a joke?"

"You can personalize it any way you'd like. You don't have your own toilet, though. Gotta share with the others down the hall," Zak said.

"This is… nice." I could pretend I had a college dorm. A silly fantasy to have but then, why had it made me excited?

"Is there any way I could get my phone back?" It felt awkward to ask, especially after he'd done so much already. I had no media presence or friends to get back to, but I wanted *something* in case Naomi reached out.

I could tell by his narrowed gaze that I wouldn't like the answer. "I'll look into it but it wouldn't hurt if you went off the grid for a while. Let the excitement die down and we'll get you through exams and come back to this after."

Zak gave me another pat on the arm. "Don't take it too hard. Could be worse, right?"

"Right…" I forced a smile that he responded to in kind. He left, saying I should get actuated with my space and some rest.

I knew why demons hated angels now. Who, in their right mind, would choose to torture themselves this way? Even if I'd been wary of Zak, I didn't hate the feeling of sunlight and radiance with him near. With it gone, I was left as a dusty moth coveting the flame. Why would anyone want to be alone after that?

I was feeling out my mattress when I heard a soft knock.

"Zak?" I opened the door. My sharp inhale was too loud to play it off as subtle.

Guy's silver eyes flickered down at me. "No. Just thought you might want this."

He held out an arm with a black duffle looped around his palm. Not just any bag.

My bag!

"Sorry about before," he said, "You were a job. Nothing personal."

His apology lacked any real conviction. I reached for it, unsure at first. Why did he have it and why was he offering it to me freely?

"Guess you did your job well," I said.

He worked his tongue on the inside of his cheek. His lips parted and I expected more but all he said was. "It would seem. Have a good night. Jess."

You too. Prick.

I closed the door and cocooned myself in blankets after that. Furious but also curious. I imagined reapers as ghoulish phantoms who only ran with spirits, hiding a wealth of otherworldly knowledge in their shadowy abyss. Guy and his pajama pants turned my upside down world diagonal.

It would be weird not waking up in the apartment tomorrow. The cats wouldn't tickle my nose with the scent of their piss, which really wasn't a loss. They weren't *really* ours. My aunt just had a weak spot for strays. A few of our favorites were welcome in the apartment but would leave through the windows as they pleased.

Naomi really should have been more concerned about shifters, now that I thought about it.

The darkness in my room grew heavier as my body sank into the mattress. Two years or not, I already felt in my gut that I was never going back home. I was just one of the many strays that used our home for refuge.

Maybe, I'd always been.

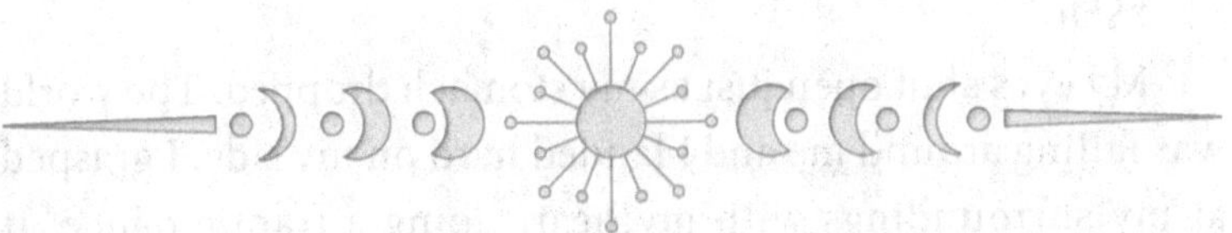

My dream that night consisted of cozy blackness and rhythmic vibrations. Nothing special or amiss, until *something* beckoned me deeper into the abyss. Not a person or even a voice. It was more like a feeling that didn't belong to me.

I drifted through the nothing, like a twig floating in black water. There didn't seem to be anything interesting to see for a while. And then, a bright spark in the distance.

The light flickered incessantly as if the darkness was a fortress to knock against. I veered from the path of aimlessness and migrated toward its warmth. Was it even possible to feel the heat while in a dream?

As I got closer, the light sounded a dull roar like rolling thunder.

"*Jessebel…*"

The darkness behind me grew colder the further I left it behind. Seeing my cooperation, the light created more of itself, spreading like spores. It ate away at the black, fighting for dominance in the empty space.

My head started ringing from the pressure building on both sides. It felt like my body wanted to split in two; starting from the top of my skull to my navel. Both elements wanted to exist but couldn't.

Then, from the black, two pale arms with blackened fingernails shot out and reached for me.

"Shit!"

My eyes shot open just as my stomach dropped. The world was falling around me and I landed hard on my side. I grasped at my surroundings with my heart doing a frantic dance. It took a moment for reality to set in, but with my face flat on the floor and a blanket tangled around my legs, the image became clear.

I silently apologized to whoever lived below me. Hopefully, it wasn't Guy. That would be mortifying.

Groaning, I pressed my palms into my eyes. There was a dull throbbing in my skull, probably from hitting the floor with it. My skin was buzzing too, like a limb falling asleep, but it was all over my body. After some deep inhales, I was back to feeling myself. Myself with a headache that is.

The generic desk I was given also came with a small, electric clock. I squinted at the glowing numbers. Good, because I didn't have a phone anymore...

After midnight? It was too early to start the day but I wasn't feeling sleepy after that. Hopefully, my downstairs neighbor slept through my abrupt tremor.

I became aware of the sweat on my back and the strong urge to pee. Not to mention, I hadn't brushed my teeth yet either. I hadn't even left my room since Guy's little visit. My exhaustion took precedence over hygiene, but no longer.

I was collecting my toiletries when it dawned on me that we weren't given individual bathrooms. That meant leaving the safety of my little box. I poked my head out of my room first; half expecting the reaper to be haunting the hallway. It wasn't totally pitch-black, thanks to the light pollution outside creeping in through the windows.

Just diagonal from my room was a door with a restroom label. Three long, quick strides, and I was in. I expected cold metal grates and ugly, yellowing tile. Still had prison on the brain, but the interior was clean and white with blue tones.

I had the place to myself and occupied a shower stall. The hot water felt soothing against my scalp. An hour might've passed, I wasn't sure. It was difficult to pull myself out of it but once I did, I brushed my hair and teeth, dried the roots of my hair with my blow dryer, and called it good.

Before leaving, I caught sight of my reflection. My dream had done a number on me. The sweat was all washed off but my eyes looked like I hadn't slept at all. I leaned over the sink, staring harder into the mirror.

Something was glowing beneath my skin and made a spider web from my cheekbones to my eyes. When I blinked, it was gone. I waited a few moments to ensure it wasn't going to happen again.

My fingers trembled against my face as I pressed into the skin, searching for more light. Maybe I had just seen things, although I knew what I was telling myself was a comforting lie. Zak said I used demon's magic, but somehow, light as well. Did that mean angel magic?

When I left, the hallway was no longer empty. The realization came when I stepped right into their path.

Holy crap.

She was *pristine*.

It was like looking at a porcelain doll. A little creepy, but also perfect. Her skin was so smooth and her hair the color of moonlight, cascaded over her shoulders. The eyes that scanned me were a deep dark color, which I assumed brown at first until they hit the light just right.

Red.

She stopped but didn't redirect to get around me. Instead, she stood with an aloof, dullness in her eyes as she slowly examined me. My ends were still damp and I wore an oversized t-shirt and shorts, but she looked like she was on her way to model for an athletic magazine. Her sports bra and leggings highlighted her toned body and creamy smooth abs. I glanced down at myself, feeling like a potato. Where was she off to that late? Or was it early?

"Hello." Her voice was soft and void of emotion. She hardly moved or even breathed. "I haven't seen your face before."

"Yeah, hi. I'm Jess. I'm… new," I said.

"I see."

I watched the vampire lean in a few inches. Her nostrils made delicate puffs as she located my scent. I was glad to have just showered, otherwise, it would've been both weird *and* embarrassing. "What are you?" she asked.

"Nothing special." I took a step back. Admitting what I was hadn't become part of my vocabulary yet.

"I smell demon blood."

"*Half*-demon," I said. She was probably used to the smell of demons as it was their job to hunt them. "I didn't catch your name?"

The vampire sported a subtle but wicked grin at my attempt to dance around her questions. Admittedly, it was sloppy. She probably knew I didn't have to ask what she was. "Mallory. It's nice to meet someone who doesn't put a name to my face."

"Oh. Are you famous?"

Her smile widened and I was able to see her sparkling, sharp fangs.

"It was so lovely to meet you. Jess, the half-demon," she said and glided away.

*　*　*

It took a while to shake off the weird vibes Mallory left behind. Luckily, I was still able to get a couple more hours of sleep before the sun came up. When I woke, I was plagued by a splitting headache again.

Zak didn't leave me with much instruction, so I hoped to catch one of my dorm mates and ask them where to go. I hurried to pick out some clothing while ignoring the pain in my skull. Makeup didn't seem necessary, especially if we were going to be sweating. My lashes were pretty thick on their own, anyway; a gift from parents I didn't know.

I roped my hair back into a bun. The new workout pants from the store were stretchy and supportive, just as I'd hoped. Women back in Haverwick would be green with envy knowing how cheap I'd gotten them. I was smaller around the waist but *wide* at the hips, so when it came to shopping for clothes, it felt like trying to fit a triangle shape into a rectangle.

My trusty gloves were last. I tugged them up to my wrists and paused. Were they all that effective anymore? Zak said I wouldn't have to worry about hurting anyone here but I wasn't brave enough to leave them behind just yet.

I wolfed down an oatmeal bar from my snack stash just in case I was running late. It felt like something was twisting inside me like I'd had too much coffee and fed my anxiety. I wish that had been the case.

Coffee sounded amazing.

I didn't run into a single soul on my way to the elevator. No one was in the lounge either, but cups had been used in the sink. Great. People had been awake long before me. I didn't waste another second and hurried outside.

As luck would have it, and maybe some divine intervention, I had an escort waiting for me on the other side of the doors. Zak in all his handsome, angelic glory, stood under the overcast sky in a casual sweat outfit. Anyone else would've resembled a marshmallow. His head tilted back as he watched birds flying away.

He sensed me then and turned sharply. When his face lit up like the morning sun, my heart made an annoying jump. "You look refreshed," he said, "Glad you got to catch up on some sleep."

I nodded, unsure of how to take that compliment. "Thanks. Where are we going?"

"I thought I'd help you find your way." He paused. "Training might be rough at first, especially during your withdrawals, but don't chicken out on me, 'kay?"

"Saying that just makes me apprehensive."

"*Ha!* My bad. But hey, I'll be here the whole way. You start to get the shakes or feel like you're gonna puke just give me a nudge."

Oh, good. Throwing up my insides was exactly how I'd wanted my first day to go.

Zak just snapped his finger in the direction east of us and moved along. A large gated area blocked us from a dirt track and a well-groomed, grass field but we let ourselves inside. He continued with his goofy banter until we reached a small group huddled together.

The number of heads was smaller than I expected. One girl stood calm and stoic with her hands behind her back. Her skin had a cool hue and her deep, blueish-green hair consisted of several smaller braids into a larger one. She turned my way once, acknowledging that I existed, and then faced forward again.

A high voice squeaked from somewhere close to me. "Hi!"

My eyes dropped to see a very short blonde girl with dyed-pink tips talking up at me. Her hazel eyes were popping out of her head and she grinned, showing all her teeth.

"My name's Tori," she said, "You're Jessebel, right?"

"Y-Yeah, Jess is fine. Good to meet you."

"Jess. Sorry. I tried bothering you earlier but you must've been sleeping like a rock." She giggled. "It sounded like you hurt yourself."

So, someone had heard me after all.

"Sorry if I was loud," I said, "I just… tripped?"

"Well stop throwing yourself around like that, you'll give me a heart attack." Her laughing stopped. "You're pretty. Are you a vampire too? Elf? No… I don't see the ears."

I snorted. It was flattering to be compared to an elf. Elves were probably the only other creatures that challenged the youth and beauty of the blood drinkers or the immortality of angels. "I mean, thank you, but no I'm neither," I said.

Tori tapped her chin. I assumed she was still trying to guess without asking. "There's definitely something about you, though."

"You can tell?" I asked, "I mean, I guess we're all something. What about you, if you don't mind me asking?"

She grinned. "It's a secret."

"Don't be rude, Vittoria." A second and velvety, female voice chimed in. I felt my stomach sink at the sight of the vampire from last night, now approaching us.

Mallory's long, white hair was tied back in the perfect pony-tail, not a strand out of place. She had someone with her this time, a boy with reddish, brown hair and a blank expression. "You shouldn't ask if you aren't willing to share," Mallory continued.

She flashed her pearly fangs as her lips curled upward. Without warning, the vampire came up to Tori and thrust her arm into her stomach. I flinched, assuming she had just committed a great assault, but when I watched Tori's face for any indication of pain, there was none.

A wispy hole in Tori's body appeared where Mallory's arm was, allowing a path all the way out to her back.

"What…" The rest of my sentence died.

"A spirit," Mallory said, "Quirky little things, ghosts."

"It's more fun when it's a surprise." Tori frowned. "You didn't have to ruin it."

How was that possible? She looked so real and tangible before me. Were wandering spirits a casual thing and my aunt just kept the house heavily saged? I slowly wrapped my head around the idea that a dead girl was standing in front of us; nothing ghoulish or ghostly about her either.

Mallory slipped her arm back and shook it like it had gotten wet. "Our new friend says she's part demon. Isn't that right, Jess?"

That got Tori's attention off of her frustration. "Oh, really? Don't demons have horns coming out of their heads?"

Mallory's tone was dripping with ulterior motives. "It's ignorant to believe that all demons look the same. Jess could just be a late bloomer."

My body tensed, sensing the danger as Mallory took a step toward me. She was doing that thing again where she wanted to invade my personal space, but I doubted it was just for a sniff. "I could always perform a taste test to be sure? I have a diverse palette."

I slid a hand over my neck. "I'll pass, thanks…"

"Don't you have a harem of human boys to get your breakfast from?" Tori scoffed, coming to my aid. "You're training to be a peacekeeper, not a connoisseur."

Mallory raised a perfectly shaped brow. "Do *you* have the same meal every day? Oh, that's right. You're unable to delight in anything but floating about."

Wow.

Tori didn't have much to say back, but I could tell from the way her eyes dimmed that it was a sensitive subject. I had zero experience with spirits, but if they lived as ghosts, they probably didn't need to eat or use the bathroom; nothing that mortals were required to do.

I wasn't sure what Mallory's deal was, but I was already over it. The words fell out of my mouth before I could stop them. "I've always been curious," I started, "As a vampire, do you like a side of STD with your liquid diet, or do you prefer a salty chance of high cholesterol?"

What was *that*?

It was too late to take it back. I don't know what compelled me to snap like that, but I could sense Tori's growing smile next to me. At least it made her happy.

The vampiress, however, sneered. There was a drawn-out silence as if Mallory wanted to kill us with the tension. "I prefer my blood spicier, actually."

The way her eyes inspected my neck made me gulp.

"Anyway," Mallory carried on, "This is my youngest brother, Darren. He's a man of few words, but perhaps you'll get along? He's not one to indulge either."

Darren looked nothing like her. Even his eyes were more amber than red. Diluted. It was usually a sign that they adapted to the synthetic blood and didn't drink straight from the live, pulsing, tap. I found that oddly comforting.

"Hello." I offered but didn't receive more than a nod.

Thankfully, more people showed up on the field. Their conversations amongst each other divided the vampire's attention. While Mallory turned her pretty head, Darren had not. His cold stare never left my face. So, I just accepted the awkwardness; too afraid to turn my back on either of them.

"I guess you know Mallory and now Darren, one of her delightful brothers," Tori said. They could easily overhear us, but Darren had no reaction. He continued to look gloomy and uninterested.

"One?" I asked, warily examining each new figure coming in. "Is anyone else in the group just as charming?"

Tori moved closer to my side. She was perfectly pleasant company, but the whole spirit thing still wigged me out. Would I feel anything if she bumped my shoulder or not? She leaned her head toward the entrance. "Yara is cool but hard to talk to. Don't take it personally. I think it's a siren thing?"

I assumed Yara was the girl with blue-toned hair based on her reverence. A siren? I was surprised to see her so far from the ocean.

Tori continued, "Max is kind of a hothead but I think it's from drama with his clan… don't tell him I said that. But Barrett is nice. Everyone likes Barrett."

The next two Tori mentioned came walking over together. One carried a heavy, furrowed brow over blue eyes and wore a permanent scowl. Had to be the hothead. Max. His hands were buried deep in his jacket pockets as if he could project his disdain for everyone with his clothing alone. A large nose took residence in the middle of his face that was framed by light hair.

I spotted a tattoo on the back of his exposed calf; a mass of symbols—*clan* symbols—I'd seen on other werewolves. The ink had been drawn so heavily that my own skin began to sting at the thought of the intense needlework.

His buddy, Barrett, also had a tattoo. The same one, but on his shoulder instead. He was chatting Max's ear off with the energy of a labrador. I could see his scalp with how short he kept his hair. "Hey! New recruit."

Barrett hustled over to Tori and me, his hand out for me to shake. "What's up? I'm Barrett."

I took a breath before taking his hand. Nothing. I didn't feel anything. The gloves had done their job just fine but I fell forward from his powerful grip.

"Jess," I said.

He grinned. "Cool. This is Max. Sandulf clan."

Ahh. Knew it.

Most wolf shifters, especially when religiously involved in their clans, forwent surnames and used clan names instead. Hopefully, they had a system down to avoid inbreeding, though.

Mallory yawned behind her dainty hand. "The mighty alpha with his pack of *one*. How adorable."

Max's growl came from deep within his chest and rumbled like the earth was shaking. When his burning, sapphire eyes reached me, I felt a surge of his dominance, almost like he had a magic of his own that compelled me to feel weak in front of him.

Wait. He was familiar.

"Hello, Mallory," Barrett said with a taunting sweetness to match her own, "How *is* the princess this morning?"

"She was excellent until you fleabags turned the air foul," she said, "Have some self-respect and bathe, then maybe your clan will want you back."

Max already looked like a ticking time bomb but Mallory kept prodding. I was expecting some sort of confrontation between the species, and yet, I still jumped out of my skin when Max leaped at Mallory with the speed and force of a truck. I know because the sound his chest made against Barrett's extended arm was deafening.

"Whoa—" Barrett staggered after almost clotheslining him. "Could we not do this today?"

"Yes, where are your manners?" Mallory pouted, not at all concerned that Max had murder in his eyes.

We were all startled by a booming voice snapping at our group. I scanned the room for whoever was reprimanding us and saw Zak giving Max a cold stare. "Guys, I suggest you behave in front of our newest recruit."

The blue-eyed wolf shoved away from Mallory. She brushed it off like it had been nothing but a mild nuisance. Max's gaze felt like icicles, stabbing at anyone he came across and I had the sinking feeling I'd seen them before. Recently.

I didn't want to catch his attention again, so I pretended to have been looking elsewhere; taking small steps toward the track. Even with my feeble attempt, I could feel Max nearing. He nudged his friend, Barrett, out of the way and he took a long inhale when he reached my back.

Good gods. Again with smelling me?

"New recruit, huh?" he asked gruffly.

I wanted to crumple like a paper ball, but I couldn't just ignore him. Putting on a brave face, I turned, only to validate my concerns. It was the same blond werewolf that I'd dodged the night of my arrest.

And he looked as happy as I was about our reunion.

"The hell are you supposed to be, anyway?" Max asked. His voice didn't seem to have any other range except for a guttural growl.

Barrett decided to lean in too, somehow lessening how menacing the situation felt by adding a second wolf. "Yeah, don't take this the wrong way, newbie, but you've got an interesting smell."

"Women love hearing that." I said.

He laughed. "Hey, I didn't say it was bad."

Max lost his patience with both of us. "Well? What are you?" he asked again.

"Come *on*." Tori resorted to a pout, including a juvenile stomp of her heel. "I'm trying to make a friend, go away."

Max hardly paid her mind. I couldn't blame him. She was too cute and small to look like my backup. His face at least loosened up some. No longer scowling, but his empty expression and dilating pupils didn't feel friendly either.

"Your shirt trick was clever," he said in a low tone, "—but don't get cocky. You aren't going to last a week here." He finally left my space but not without adding another dig. "Scared little girls should stay at home."

Max walked off with Barrett close behind, asking if we knew each other and what the "shirt trick" was. Then, I saw his eyes widen. "Oh, shit?" Barrett's voice was filled with delight. "She's *that* chick—"

He was silenced by Max smacking the back of his head. Barrett muttered some choice words but peeked over his shoulder at me one last time. I knew he was referring to the flannel I'd chucked onto the bus to get rid of him, which meant he definitely remembered me.

Max had been right, though. I *was* scared.

As powerful as demons were, a spell or two could have me trapped and bound. Depending on the severity of the spell, it could be for minutes or eternity. Not to mention, Zak, or any angel present, could zap me out of existence if they wanted.

It was a little late to back out, now. I'd already committed to the madness.

"Bring it in, guys." Zak waved us all toward him. "Let me introduce you to Jess Winters. She's new so she's a wee bit behind. But I think you'll find her to be exceptionally exceptional."

Tori bumped into me with her shoulder, lifting her brows at me. I felt her too.

How curious.

Zak gestured to her first. "This is Vittoria Hanson, but you all know her as Tori. It looks like you two already met. And Guy Shepherd over here, you remember him. Hi, Guy!"

Guy dragged a hand down his face, shielding his vision or ours. I let out a quiet snort. Seeing an agent of Death show embarrassment made him a lot more human and less sentient.

"This is the lovely Miss Yara." When Zak gestured to the green-haired girl he never finished with her last name. She gave me a quick lift of her hand, brief and polite.

"Over here, Barrett Sandulf and Maximillien Sandulf. Call him Max or he gets mad."

Barrett waved. Max did not.

Zak listed a couple of other names and I met everyone's eyes; knowing full well I'd probably forget names for a few months at least. I'd almost drowned out Zak's voice until one name caught my attention.

"... Blaxill."

I froze. Blaxill?

Like, Roman Blaxill?

Mallory's twinkling fingers in my direction were as creepy as the cheery expression she wore. Then, Darren was a Blaxill too? Now it made sense why she was pleasantly surprised that I hadn't recognized her right away. Her father was only one of the most famous vampires in the world.

And I'd just asked her if she enjoyed drinking STDs.

The friendly introductions were over and Zak had us run the track.

The wolves took the lead, soon to be followed by the vampires. I thought everyone was going to continue on foot like me until Mallory launched herself from the ground; cutting her time in half. Occasionally, she would add a flip or two like a flying acrobat, and I watched from below with slight envy.

The others joined in with their alternative forms of running. Max and Barrett both hunched over like they were about to transform into wolves any second. I thought I was fast, especially after outrunning Max once before, but I was barely keeping up. Tori was kind enough to keep pace with me.

On our final lap, we cooled down by walking in circles together. I put my hands on my hips and tried to catch my breath. My legs hadn't felt that heavy the other day when I was booking it across town.

"Hey," Tori said in a hushed tone, "Don't expect Zak to go easy on ya' just because he's cute. He's ruthless deep down."

My cheeks burned while she snickered at me. I knew I couldn't have been the only one who found Zak attractive. He had the face of a god. It wasn't a big deal, it was just that Heaven knew what it was doing when it made him. I was simply appreciating art.

"Duly noted," I said.

Tori hummed happily to herself and reached for her toes, stretching out her legs. When she caught me scratching my head over it she laughed. "It's just a habit. I don't really feel anything."

I broke my stare. "You don't?"

"Nah, well, *sometimes*. But it's not painful or anything."

"How are you so…"

"Solid?" Tori flashed a proud smile. "I know. I can pretty much do normal stuff. Except I don't need to eat anymore, which does kind of suck. All I need to regain my energy is rest. But I miss pizza, ya know?"

I nodded, feeling guilty about my previous dinner with Zak.

She went on to talk about the one time she had tried to eat food, resulting in traumatic failures, but we were interrupted by another unearthly presence.

Guy didn't have the shine of sweat like I knew I did. The only difference after running that much was the wind had moved his hair a fraction. He pulled the strands back in a small ponytail, revealing some softer features that I hadn't noticed last night. I was too focused on catching his face changing into a skeleton again.

In his hand was, what looked like, a purple teddy bear. He pressed the toy to Tori's chest as he passed, muttering under his breath. "Your physical form only lasts a few minutes at most, don't forget."

Tori hooked the bear to her pants like it was a totally normal occurrence. An accessory, even. "Killjoy." She rolled her eyes. "Don't mind him, Jess. He's just a big grump."

I chuckled awkwardly, unaware of whatever dynamic they had. What was up with the bear? She looked young but I couldn't imagine her needing a support toy to cuddle at night. It was cute enough; rounded ears, beady eyes, and four plush arms and legs.

But *why*?

Guy let out an exasperated breath, only turning back once to look at me.

"You look better this morning, Jess," he said, "Less like a lost sheep."

One of my eyes twitched. "Gee, thanks?"

The corner of his lips crept upward before he faced away. Tori on the other hand crossed her arms and frowned. "Get used to his mood swings," she said, "He can be a real butthead when he wants to be."

"How long have you two known each other?" I asked.

"Forever." Her eyes wavered and she twirled the ends of her pink-tipped hair in her hand, "Forever for me, anyway. We used to be close until I died. Ghosts make him uneasy."

"A reaper uneasy around ghosts?"

"I know, right? When did you two meet?"

I paused. "He sort of arrested me."

She laughed. "For real? You must've been *really* naughty."

"Was Guy the one who retrieved you?" I asked, "When you…"

I didn't want to mention someone's death right in front of them. Though, I'd never been in that kind of awkward situation before.

"Yeah," Tori said, "but I don't like thinking about it. Too gloomy."

"Fair enough," I said, "So, how does training usually go?"

"Besides making our muscles ache? Not mine," she said haughtily, not out of breath like I was, "Combat. Oh, and some basic criminology and such. I know this is all new and scary but like, you're in good company."

"Yeah." I focused on the grass at my feet. Suppressing myself was practically second nature. I didn't have to now. Was I happy or terrified about that?

"So," Tori said suddenly, breaking me from my spell and I almost tripped, "What makes you scared? Zak must have noticed something about you."

"Uh… I hurt people if I touch them," I said, "At least, I think that's how it works."

"Is that why you wear gloves?" she asked.

"Yeah."

"Is it an automatic thing then? You can't control it?"

"I'm not sure, actually," I said.

"Oh. Well, either way. Sounds useful." Tori bobbed her head, agreeing with herself. "Zak wouldn't have recruited you if he didn't think so."

Zak did seem convinced that I would be useful. I wasn't so optimistic. What else could I actually *do*? There was that weird, smokey magic stuff, but I had no idea how to conjure it at will. Was it something all demons could do?

We circled back around to meet Zak in the middle. His smile was a flat line across his face this time. I wasn't sure what had changed since a few minutes ago, but the air felt tense.

He curled a finger toward him.

"Jess and… Guy. The rest of you split up. Practice sparring for a bit."

Max contributed a low huff, but everyone obeyed. I really wanted to see what sparring looked like between my peers; to see if I could survive the daily onslaught, but I guess Zak had something else in store.

When Guy made his way next to me, he lifted his shoulders lazily. At least I wasn't the only one who didn't have a clue.

"You're going to take an assessment test," Zak explained. "It's just Jarmiel and me observing, so don't get too nervous."

I looked past him and saw his angel buddy looking clean-cut and sharp as he appeared on the field. He greeted me with a quick, "Winters," and carried a clipboard close to his chest.

But Jarmiel hadn't been alone.

"Not even going to introduce me, Zakiel?" The voice was female; firm, like Jarmiel, except she had a hint of playfulness that the angel did not.

"*And* Lisha," Zak said. It wasn't like him to turn his nose up to anyone, so I was taken aback when he snubbed her.

Lisha was a vision of night; black hair, dark skin, and vibrant, violet eyes with pupils like long, vertical slits. The hair closest to her face was pinned all the way back and I saw something glistening across her neck, like layers of deep, purple amethysts.

Scales.

"Winters," she addressed me, "Or do you prefer Jessebel?"

"Jess, please," I said. She was a beautiful woman, in a regal, unapproachable kind of way. There was something about her that I felt I needed to be reverent toward. Was she a god? Not like I knew much about gods, mysterious bastards.

"I've heard a lot about you," she said, "Not enough, though."

Lisha's eyes shot toward Zak.

"Lisha is only here so she can lure you to *her* team," Zak said, "Anyway, Jess, I've asked Guy to help with your *demon*-stration. Get it? Demon… stra—anyway, it's not a formal demonstration. We just want to see where you're at before we start training you."

He never said anything about a test. What if I did something too extreme or nothing at all, and I let Zak down? Did the video of me not "demonstrate" enough? It wasn't like I actively practiced any demon magic; only by accident.

Zak slapped Guy on the back. From the volume of the impact and the way his hand lingered on his shoulder, it felt more like a threat. His approach with me was much gentler. "Do your best. And don't go easy on this one." He thrust his thumb over his back at Guy, who didn't appear nervous about what was to come. "Oh. And you don't want these."

Zak smoothly cradled both of my wrists and slid my gloves off. Gone. Just like that.

"Wait—" I went to snatch them back but he stopped my hand, making us high-five instead. He'd already pivoted his back to me. He just gave them back and now he was stealing them again?

"Trust yourself," he said, keeping our palms touching long enough for me to feel a charge. I gasped, realizing I'd just fed off his energy.

A shot of adrenaline couldn't hurt before getting my ass kicked…

Guy shook his head but when he looked back at me, his expression changed. His brows twitched, like he noticed something on my face. "No hard feelings, newbie?"

"Why?" I asked, "Not taking my soul today, are you?"

I meant it as a joke since he started it by getting playful with his competitiveness but the reaper smirked.

* * *

We moved away from the track to our own little patch of dirt. Zak perched like an owl atop the nearby fence, which I found both silly and impressive. I assumed he wanted the best view of whatever was about to happen.

A circle was marked for us on the ground. Guy and I stood inside the lines facing each other. Waiting. My arms hung awkwardly at my sides. Jarmiel started attaching red circles to Guy's body; his back, chest, shoulders, and legs. Why was he getting the extra armor and not me?

"Okay, Jess," Zak called down, "See the targets on Guy? All I need you to do is hit as many as you can before he knocks you out of bounds. You'll have three chances to do so. Use any means necessary."

Jarmiel grumbled.

"She can handle it," Zak said.

Jarmiel's glance in my direction failed to encourage me like he was watching a sick animal about to be put down. *Good gods...* I shook it off. The test itself sounded simple enough. It was basically a game kids could play. I located the easiest circles to get to on Guy's arms, chest, and thighs. They were large enough targets. Reaching one shouldn't be a problem, but I knew it would turn out easier said than done.

My aunt taught me *some* self-defense, but her tactics focused on flight, not the fighting itself. A hostile vampire would go for the throat, using claws or fangs; sometimes targeting their victim's soft core. Sadly, the most common attacks involved vampires, so I was clueless about reapers.

Guy watched me from across the mat. I'd seen him in action once when he pulled me out of my aunt's teleportation circle. Back then, I hadn't been ready for a brawl. I took a deep breath and flexed every muscle, waking them up.

Still, it would've been nice to surprise him with an explosion of power. It wasn't like I could kill a reaper, right? I closed my eyes and searched for any inkling of my inner darkness. It was similar to reliving my dream last night. Behind my eyes were black, but there was substance to it. Movement. A flow, like a watery current. I called into the dark with my mind, and received a low rumble in response.

And a spark.

When I opened my eyes, I saw the world flying away from me.

My back came crashing down. The dirt did nothing to soften the blow. A harsh gasp from my chest left me hoarse and confused. All I could do was stare at the sky, clueless as to how I got there.

Guy appeared in front of my lame body, as swift and unsuspecting as my fall. He offered me his hand but I just glared and rolled myself up. Call me petty. I was outside of the white lines; my ass and my pride were injured.

"Sorry," Guy said, sounding the exact opposite.

I mumbled. "Just get back to your side."

"Oh? I shall then."

He did. I still wasn't sure what Guy had done to me. My stomach was sore like I'd been hit pretty hard by something. I heard Mallory's bell-like chuckle from across the field and groaned.

One of my attempts was already over.

"Come on, Jess," Zak said, "Don't let him get cocky."

Not wanting Guy to toy with me the entire time, I moved first on our second round. The taste of dirt on my tongue kept my anger alive. I stuck to the middle, giving myself a chance to stay inside the lines even if I got hit. Guy remained motionless.

Then, I felt a change in the air. He raised his arm and held it out like half of a cross. The certainty on his face sent a chill through me. I braced for whatever was coming my way, even if I couldn't see it.

He swept his arm to the right, so I went left. A sharp wind blew past me. Something had definitely been there in front of me. Guy twisted his arm back to come for another swing. I didn't know if I should run forward or back—

"*Oof!*"

He caught me in my overthinking again. That time, I was hit across the chest. I tumbled and almost rolled out of bounds for the second time. *Dammit.* I couldn't let him keep doing that. I clutched my shoulder, worried about how I looked in front of my new commander. If Zak believed in me, I wanted to prove that he hadn't made a mistake, that *I* wasn't a mistake.

"That was a close one," Guy said, "You learn quickly."

I kicked off the line before he could nudge me out. Guy twirled his hand around like he was carrying a baton. What was he wielding and why couldn't I see it? Was I doomed to keep dodging blindly?

I ran at him again. His movements became swifter to match mine. I dodged twice before getting hit again, but I was close enough to reach him. One of his targets was inches from my hand, and then, I was blocked at the last second.

He spun both hands around, and I finally saw it.

The object moved through the air, distorting him with a blur. Not sure what I did differently this time, but the image was becoming clear. Honestly, I should have known right away what it was.

His scythe.

It warped into reality, showing me its dark, reflective metal. The malicious blade curved to a pointed end. Crazy to think that weapon was the last thing a living soul saw before being parted from mortality. Guy quickly used the distraction to his advantage and catapulted me out of bounds with the butt-end of the scythe.

"*Fudge…*" I wheezed, back on the ground, "I don't like you."

"Come on. One last shot."

Irritation overshadowed my pain. Even if I could just touch him *once*, I'd be satisfied. I didn't care about everyone's expectations anymore; *I* couldn't leave this ring with a zero.

When I ran toward him, he behaved the same, like he had a card up his sleeve. I wasn't sure if he'd meant to unveil his weapon or if he hadn't noticed. He didn't strike with the intention of cutting me. *Thank the gods*. But he also wasn't paying close enough attention to where my eyes were moving. It was my turn to smile.

As I suspected, he still didn't know I could see it. Not until too late, anyway. I dodged a low sweep with a jump and then lunged at the bastard with all my strength.

To his surprise, and mine, his body gave to my weight.

He didn't topple over completely, like I'd hoped, but I moved him back a few feet. We stood there with my arms wrapped around him in a bizarre embrace. I blinked, wondering what to do next. He didn't look heavy, so why couldn't I lift him or push him over with my half-demon strength?

So, I did what anyone would do to thwart a man while in a panic.

By any means necessary, right?

My knee came up toward his crotch and he immediately caved into me with a loud grunt. Even servants of death experienced biological pain. Good to know. It gave me the time I needed to push him to the ground. I trapped him beneath me with legs on either side of him, surprised by my own boldness.

He spoke up at me through gritted teeth. "That was a cheap shot."

"And your invisible scythe *wasn't*?" I snapped back and punched one of the targets on his shoulder. Twice. Three times. Every hit made him pulse against the ground, and I thought I might've had the upper hand.

He decided to forgo the scythe altogether and focused on getting me off of him. Guy dropped the staff and rolled us over in one, swift movement that made him the dominant one. Both of my arms were pinned out to the sides. His fingers felt like ice against my skin.

Cold, cold, cold!

There was no warmth, unlike the abundance of sunshine with Zak. I wiggled desperately, releasing quick, sharp breaths. The dread bled from my chest like poison the longer we were touching. I thought I'd go mad being like that much longer, but then, the frost in my veins became bearable. Constant, unsuspecting, and calming.

The glare on Guy's face mellowed as did the shock from his touch. He looked down at me in wonder just as I stopped struggling. Keeping eye contact, he glided this thumb over the veins in my wrist, as if performing a careful experiment.

My chest reached for his with every breath, entranced by his examination of me as well. Guy cleared his throat. "Giving up already?"

I wormed them upward and planted my feet on his stomach, kicking his middle target repeatedly, like a killer rabbit. My legs were always the strongest part of my body, but I felt my strength had increased. He grimaced and his grip slipped once, but as soon as he recovered, he clamped on to keep himself from being kicked off.

Then, I saw it again. The sparks of dark matter reappeared briefly on my body.

It sizzled off of me like steam, not forming a cloud like before. I was excited at first but then panicked, remembering what it had done to the monster before. Lights traveled up my arms, making the white-web effect with my veins again.

With an unladylike growl and an effort to pull a leg muscle, I tried to launch him to the side. It worked, but he still held my arms. We tumbled together toward the line. The magic subsided.

I lost.

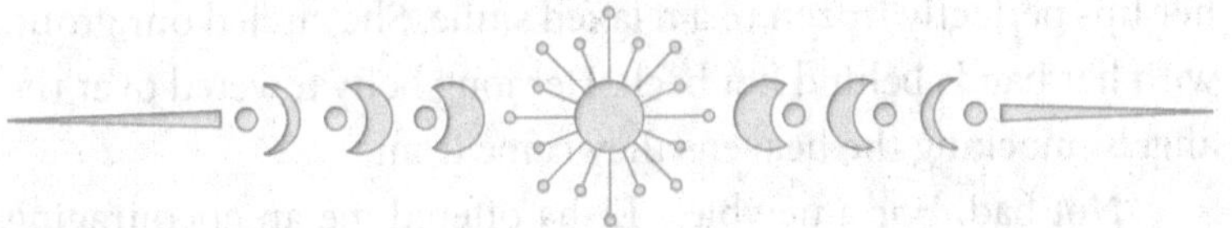

Zak was the solo clapper in our three-man audience.

Guy helped me to my feet after I let go of my ego. At least I'd gotten to hit him a couple of times. His cool touch hardly phased me that time. Strange; I was so used to being the one with the scary hands.

"You're a little tiger, Jess," Zak said with a beaming smile, "Gave him a good scratch too."

Guy had no compliments. His scythe was mysteriously back in his hand. "Can you actually see this?" He watched for my reaction while I stared directly at it while rubbing all my bruised limbs. "You can. Interesting."

"Am I not supposed to?" I asked.

Guy didn't answer. The scythe had been deliberately hidden but I could still see it? I wanted him to give me an explanation, but in the next moment, we were surrounded by angels.

Zak leapt from his spot on the fence but Jarmiel swatted him out of the way. "Any injuries?" he asked me. It took me a moment to realize he was showing actual concern for me. His placid voice never gave his emotions away.

"N-nothing terrible," I said.

"I told you she'd be fine," Zak said, "I'm more concerned about Guy reproducing."

Guy and I both winced at that. The nut shot may not have been the coolest technique on my part, but I'd been desperate.

Lisha, the dark goddess who had come out of nowhere, had her lips perfectly frozen in a relaxed smile. She circled our group with her hands behind her back. Her long body towered over the angels, mocking the heavens they came from.

"Not bad. For a newbie." Lisha offered me an encouraging nod. I did the same, wondering if that was some shifter custom to do so. She hummed a laugh while Zak let out an exaggerated sigh.

"Yeah, yeah. I know what you're trying to do, Lish," he said, "Don't even think about it."

"Jarmiel, do you hear this?" Lisha chuckled. "What an *angel* your friend is."

Jarmiel kept his gaze down at his clipboard. "His youthful earth years are unbecoming. Seems he needs a competitive playmate."

"Aw, Zakiel. I didn't know you revered me so," she said, "I'm honored to be your playmate."

"A fearsome creature you may be, but you can't steal this one." Zak stood at my side. It would've been cute, if I hadn't felt like I was watching two toddlers fighting over a toy.

"I never *steal*. I only ever come offering more." Lisha gave us a wink before turning on her heel. "If she doesn't improve under your watch, you know where to find me."

"Who is she?" I asked as soon as she was out of earshot.

"One of your captains," Jarmiel said, "They've appointed their own teams, like Zakiel. Though, his energy could be put to better use elsewhere."

There seemed to be more meaning behind his last sentence but Zak just lifted his shoulders. "Helping Jess is my top priority."

I wasn't positive, but I thought I caught Jarmiel's eye roll.

"If you're quite finished, I'd like to take Miss Winters for the remainder of the day," he said, "She needs to review the rules and expectations here at EXO."

Zak made a pained moan but didn't fight him on it. "See you around, Jess. Good work."

I guess I should have been grateful to sit in a classroom after all of that. My body ached as I followed Jarmiel to the tower. We reached level 5 and every room we passed was sealed, leaving me to wonder what else went on in these halls.

We stopped at a door and he opened it for me. Inside was tidy, if not a little barren. "Sorry it's going to be such a lonesome session," Jarmiel said, "Zakiel focuses so much on everyone's physical capabilities that he slacks on the other important details. We'll get you caught up with everyone else as soon as we can."

I settled into one of the desks and Jarmiel dimmed the lights. It was a little exciting to be in an actual classroom, but without other students, it didn't feel so different from my homeschooling.

Jarmiel turned on a bright projector that displayed an image on the wall. "Let's go over some rules," he began, "Any excessive use of your supernatural abilities outside of training is prohibited. Don't be tardy. Follow instructions…"

I'll admit, I zoned out a bit as he went on. In my defense, most of them sounded like common sense. Jarmiel paused and I didn't know how long ago that was. "Am I boring you?"

"No, sir." I said, suddenly hyper-focused.

He continued. "Training is required of every aspiring peacekeeper. If you do not pass the test, you will have to retake it. While you have freedom over your spare time, we still expect you to adhere to the standards and respect everyone's schedules. Since you are under Zakiel's and my watch for the time being, you may roam the grounds and facilities here but do not leave EXO unless granted permission to do so. If you become an official peacekeeper after basics, that restriction will be lifted."

My heart skipped a little. A few weeks and one certificate later, I could go out and look for Naomi.

Jarmiel stopped again, as if he read that thought, "After you pass, you will be expected to keep up your own schedules in physical wellness. Your next priority will be earning a badge. It involves more specialized training and allows you to participate in more complicated missions. For example, Zakiel and I were sent to find the Ghoul you encountered."

"But Max was there," I said, remembering that quite well.

"Yes. He passed his peacekeeper test." Jarmiel clicked a small remote in his hand that changed the slide on the projector. "Mr. Shepherd and Miss Blaxell also."

"Why do we all train together then?" I asked.

"They volunteer," he said, "It earns them rank points, keeps them in shape, and increases pay by a small amount."

Didn't take Mallory to be one for charity.

He motioned to the chart now illuminated against the wall. I skimmed the bullet points, broken up into several different categories; supernatural or not, which type of supernatural, and potential threat levels. "The most common threats under EXO's jurisdiction consist of lesser demons, supernaturals, gang activity along with cultists. Beginner recruits are allowed to handle them in groups. Around level three is when a superior will lead the team. Anything above a three, only members with their badge can participate. That would be someone like Zakiel."

"How do you get a badge?" I asked.

"Two years of service and a performance review. I wouldn't worry about it until after you pass the test."

I jumped to another topic. "Sorry, but what was that Ghoul doing at Peter's house, anyway? Haverwick is a small town and hasn't attracted big monsters before."

"Something important to note, especially considering your position, Miss Winters, is to never lump all demons together," he said, "Some aren't violent at all, believe it or not. The level system merely gauges the target's predicted strength. Their actions rely heavily on their origins."

"Origins?"

He nodded. "A minion who serves The Demon Lord of Slothfulness would not commit the same crimes as those from the Wrath Kingdom. If they bother to commit any at all."

I laughed, but his confused expression took me off guard.

He hadn't meant to be funny.

"So, what's expected of me?" I asked.

"A mission will be assigned to you, and you will carry it out using your best judgment or that of your captain. Assuming we've trained you well."

"Does that include… killing?"

"When the need arises, we remove their physical form from this realm. Yes." Jarmiel delivered with a solemn nod. "Their souls, however, are out of jurisdiction."

"So, they're allowed to go back to Hell?"

"Yes." Jarmiel said, "Nowhere worse we could send them."

Touche.

"Why doesn't EXO use weapons for this sort of thing?" I asked, "Like magic bullets or something."

"Purifiers do. They can bless certain objects to have similar properties as angel magic does," Jarmiel said, "Demons are only at half strength on Terra, and even weaker when possessing a host. Even still, regular weapons can't penetrate the skin. If our weapons do somehow succeed, the demon's rapid healing renders them useless, anyway."

The more we discussed killing demons the more squeamish I got. In a way, he was just explaining how they would kill *me*. I hadn't taken a bullet before and I wasn't interested in testing out the theory.

"Jarmiel." I raised my hand for the first time during that entire meeting. "If the war is over, why are the demons still fighting? That doesn't sound 'over' to me."

It was like the uprising never stopped, just slowed.

He glanced at the clock on the wall and frowned. "I'm afraid we must visit that discussion another time. But the short answer, Miss Winters, is that the war *isn't* over. We only defeated *one* Lord of Hell. And there are many."

"Which one?"

"Hm?"

"Which lord?" I asked again. I don't know why I needed to know that, but I was curious.

"History refers to him as The Devourer. To us, he is The Demon Lord of all Sin."

11

That night, I searched my bag for the candles Naomi shoved inside and positioned them around my bed. Most of the spells I'd seen Naomi do in the past involved candles, oils, plants, and crystals. I had candles.

If I couldn't reach her with a phone, there was another way.

One by one, I lit them all while muttering at the crappy lighter. To be honest, I couldn't even remember how the communication spell worked. What else was there? I knew there was a rock. Or was it a crystal… *Ha!*

I snatched the warm-colored stone hiding in my socks. It had a smooth, caramel surface, except for the rune carved in its center. As I held it in my hand, I wondered why Naomi hadn't used a spell to communicate with *me* first.

What if something bad happened to her?

I turned out the lights and carefully sat in the middle of my candles, so my pajamas didn't catch fire. It would be nice to know if Naomi was okay and to let her know that I was fine too. She wouldn't be thrilled about EXO but I think she'd get over it knowing I was alive.

I took a deep breath and focused on my yellow rock.

The flames remained perfectly still and unimpressed.

Okay. So, I hadn't remembered any fancy words Naomi would use. She said the root of all magic was through the spirit and mind, then the elements, and so on. Could I just *think* about her name really hard and she'd eventually hear me?

I closed my eyes.

"Naomi," I whispered into the void. "If you can hear me, just…call me back?"

That was extremely lame.

The stone in my palm should have been glowing or something but it remained dull and cold. I scoffed and chucked it away from me. My make-shift ritual felt more ridiculous the longer I sat there. I was missing something to get the magic going. Or, in the gravest of circumstances, Naomi was just too far to reach.

"You're the witch. Why haven't you done *anything*?" I scolded the empty air. "Do you care at all that I'm gone?"

Of course she cared. I sighed, letting the aggression flow out of my chest. That wasn't fair. Naomi revolved her entire life around me. She hadn't had much of a life at all, when I thought about it. We just had our pretend life together.

I hadn't a clue where her broomstick had taken her. It couldn't be a location we'd been to before. That was a rule whenever we discussed uprooting.

Candles still decorated the floor but I snuffed them out and danced around them to reach my bed. I curled up in bed and everything was still, except for my mind which was stirring. Should I be worried? I tossed and turned, unable to stop thinking about Naomi. Was she hurt or had she abandoned me?

I groaned into my pillow. There was nothing I could do about it yet. Not unless I sprang free from EXO and risked Zak hunting me down with much less *mercy* this time. Even then, I didn't know where to start my search for my slippery aunt.

"…*Jes…bel…*"

Unlike most, who would bolt upright in their beds at the sound of a voice in their room, I lay frozen. My body ran cold while my pores produced sweat. It could just be one of the others outside my door. Tori, maybe? She may be a ghost but she didn't sound that eerie.

"*Jess...bel...*"

I sat up that time, wishing I'd left some candles lit. The voice sounded like it came outside my door. It had a scratch to it, like they needed a cough drop. I wanted it to be Naomi, finally connecting through the stone, but it didn't sound like her either.

The doorknob shifted once. I clutched my blanket, waiting to see if it would actually turn all the way. What would I do then?

"*Come out... little demon...*" The knob returned to its normal position with a soft *click*.

A pregnant pause.

I waited for more sounds, eyes glued to the door, before tiptoeing to my chair and grabbing the sweater that hung off it. It covered most of my body with its obnoxious length. Great, but a weapon would be greater. Was I being punked by someone on the same floor as me? Security seemed too tight for something sinister to creep through.

I took a few shaky breaths before opening the door to the hallway. No one was there. It wasn't that late at night so I was surprised *no one* was up and about. Just to be sure, I stepped out into the hall and looked down in both directions. *Is this how stupid people die in horror movies?* Probably.

The silence was broken by something thumping softly against the carpet.

That hadn't been me.

Naomi said the chance of attracting dark spirits while using communication spells was slim, but *not* impossible. It would be just like me to fudge up the spell to that extent. I looked back to my left, feeling my muscles stiffening. Still, no one was there.

Not a person, anyway.

In the middle of the hallway, sitting upright with a lopsided head was Tori's purple teddy bear. We were in a standoff, while my brain processed the threat level of the plush toy. It was just a doll but the timing of everything was creepy.

I was not prepared when the bear suddenly charged at me.

I screeched and fell back. "Holy shit!"

The bear looked so ridiculous, teetering toward me like an uncoordinated toddler. Its pillowy arms waved in the air as it closed in, but it never reached me.

Just as abruptly, the figure of a man with mousy hair sprang into view. His long arms shielded my body from my cuddly attacker.

"Guy?" I gaped up at the reaper. Could suddenly appearing places be another one of his tricks? He remained crouched over me like a mama bird protecting its young.

"It's just me!" The bear actually spoke. I peered around Guy's legs, recognizing that voice right away.

"Tori," Guy grumbled. I didn't realize I was clinging to his t-shirt until he tried to move. My fingers wrinkled the fabric in my death grip until I quickly released it. Not embarrassing at all. He ran an open palm down his tired face. "What were you thinking?"

Tori's voice giggled from within the stuffed animal. "I'm sorry, I couldn't help myself."

"I'm so confused," I said.

"The doll is her stand-in," Guy said, brows pinching together, "It's dangerous for a soul to exist without a vessel and she can't manifest her physical form for long."

"Really?" I checked out her tiny, stuffed figure again. "Fascinating."

Tori waddled closer. Now that the initial alarm was out of the way, her appearance was not at all life-threatening. When she waved I couldn't help but chuckle.

"It has to be an item of emotional value from her previous life," Guy further explained, "And functional. She can move around this way, even if it's silly."

Tori pointed a mitten up at him. "At least I'm still cute, unlike you, bedhead."

He snatched her from the ground and her paws flailed in circles. His lazy eyes were back as well as his lack of enthusiasm. "Sorry for this disturbance, Jess."

I shrugged. "Thanks for coming to my rescue. Are you always ready to pull the trigger like that?"

"Not really," he said, "I'm going to get a couple more hours of sleep. You should too."

Tori's beady eyes remained unblinking. "Why *did* you show up like that? Flashy isn't your style."

He brushed the question aside. "Go to bed."

"Yeah, but why?"

"Tori."

"Your face is turning red. Wait—"

Guy walked briskly before I could hear any more. He opened Tori's door and chucked her weightless body inside. Her landing sounded soft on her bed despite his harshness. He sighed and turned to me. "In the future, I would avoid attempting spells you're unfamiliar with."

I flinched. "How did—"

"There are people here who can sense shifts in energies. If you do anything on a grander scale, I'm sure you'll set off the alarms."

"I see…" So much for being discreet.

Guy paused by Tori's doorway. "What were you trying to do anyway?"

Telling the same reaper who arrested me that I was trying to communicate with my aunt didn't sound like the best idea. I wasn't sure what she was in for if EXO found her before I did. "It was nothing special. Just practicing simple sleeping spells."

If he believed me or not, he didn't show it. "Goodnight, Jess."

He returned to bed without pestering me further. I locked myself back in my room as well, almost tripping on the candles I had forgotten were there. What was Guy's deal anyway? I couldn't tell if he liked me or not. He couldn't feel totally indifferent if he came to help when he thought I was in danger.

Not that it mattered.

I decided to clean up the failed ritual on my floor since I wasn't tired. The last thing to find was my stone that rolled under the bed. When I lifted my comforter, I immediately saw the pulsing glow.

Did it work?

I snatched the rock, feeling the magic energy beginning to surface. "Naomi? Aunty?"

The light softened until it completely faded away.

12

One week, down.

And so was my face; down in the dirt, that is. My gloves were shredded from the number of times I had to catch myself from planting my nose in the ground. A bitter taste of grass lingered on my tongue.

"You're really coming along, aren't you, Jess?" Mallory taunted as she kept me under her heel. "You almost hit me that time."

She flicked her white hair to the side before letting me up. We were about to start a new round of combat practice but before Mallory could call dibs again, Zak requested that I be his partner. I thanked the heavenly gods for that one.

The days flew by on a similar schedule. I'd shower late at night, eat in the cafeteria, and get my ass handed to me in training with my peers. Each of them welcomed a new method of pain. I did my part to avoid attention from the angry werewolf or vampire queen, but Mallory was always enthusiastic to "help" me practice.

It didn't help that my physical abilities were on the decline. I had a guess it was due to my withdrawals. Everything felt heavier like I had stones strapped to my ankles. Zak gave me small doses of my aunt's medicine until the other day, then we went cold turkey.

The headaches worsened, like a nail being pounded into the front of my skull. My skin and hair had faded in color. Instead of red tones, or even soft brown, I looked dry and ashen. The food at EXO was filling but left me feeling starved. I should have been healthier from all the exercise not falling apart.

The withdrawals had to end soon…

Before I began training with Zak, he cracked his neck and removed his sweater. I half expected him to glitter gold. "We only have seven more weeks to get you in top shape for the exam. Sounds like a lot, but it'll blow by fast," he said, "Hope you're ready for me."

Not really, I wanted to say. I knew I couldn't rely on his favoritism forever. Eventually, EXO would task me with something more dangerous than Mallory.

"Okay, J-J-J-JESS." Zak clapped his hands as he cheered. "We're gonna go over some simple defensive tactics. Did your aunt ever teach you any cool tricks?"

The last thing I wanted to do was keep moving, but I attempted to mirror Zak's energy.

"Only some," I said.

He chuckled. "Okay, let's have you face me first. We have a lot to go over before tapping into your special abilities. Let's pretend I'm coming at you. No weapons. Just act like I'm some creep on the street or something."

I almost laughed. Zak couldn't look villainous if he tried.

He moved toward me and his expression changed. His eyes lost their light and his smile faded. I lost the strength in my stance. *Nevermind.* He could pull off the villainous type just fine.

"Keep your knees bent." He instructed. "Eyes up, chin down. Hold up your fists for me."

I scrambled to get in position before he reached me. When his arm came up my immediate action was to flinch and fall back.

Zak moved his pointer finger discouragingly. "Hey. If you're going to defend yourself instead, don't leave your head so exposed. Any vampire, shifter, demon, *angel*, can hit like a truck and one swing to the head could be fatal or knock you out cold."

Yeah. Mallory didn't exactly hit like a fairy.

He did not hold back. Zak's hits felt like blocking cannon fire. I knew if he held back it would only be a disservice, but *damn*. It was a tough call between embarrassment and frustration that I couldn't improve, even after further instruction. Zak mentioned it wasn't for lack of understanding the technique. I was just… slowing down.

That is, until our last round when I'd gotten daring and tried punching Zak's chin. He grabbed my fist and used my momentum to pull me forward. His other arm curled around my neck in a chokehold.

"We'll practice more tomorrow," he said, "Nicely done."

I tried to gulp but it got stuck in my throat. Despite us both perspiring, his breath on my neck gave me goosebumps. Our position was far from romantic, but his entire body pressed against mine kept me from thinking straight.

Zak released me and casually wiped his brow. "I was thinking we could stick around after training and practice that little magic trick you used against the Ghoul. We might need a lot of open space… Jess?"

A sharp pain struck the front of my skull, harder that time, and traveled to my toes. I gasped. My vision turned purple. I felt myself falling forward but caught myself on my knees.

"Jess?" Zak reached for me again. As soon as his arms lifted me up, I dug my fingers into his shoulders. I was going to black out. I just knew it. My head felt muddled and made me dizzy. Zak was the lighthouse keeping me from drifting toward the dark sea.

I *needed* him.

Zak's fresh, citrusy scent helped calm my mind. To avoid the pain, I imagined an orange grove surrounded by wet soil, the woodsy aroma from the bark, and morning dew on the leaves. He was at the center of it all like a ball of sunshine keeping everything alive.

Finally, I felt my desperation dwindling. The pain in my head subsided. When I opened my eyes, I was looking directly into Zak's chest.

No wonder his scent was so strong. I was literally sticking my face in it. *Oh, gods.* I wanted to die. It was nice, don't get me wrong, but if it were possible to explode from embarrassment, I would've splattered all over the yard.

His chin rested on the top of my head while his arms secured me in place. I didn't know why he was allowing it to happen but it went on for too long. I sprang back like a frightened cat. "I'm sorry! I-I don't know why I did that," I said.

"Careful. Don't fall over." Zak's grin was crooked. I felt like I'd crossed a line. He was still a commander for EXO. An *angel.* What if I'd made him uncomfortable or put him in an awkward spot? Unfortunately, several faces had observed what went down between Zak and me. Max wiped his dripping scalp and scowled. His sparring partner, Barrett, was still distracted and didn't quite catch Max's next blow to the stomach.

Tori levitated off her toes to reach Guy's ear. She whispered something behind her cupped hand. I could only imagine what. Pining for their acceptance felt icky, but I couldn't help desiring it too. If I had to be there, I wanted to find my place in our group.

"Let's get you to Clove," Zak said, "We're overdue for a visit, anyway."

* * *

Zak's first thought after hugging me was to see a doctor.

Clove was EXO's supernatural medical specialist. I couldn't remember the last time I went to see anyone about my health.

Naomi had her natural remedies and with my elevated healing, a need never arose.

Inside of EXO tower was an entire floor dedicated to this Clove person. Luckily, we got to ride an elevator all the way up. Severe injuries must have been dealt with off-base seeing as the hike to the medical floor was inconveniently near the top.

As soon as we entered the hall, I was hit with an unpleasant, chemical scent. The sparkling white tile irritated my eyes. I felt another jolt through my body and leaned against the wall.

Zak made to assist me again. "Easy does it," he said.

"I'm good."

I tried being as polite as I could while pulling away. Leaving his embrace earlier was worse than stepping out of a hot shower. I wasn't sure I had the strength a second time. Besides, I didn't want to get him in trouble with any more hugging. "Does Clove know that I'm…"

"A demon?" he asked, "Yeah. Don't worry about that."

I nodded. "You don't seem surprised this is happening."

"I'm not. You need energy to survive as a demon, half or not. I'm not just talking about human food." When I staggered, Zak lifted me off of the wall and I didn't protest that time. "Hang on. Almost there."

The hallway felt like the boardwalk to eternity, or had that been my imagination stirring? What if it was like the movies, where they bring me to a friendly facility only to cut me up and divvy out my organs? It sounded bonkers but that shit was real.

We approached a pair of double doors with a security lock. All Zak had to do was knock and say, "Hey, Clove!" and someone buzzed us in.

"Come in." A female voice said.

I chewed my bottom lip while gazing at the many diagrams of other supernaturals that hung on the walls. Machines hummed, warmed up, and ready to perform. I tried my best to ignore the test tube cabinets and shiny torture utensils lying in trays along the counters.

"Jessebel Winters. Have a seat."

I hadn't spotted the woman yet in the sea of shelves, but I did find the chair verbally offered to me. It came with restraints; straps and metal clamps for the ankles and wrists.

Cozy.

When I hesitated, Zak gave me a bump on the shoulder.

"Jess, this is Clove." He introduced me to a stiff woman in a lab coat who skirted around a bookshelf. Behind her sheet of black hair were a pair of transparent wings. Equally glossy to match her black mane were antennae. They peered out from her scalp and bounced along with her movements.

Clove's pointed nose stabbed in our direction, her cheek-bones and chin just as sharp. All common traits among fairies. The adorable, silver freckles, like rhinestones under her eyes, didn't suit her otherwise cold demeanor.

"Hello," I said, but Clove gestured one tiny hand toward the chair again. She waited until I complied to move one of the straps across my chest.

"How are you feeling?" she asked, "Zakiel texted me that you're blacking out."

"Yeah…" Sitting helped even if the straps concerned me. "Are these really necessary?"

"Considering past experiences with patients like yourself, yes." She lifted my eyelid and shone a small flashlight through my brain. "Has this been happening a lot or just recently?"

"Recently," I said. A cabinet of needles and tubes taunted me from behind her. It was kept cool and left a layer of fog on the glass windows. Some of the tubes already contained varying shades of blood, labeled differently with letters and numbers that meant nothing to me.

Blood wasn't just the liquid that kept our fleshy bodies functioning. It was treated as currency, especially in the vampire market. The younger, fresher, and healthier, the better. But blood was also used for much crueler intentions like spells, curses, and other rituals. I got a lot of my horror stories from Naomi.

"Our samples never leave this room." Clove's slender finger pointed to the cabinet I'd been eyeballing. "I do all the testing myself. We won't poke you today, though."

I sighed, relieved. "You alone?"

"It would be easier if I were a vampire. I know." She sounded tired like it was something she had to repeat often. "But I do just fine without having to sample my samples."

I smacked my lips, imagining a taste-testing clinic run by vampires. I'd heard of such ideas but they hadn't been popular with the public. With Roman Blaxill's vampire involvement with the medical field, that could change.

Clove did a routine check of my vitals. I took a deep inhale and forced my neck to relax against my headrest. Zak's eyes lingered on me, but they had a faraway look about them. He was miles away.

"You're staying?" I asked him.

"Would you prefer I didn't?" he asked.

"No, but you probably have better things to do."

"What could be more fun than this?" He grinned. "You're kind of my responsibility, so I'm gonna make sure you're okay. Besides, we don't want to stress Jarmiel into an early grave."

I could tell something else was weighing on Zak's shoulders. His heavenly glow was decent camouflage, but even his obnoxious peppiness had gone down a notch to follow his slouching figure. "You seem tired," I said, "I hope it's not because of me."

"Says the girl who almost passed out in the hallway," he countered.

"*Neither* of you looks well," Clove stated. "Even angels need to take care of themselves. Work problems, Zakiel?"

He let out a breath that shrank his chest like a balloon. "Something like that. This guy's slippery."

"What guy?" I asked.

"We've been looking for someone. A criminal who tampers with the dead." Zak paused. "We call him The Necromancer for obvious reasons. That creature you saw the other night was one of his Ghouls. He makes them from bodies he collects. Real nasty business."

Anyone could guess that after taking one look at the Ghoul, but it was still disturbing to hear. "The Necromancer planned for that thing to be at Peter's house?" I asked.

What business did a notorious necro-freak have in a place like Haverwick?

"The attacks seem to be random," Zak said, "He doesn't target anywhere more than once and takes new corpses every time."

"So, he controls the dead and is slowly making an army?" I shivered, imagining a hoard of Ghouls. The Necromancer had to have a strong stomach and a gaping hole for a heart to create that level of patchwork.

"Seems that way," Zak spoke so softly I could barely hear him. He ran his thumb over his chin, pinching the skin until it made a butt. I felt bad making him speak more about it but I was too invested now. "We've also run into individual puppets before. They're silent, sometimes indistinguishable from the average person, depending on how recently they died. The longer they're dead before reanimation, the more stumbly and drooly they are"

"Is he working alone?" I asked, "Can't the reapers do anything about this?"

His laugh was strained. "Oh, they're mad. It's going to cause a war on the other side any day now. As far as we know, he is on his own aside from his *creations*. You'd think having Ghouls around that he'd be easy to find."

He stopped and a smile spread across his face. "You handled the Ghoul, no problem."

"I wouldn't say it was *no* problem." I cringed at my own humble brag. Another minute in that driveway and I would have been toast. "I didn't know I could… What happened to me anyway?"

Clove wrapped up her examination and jotted some notes on a clipboard. The sound of her furious scribbles shocked me back into our current reality. "Something happened?" she asked.

"She has a connection to dark matter. And like any magic, it can be tricky," he said, "It could have something to do with your blackouts."

Clove clicked her tongue. "*Magic*…What have you been eating Jessebel?"

For some reason, I drew a blank. Before EXO, I hadn't been much of a breakfast person but that cafeteria changed my mind.

"Waffles?" I said.

Her beady eyes darted across my face.

"What do you do for actual nourishment, I mean? Are you at least eating red meat?"

"Jess has been on a *homemade* supplement most of her life," Zak said, helping me with my brain fart, "We've been weaning her off. It's only been a couple days without."

"That's something to tell me." She raised one of her thin brows. "Do we know what's in it?"

"Not really." I felt a pool of dread in my stomach. The real question was, did we *want* to know?

Zak's eyes softened but Clove wasn't as tactful.

"Demons *feed* off humans. Souls," she said, "Not a practice we normally encourage. This supplement you have may have been acting like synthetic blood for vampires. By the looks of things, it's not enough to sustain your body anymore. You're starving."

I looked to Zak for a positive retort.

"It's possible that when you used your demon magic to kill the Ghoul it screwed with your diet," he said.

"Wait. Am I *dying*?" I asked, shifting in my seat.

So, I was just going to wither away unless I hunted people like livestock? My stomach acids sizzled. How could it possibly be what my body wants when the idea made me physically ill? How was I so sure Naomi hadn't ever.

No. She wouldn't have fed me actual *human beings* in secret; disguised as filets or ground organs in my tea. No way in hell. When would she have had the time to visit the human meat market? Illegal, by the way, if that wasn't obvious.

But I sure came up with those ideas fast…

"So we up the dosage, right?" I asked, "I mean, I can't *eat* people."

I gagged, and that was Zak's cue to come to the rescue. He pushed off the wall behind him and took the other side of my chair. "Keep your breakfast down. We're not jumping to cannibalism."

Clove hurried off to a room in the back while I focused on not throwing up. Zak held up an open palm and wiggled his fingers. "Your touch," he said, "Remember? What demons actually need is the soul, or life force, and your contact with others can help you do so. Weaker demons tend to eat flesh because they lack the magic or intelligence to extract it any other way."

"How lovely," I said, feeling my own spirit flattening, "Doesn't that mean I still have to kill someone?"

Would there be a point to living if it meant I had to kill others to do it? That was how the food chain worked, but it was all wrong. *Evil.* If that was how demons worked, then how did angels survive? They weren't human either.

"A vampire doesn't have to kill to feed," Zak said, "It's a choice. The human body will replenish blood. The same goes for soul matter."

When I could only pull off looking more confused he winced. "*Ah*… sorry, let me explain. The soul's core is separate from the surrounding soul matter. Think of it like eating an apple. You can chew the outside, just don't bite the core."

"Who bites the core?" I asked.

"It's just an example."

"That doesn't seem scientifically sound."

Zak raised a brow. "Peter is still alive, isn't he?"

Clove made an abrupt return carrying an armful of wires that she dumped on the counter. She removed the awful straps from my arms. "We're going to test something. Zakiel, over here."

Once I was freed, Zak placed himself right in front of me while Clove taped the wires she brought to our bodies. I averted my eyes when she reached inside of Zak's shirt.

Just kidding. I totally looked *and* discovered a new appreciation for collarbones.

But then, Clove said something like, "Just remove it."

His caramel hair looked like straw blown by the wind after he pulled the shirt over his head. He could've been hiding a gut under there and he still be gorgeous, but the four-pack he nurtured was nice. I dropped my head to stare at his shoes instead. It felt like an even worse sin to ogle at an angel's body. Even so, I couldn't erase the image of his solid chest from my mind.

Once Clove had us all hooked up like bugs in a mangled spiderweb, a Chief Communications Strategist monitor *beeped* to life. I realized quickly that the tones were in tune with my pulse. *Gods. I need help.*

"What do you know about succubi?" Clove asked.

"Just that they're trademarked as the demons of debauchery," I said.

"Remove your gloves," she instructed while scratching one of her long antennae. "Take Zakiel's hand and we'll see if anything changes."

I didn't move. Zak had to, gently, wrestle one of my stubbornly clenched fists and tried interlacing our fingers. "C'mon. I don't have cooties," he laughed, "We're trying to help you."

He was right. It shouldn't have been a big deal, but I still felt awkward about it.

"I'm not going to hurt him, right?" I asked.

"Zakiel is a durable subject," Clove answered.

Zak winked at me while she couldn't see. "I don't know how to take that compliment, Clove."

After about a minute, Clove glanced at the machine a few times and mulled. "Try again, Jess. Picture the energy beneath the surface."

Beneath the surface?

He's already half-naked!

I closed my eyes just as the loud beeping started up again. That was my heart rate alright.

"Hey," Zak's calm humor entered my ears, "Everything's fine."

I could hear him stifling his chuckle and made the mistake of looking up again; enchanted by the brown crystals in the middle of his face. His thumb made circles in the back of my hand which, by some miracle, slowed my heart.

It was just like before with the sunshine and orange fields. The more I focused on Zak's hand, the more warmth traveled up my arm. It flowed through my veins like liquid fire until all of me felt awakened by the internal sun. The aching I'd been feeling for days was gone.

"Feel anything yet, Zakiel?" Clove asked.

"Just a tickle," he said.

Clove waited by the monitor with her eyes peeled. "Picking up some readings now. How do you feel, Jessebel?"

"Better," I admitted.

Her lips curled. "Good. You'll need to learn how to nourish yourself regularly and safely. The hardest part for you will be portion control. Not for you but for others."

"How do I do that?"

"Practice and listen to your gut."

Great.

Clove removed us from her machines and Zak threw his shirt back on. My heart could finally catch a break. How many people had been so lucky to see The Angel of Mercy like that. I might've been obsessing, just a little.

"I would avoid any intimate relationships until you've learned how to prevent absorbing someone's vitality when you touch them," Clove said, like she could read my impure thoughts.

"I… agree," I said, "But how do I practice that without risk?"

Zak interjected. "You haven't forgotten about me, right?"

"You want us to do *this* during training?" My voice cracked. If he wanted me to start holding hands with Mallory, I'd quit.

"Well, yeah. It's not just going to keep you alive. It should make you stronger too. It may even be why you were able to use demon magic in the first place." He drummed his fingers on my knuckles. "It's only evil if you make it so. It saved your life. You get control of this, and you won't have to worry about accidents again."

Zak's eyes burned with determination. I knew he wanted to use me. That was the whole reason I was there, but an angel wanting me to eat souls and use demon magic felt backwards. "We'll practice everyday. Consider it extended training," he said.

Clove already had the area looking organized during our conversation. She paused from her fluttering to rest her wings against the wall. "If anything new develops, or you lose consciousness again, come see me right away. I wouldn't be surprised if your body experiences more sudden changes."

What *else*? Horns and a tail?

"Sounds good," I said.

"I'd also like to get some bloodwork done, once you're feeling up to it."

"Do we have to?"

"If you want to be a peacekeeper, yes," she said.

I swallowed. She said she did all the testing herself. No one else should've had access. If anything, they could use my blood to learn more about me. Maybe that was why I hesitated.

"Thanks for everything, Clove," Zak said.

She gave him a nod and shortly after we were dismissed.

13

W hen we left the building, I caught my reflection in one of the windows. I was shocked to see how quickly the positive effects Zak's energy had, even cosmetically. My hair was voluminous instead of dingy and frizzy. The darkness under my eyes dispersed and my skin was glowing.

I was healthy again.

Prettier.

Not just pretty. I felt *hot*. Had I always looked like that or was I high after taking bits of Zak's soul? I'm sure angel juice could erase years off a person. When we had arrived at Clove's earlier I was barely making it through the doors and now I was leaving with a full-on strut. What was I supposed to do now, ask everyone to donate their life force to my beauty and survival fund?

"How are you so okay with this?" I asked Zak suddenly on our walk back to the dorms. There was no context leading up to that so it was natural for him to act confused.

"What do you mean?" Zak smiled innocently.

"Me. Demons. Everything." Everything I knew about good and evil, light and dark. Mine and Zak's partnership didn't make sense. I didn't think I was *evil*, personally, but who was to say?

I couldn't be sure, but it seemed like he was trying to avoid eye contact. What if he felt awkward after everything? He always seemed chipper and composed but what if he felt violated? The thought made me sick to my stomach.

He didn't like me touching him…

"Not many demons want or even have the opportunity to come to EXO," he said, revealing no disgust in his voice, "This feels different."

"You've asked them?"

"Not *every* demon I see. You're still special, I promise."

"Ha-ha." I snorted, trying to keep things light like he was but I couldn't stop myself from fumbling with my hands, "Jarmiel said it was strange that I had a will of my own and that's why you asked me."

Zak shrugged. "I think it's cool that you're here."

Still refused to look at me.

"*Cool?* What if I do something really bad?" I asked.

"You won't."

"How can you know that?"

He grabbed me by the shoulders, making us come to a halt. Finally, his eyes bore into mine. The brown from his crystalline eyes looked like candy caramel in the sun, melting into my soul. "I told you, I didn't sense any malice inside you. Be comforted, because I've never been wrong. About that at least."

I wanted to believe too, especially with him holding me there, planted in his convictions. There was so much about me that I was figuring out for the first time. My aunt knew and had all those years to help me. She hid me under a blanket of denial and magic. Zak wasn't hiding me at all.

But why?

The more Zak's stupid smile grew, the less upset about it I became.

I let out a sigh. "Sorry. I'm frazzled."

"It's a lot. I get it." We stood for a while longer. His fingers on my shoulder softened and I could've sworn we'd gravitated closer. My heart skipped a beat, terrified to be in the vortex of Mercy's gaze, but not wanting to escape either.

He pulled away first. "Wanna grab some dinner? I know you're not hungry after your angel sampler but I'm starving."

Zak needed to be renamed as The Angel of Tactlessness.

"I guess I should thank you for that," I said, "I feel remarkably better."

"Anytime you feel like you're about to faint, just call me."

I didn't want to get caught up in any cutesy feelings, especially when he was supposed to be my commander. Captain. Whatever. But I couldn't help wanting to be closer to him. Everything felt better with him around, like he was a literal sun and I the flower. As long as we didn't cross any lines, I could admire him in secret, right?

He immediately started walking toward the cafeteria but I stopped. "You don't want to clean up first?" I asked.

Zak's eyes were already half-lidded and I had to slow down so as to not walk ahead. What if I'd taken too much energy from him that time? I felt bad making him tend to my stupid needs when he was clearly exhausted.

Could he ever stop being nice?

"If *you* can stand sitting next to me and my post-workout stink, then I'm good," he said.

I wasn't convinced but if I knew anything for certain about the angel, he liked his food. He'd be right as rain after a snack.

"If you say so," I said.

Zak suggested something other than pizza. Pasta.

Same food groups, but whatever.

My stomach was full but I was hyper-aware of the feeling of lacking that followed. Cheese and carbs, my beloved comforts, just didn't hold up to the life energy I took from Zak earlier.

I feast on souls….

I shuddered.

Zak finished well before I had and talked over his empty plate. "We'll have to see how stealing energy can benefit you in combat. It would mean having to touch an enemy or comrade. Both sound risky. Undercover work might suit you."

With an ability like that, being undercover made sense. I imagined a dark seductress sleeping in some evil dictator's bed chambers, slowly draining him of life. "Maybe. I don't think I could do it, though," I said.

Zak chuckled. "No? Why not?"

"I'm not sure I'm comfortable using my body for that."

He choked on his drink.

"Hang on! I'd never prostitute you off." Zak sputtered his carbonated liquids and stumbled over his words. His eyes dropped, doing that annoying thing again where we didn't look at each other. He rubbed his chin with his veiny hand. "I can see why you'd have those thoughts, though. *Ah.* This is why Lisha would be a better teacher for you. I'm already messing this up."

"That's not true." I started but changed the subject before I said anything too heartfelt like he made me feel safe. Zak didn't need to know how much I'd grown to like him. "You *swear* it doesn't hurt when I'm stealing your soul from your hand?"

It was something I didn't want to have to ask Peter, thanks to my lingering guilt.

"No. Then again, I don't think you were really trying," he said.

"I don't want to *try* and kill you," I said, "What does it feel like?"

His eyes flickered to mine once before returning to his barren plate. "Hm. Like a soft tug of a rope, pulling from the center.

It's not unpleasant, but for someone unawares, it could be tricky getting untangled from."

Damn. So, Peter wouldn't have known something was wrong until it was too late?

I think Zak felt my stir of emotions and decided to make it better by saying, "But hey, after some practice, you can have a boyfriend and not kill him."

My glowing cheeks were probably blinding him so I hid behind my hands. "Why are you like this?"

"You are embarrassed easily, for a Demon," he said.

"Shut up."

"That's not very nice."

Shit. He was right. I shouldn't have been so comfortable as to disrespect an angel, but when I looked up to apologize he was still grinning. "You spook easily too," he said, "I'm only teasing. Or am I?"

"I really don't know." I folded into my chair. Did one have to be playful and obnoxiously optimistic to claim the title of a merciful angel?

"Lisha wouldn't tease you as much but she's also not as much fun as I am," Zak muttered.

"What's your deal with her?" I asked, "You tease each other a lot too."

His brows touched. "She's my rival."

"Rival?"

"Yeah. Everyone needs a good, healthy, rivalry."

It was my turn to laugh. I'd thought there was some serious bad blood between them but they had just been playing. "So you just mess with each other?"

"*Mhm.* She could probably kick my behind in a real fight."

"You're an angel, though," I said, "What is she?"

He leaned across the table, darkening his gaze as if he were about to reveal the biggest secret of the universe. "A rarity even in our world. An ancient glory that made both heaven and hell once tremble. A wrathful goddess of the stars and mountains."

I rolled my eyes at his theatrics. "Okay, and that is?"

Zak just smirked. The way his crystal irises glimmered reminded me of the jewel-like scales from Lisha's neck.

* * *

I never did get an answer.

It was much later when we decided to walk back. Zak provoked me further about my blushing problem, to the point where I almost said "To hell with it" and punched him.

I didn't but it was tempting.

Zak took a breath from his ceaseless chuckling. "Sorry. Just trying to thicken your skin. You might get stupid comments from your peers about being a succubus. I hope you know that *my* teasing comes from a good place."

I smiled, feeling genuinely grateful for him. It would have been scary if Zak hadn't found me. If I'd lost Naomi in the portal and was left to my own devices, I would've been alone. Sure, I could hide out and take my meds, but eventually it would run out. I'd need money for supplies. The image of me dying until I lost control and attacked someone made me gulp..

Wait. I had to replay what Zak had just said in my head.

"Did you say succubus?" I asked. Clove had brought them up too.

"Yeah."

"*Sex* demons? Really?"

Zak shrugged. "They're known for stealing their victim's souls through touch. They also enjoy tormenting them to the brink of insanity, but I digress."

"But I don't—"

"Yeah, I know you wouldn't do that. Succubus or not, you can handle it. You're a tough cookie." His small words of encouragement shielded me briefly from the horrifying realization that I could be related to the winged demons of lust. It made the most sense. Hadn't I been in Peter's bed when everything went horribly wrong?

Gods... But regardless of how stressful all the revelations had been, I felt like EXO was where I needed to be. I had no freaking idea what I was doing before. Whether or not I could be useful to EXO was yet to be seen but part of me really hoped I could be.

"Thanks," I said, "I'd be pretty lost without you... and EXO."

"Speaking of lost things, why do you think it's so hard to reach your aunt? " Zak asked.

The air had gotten colder and made my skin prickly. I looked up at the stars getting brighter in the sky, envious of their clarity. "I don't know. I know she had plans to keep us off the grid, but now I'm out of the equation."

"I see." He breathed out his nose. "We'll find her. I'd like to talk to her too."

It was kind, but would his offer keep me indebted to EXO? I wanted answers from Naomi too, but what did the angels have in mind for her? If Zak was gracious with me, maybe he'd go easy on her too.

Zak came to a halt outside of the dorms. "Thanks for joining me. I hate eating alone."

I snorted but was still flattered. "Like you don't have *plenty* of willing participants at your disposal."

His eyes narrowed playfully. "Are you judging me for my angelic charms?"

"I just didn't know angels could be so conceited."

"It's called *self-enlightenment*, Jess."

I cracked a smile, enjoying our little exchange. Probably too much. I did feel a twinge of jealousy knowing he was like that with everyone. It was stupid but a real and fleeting feeling I had. He was just naturally a nice person.

"Glad we could get some answers today," he said, "I hope you're feeling better about things."

"Me too, I—"

But I stopped.

A dark figure loomed behind Zak. The man showed up without a sound. He was tall, dark-haired, and had red eyes that glittered at the moon.

"Cupcake?" he said.

No way. The creep from jail?

His dry voice was a startling greeting to my ears. "What are the fucking odds?"

What was he doing there? He couldn't have been released already. At least, from my first impression of him, he'd gotten into some real trouble.

The vampire strolled toward us with all the leisure in the world. I could feel Zak's intense stare and took that to mean he wasn't thrilled either. "Aiden."

Aiden. That was his name.

"Not happy to see me?" Aiden's smile revealed his canines. "It's good to be home, Zakiel."

Zak deflected his loud satire. "This is the last time. Be on your best behavior."

Last time? What did that mean?

Aiden carried an air of trouble with him, significantly more potent than when we'd been confined. The deep ruby color of his eyes was striking, even in the night. "We all know Daddy won't let that happen," Aiden said, "but if you keep recruiting pretty things, I might play along."

He cast his eyes down at me. I hadn't said anything, but watched in disbelief as he opened the doors behind me. His slow turning of the knob was as irritating as it was painful. I knew where Aiden was going, and yet, my heart sank even lower when he finally let himself inside.

He was going to live there. With me. In the same building.

Aiden sang and let the door slowly shut behind him. "Later, Cupcake."

14

We met outside that day with the brisk morning air. Tori greeted me with a timid smile. I knew the weather didn't affect her spirit body and was slightly jealous. A few days had passed and no fainting spells for me. That had a lot to do with mine and Zak's one on one's.

Our "lessons" consisted of us holding hands and me pretending to know how to control the ebb and flow of his energy. I appreciated that it took place away from the group but hopefully that wouldn't get Zak into a compromising situation. Especially with his position and the other angels…

Tori looked very human that day, as in, not like a stuffed animal. I eyed the bear taking its place on her hip, and half expected it to move again. "Sorry about the other night," she said, "I hope you know it was just for laughs. I didn't think a demon would be so jumpy."

"It *was* funny," I said.

After I shit myself.

"You seem distant this week. Just making sure it wasn't because of me," she said.

"No. No, I've… had a lot on my mind." I gave her a reassuring smile. When I thought back on it, my reaction to her joke wasn't classy. And the way I grabbed Guy. *Ugh.*

He probably thought I was such a loser, cowering behind him. My job, eventually, was to protect people from the scary stuff, not hide from them. I had to get used to tense situations.

That was going to prove harder with Aiden around.

When I asked Zak last night why he was there in the first place, he said: *"He's Blaxill's eldest. We have the whole trio."*

Mallory already had a weird fixation with me but now her creepy brother too. Aiden acted indifferent toward everyone, even his brother, Darren. Mallory was his only cohort. She seemed to be the only one on Aiden's level, as they snickered constantly together.

Tori and I arrived together on the field but were welcomed with turning heads and piercing stares. That had become the norm since I fainted. Was it because of Zak? I practically groped the guy in front of everyone the other day, and then abruptly left.

Zak's bountiful enthusiasm as he bossed us around made it easier to ignore everyone else at least. Although outwardly admiring him wouldn't help my case. Tori hadn't mentioned anything, but I caught her glancing between Zak and me several times. I kept my excitement in check whenever he called my name for something, but that didn't fool everyone.

"Does someone have a crush on the teacher?" Aiden asked.

Tori left my side for maybe a second when he creeped up behind me. He'd done that a few times now, like he enjoyed startling me. I didn't want to overthink it, though.

"No. Not that it's your business," I said.

"Liar."

He didn't press any further and slunk off to stand beside his sister. *Creep.* I huffed. It wasn't like the age gap between any of us was that extreme. Discounting spiritual years, anyway. I wasn't pining after someone's grandfather. Just an angel.

Just an angel.

I knew it wasn't the last of Aiden's adorable jabs. The not-so-judgemental part of me wanted to give everyone a chance, but Aiden had a vibe. He looked like a guy who would treat his dates to a fancy dinner but drizzle *them* over his dessert.

Okay. *That* may have been a purely judgemental thought. I didn't know him at all. All I had was the minute we were in jail together and I wouldn't label it a pleasant experience. He could just be eccentric or enjoys messing with people. Deep down, he might be a nice person.

I met his eyes from across the field and he gave me a slow lick of his lip.

Nope. My judgment stands.

After warming up, an obstacle course had been set up in the grass. It wasn't made of much, probably because the absurdly strong and flexible simply blew through it. Drones carried small targets high in the sky and Mallory danced her way into the air. She didn't miss a single one with her wide kicks and daggers for fingernails.

I remained on the ground; climbing over walls, crawling under wires, jumping on beams—anything you could think of that still respected gravity. The last area had a tall and narrow platform set up for us to run across, because why not?

The weak surface did not complement my anxious attempt to remain swift and balanced. I made it about halfway when a figure dropped from above and landed, perfectly perched on my beam, like a cat.

"Boo," Max growled.

My legs shook from the surprise and I lost my footing. His blue eyes followed me as I fell. I starfished on the grass, wondering if I would have permanent back problems from training. Max hadn't left his post. He must have been enjoying the view. I grumbled a few rude names to call him while pushing myself up.

The werewolf dropped right on top of me and caged me under all four of his limbs. I pressed myself back into the dirt and shielded my face, wondering if he'd heard what I'd called his mother.

His hot breath hit my knuckles. "If I were hunting you, you'd be dead already. *Demon*."

I scoffed. *How did he know?* Not that we kept it a big secret. "Could you get off me?"

"Are you even trying? I expected more from something like you."

I wormed my way out from under him, ignoring how he'd tried using his words as a knife. Why target me? And what made him any less monstrous than me? We hadn't even spoken all that much. Was he still being petty over the whole bloody flannel on the bus thing?

His head jerked to the side like he had heard something. Without even standing up all the way, he leaped back into the air and reached the beam. *Good riddance.*

Max was right, though. I hadn't done much to impress and I'd been quiet about what happened after I fainted. In truth, I hadn't wanted to announce that I could be a succubus. Even Zak expressed concern about the word getting out, more than the general title of half-demon.

I grasped at the grass and pulled myself back up. The leathery blades felt crispy all of a sudden. Did grass die that quickly after being crushed? I didn't pay much mind. Winter would arrive any day; everything was drying up.

When I finally finished the course, I drowned myself in my ice-cold water bottle. The whole time I kept imagining how much more satisfying touching Zak's hand would be, as opposed to the liquid relieving my parched tongue. Maybe his arms too…

I couldn't even remember how Peter had felt before. Warm, *I think*, but not like Zak. Did souls have variations, like flavors of soda? If I had to compare the two, Zak was like a warm cup of sunny, rich butterscotch, and Peter had been tap water.

Gods. I was equating the worth of souls to food and drink.

Zak shouted for the group to get organized again, but I took my time. I worried for my own soul, the good half of it anyway, after having compared Peter's to sink water. My body ached too, reminding me that my strength came from other souls and I'd spent it sweating, jumping, and climbing.

I hated it.

Zak had welcomed me so easily, demon blood and all. Why was it so hard to accept my own circumstances? How could he not see me as something to hate?

A scratchy voice tickled the back of my ear.

"You look thirsty, Cupcake."

Not again. Aiden chuckled at my gloomy state. He leaned back on his heels while his crimson gaze traveled shamelessly around my body. "I just came to sympathize," he said.

"They have gallons of the synthetic stuff to help with *your* problem," I said, even though I knew he likely only drank organic, "And stop calling me Cupcake."

His grimace scrunched his handsome face. "I'll pass. So, you ended up here of all places?"

"You did too."

"C'mon, we're not in the pod anymore. You don't have to be skittish with me."

My dismissiveness seemed to only humor him further. I preferred our circumstances back then. At least then he'd been handcuffed. "You still had someone's blood on your lip when we met."

Aiden's head leaned to one side and he stepped closer. "What were you lookin' at my lips for?"

His eyes narrowed as my internal temperatures skyrocketed. I came up with something quick to retort, "I couldn't help there was an obvious mess on your face."

"Not used to vampires in your neck of the woods?"

"Are they alive?" I asked.

"She lived," he paused, "I think."

"You *think*?"

He raised his shoulders. "I'm not a paramedic, Cupcake. Maybe it was an *accident*. You can understand that, can't you?"

My tongue went from mostly dry to a sandy desert. Did he know about Peter? A few words from his sly lips and I was plagued with images of Peter's face struggling to breathe.

A clever grin crept across Aiden's face. If he'd intended to provoke me, then he was a bigger tool than I thought. I took a long, angry drag from my water bottle. If I couldn't stop the images from coming, I'd drown them.

"Sorry, am I being presumptuous thinking we have something in common?" Aiden asked in the same tone of innocence and mockery as Mallory. When I continued to remain silent and crossed my arms he shook his head. "Let's start over. I could really use a friend while I'm stuck here. Looks like you could too."

My lack of companions around me reaffirmed how alone I felt. Tori was great, but flighty? However, most vampires made "friends" outside of their circles to get free, consensual meals. In another life, and if he hadn't been interested in my blood, I might've enjoyed the attention. His raven colored hair did him a lot of favors. As far as male beauty went, he had the longest lashes I'd ever seen and a facial structure that anyone would envy.

Still, I didn't want to become a vampire's personal blood bag.

"You don't want my blood," I said, "I doubt it tastes any good."

"Now, who's being presumptuous?" Aiden's eyes paused at my throat. "I happen to have an adventurous palate."

"That's great for you. I'm not interested."

I turned sharply but he inserted his body in my path. My face came close to his chest. His ruby eyes glittered down at me from beneath his umbrella lashes. "You don't really care about this shit, do you?" he asked, sounding like a normal person and not a gravelly seducer.

"What?" I grumbled, wanting to return to the group. I'd even welcome Max's perpetual glaring.

"Just a wild guess. You're no more a volunteer here than I am."

Aiden and his siblings all seemed pretty passive toward their duties at EXO. I mean, Mallory enjoyed showing off, but none of them seemed thrilled about the goal of defending the innocent. Which begged the question, what had *they* done to get "recruited?"

"Just ask someone else to feed you," I said. Could Zak see us?

Aiden caught me looking for the angel, anyway, and laughed with his head tilted back. "*Please* don't tell me you're actually sweet for Mr. Sunshine over there?"

A heavy stone sank in my stomach.

"You know you're just a tool to him," Aiden said, "At least a friendship with me comes with equal exchange. I give as much as I get, Cupcake. Wouldn't that make life easier for both of us?"

I didn't have to keep listening to him. When I made to leave, his lanky body stuck to me like a shadow; playfully mirroring my movements. Aiden took it one step further and nipped at the air just above my head.

"You bite me and I'll scream." My attempt to sound threatening only made his smile grow. It was a weak threat. I should've offered to stake his heart.

"I certainly hope so," was his smooth response.

"Aiden." Guy appeared like a dark shadow behind the vampire, not as tall but equally imposing. He hadn't arrived on his cloud chariot like my latest rescue from Tori's bear but his timing had been perfect. "Jess needs to focus," he said, "You'd benefit from the same."

Aiden lingered for a few seconds longer even with the reaper staring him down. I couldn't hear any of us breathing. The tense moment couldn't end soon enough.

"*Jess?*" Aiden finally said, singing my name. "That's a nice name. Jess, Jess, Jessssssss."

I frowned. "Will you stop calling me Cupcake?"

He just smiled before dragging himself back to the group. Guy watched as well and pinched his forehead like he was experiencing a migraine. "You're going to be trouble aren't you?"

"*Me?*" I asked.

What about him?

Guy was either deep in thought over how much of a nuisance I was or wanted to distance himself from the situation because he never answered.

* * *

To my surprise, Jarmiel pulled me early from training.

At least *he* wanted to talk to me.

I had a feeling I was in trouble, though, unless I read his harsh, yet beautiful, expression wrong. He'd shown disappointment in Zak's involvement with me from the beginning, but any excuse to sit sounded nice. I recovered quickly but the aggressive training still drained me.

He brought me to the same classroom we used last time and made no mention of Zak. I decided not to mention it either. Less attention we received, the better.

Nothing; that was what that hug between Zak and me had been.

"You have homework this week," Jarmiel said, "We should be caught up with the others soon and you can join their classes."

We reviewed previous classes together. I was still curious about the average day for a peacekeeper, but I supposed that came with experience. After Jarmiel finished going over the rules with me, again, I took advantage of the transition into his next lesson.

"Jarmiel, you said that demons work differently and that depends on their origins?" I started.

"Yes."

"Are Ghouls demons?"

"Interesting. Why do you ask?"

"Zak said The Necromancer made them," I said.

"He did, did he?" Jarmiel took a long breath. "Yes, Ghoul bodies aren't biologically demonic. In fact, they're entirely human. When they become possessed by The Necromancer's magic, that changes, but we don't know if he's conjuring demons to inhabit them or if the Ghouls remain mindless puppets."

"Would they be more powerful if demons possessed them?" I asked.

"Depends on the demon. A demon on the surface of Terra has only half their normal strength. When they possess human vessels, they regress even further."

"Why?"

"We believe it has a lot to do with the World Soul." Jarmiel took a break from the projector we clearly forgot about and went for a textbook instead. He opened a thick one and laid it out for me on my desk. "Of course, these are just drawings, but close to the real thing."

The pages looked like beautifully drawn, ethereal trees. But the longer I looked, the more confused I became. I thought I could make out other organic shapes, like *organs*, from their transparent frames. They were all connected, like roots leading to one, larger being.

The World Soul.

I was not expecting a mythical history lesson.

Angels and demons made their public debuts, but the World Soul remained fantastical, and was still treated reverently amongst religious sects. Probably because no one *living* had ever seen it.

Faith required.

"The World Soul needs all elements in balance, specifically light and dark matter. Both are necessary to survive, like a plant that needs the sun and the rain. Heaven provides pure light while Hell resides in pure darkness. Within those realms, angels and demons are at their full strength. On Terra, however, where the light and dark mix, we adapt to half the available matter. Does that make sense?"

Uh, huh… I nodded. "I think so."

"Even you won't have access to your full capabilities unless you return to Hell. Your comfort in living on this plane probably comes from your remaining half lineage, whatever that may be exactly," he said, "I often forget that your upbringing wasn't an informative one. Feel free to ask questions and I'll answer what I can."

What he can.

Did that mean he was going to be selective in what he told me?

"So, being half means I'm even weaker?" I asked.

"That remains to be seen."

"What happens to the World Soul if things aren't in balance? Like, if there's more light than dark, or the other way around?"

"The World Soul has a system in place," Jarmiel said, and I think he noticed my hand starting to raise because then he added, "Reapers, yes. They enforce the World Soul's will, keeping the balance between Heaven and Hell."

"So there's angels and demons feeding the World Soul, and reapers keeping things in order… Why humans? Why supernaturals?" I knew I was asking a loaded question, but if I had a wise angel at my disposal, why not try discovering the meaning of life?

"Humans are born of the World Soul, pure and impressionable. We don't know why the World Soul creates, just that it does. And has. As humans are exposed to both light and dark matter, their souls begin to change. Eventually, they find homes in Heaven or Hell, and thus the cycle continues."

"So the great judgment everyone talks about is a soul having more light or dark matter?"

"Like likes like. Supernatural beings have struggled with this knowledge since they began as demonic experiments."

"They did?" I asked.

He nodded. "The demon lords manipulated humans into beings *like* themselves through rather cruel acts of sorcery. I believe it was to mock the World Soul while coveting the power of creation."

"That doesn't seem fair," I muttered. Assuming everyone wanted to get to Heaven, anyway. I didn't even know where I'd end up when I died but at least fifty percent of me wore Hell's brand.

Jarmiel's soft smile appeared unexpectedly. "Why do you say that?"

"Well, it's like getting shot in the foot before a race, right?" I didn't think he would be the sensitive one, especially toward supernaturals.

"It would seem, but the race isn't lost. We're a bit off-topic now." His warmth faded and he didn't explain further.

"Sorry," I said, trying to disguise the disappointment in my tone, "It's just interesting. No one talks about the World Soul."

"A pity. Is your aunt religious? I'd assume that a witch would believe in some higher power or another."

I snorted. "Yes and no. Worship isn't really her jam, unless there's a cat god I don't know about."

Jarmiel paused for a moment and I raised a brow.

"There is?" I asked.

"I suppose. In another realm or universe."

"Holy crap."

He smirked at my wide-eyed expression. "I wouldn't search beyond your realm as it is already vast and treacherous."

"What counts as *my* realm?"

I think he debated on humoring me because he glanced at his projector and swayed a bit. He switched the lights back on. "Since you're currently living, it's here. All around you," he said, "Terra was made for mortal existence. Reapers are protectors of the World Soul and use Death as their tool. Heaven and Hell are made for immortality and take responsibility for the souls that pass on, as I said before."

"Do I even try if I'm already a demon?" I liked the idea of mystical god-trees but if I was already bound for Hell, what was the point?

"You mean, to enter Heaven?" Jarmiel's pensive gaze scanned across my face. "I don't think I have these answers for you, Miss Winters."

As much as I appreciated his honesty, it sucked. I'd rather not see Hell if I could help it. How could anyone fight fate that was imprinted on their very blood?

"If you want one angel's *opinion*," Jarmiel started again, "I wouldn't give up hope. Though, I've never met a demon who longed for Heaven, we already know you to be peculiar. Being in Zakiel's company should have worn you down, not lifted you up. Although, he tires *me*."

His confidence and jokes brought peace back into my mind. I even grinned. There was an air of adoration when Jarmiel spoke of Zak, only when out of earshot.

"What is Heaven like?" I asked.

Jarmiel turned his attention to the windows. His golden eyes reflected the sun, making the crystal lines twinkle and dance. I already knew he was a naturally gorgeous man, in all angelic fashion, but he'd never looked so serene. "This temporary mortality fogs my memories, but it is beautiful. Let's carry on. If you wish to return to the topic another time, I could oblige."

Just like that, we were back into work mode. Jarmiel's volume elevated to prove his point. "Now, demonology is a sensitive topic to teach as demons can invade weak minds who explore such literature. The shortest incantation can entice any simple dark spirit. So, before going further, I advise honing your mind to be aware of intrusive thoughts. It's as simple as practicing discipline."

"Simple. Right." Naomi used to say something similar. She let me know why I was different from other people, but she refused to let me explore deeper than that. No books. No names. As a child, it was easy to accept. Demons were scary and I didn't want that.

"Do demon lords invade minds too?" I asked.

Jarmiel's shoulders slumped. I think he could tell that I was about to take us down another tangent, but he nodded. "Some could care less and leave the meddling to their underlings. Others enjoy the torment."

"What did The Devourer want when he started the war?"

"To bleed darkness into all three realms and create whatever he desired with no other gods to oppose him. In other words, control." Jarmiel listed the facts off like he was a textbook himself. "He failed but there are plenty of others eager to continue his work."

"That's why the war isn't over. They're all coming to take his place."

When Jarmiel confirmed, I swallowed. Why wasn't news like that being broadcast? All we ever heard about was the good angels were doing, and occasionally, putting down supernatural politicians.

Jarmiel once again seemed to understand my thoughts. "It's another reason EXO exists; to prepare for what's to come and, hopefully, prevent another catastrophe. Any other questions, Miss Winters?"

My head shot up from my desk. Apparently, I had been burning holes into the wood. "So many… Which hell kingdom do I come from?"

He took a moment to mull over the bookshelf behind his desk, running his fingers along each spine. "It would be hasty of me to assume, however… The Kingdom of Lust. Dangerous, hungry, and unforgiving. Its inhabitants experience all the pleasures of the world but are never satisfied, only being rewarded with eternal emptiness and frustration. Considering your ability to tamper with souls through touch. It's very possible you're the successful offspring of an incubus or succubus."

I groaned. There I'd been, hoping there was more to it all, but I was just the result of some flying ejaculation with horns.

Jarmiel selected a few books from his collection, creating a slow-growing pile in his arms. "It's only natural to be curious. I do wonder how much your aunt truly knows. Sheltering you was a good way to keep demons from finding you."

She'd been trying to hide me from angels as well. I sat on the edge of my seat waiting for him to proceed with something more uplifting. My eyes grew in sync with the number of books he continued to stack. He returned to my desk and dropped the heap in front of me, making the wood creak under the weight.

"Take these," he said, "One book for each kingdom. For personal study."

I gazed sorrowfully at him but it did nothing to crack the rigid angel. He was supposed to be the strict and responsible one. Why was he allowing me to take demonology books home? "But I thought you said—"

"It *is* unwise." He moved his head from side to side. "It *is* dangerous."

"You're really letting me read these?" I asked to be sure. Jarmiel was a smart man. He had to know what he was doing. It was like handing a demon ambition. I had no idea why the angels kept giving me chances. Unless Jarmiel was testing me.

Jarmiel's golden gaze didn't lift from the ground like he was trapped in a bittersweet daydream. "Leaving someone in the bowels of ignorance can be quite cruel. Or a blessing. I'll let you decide, as it is your right."

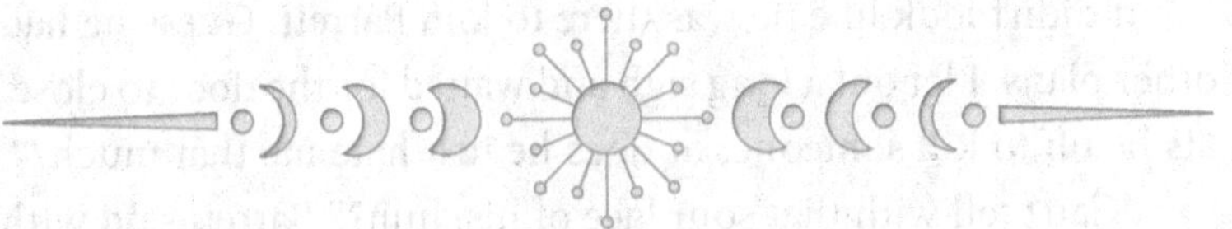

Jarmiel lent me a satchel to lug my books back to the dorms after our session ended; bless him. The weight was fine, but the quantity was obnoxious. I couldn't have kept them all together otherwise.

The bag banged around my legs awkwardly, reminding me of my sore muscles. What was so great about demon strength if everything still hurt?

Naomi's shop had been stimulating but only to the senses, never physically taxing. I played various scenarios in my head of how a conversation with my aunt would go while walking back to the dorms. Would she avoid my questions as she always had? Would I still go with her if she refused to give me answers, or would I stay with Zak?

I wasn't so sure.

When I entered the lounge it was already occupied by the wolves. Barrett sat in front of the tv and waved in my direction. The large bowl of popcorn in his lap smelled like it was drenched in butter. "Hi, newbie. You look beat."

I received a passive leer from Max as he stomped out of the kitchen carrying a massive energy drink. The hostile aura could be felt from across the room. He wore his superiority complex around like an accessory. Was it just an alpha thing?

Max bumped into my shoulder as he left the way I came in. "You're still here?"

It didn't look like he was there to join Barrett. Guess he had other plans. I let out a long sigh and waited for the door to close. "Is he off to kill someone, or does he just hate me that much?"

"Can't tell with that sour face of his, huh?" Barrett said with a small grin, "He's just… going to the gym."

His hesitation made it sound like Max was certainly *not* visiting the gym, but I didn't question what that was. Not my business.

Although, a nap and a candy bar could help his shitty attitude.

I felt Barrett's eyes linger on me like a child, or puppy, noticing a new toy. He'd been friendly so far, but I didn't feel cute or clean enough to entertain any socializing. With an awkward "See ya," I tried hurrying toward the stairs.

"Need any help?" Barrett asked, appearing just behind me. He motioned to the heavy bag I had and started lifting it before I could even answer.

"Oh. Thanks."

He wore a cheesy smile and waited to be escorted to my room. We skipped the elevator and hiked to the third floor together while making small talk. He raved about the movie he was watching and then asked what kind of movies I liked.

"Hey, so…" Barrett rubbed his nearly bald head before handing the bag back. "Sorry about Max. He's a good guy, I swear, but he's very, uh, *passionate*?"

"Does he get any better?" I asked.

"Not really. But give him a good beating and I'm sure he'll respect you. Not saying you owe him anything but it's fun humbling people sometimes." Barrett laughed. "I'd pay to see that."

Watching Barrett defend his friend was almost cute. Too bad his friend was a douchebag.

"Alright, I'll see you around," I said, "Thanks, again."

Barrett left and I could finally relax in my room. Not that class with Jarmiel had been tiring. Really, I could spend hours focusing on the World Soul. It was interesting and magical, but I had, as Jarmiel put it, "other priorities."

I was becoming increasingly aware of the power differences between myself and the others, especially when I hadn't taken any energy from Zak. With more training I could improve, but would it be enough? What I needed was power and that meant…

Souls.

The solution was simple, I just didn't want to do it. How hard was it to touch someone? Zak made himself perfectly accessible. *Easy* and yet, I still couldn't fully embrace it.

Instead of dwelling on self pity, I took a hot shower, put on a cozy sweater, and opened some chocolate candies before reading at my desk. Demonology hardly counted as escapism, but at least the material held my attention.

Evenings like that made me realize just how good I had it. Warm clothing and my favorite snacks wouldn't have been provided in jail. Maybe it was as good as it would ever be, especially if Hell was all I had left to look forward to.

Instead of dreading my afterlife, I thought about Zak again. My feelings for the goofy angel blossomed brightly in my chest. I wanted to trust him, and I wanted him to trust me. If I could be anything like him, maybe I'd have a chance to escape my fate.

Wishful thinking.

I opened the first of Jarmiel's heavy textbooks. Not all were part of the Demon Kingdom and that one in particular focused on various supernaturals. In the likely scenario that one of Blaxill's children tried to eat me, I read up on vampires to be prepared.

Like most supernaturals, vampires began as myths or scary stories to tell children. According to the text, however, now their numbers competed with the humans. The only drawback; vampires lived half as long.

Vampires were stronger, faster, and more durable until they reached expiration. The cause was still unknown. Another myth was that it was part of a curse on the vampires. The next bit was interesting:

"Healing properties were discovered in vampire venom, but at this time, it has been deemed too dangerous for medical use. In a recent study, seventy-eight percent of the test subjects either perished or succumbed to vampirism."

No wonder the protestors were upset about Roman Blaxill's pharmaceutical movement. On the other hand, if he found a way to make the venom safe, it could save a lot of lives. It would be the end of cancer and pandemics.

The next passage highlighted ways a vampire could die before their expiration.

"Decapitation or the removal of heart…" I read aloud to myself. Well, *that* would do it for just about anyone, wouldn't it? I closed the book, having no plans to cut off Mallory's head anytime soon.

The demonology texts waited on my desk. Taunting me. They were simple in appearance; black leather covers and thick parchment. I expected cryptic symbols or for them to be hissing with magic. They must have been the censored editions.

I grabbed the book labeled "Avidus, Kingdom of Lust."

Already, my fingers were shaking. Letters were printed in a maroon ink that seemed to dance off the page. The illusion hurt my eyes but I searched the list of names and references in the index.

Ah, yes. The succubus.

A chapter opened with illustrations of the sex-crazed demons. The succubus and incubus, female and male bodies, were completely nude, colored in the same reddish-brown ink. Their faces were sculpted to be appealing to anything that breathed, but not in the same way as the angel's beauty.

Zak made my heart race like a child excited for presents during the holidays. The demons, dangerously gorgeous and frighteningly monstrous, gave me more of a thrill. I felt cautious of how lovely they were. It could be because of their gargoyle wings, long tails, or sharp and devilish horns.

My gaze lingered on the chiseled incubus for too long. Their seductive powers worked even in 2-D! Before I could creep myself out further, I quickly flipped the page, and ran into a title called: "Kiss of Death."

That didn't sound fun but I continued anyway. The lust demons were notoriously powerful in their realm, able to steal life from their mortal victims through seduction, and without having to be right in front of them. *Dreams?*

I shuddered at the thought. The Incubi especially, the male demons, hunted while their prey slept; giving them dreams of fiery passion to keep them distracted. Poor, horny bastards wouldn't see it coming. I wanted the text to explain *how* the demons were able to do that, but it wasn't a Demons for Dummies or How To Eat Mortals guide.

It did make me wonder about my own parents, though. The phantom faces I'd grown to recognize from Naomi's photos felt like strangers now. Humans couldn't have made me and I don't know why I ever believed that.

I skimmed the next section; searching for… something. Anything to explain my existence. The succubi were known for attempting to breed with humans and, sadly, not in the most consensual fashion. At least, no one thought they were going to wake up from a good dream *pregnant*.

If a succubus *wasn't* looking to breed, then they were just gathering soul energy, like bees to a flower. The list of feeding methods made me blush all over again. "Good gods…" I winced at the drawing of a human woman wrestling with two incubi. Their limbs were entwined in a position I could only assume gave her pleasure, considering the drunk look on her face. Wouldn't that hurt, or was I just a prude?

No wonder Jarmiel had wanted me to study on my own.

The success rate of demon offspring was nearly impossible, especially when a human vessel carried the child. I could have been a miracle baby but I didn't inherit the horns. No wings. No tail. I liked my face okay, but I didn't compare to the naked drawings and I couldn't snoop on people's dreams. Not that I ever tried.

But I *had* kissed Peter, and he *had* almost died. If I'd known better then…

Just as I thought that, I flipped another page and my heart sank. *"In most cases, succubi visit their victims several times before killing them. Life force replenishes slowly over time. Long-term damage to victims includes loss of self, personality changes, depression—"*

Thud.

Guilt weighed me down until my forehead met my desk. Was Peter alive but forever in pain because of what I did? Could I change anything?

Somehow, sitting like that increased my drowsiness. I fell asleep with the "Ritualistic Dismemberment" chapter pressed against my face.

That wasn't the weirdest part.

I sensed something moving in my room. The pages from my book peeled away from my cheeks as I sat up. Everything was much darker than I had left it. If it was Tori and her teddy bear again I was going to bury her in my sock drawer until morning.

Heart pounding, I swiveled in my chair to catch any shift in the shadows.

An unnatural breeze hit my back and startled me out of my chair. The book was flipping its own pages on my desk. The window was locked. It couldn't have been a draft but the pages moved too rhythmically anyway.

I took a second to catch my breath.

"Tori?" I asked. May as well get comfortable with the idea of poltergeists.

No response.

I was about to stuff the books back into their bag and return them to Jarmiel, but curiosity guided my eyes to the opened pages. No more naked demons. There was a bold name above the text and I leaned over to get a closer look. *Asmo—*

Lights flickered in my room. A power outage? Now?

I should never have opened the books.

The name lay flat on display, tempting me to read once more. *The Great Demon Lord of Lust, Asmodai.*

A blanket of darkness covered the room, save for a strange glow that brightened in one corner. Silver lights created the illusion of winter starlight. The heavy scent of magic settled in the air; its burning taste settled on the back of my tongue.

Someone used a spell. *Here?*

"Naomi?" I noticed one corner of the room that just looked… wrong. It bristled, like a photograph getting crumpled. Something cut through the scene, further giving it a paper-like effect. The sharp object ripped a wider opening, and a dark figure forced its way through. He wriggled in like a roach finding its way under a crack. My spine stiffened so hard I didn't think I'd be able to move ever again. Who and what the hell was that?

His wild, ashen hair took refuge under a black shroud. He slowly turned his head in my direction. I could see his cracked lips pulling up into a grin. And those *eyes…*

Orange with a hint of madness.

The words he spoke crackled like burning wood.

"You're getting warmer…"

16

When I woke the next morning, I felt like a piece of marinated poultry that sat in rosemary overnight.

Which I had. I used most of Naomi's herb stash to keep the nightmares away. It worked, apparently. I was able to fall back asleep without a creep smiling at me in the corner. The crap I was reading would've given anyone nightmares.

It had been a dream… *had* to be.

But it felt so real.

My feet barely touched the floor when I recoiled back into bed.

"What the hell?"

Jarmiel's books had been scattered everywhere. I'd placed them outside my door after last night, but there they were in front of me again. Part of me really hoped someone outside saw them in the hall and chucked them unceremoniously back into my room, but my door was locked.

Enough of this.

I shoved them back into the bag they'd arrived in, saving the opened book for last because I was chicken. It wasn't the book of "Lust" like in my dream. It was one labeled Invidia: Kingdom of Envy.

My pulse quickened. I hadn't touched that book last night but as soon as my fingers were on the pages, the similar feeling of someone watching me from inside my room resurfaced. Was something really trying to communicate through the damned books?

Jarmiel said it could happen.

He's taking these back… today!

I carried the heavy bag downstairs and stormed outside, motivated by my new sense of urgency. The brisk morning air grazed my cheeks but I was stopped by a line of peacekeepers waiting for me.

Us, actually.

Tori and Guy stood beside each other, both wearing puzzled expressions. I let my bag slump off my shoulders to greet them. "Morning. Are we in trouble?"

"We're about to find out," Tori said but her eyes were wide with glee, not terror.

Guy looked about the same as he did any morning. His lazy eyes turned to me. "Sleep well, Jess?"

I hadn't realized before but the man didn't blink. For looking so tired all the time it didn't seem like his eyelids knew *how* to close. I engaged in a staring contest with him to prove my point further. "I've slept better," I said before surrendering.

Both Zak and Jarmiel dressed in black bodysuits with sculpted padding. Zak looked sexy as hell. Though, I couldn't imagine saying something so irreverent to his angelic face.

"Books won't be necessary today, Miss Winters," Jarmiel said.

I tore my gaze away from Zak. "O-Oh. No, I know, I just wanted to return them."

"You read them all?"

"I read enough."

I forced a smile and Jarmiel's brow furrowed. "Why don't you place them back inside for now," he said, "We have business to take care of today."

I knew he'd agree with me once I told him what happened, but the look on his, and Zak's, face stopped me from explaining. Something serious must've happened. The twinkle remained in Zak's brown eyes but he delivered no jovial introductions.

I left the books back inside the lounge just in time for the remaining trainees to arrive.

"Morning troops," Zak said, "We're getting suited up today. Meet us in the gym"

Tori clapped her hands together. Guy was slow to follow after her and the angels. I must've been dragging my feet as well because someone pushed ahead of me.

Max. I scoffed and let it roll off my shoulders. He had some incessant need to exude toughness in the least mature ways possible.

"Hey, newbie."

Barrett arrived next to me, feeling like a hot and cold contrast to his friend. His next question was directed at the back of Max's head. "We're getting new suits today? Don't we have to pass exams first?"

"Whatever's changed their mind isn't something to take lightly," Max said. His icy blue stare pierced us both when he glanced over his shoulder.

Barrett leaned down to reach my ear. "We're going to look awesome, though," he whispered.

The angels had looked pretty cool in their getup. The material fit snug but no one stretched or pulled at it with discomfort. I had a perfect view of Zak's toned shoulders when cool fingers brushed against the back of my neck like tiny ice cubes.

"Careful. Someone might notice." Mallory floated ahead like a phantom in white. Her faint smile and narrowed red eyes told me that I'd been caught. She tilted her head toward Zak and lifted a finger to her lips.

My mouth opened but only air came out. Zak had gorgeous features and a friendly soul. How could anyone *not* like him? I'd never do anything about it, anyway.

We stopped outside one of the low-standing buildings where peacekeepers and purifiers formed lines outside the doors. Inside had been emptied to make room for booths and tents walled with black fabric. Each table had stacks of silver cases sitting behind them.

"We made updates to the gear months back," Zak began explaining to us, "but after a recent case, we decided it was best to assign everyone their suit now. They're built to help you withstand most attacks, teeth, claws, knives, and bullets, of course, don't rely on them to save you. We have varying styles depending on your individual mobility and comfort. Grab your size and head to the changing stations."

I had my eye on a suit that another woman wore. Hers had a high neck, perfect for discouraging vampires. It also didn't have sleeves like Zak's, but came with sturdy looking gloves, reaching below her elbows.

My eyes finally reached the wearer's face. *Lisha!* She stood tall and drew her hands behind her back. Her attention lingered on several faces that crossed her path. When I did, she gave me a slight and formal nod.

After waiting in line my turn arrived, and two cases were handed to me. "Pick your preference. Changing areas that way," the member behind the booth instructed.

Tori, Mallory, and Yara, whom I hadn't spoken with yet, were already heading in that direction. No one seemed to mind getting naked while in the tents. I on the other hand had never changed in front of anyone before.

Unless running around Haverwick topless counts?

The first box had a suit similar to Zak's; fully-body but with a little stretch. Originally, I'd thought the more coverage the better, but I soon changed my tune when the fabric reached my thighs.

When I had to zip up the front, it got stuck on the fleshy roadblocks attached to my chest. Mallory, with her slim, proportionate, and fully nude figure, noticed my struggle. She sauntered on over and gripped the zipper stuck at my bulging cleavage while her other hand smashed my breasts flat.

With one hard yank upward, the zipper hit my collarbone and I was corseted in.

I wheezed. "Thanks."

She let me deal with getting it off, which was somehow harder than getting it on. I tossed that suit away. A "no" for me.

"Girl, your *body*." Tori suddenly chirped.

Several heads in the tent turned at Tori's discovery. I closed my arms over my chest. "What?"

"Uh, you're hot, that's what," she said, as if she'd never seen her own figure before. Granted, she wasn't as developed that way. "If I looked like that I'd never wear clothes."

It was Yara who spoke up on my behalf. Her voice poured out, fluid and smooth, like hot caramel and brewed coffee. "Focus, ghost-girl. We don't have time to waste."

Tori pouted. "*Okay*."

Yara tossed her eyes upward but her expression was full of humor. I mouthed "thank you," to silently appreciate her efforts, but not at the expense of Tori's feelings. She saw and smiled before returning to her business.

My second suit proved to be much easier to navigate and revealed my shoulders. Just like the one Lisha had. The zipper parked at the base of the spine instead. I liked the freedom in my joints and moved my limbs out and around, testing the limits.

Yes.

When I stepped out, I threw my hair back in a ponytail and glanced at the standing mirror by the tent. I looked like an expensive super-soldier. The gloves even made me feel extra secure. Where did EXO get the money to make suits like that for every member?

I liked seeing myself, though. Powerful. Professional. In my heart, I still felt like a poser but at least now I looked the part.

Zak's approving smile when I rejoined the group made my chest burn with pride. I should've been more concerned about *why* we were receiving our suits early.

Guy left his dressing tent next and I had to shut my mouth or leave it hanging open.

I almost didn't recognize him. No more baggy clothes or disheveled hair. He emerged as an entirely new man with five-plus years of maturity on his face. Or maybe I could finally see his strong jawline.

The suits seemed to complement everyone.

Save for one.

Aiden crawled out looking like a miserable cat that had been forced to wear a sweater. His rebel spirit reflected poorly on the unified garb. Disdain dripped from his person.

I had to suffocate a snort.

"Not to your liking, Aiden?" Zak asked. I knew he enjoyed himself at that moment. Even Darren, who sometimes I forget about completely because he was so quiet, hid his mouth behind his hand.

Aiden grumbled, pulling at his neckline. "It itches."

"Well, you look *great*," Zak said, "Okay, my team. Return what you aren't keeping and sign out the suits you are. When you're finished, meet with everyone else in the assembly hall."

We did as we were told. A new and heavy tone settled within our group as we filed into an auditorium. Lisha's team was stationed next to ours and I hadn't known until then just how small the supernatural portion of EXO was. Most of the faces in the room were purifiers. Their suits were thinner than ours like they didn't expect to deal much in combat.

I shouldn't have been at all surprised by their unwelcoming gaze. Not a single smile from the crowd was given to anyone in our group. I blamed the seriousness of the situation for the time being.

Tori had taken her teddy bear form again and jumped onto Guy's shoulder, "What do you think's going on?" she asked.

"We're about to see." He muttered. Not only did he carry her but it seemed he had to hold her suitcase as well. She huddled closer to his ear and waited.

A small stage sat high enough for us to see who entered. I heard a unified clack of shoes. A godlike man in stature with rich, brown skin and striking white hair pulled back in two, thick braids took centerstage. He spoke with a thunderous and firm voice.

"Good morning. I apologize for arriving on short notice."

He seems important, I thought. I heard someone muffling their chuckle. Lisha stared at me again. She sidestepped through people until she reached my side. "That is Raguel," she said, "One of the three heads of the Angel Council. He is a big deal."

I gulped. "I-I see. Thank you."

An unpleasant prickle danced across my skin. It reminded me of the first time I saw Zak and Jarmiel. I still wanted to know what *she* was. Zak kept it secret but I had a feeling he was just playing again. Although, I hadn't seen anyone quite like Lisha before. The dark scales that covered her neck seemed like an expensive piece of jewelry.

Her slitted eyes shifted back up. "Pay attention, recruit."

My head focused back on the stage at record speed. Raguel continued, his voice booming without the use of a mic, "As some of you know, suspicious activity from the other realms has been higher than usual. After a recent report, we may have located one source of the rising attacks."

He motioned to someone in the back and a large hologram appeared behind him. We were all hit with a bright, 3D portrait of a younger looking man in a hoodie. For how advanced their technology was, the image itself was poor and didn't reveal his whole face.

My gasp stirred both Guy and Lisha at my sides, but they kept silent.

Crappy photo or not, I felt like I knew this person. The blurred image triggered memories from my nightmare. I felt ridiculous assuming since it could be any skinny guy in his twenties.

But still.

"Many of you have already adopted a name for him. The Necromancer," Raguel said, "He was last seen a week ago with more of the undead abominations."

The Ghouls. My fingers twitched at my sides. Raguel motioned again and the image switched. The projection became life-size sculptures of the mutilated bodies. Some had three heads instead of one.

"The man portrayed also seems to be in possession of a very dangerous object," he said, "A blade made of dark matter. We do not know all that it can do yet, but judging by the similar markings on these bodies, we believe it gives him the power to reanimate and possess. While the attacks seemed random in the past, our latest theory indicates that he is targeting EXO members. I know many of us have lost friends and are frustrated that this man hasn't been stopped, which is why we're preparing for anything by giving you new uniforms earlier than expected."

His thick, protruding brow darkened his gaze, making his crystalized eyes glow and burn into our minds. Mine, at least. I couldn't seem to keep still.

"If our theory is correct, we could experience another attack close to home," Raguel said, "We are putting together more teams to track him down as we speak. As for the recruits who have not yet passed their exams, you're granted permission to use the means necessary for self-defense. This does not mean purposefully engaging with Ghouls or the culprit if spotted. You will retreat, signal for assistance, and fight only when those first options are ruled out. Is that clear?"

"Yes, sir." The room echoed.

As soon as the assembly ended, Zak whisked me away from the group. He didn't say why but it seemed urgent. Jarmiel stayed close as well, with tired eyes and a glistening forehead. Neither said much but their pace was faster than a casual stride. The room still buzzed with murmurings about Raguel's announcement.

"Where are we going?" I asked finally.

"Oh, just—" but someone cut Zak off.

We all came to a halt as the massive frame of the angel blocked our path. Raguel. I looked back at the stage, wondering how he'd appeared so quickly.

"Winters," Raguel said, revealing zero emotion, "And you two. Would you follow me, please?"

Zak kept trying to make small talk with him but he replied with one-word answers. He took us far away from the others, heading toward the building with Zak's office. I did my best not to panic but the entire walk felt like the burning end of an explosive.

We arrived too soon. I shifted my gaze to the angels at my sides and noticed a few peacekeepers had followed us. They closed the door after we entered Zak's room.

"Sit," Raguel instructed.

Three chairs already awaited us. Watching Jarmiel lower his tall frame into his seat would've been funny under normal circumstances, like a penguin trying to bend in half. Zak, on the other hand, plopped down, feet landing hard on the carpeted floor.

Raguel made a slow turn about the desk before taking his own seat in Zak's chair.

"Care to explain why a *demon* is sitting in your office, Zakiel?"

17

T he room vibrated as Raguel's aura radiated a powerful light.

His eyes were balls of white fire ready to burn me out of existence. I grasped the arms of my chair, feeling the need to flee, when glowing chains materialized in front of me. The heavenly metal wrapped around all three of us but only hovered threateningly, never touching our skin. I could feel its searing temperature wanting to burn through my new clothes and sizzle my hair.

Thick beads of sweat fell from my face. I was in a furnace. Wait, no. Was I actually freezing? I couldn't tell anymore. With a lame attempt, I wiggled in my chair to get further away from the chains, but someone's finger tapped the back of my hand. Zak's gentle touch lingered on my skin for a moment until my heart rate was no longer skyrocketing.

He chuckled at the holy man in front of us. "Raguel, is this really necessary?"

Raguel stood and the long braids resting on his shoulders seemed to hover. "I don't know what I find more insulting, that you tried to lie to me, or that you're *still* trying to. You even got Jarmiel to follow along in this scheme of yours. This is an abuse of your power."

"I *asked* for his help," Zak said.

Raguel scoffed, turning to the second angel. "And you complied?"

Jarmiel's head dropped. "Yes."

My heart hurt for him, just a bit. He looked like someone's pride and joy getting scolded for the first time. Raguel pressed his fists into the desk and sparks sprang from his golden rings. "*Why* am I having this conversation at all? A *demon*, Zakiel?"

I bit my tongue; unsure if saying anything on my behalf would make things worse. The chains continued to irritate every cell in my body.

"Okay, first, I didn't lie. I just avoided telling you for a while," Zak started, "Second, I can explain."

"Please do." Raguel's stern face matched his stern tone.

I gulped. *Gods, give me strength.*

"Jess is no ordinary demon. We're not entirely sure what that means yet, but Jarmiel wouldn't have agreed to help me if he didn't feel the same. I'm sure you can sense it too."

The white-haired angel still fumed, but only through sharp breaths out his nose.

"Do *you* sense any malice from her?" Zak asked.

Raguel's body shook like he wanted to yell but held back. "It's not always as simple as a feeling, Zakiel. Hell gets more clever by the day. So, one of their kind sends an innocent face to your door, and our greatest angels falter?"

Zak angled his chin to look down at me while I peered up at him in my stupified state. "Do you allow fear to counsel you now? That's unlike you, Raguel," he said.

The tone of the room suddenly changed.

"Zakiel," Jarmiel whispered sharply. Even I was taken aback. That had sounded an awful lot like an insult.

Raguel's silence made my insides tighten, but Zak continued. "You seem to think I've adopted the shortcomings of mortals, like fear, but perhaps it is you?"

"Watch your words," Raguel said.

"Humans fear what they don't know. We're supposed to be different. See for yourself that she isn't a threat to you."

Raguel took a deep breath. After a moment, his eyes dimmed almost back to their normal state. I flexed under my chains as Raguel came back around his desk to stand in front of me. A flurry erupted in my veins as something inside wanted desperately to escape the imposing angel.

"Not being a threat to me is easy enough," he said, "She can still be a threat to others."

Zak raised a brow. "If that's your argument, then so can any of our peacekeepers."

"That is a different issue entirely."

"Is it?"

Raguel's light flickered again but I finally spoke up. "I don't want to hurt anyone."

Whether he believed that or not, it was impossible to tell with his harsh stare. He used my armrests as balance as he leaned to better examine my face. I could barely meet his gaze. The heat from my chains made my eyes prickle from the intensity.

"If that's indeed the case, then you're still in the wrong place," Raguel said, "Part of a peacekeeper's job comes with the strong possibility of violence."

"But not against humans."

He blinked. Finally, he seemed to be considering something other than banishing me. "That's... correct."

Zak waved a taunting finger from his restrained hand. "It also just so happens that I've already extended my mercy."

Raguel's mouth opened once before shutting again. I had a chest spasm when he suddenly snorted.

He pushed off of my chair so his back was against his desk. A harsh laugh left his lips next. From there, his frustration grew into a half-hearted series of chuckles. "So, you *had* planned on telling me but only after you had her secured." Raguel shook his head. "If I didn't know any better, I'd say she bewitched you, Zakiel. Bless your soul."

Zak wore the smile of a charming prince, but he fooled us all with his cunning. "You guys get so jumpy about the littlest things, I wanted time to prove a point. She also took on one of The Necromancer's Ghouls by herself," he said like a proud father, "A big one too."

Raguel made a humored frown. He pinched his chin between his thumb and pointer finger. "This true, girl?" he asked.

"Sort of," I said.

Technically, the thing had still been alive.

Raguel's brow softened as he continued to study me. The chains across me, Jarmiel, and Zak turned back into tiny balls of light that vanished in the air. I rubbed my exposed flesh that had turned pink and took a big gulp of air.

"Lisha informed me of your progress here. Sloppy and inexperienced, she says, but your determination against the reaper was admirable." Raguel spoke slowly like the words were painful to utter.

"Really?" I asked, remembering the test not going well at all.

"Your scores were some of the lowest I've seen, but that's not uncommon for recruits with zero experience. With a demon's strength, I expect better from now on."

Did he just refer to me as a recruit?

"You're letting me stay?" I asked.

Raguel's eyes rolled to one side. "I don't have a say in it at the moment, thanks to Zakiel's questionable methods, but he hasn't given me a reason not to trust him. This doesn't mean that I trust *you*. Prove to me that you're more than a demon, Jessebel Winters."

His frosty eyes scanned all three of our faces.

"This is on you two, should things go poorly," he said, pointing to the angels, "but I too am curious. The chains should have caused you to catch fire at least. What sort of evolved demon breed are you?"

My eyes grew out of my head. He'd intended to set me ablaze? Rude.

"We don't know but that makes her special, right?" Zak asked.

"If that's the case, I'd like to get her bloodwork done."

My heart sank, but why? It wasn't like they could find out anything worse.

I was already a demon.

Zak sounded less chipper about that part. "We'll see to it before exams."

"Uriah won't like this," Raguel said.

I remembered that name from EXO's historic video. Barely. Of the three angels around me, they seemed to revere Uriah as someone in a higher position than them. Zak lifted his shoulders. "Ahh, he's strict but he's curious too. I'm sure he'll see the benefit of studying her."

Raguel pressed his lips together. We all watched him reviewing the last ten minutes in his mind. For the moment, it seemed like we were safe. I was safe. And it was thanks to Zak. I felt the weight of his generosity building up brick by brick.

Zak and Jarmiel had been willing to go against their own… For me?

Raguel stepped forward, away from the desk again, "I apologize but I'd like to experience your aura for myself."

He presented his hand to me and I knew the drill. It didn't make it easier to surrender. I still didn't trust my touch. Everything that happened after was still unpredictable.

It felt like a rush of wind blowing up my arm. Not only was his grip intense but his energy as well. I watched his holy face closely for signs of distress but he revealed nothing. "It's as you say. Her soul isn't malicious but very disorganized," he mulled, "How is it something like you has come to be? Who were your parents?"

"I don't actually know," I said, sounding like a broken record.

His voice growled a bit, or was he grumbling? "Do you want to be here? This isn't purely to appease Zakiel?"

Since he mentioned it, maybe I had wanted to please Zak. The thought of disappointing him made me physically ill. If I ran, he would think I was a coward. Those were thoughts I haunted myself with as well. I didn't want to keep running; from the world or myself.

Raguel cracked a smile and dropped my hand. "I suppose that doesn't matter. Looks like you're stuck here for now."

He turned away, making a slow lap to the chair behind his desk again.

Much to my displeasure, my voice quieted like a mouse. "I don't want to be something people hate. I'll learn how you do things here."

Raguel took a longer pause than I had. He lowered himself into his seat and drummed his large fingers against the wood. My nerves settled like dust on a shelf. Things were still while the wrinkles around his face softened even more.

He sighed. "I'll need you in top shape, and quickly. Training a demon will be tricky. I hope you all realize what you've gotten yourself into."

I just nodded.

"Do not abuse this chance, Winters. Pass your peacekeeper test. I will hold a council meeting following your success, regardless of your contract with Zakiel," Raguel said, "Now, all of you get up."

I rose from my chair. His presence was still a bit too bright. Too godly. But I forced myself to keep my head up so he knew I was sincere. "I'll do my best, sir," I said.

"Then you're all dismissed."

Jarmiel made a swift path toward the door but Zak hesitated. "Wait, isn't this my office? Hey, Raguel, we should get a drink! I missed that handsome face."

The silence from the braided angel was deafening. I made a dash for the hallway after Jarmiel.

18

"That was awful."

I held my head between my hands, still processing what had happened. For a moment there, I thought Raguel was going to kill me. I had to check my arms a few times to make sure his heavenly chains hadn't actually burned me.

The three of us took an elevator to the first floor and headed outside. Peacekeepers and purifiers walked purposefully around campus in their new uniforms; separate from each other, yet unified.

Zak puffed out his cheeks. "He didn't even want lunch. What a grump."

"I thought you sent the paperwork," Jarmiel said. He kept his sights on the sidewalk ahead of us. A flustered vein appeared on his forehead again.

"It's not my fault if people don't read their mail."

"Will you take *anything* seriously?"

A chime went off from Jarmiel's jacket pocket, distracting him from his frustrations. He groaned. "It's Uriah. I'm not answering this alone."

"Fine." Zak stopped and thumped his heel like a disgruntled rabbit. "Go on ahead, Jess. Get something to eat with one of your roommates and get better acquainted with your suit. Looks good on you, by the way."

Jarmiel simmered once more. "Zakiel could show more enthusiasm for his trainee's highlighted figure."

It took me a second to hear what he actually said because his tone was so bland. The satirical translation I heard was: *Zak thinks I look good.*

Zak was at a loss for words, for once. He looked like he wanted to laugh at his partner's attempt at humor but froze up. Finally, he said, "You're saucy when you're angry. And inappropriate. I don't hate it, though."

Jarmiel revealed his victory with a faint grin. "We'll discuss which of us is more inappropriate with the council. Phone call. Now."

He barely lifted his hand as a farewell before dragging Zak away. Disappointment followed me soon after but I knew it was best not to feed into the hopeless fantasy. Zak spared me plenty of his time.

I made several shameless examinations of myself in every reflection along the building's windowed walls. Maybe it was because my aunt never encouraged dating and I wasn't used to being seen as desirable, but I couldn't stop smiling. I hadn't felt giddy over something so silly. Ever.

My mood soured when I entered the dorms again and saw my bag of books waiting for me. I didn't want to keep those things around, especially while I slept. Those heavy suckers were slung over my shoulder and I headed right back outside.

Jarmiel wasn't there to escort me so I'd have to find his classroom from memory. It wasn't a large campus. Everything except for where I slept and the gym was in the tower. Having just been there in that tense situation with Raguel, I wasn't eager to be back.

I crossed the courtyard and chuckled to myself. What would Naomi think of my new outfit? Her horrified face would be something to behold. If we had just taken the bus instead like I suggested, we could still be together.

"Demon."

I slowed my pace.

It was daylight and I was surrounded by protectors of supernatural and human society, but I sensed something off. A man stood behind me, wearing a purifier's uniform, white against my black. His aura was weaker than my company of angels and supernaturals. Very human.

I could feel his thoughts.

Negative. Fearful.

"That's what you are, right?" The man spoke again. More hostile entities formed around him. All purifiers.

I gripped my bag strap tighter. "Who's asking?"

He scoffed, causing those who followed him there to chuckle. "What trick did you use to brainwash the angels?"

"I'm just returning some books."

"You're not fooling me," he said, "You have Zakiel wrapped around your finger. It's disgraceful to him and to our cause. If anything, you're more dangerous than this '*Necromancer*' everyone's fussing about."

The peace I'd felt in EXO until now seemed like a farce, and the purifiers were the reality. Zak probably didn't gossip about me much, which I appreciated. But now that others were catching wind of what I was, the true face of these hunters was looking me in the eye.

They didn't want me.

He took a step forward. I'm not sure why I felt nervous. One touch and I could probably knock him on his ass. Humans were never going to be as deadly to me physically, but I wasn't ruling out their potential.

"There's no place for you here, foul servant of darkness," he said. I could tell it was the tone he practiced when casting out malevolent spirits. It had a ceremonial chime to it. "Depart and never return."

Considering it was a sunny day and I was standing there, not being evil, it was almost laughable. A songbird chirped over our heads.

"Okay, then. I'm gonna go elsewhere." I pivoted on my heel; not giving him my back but not facing him either. The purifier looked taken aback but luckily didn't follow after me. I re-entered the tower without a second thought.

Perhaps it had been survival instincts, but I knew exactly which floor to ride the elevator to and even turned down the correct hallway that would eventually lead to Jarmiel's room. My heavy sigh traveled down the narrow walls.

That had only been a small group of humans from EXO. What about when the rest wanted to rally against me? I imagined the mobs outside of the court halls and shuddered. A pathetic longing for Zak to be nearby shook me. It wasn't his burden to carry. I needed to get stronger.

When I did find Jarmiel's classroom the door was locked. I was hesitant to set the books down outside of his door. It wasn't like I hated learning from the texts. I just wished they wouldn't do creepy shit.

Really, I think I was stalling.

I wasn't looking forward to the walk back; a sure way to endure more taunting from the purifiers. On the other hand I also didn't want to be stuck in that hall forever. Damn. I really was relying on Zak too much. Funny, as I barely trusted the angel not that long ago.

A shadow appeared next to me; too close to be some casual passerby. My thoughts immediately went to the purifiers I'd just snubbed. *No way.* Had he really followed me?

I whipped around, one arm raised at eye level. Hurting him wasn't the goal but I wasn't about to let him try casting out my soul. I extended my elbow with the intent of shoving whoever it was away.

Cold fingers lightly blocked my force, sending an icy wave up to my shoulders. I knew right away it was Guy. The reaper's dark and lazy lids were slightly wider that time. He was still in his suit as well with his hair knotted behind his head.

"What're you doing here?" I asked.

"Is this how you normally greet people?"

"Sorry." I relaxed my stance, feeling stupid. "You snuck up on me. I'm a little tense."

"I can see that. Nice reflexes, though." He smirked. "I'm sure your choice in literature had nothing to do with your nerves?"

Oh, yeah. My books.

I dropped the bag and kept my arms close to my chest. "They were recommended to me. What're you doing here?"

"Zak isn't with you this time," Guy noted.

"No."

"You know they're enforcing a buddy system, right? Partner at all times until The Necromancer's caught."

"Oh, yeah?" I looked over his shoulder. "Where's *your* buddy?"

He did a half-circle scan around the room, before landing back on me. "Ah, there you are. Guess we're both safe."

I laughed. That was cute for someone so stoic.

"I'm guessing you saw what happened outside?" I asked.

"It *was* in a public area and in the middle of campus," Guy shrugged. "Do you mind me asking what that was about?"

"It wasn't obvious?"

"Faris approaching you doesn't shock me. He'll chastise someone if their shirt is wrinkled."

"So, his name's Faris?" At least he was notorious around EXO and I wasn't too special. Still, a purifier reacting to a demon being in his home made sense to me, even if I didn't consider myself a threat to him.

Guy's dark-rimmed eyes shut halfway as his smirk widened. "Not gonna try cursing him with more spells in your room, are you?"

"I'm not adept enough for that."

"What's the story then?"

I leaned against Jarmiel's door, hitting my head on the wood. No one else was around, what could a little venting hurt? "Can you promise not to laugh?"

Guy straightened up, like he was ready to catch a ball being thrown, but said nothing.

"You're not promising," I said.

"I take promises very seriously," he said, "I might laugh, but only because you're being so reserved about it."

"Fine." It was agony, but I managed to say something. "It's possible that I'm… I could be, or might be related to a… *succubus*…"

"Hm?"

"Succubus," I said a little louder but equally as pained, "That's why Jarmiel gave me these books to see if anything registered. They freaked me out so I brought them back. Anyway, people like Faris are realizing I'm a demon and aren't very happy about it."

I watched as a rose-colored blush dusted over Guy's ghostly face. His eyes widened, but he was excellent at keeping the rest of himself still. For a moment.

"I see," he stopped to cough, "That's—"

"I said not to laugh!"

Mortified, I raced toward the elevators. Guy stayed close behind me. "Okay, so that's a sensitive topic," he said, "But succubus makes a lot of sense."

I dropped my shoulders and sulked. It wasn't the fairytale I had in mind for my biological making. While we waited for the doors to open, I asked him, "How?"

"They're known for bewitching others. Is that not something you've noticed?"

"Have I noticed that I'm bewitching?" I didn't understand. Was he complimenting me? "If that were true, Max would be a little nicer to me. And Faris."

The doors opened and we rode the elevator back down together. I couldn't help but feel like Guy had been stalking me on some level. How else would he have known where I was, or where I was headed? Oh, well. I was glad for the company.

"Max isn't nice to anyone," Guy said, "Have you watched a nature documentary? Creatures are aggressive when it comes to mating and territory. Bewitching others can just as easily curse someone with obsession. I'm just saying, it won't always have a positive outcome."

I hadn't even considered the *negatives* of someone finding me appealing. The horrifying image of Max's wolf form pursuing me visited my thoughts again, only this time, he was hunting for a "mate." *Gods*. Never.

"I don't think anyone's obsessed with me," I said. If anything, *I* was the freak with an angel obsession. Equally in awe as well as fearful for my life.

"It's something to watch out for. If you are what you say, don't you need to—?" Guy cleared his throat again but didn't finish. He didn't have to. I knew where it was going.

Don't sex demons need sex?

"I haven't really tried," I explained, feeling awkward bringing up intimacy with a reaper I hardly knew, "I didn't date much."

Our stroll back to the dorms was tense, but not due to each other's awkwardness. The purifier from earlier, Faris, was gone but I recognized his cronies glaring as we passed. While the intense stares came for me, they almost immediately diverted once they saw Guy.

No one dared approach.

"No one's asked you out before?" A dark chuckle escaped his lips that might have been a scoff, but I didn't know to whom or at what. "Is that a yes?"

"*One* guy," I said, "And it blew up in my face but you already knew that."

His smile dropped. "I see. I'm sure that was traumatic."

Considering I hadn't been able to get over it yet, trauma was an accurate label but the deepness of his vocals was oddly soothing. "Thanks."

It hadn't been long since my visit with Clove but I could feel the fatigue creeping back in. The warm, glowing energy from Zak was on my mind more than I wanted to admit. Sitting around until I passed out again sounded stupid. I wasn't ready to start asking for energy, but stealing it secretly felt too icky.

We made it back to the dorms safely but I found myself wanting to talk with him more. "Thanks for walking with me. Could you maybe not mention the whole succubus thing to anyone?"

"Sure, but they'll figure it out. If they haven't already."

"Are reapers ever afraid of demons?" I asked.

Guy listened but made his way inside and toward the fridge. I couldn't imagine what had brought a reaper to EXO. He had an entire existence in a realm that I knew nothing about. "Demons can be scary. I haven't actually seen many on this plane. I've dealt with a lot more supernaturals flooding the underground world. Gangs, drugs, you name it."

I remembered how he mopped the floor with me during my assessment test. If that was him holding back, what was he like against a real monster?

"Zak said that you volunteered to be here. Why?"

He popped open the fridge and offered a water bottle to me. I still wasn't used to seeing him in anything besides his cozy clothes and sleepy hair. It was weird being able to see most of his face and his suit made him look the part of a dark, lethal reaper.

"It's a long story," he said, "What do you know about us?"

"I know you can separate spirits from their body with your big sticks."

He laughed and opened the water for himself. "Big sticks?"

"You couldn't have found a nicer way to transfer souls, like with candy or puppies?" I asked.

"Puppies?"

"You know what I mean. Scythes are scary and dying people are already freaked out."

Guy took a calculating sip. I had a feeling he enjoyed watching me get flustered as he leered over his drink. "I'll put in a good word and see what we can do about your puppies. Maybe by the time you die, I'll have something fluffy in store."

"Hey, hey, don't joke about that," I said, but I just made him laugh more.

Of course, he would find mortality humorous. It wasn't *his* problem.

"Sorry," he said, "Sometimes, you have to laugh. It'd serve everyone better if they found humor in the inevitable."

"Ha-ha." I frowned.

Guy's gray eyes gleamed. I meandered toward the bar table and took a seat on one of the stools. Still, cross about his crudeness, I rested my elbows on the counter with extra sass. "So other than making jokes and arresting girls, what's your deal?" I asked.

"Still mad about that?"

"Annoyed is a better word."

"You're not just a girl, let's be real." Guy approached my counter and tapped the surface once. "It's like you said. I volunteered. Zak and I are friends-ish."

"You got bored at your day job?"

"Part of it has to do with my personal agenda. Another is Tori," he said, "There aren't many safe places for a wandering spirit on Terra. EXO found a use for her."

His voice had gotten sharper, whether he noticed or not. I didn't want to pry further about his female companion. Were they romantic in some way? She seemed more like a little sister.

"And you?" I asked.

"There's been curious activity from the other realms. Here in particular. Figured I'd gain the most knowledge from seeing it first hand."

"You're talking about The Necromancer?"

"He's one problem," he said, "Anyone who tries challenging Death on Death's territory is a problem."

If Death were to be insulted by anyone, a sorcerer meddling with the dead would probably do it. "Who does your job while you're away?"

"There are many. Think of us as employees for one giant organization or a bunch of worker bees to a hive. Not much changes in my absence." Guy drank the rest of his bottle before adding, "I like it here. It's not surprising how many reluctant souls there are but the job gets depressing."

I looked up but he was studying his fingernails. If that was more depressing than hunting demons and vampire drug lords or experiencing mortality in general, then a reaper's job must really suck. "I'm nervous to die but knowing there's an after has to give people a little hope, right?" I asked.

Guy took slow steps around the bar, making the anticipation of his next words even worse. I squeezed my water bottle too tight, making a loud crackling sound from the plastic. When he'd gotten close enough to me, his voice carried like a dark ocean rumbling in my ears.

"For some, *after* isn't a pleasant place to be."

19

I felt eyes everywhere. That, or I'd adopted more of my aunt's extreme paranoia.

The whispers were constant. People from the cafeteria, class, and even on the way to training, all quieted when I got close. Was it merely self-absorption in assuming they'd all been talking about me?

My group with Zak felt the least invasive, believe it or not. Even with Aiden's taunting and Max's in a constant state of being pissed-off. Mallory became a pleasant breath of fresh arrogance compared to the looks I received from any purifier.

It was time for mine and Zak's special training. After we found a secluded spot next to the field, he walked off and reappeared carrying cinder blocks. I watched with growing curiosity as he set them in front of me. One wouldn't have been too difficult to break but after seeing him set down three more, I heard my bones cry.

"Let's test your strength before and after you borrow some spirit energy," Zak said, "See what you can accomplish as you are now. Just chop down what you can."

I inhaled and stepped up to the blocks. With a sturdy stance, knees bent, I brought my arm down and broke through the first but only cracked the second.

When Zak didn't say anything, I panicked. "That bad?"

He shook his head. "I mean, our purifiers have been able to do a little more and they're *not* demons, so…"

Great. Even the purifiers were better. Peacekeepers were supposed to be the brute strength of EXO. They were going to run out of uses for me. I didn't want to end up back in jail, with no chance of ever finding Naomi. Although, the longer I was away from her, the less I found myself wanting to go back to our life before.

Was that wrong of me?

Zak reassembled the stack with some new blocks and held his hands out to me. "Don't sweat it. This is the first time we're really experimenting with it. Here. Take enough to make an impact." When I didn't return his graceful smile he added; "You won't hurt me. I promise."

I inhaled through my nose and removed the new arm protectors that came with my suit. Our fingers glided over one another's and I felt his energy right away. My heart hesitated but my instincts did not. His essence became the air I breathed. The taste of citrus and summer warmed my tongue. I wondered if his lips tasted like citrus too. They looked pillowy enough to promise a soft landing.

"You good?" Zak tilted his head at me when I quickly stepped back.

I just thought about kissing you, so no!

The same thing happened with Guy too. I couldn't be *that* desperate for attention. Or was it a succubus thing? The "Kiss of Death," just like it said in Jarmiel's textbooks. From my brief and deadly experience, I knew I *enjoyed* kissing. I hadn't noticed a demonic obsession towards it, though.

Gods, but I felt so much better with Zak's energy, even if my thoughts embarrassed me.

I focused back on the blocks. My open palm came down on the hard surface and I was able to break through all three. Pride pulsed in my veins, drowning my earlier concerns. It wasn't enough. I wanted to fight a titan made of stone and feel it crack under my fist.

"Not bad at all," Zak said, "The energy you consume gives you extra strength, but it's temporary. We'll have to keep an eye on that."

We practiced that a few more times; each set of blocks became harder to break. Whenever I felt exhausted, we'd hold hands again. I appreciated him teaching me how to use my quirks in a beneficial way. Naomi would never. It made everything a little easier to bear, like there was a purpose other than being a monster.

"What about controlling how much energy I take from someone?" I asked after dusting my palms on my pants, "With you, it comes easy but when I… with Peter…"

"What made you stop with Peter?" he asked.

"When he stopped breathing."

He must have heard the sadness in my voice because his smile faded. "Since you're already sensitive to it, I think control will come easily. Just listen to yourself. As soon as the feeling comes, stop. We'll figure out a way to practice that. I still wouldn't mess with humans. They won't be able to pull you off like I can."

I wet my lips, hesitating with my next question. "What about dark and light matter?"

"You're talking about what you did in the video, right?"

I still couldn't meet his eyes after thinking about his lips before, but I gave him a nod. He shooed me a few feet away from him and lifted an arm. A piercing sound, followed by static came from his hand. Just like Guy's scythe, a long object constructed itself from nothing. Zak's looked like a sword made out of pure light. Staring for too long made me blink purple spots.

"I can make this sword and my wings. It's a mental and spiritual game as much as it is a physical one." He swished the sword once and a wave of heat sliced across my middle. "If I'm not mentally in check, it'll go off like a firework and maybe even burn me too in its rebellion."

"Light would do that?" I asked.

"Light is *all* about disruption and disorder." Zak chuckled. "Imagine your room at night, dark and quiet. You're in a state of tranquility, and then, the sun rises. In less than a second, it obliterates the dark and everything is awake with color. It's a devastating process if you think about it."

The man was poetic about sunshine. Not surprising.

Charges of electricity from the sword grazed my skin. The light was like a wild beast behind tight reigns, which wasn't what I imagined an angel's power to be, but then, Zak arrived in a similar fashion to disrupt my life. Its temperament reminded me of my own power when the gold lights lashed out, but mine had been covered in darkness too.

The sword severed itself in half and retreated back into his hands. A pulsing glow traveled up his arms and ended in his soft, brown eyes. He showed some teeth in his grin. "Light is meant to be shared. If I understand correctly, dark matter is conjured differently and behaves differently. Demons use it because it requires the consumption of something, and boy, do they like to consume."

"Like a sacrifice?"

"Bingo. Light can be made but dark matter simply exists and takes. Ah… Jarmiel might be better at explaining this stuff."

I had a list of questions but Zak wanted to spar again.

After our afternoon finished, I returned to the dorms and washed up. As warm water poured over my head, I debated sharing my concerns about the purifiers with Zak. Faris had been the only one to approach me, and even that hadn't amounted to much.

I toweled off and was about to leave when Tori's head, only her head, popped through the bathroom door.

My alarmed yelp echoed off the tiled floors. "Tori!"

"Oops, sorry."

She quickly tucked her head back and opened the door like normal. Her purple bear was hooked on her belt, dancing on her hip as she waved frantically around me like a startled bird. "I thought you might be here."

Just behind her, Yara walked by in midnight green sweatpants. "You're not supposed to do that anymore," she said.

Tori set her hands on her hips until Yara disappeared down the hall. "Sorry, I'm just bored and want to hang out."

I didn't really believe I'd been her first choice, but it was another chance at getting to know my group better. Her pleading eyes turned to me and I couldn't say no. So, I agreed, under the condition that I could get dressed first.

She beamed and waited for me in her room across the hall. What did girls talk about in their spare time? I slipped into some sweats and kept my wet hair in a thick braid before knocking on her door.

We sat on Tori's floor and exchanged easy questions. "How was your day?" "Did you see Zak scold Aiden during training?" "What face moisturizer does Yara use?"

The speed in which her sentences flowed exhausted my brain muscles.

"— so then, I tried painting my nails the other day but the color just faded." Tori took a breath she didn't need. "Waste of money and time. Anyway, should we go do something? Get food?"

"You want food?" I asked, remembering the drama with Mallory over her inability to eat.

"I mean, *yes* but I can't," she said, "I just don't want to waste a weekend being lame at home ya' know?"

I could understand that. Sneaking out to Peter's party had been my little act of rebellion. Before that, my previous teen years dragged by without much excitement.

"Can I ask you something?" Tori bumped her silent heels together. "What were you and Guy up to the other day? He rarely talks to *anyone* for long periods of time."

She must have been talking about when he saved me from seeing Faris again. "Oh. We were just heading in the same direction. Actually, I was using him to deflect purifiers."

"Really?" A more somber expression brushed across her soft features. "He seems to like you. So does Aiden. In a creepy way."

"Lucky me. What makes you say that?"

"He's always doing these annoying worried glances, like a mom hovering over her toddler," she said.

"Aiden?"

That wasn't how I remembered Aiden looking at me. More like a child eyeballing a birthday cake before a party. Tori shook her head like she had a bug. "What? *No*. Ew. He looks at you like he's gonna murder you."

Or that.

"Why does Aiden come back if he hates it here?" I asked.

"Who knows? He doesn't talk to anyone, just his sister and now you." Tori tucked her knees to her chest and gazed at the carpet. "It's probably because you're pretty."

I wanted to laugh. If prettiness was my problem, then maybe I had no reason to worry about all the purifiers gossiping behind my back. "Thanks but I don't think that's why."

"Are you one of *those* girls who's oblivious to your own annoyingly beautiful existence?" Tori leered at me from behind her raised knees.

My laughter only increased until I made a rather unflattering snort.

She's funny.

"You know *you're* pretty and even have cool pink hair. I can't pull that off," I said.

She wiggled her shoulders at that. "Yeah, well… I'm stuck with it. I bet school was fun for you. Were you super popular?"

"Definitely not."

It was like Tori could smell drama brewing and she inched closer to me. "I'm not buying it. No one can talk about anything else, so how were you ignored before?"

"My aunt and I didn't get out much. Being popular would've been against the rules."

"Why—*oh*, right." She trailed off. "People would freak if they knew about you, huh? Were you in a sketchy part of town? I was in Cosoco. Shady stuff happened there all the time."

"By the Outskirts?" I asked. The peak of civilization's rebuild hosted a depressingly small population. Volhold sat in the middle like a shining castle, but the further you branched out to the smaller cities and toward the Outskirts, the darker it got. Haverwick was middle territory; neither shiny nor abundant in crime.

Beyond the Outskirts were the Wastelands; areas that never fully recovered after the war. At the rim of the Outskirts was a literal drop separating *us* from *it*. The "legend" was that the angels raised us toward Heaven while others believed the tainted earth sank deeper to Hell.

People also claimed demons polluted the air in the Wastelands with Hell's poison. Supposedly lawless and barren, except for criminals, devil worshippers, and monsters. No reporters or journalists ventured out there so how would we really know?

Just had to take the angel's word for it.

"Yup. The Outskirts," Tori said, "What about you? Where did you live?"

"Haverwick. The mountains were nice."

Much better than looking at the same buildings blocking the sky every day.

Tori's youthfulness shone brightly. Her knee bumped mine when she leaned in. "I'm surprised you stayed so close to the main cities if you were trying to be discreet. Were you on the run? What about—*oops*."

I forgot she was a ghost for a moment. The physical form she manifested was incredibly real but her body vanished from sight, and then something stirred from atop her bed. The teddy bear grumbled using her voice to speak. "I guess I need to rest up again. So embarrassing."

"Is there a way to prolong your manifestations?" I asked.

The bear hopped down from the mattress to resume her spot by me. "I used to last ten minutes before, so it's getting better. Sorry if this freaks you out."

"The bear's growing on me." I went to pinch the bear's fluffy ears until I thought about the person inside. "Hey, going out might be fun, if you still want to."

Tori's small frame sprang a foot in the air. "I'll literally do anything. Want to see a movie?"

"Oh…" I stopped. Jarmiel and Zak both said I couldn't leave campus on my own yet. I'd forgotten that everyone else could. "I don't know if I can, actually."

"Are you a convict?"

"N-No. I wouldn't say that, exactly."

She just giggled. "Okay, we can go to the cafeteria then. Maybe some of the cute guys from Lisha's team will be there."

Cute boys?

I hadn't realized we were on a mission.

She waited patiently while I ran to my room to grab a nicer sweater. I felt spicy after all the flattery. When I reemerged, Tori climbed up my leg like I'd seen her do with Guy. She perched on my shoulder like a pet owl. A few weeks back, I never would've imagined having dinner with a stuffed animal.

"I'm not letting go of the convict theory, just so you know," Tori said.

*　*　*

We headed downstairs and ran into Aiden and Mallory. They resembled both sides of the moon; one bright and the other pitch darkness. Mallory's outfit belonged in a fashion magazine; the Fall/Winter edition. Styles people might ogle over the pictures for but never actually wear. The short dress squeezed her thin waist, stark white as her hair. Her boots, also white, reached her knees.

A long leather jacket draped over her and a fur shawl posed as the cherry on top.

I shivered.

She probably skinned the beast herself.

"Jess." Mallory greeted coldly. "You're making friends. How sweet."

Tori and I gave her the bare minimum of a response for courtesy's sake. Aiden took his sister's side as the dark knight drowning in black. An oversized shirt and coat hung off his body.

"Care to join us, Cupcake?" Mischief crept along his face. "You can bring your… pet."

Mallory snorted.

"Screw you, dude." Tori's mitten hand didn't possess any digits but I had a feeling I knew which she held up.

"Where are you going?" I asked, not actually interested but curious where anyone went dressed like that.

"Business gathering for dad," Mallory said, "We show our faces at his dinner parties, but the real treat comes afterwards. Come if you'd like. I'm not responsible if anything happens to you."

She flashed us her fangs and Tori's stuffed body shifted deeper into my neck.

"Have fun with that," I said, "We have our own plans."

Mallory whipped a strand of her hair back, seemingly unsurprised, but her older brother pouted his lips. "I guess Cupcakes make for better desserts, don't they?"

It sounded like a joke but the way he sucked in his lips made my stomach drop. Even his sister rolled her frosty eyes at that. "It's unsettling seeing you so desperate, Aiden," Mallory jabbed, "Let's go."

20

*O*ur dinner consisted of salad and cookies while Tori pretended to sip a smoothie.

She was able to manifest during that and I wasn't only sitting by a toy, thankfully. When I told her about my run-in with Faris, she groaned loudly in recognition. "Faris is the *worst*. Always has some holy stick up his butt," she said.

I nibbled on a piece of cold lettuce when I felt a shift in the air. Tori stopped talking; very odd considering she hadn't all evening. The dining area had been scarce, but the murmuring grew like a disturbed beehive.

"Wait here," Tori said. I blinked once, and she disappeared. Her stuffed bear on the chair went limp as well. A second of quiet awkwardness later and Tori's voice whispered next to my ear.

"*Jess.*"

Like her previous antics, I jumped out of my skin. "*Shit…* Yes?"

"You have to see this," she said and a glowing phone screen floated by my face.

"Did you take this from someone?"

"Well, I didn't bring *my* phone."

"Tori…"

"Just look!"

I redirected my concern to the display on her screen.

Oh gods. It was me.

I rewatched myself with the Ghoul and the cloud of magic. My frantic delivery and terrified screeches were painful to witness a second time. The rest of the cafeteria who noticed me in the room had mixed reviews on their faces. Some looked mystified while others huddled tighter in their groups.

More whispering.

"Wow…" Tori's voice was still present without a body but she quickly disposed of the phone and joined me, physically, back at the table. Her bright eyes darted around and I almost wished she'd go back to her spirit form, which was far less obvious. "Why haven't you shown us this badassery during training?" she asked.

"Who sent the video? How did they even get this?" I asked, not actually expecting her to know the answer. It was only now circulating, so I had to imagine that Jarmiel and Zak had kept it under wraps.

"It's a random number. Not even a number, just some weird address. All of our devices are from EXO. Someone must've…" Tori forced a smile and her pixie voice dropped an octave. "Let's get going?"

I noticed her anxious glances around us and nodded. Something wasn't right. Tori manifested for as long as she could before returning to her bear. By then, we were already outside.

Why did someone leak the video? How had they gotten to it in the first place? Was it an accident or intentional? Zak warned me about something like this on my first day but I'd thought it had been an excuse to keep my phone.

I don't know what I was expecting when we returned to the dorms.

It was quiet at first until Barrett bounded down the stairs like an elephant or stampede and had a giant grin on his face. He bounced on his heels, making me dizzy with his excitement. "There you are. I thought you were holding out on us and sure enough."

Another phone was waved in my face. The video had been sent to him as well, confirming my fears. "I thought you were a goner, which you aren't obviously, because you're standing here, but then, *BAM!*" Barrett reenacted the impact with his arms. "You blasted the hell out of that thing. What was that? Magic?"

My mouth opened a few times but words escaped me. "I… I've been trying to figure that out myself."

Barrett's excitable movements slowed. "Shit. I didn't mean to put you on the spot. It's just, you took on a Ghoul by yourself. Only the angels have done that."

"Technically it was still alive—"

I forgot Tori was back on my shoulder again until she cut me off. "I haven't seen Zak training you in magic," she said.

"Yeah. Why isn't he taking advantage of that?" Barrett glared at the ceiling in thought. "I know it's demon magic, but I mean, if you're using it for us…"

"It doesn't scare you?" I asked.

He cocked a brow. "You're asking the shapeshifting man-beast if your cute sparkles scare him?"

"They *should*," Tori said, "They stopped a Ghoul bigger than you."

Barrett waved his hands in front of him defensively. "Hey, I'm just sayin', I'm scary too. And I'm definitely showing this to Max."

My shoulders dropped heavier than a bag of bricks. If everyone got the same video then he probably already saw it. "Do you have to?"

"Yeah, to rub it in his face," Barrett said.

"Rub what in his face?"

"He thinks—well, you know," he paused, as if hoping I'd answer for him, "You're still new and we didn't know if you could hack it as a peacekeeper. I thought it was just his pride talking since you escaped him so easily during your arrest."

Barrett's face puckered like his own words tasted sour. "Uh, anyway. I was just about to turn on a movie if you guys want to watch? You can join too, Guy."

Tori squeaked and we both turned our heads to see Guy observing from the stairwell. He'd been resting his shoulder against the doorway for who knew how long. If anything was on his mind, his aloof expression revealed nothing.

"He *hates* movies," Tori muttered but he ignored her. Guy's gaze was lingering on my face, making my insides twist. Goosebumps traveled up my arms. His look was calm but I could see the storms rolling behind in his darkening eyes.

Was he waiting to see if I'd agree to Barrett's offer?

"Maybe," I stopped when Yara glided out of the elevator.

Her teal-accented hair had been released from their tight braids. Waves of curly hair bounced around her face like she carried a moving ocean with her. A playful smirk dressed her face. "Hey, killer."

I let out a sigh. She saw the video too.

"Couldn't ignore the notification." She took herself to the kitchen, not relishing in the news like everyone else seemed to. "You look pale. Did you not know about the video?"

I shook my head. Honestly, it felt like whoever shared the video hadn't had the best intentions. If it was an effort to make me look bad, it hadn't worked in the eyes of my team. I couldn't say the same for any purifiers that might've seen.

"I knew the video existed but I don't know who shared it or why. No one told me anything."

Barrett's brow now furrowed like he'd just realized the negatives of the situation. "You saw it before?"

"Yeah. Some guys took it on their phones."

"I mean, that shit travels fast," he said, "If it *wasn't* wiped from their phones, then someone has great data retrieval skills."

"I can't tell if someone wanted to hurt you with this or make you look cooler," Tori said, "I feel like it'll keep creeps like Faris away."

"Faris?"

We all turned to Yara piping in from the kitchen. "Any purifier messing with you hasn't seen real evil." Her words, sharp as they were, strung smoothly together like a song, and the melody captivated my attention without much effort. I had to strain my ears to focus on the actual point she was making.

"You're not the only one purifiers have shared displeasure with," Barrett snorted, "Usually we're just ignored, though. Welcome to the club of outcasts."

"An outcast surrounded by outcasts takes the fire out of the name," Yara added.

I don't know why, but my heart burned a few degrees hotter. Just outside, eyes followed me with suspicion and fear, but the second I returned to the dorms.

"Most of us are wolves in sheep's clothing," Yara said, "Maybe it's his adorable face but Barrett's a real brute."

"Hey." He sounded upset at first but then he smiled. "I'm adorable?"

Yara's chuckle at that made my head buzz and she caught me rubbing my temples. "My bad. Sorry if I haven't said much before. It's because of *this*." She pointed to my face and made a swirling motion. "I manage it the best I can but that usually means I can't say as much."

"Is that a siren thing?" I asked.

"Yes. A siren thing. What about you?"

That explained her usually silent nature. I'd thought it was only the siren's songs that were dangerous, but maybe that had been old tales mixing with truth. Shame settled in my chest, realizing that I'd probably judged many supernaturals unfairly, just as I feared everyone did with me.

I debated telling them about the succubi theory. Yara was right, after all. What did I have to be nervous about around them? "Luckily, I don't need to eat people," I said, starting off strong, "but I do need their energy."

"Energy?" Barrett's head dropped to one side.

"Soul energy," Yara said. Her piercing eyes checked my face to see if she'd been wrong. I just nodded. Back in his creepy corner, I sensed Guy's interest peaking. He didn't shift his features at all but I could feel his own, bizarre energy buzzing.

"Is that hard to do?" Barrett asked.

"The process is a bit *too* easy. When I touch people, it just happens," I said, before quickly adding, "Zak and I are working on it."

The werewolf made a sympathetic groan. "Too bad we don't have another demon to help you figure things out. It's weird. You don't smell like a demon. Or act like one."

Yara stepped away to tend to a screaming tea kettle on the stove. She took a mug from one of the cabinets and began to pour. "Are you saying she's lying?"

"No, but I've smelled demons before. Their stink burns my nose hairs." His face scrunched in protest. "She's too sweet, like caramel that cooked too long."

Cupcake? I scoffed at myself, hating Aiden's nickname for me even more. Seemed like every supernatural being with a nose agreed on my scent. "Jarmiel and Zak feel the same way but we don't have answers yet," I said, "I'm just happy to skip the whole cannibalism thing."

I caught Barrett's wicked little eye raise. "Is it actually cannibalism if you're *not* human? My ancestors ate people. *A lot* of people. Gnarly stuff." He slid the bowl of fresh popcorn toward me from across the counter and grinned. He and Yara had been active in the kitchen all whilst keeping a conversation. It was impressive, really. "Those were dark times, though. Don't look so down, newbie. Yeah, you're a demon. Whatever. But have you seen a wolf's fist shift?"

Yara's cool-toned lips sampled her freshly brewed tea while Barrett's entire body shivered. "When was yours?" she asked.

"I was twelve. Worst birthday present ever."

"So young?" I thought about myself at twelve and experiencing what had happened with Peter. Even at twenty-one, I'd been a mess, and that hadn't included my body going through a painful metamorphosis.

He shrugged. "Just means I became a man before all my friends."

"Is that what it means?" Yara snickered and Barrett playfully bumped shoulders with her. "Hey, don't make me spill my tea."

I lost track of Tori for a moment, having not heard her in a while. Yara's voice was still messing with my head. When I looked around, I found her next to Guy. He listened to his ghost companion but it was like we could sense when the other was looking. I turned away just as he started to smile, catching me in the act.

"Have either of you dealt with demons before?" I asked while Barrett and Yara were still lingering.

Things had been going well so far, and then I hit a tripwire. Barrett got quiet before releasing a struggling cough. "Our pack had run-ins before, yeah. It's a sore spot for us, especially Ma—" he stopped before finishing his friend's name, "What I don't get is that you don't smell like one and you're not exactly brimming with bloodlust. It's like you're not a demon at all."

Yara's eyes glazed over for a moment. "Not all demons are frothing wildlings. Some are deceptively lovely, cunning and very patient. Much like my kin."

My lips parted but I didn't have the words. The mutual acceptance I'd felt earlier crumbled. Denying her suggestion seemed just as damning. She adjusted her hair over her shoulder and pushed away from the counter. "Enjoy the movie, everyone."

"You're leaving?" Barrett asked, "We haven't even started."

"I just came to make my tea," she said, "Goodnight."

* * *

The remaining crew, including myself, took over the living room. Even Guy.

Tori balled up her tiny, ethereal body in a chair while Barrett, Guy, and I fit on the L-shaped couch. Barrett sat with his broad shoulders to my left, completely captivated by his snack and the film.

I felt a sliver of regret agreeing to stay, especially after how the last conversation ended. It was only fair that they would be wary of me. Hell, I was wary of them too.

Guy took the spot to my right. I noticed the space difference between us versus me and Barrett. There was plenty of space on the couch but he'd decided to be close. He was back in loose clothing and his memorable plaid pajama pants. Respect for being comfortable, but he reminded me of an old man at home in a twenty-something body.

I peered up at him. "Is it true that you hate movies?"

For the last while, I'd felt him wanting to say something. It had me anxious, like when Naomi was upset about something and gave me the silent treatment until she was ready to unload.

Guy hummed softly and I felt my ears vibrate. "Not all movies. Just the movies Tori likes."

"Ah." I cracked a smile.

"How are you feeling?"

"About?"

"The video. I assume that wasn't your doing." We'd both taken to whispering but it didn't seem to bother Barrett.

"Oh. Yeah, I don't know," I said, "I'm not sure what the purpose was so I'm a little nervous, I guess."

"It won't take long to find who did it," Guy said and I felt oddly touched by his determination. Whether it was for my benefit or not. We sat in silence after that. Barrett's popcorn and Tori's commentary couldn't keep me engaged enough in the movie. I must've gotten very comfortable because my eyes started to close.

"*Jessebel…*"

An eerie voice sang and tickled my mind but I assumed it was the movie. My head sank deeper into the cushion supporting my back. The credits were rolling and I could hear Tori and Barrett arguing over something. It sounded ridiculous and I quietly smiled to myself.

"*Jessebel.*"

I shot up from the couch, alerting the others. That voice had been right against my ear. My heart was pounding. I waited to hear it again. It refused to speak but I could feel a presence there. Waiting.

My knees shook. At what point did I take voices in my head as a sign of insanity?

"You good?" Barrett asked.

"Yeah," I said, "I'm just more tired than I thought."

A cold hand felt for my wrist. I didn't flinch or pull away.

"Jess?" Guy seemed to need more verification.

"Yes, I'm fine."

His lips slanted downward. I hadn't gotten away with it, apparently. Barrett and Tori were fooled, or pretended to be, so I thanked them for the popcorn and hurried out of the room. I wasn't sure why I ran. It wasn't like I wanted to be alone.

Dread pooled in my chest like I knew something was coming. I made it to my floor when the worst headache of my life decided to stab my brain. Everything around me went black.

No. It was happening again.

Already?

There hadn't been as much build-up that time. I used the wall to hold my ground until the pain subsided. An icy breeze came from behind me and I groaned. "I said I was fine."

I glanced over my shoulder to see Guy crossing his arms like a disappointed, marble statue. He took a step forward, making me feel naked under his watch. Did he pick up on the voice I'd heard in my head?

"So you said. What happened?" he asked.

"It's the same as last time," I said. But worse, it seemed.

Guy nodded. Now that my second stomach cried for more spirit energy, I could sense Guy's like a freshly baked pie under my nose. His spirit was calm like a glassy lake under the moonlight. Strange for Death to have any energy in the first place.

Thinking about Barrett's and Tori's vibrancy that I had left behind made my muscles constrict. Phantom nails clawed at my stomach lining, ignoring the food I'd given myself already. I knew what relief awaited me if I simply allowed myself to touch one of them. The desire was slowly possessing my body, slowing my movements as if it knew there was no energy to savor in my bedroom.

I *craved* their life.

Disgusting.

I hadn't looked away from his eyes but I felt something wet slide down my cheek. How much of my aunt's medicine did I have left? I didn't know who I was anymore.

Not wanting to dump my emotional shit on Guy, I hid my face to focus on my closed room. An uncontrollable sob wracked my body but I was able to hide my face, at least. I just wished I could've held it in long enough to open my door first.

"Jess, stop."

I fumbled with the knob, got angry, and snapped. "Fine. I'm not *fine*. None of this is fine!"

A pair of arms came around me. The sudden gesture caused me to choke on my breath. Guy locked himself in by grabbing his opposite elbow before I could shake him off. I'd forgotten how strong he was from our last scuffle.

"At least you're being honest, now." His voice was cool against my emotional meltdown. The still waters of his energy seeped into mine until I became as peaceful as the calm current. I wondered if I could feel his heartbeat. Did he even have one? I let myself sink back into him; a slow surrender.

There. The drum in his chest was slower than mine, but it was there.

A heart.

"You're right. It's not fine," Guy said, "It's complicated. Now, what do you need?"

"I don't want to do this." I didn't want to eat souls. I didn't want to know that souls tasted differently; special to their owners. I didn't want the euphoria that followed when I allowed myself to partake. I didn't want to see Peter's dying face every time I touched someone.

Guy's voice rumbled in my ear and kept me in a trance. "You have two options. You can master what is undoubtedly a part of you or let it consume you. Just know, I am all that awaits you should you choose the latter."

In the moment, with Guy's arms around me, Death didn't seem so bad. I felt like I was out at sea and not in a hallway. It was quiet. Peaceful. I didn't have to worry about anything.

"I have to hurt people. How can that ever be a good thing?" I asked. When I really thought about it, the answer was right in front of me. The reason I'd been able to stop the Ghoul wasn't just a freak accident. If I hadn't stolen life from Peter that night, the demon magic wouldn't have saved me.

I would have been a bloody puddle in his driveway.

Guy didn't respond. He wasn't going to fall for the bait and tell me I was wrong. That was fine. He was allowed to be cold and direct. Neither of us moved or did anything for a while. I worried that when he finally did let go, I would fall apart.

"Jess." His call tempted me to face him. I made a half circle as his arms loosened. It felt as though a magnetic pull was helping me along and kept me turning until our toes touched. "As a peacekeeper, I can't leave if this isn't under control. So, I'll ask again. What do you need?"

I could feel the swelling from my eyes getting puffy. He probably thought I was pathetic but there was nothing to do about it now.

"Can I see your hand?"

He didn't wait for a reason; just held it out to me. His hand was smooth, like the flat end of an ice sculpture. I'd felt his aura many times but it was always brief and sometimes alarming. There was no instant warmth like there had been with Zak. The steady transference from his hand to mine still brought the soothing satisfaction I needed.

I let out a soft breath. It was working, and yet, I found myself wanting more. What if I held both of his hands? My eyes landed on his lips for some reason and I felt my insides catch fire.

I dropped his hand. It wasn't a lot of energy but the aching hunger was gone. "Thanks…"

"That's it? You made it sound so terrible."

"Maybe messing with people's souls isn't weird for *you* but it is for me."

His only response was a smirk and the flustered heat returned to my cheeks. I pretended to yawn into my elbow and finally opened my door properly. "Well, goodnight."

Even though I'd ended the conversation, he didn't leave. Guy's eyes reflected the hallway lights and I saw the faint lines that made them angelic. I still hadn't asked him about it. The crystal texture wasn't as prominent as Zak's or Jarmiel's but they were pretty, like cracked glass.

Since he insisted on standing there I continued, "Guy. You've existed for… a while?"

"That's rude."

"Do you know what demon magic *is*?"

"Magic is usually just the manipulation of exotic matter. Demons meddle with dark matter," he started, "It in itself isn't evil but Demons tend to do evil with it. Those powerful enough can bring it to a solid form."

Guy's scythe emerged, cutting through reality like a curtain of smoke. It waited obediently beside him. "Its elemental counterpart is light, which you've seen Zak use before. Their wings or weapons are just hyper controlled light. I also use *magic* specific to reapers."

"So, I could make myself a pair of wings too?"

"If you can manage."

That felt oddly backhanded. When I squinted at him he explained further, "You lack control. Angels and demons are eternal beings. They've had plenty of time learning how to shape their matter. What you did was chaotic. An explosive burst. Anyone in the crossfire would've died."

It wasn't quite a dagger to the heart I felt, but a tiny needle poking into my chest. Was all of Zak's kindness because he'd wanted to be gentle with a ticking time bomb? I shouldn't have been upset over it but I was.

Zak had always been doing his job. I knew that.

"My scythe works similarly," Guy said, grasping the staff and holding it out to me, "Matter manipulation isn't easy. Those who can usually stick to one or two forms."

"Why is that?"

"Not sure. Could be another silent law in the universe that every speck of matter obeys. Since every form seems specially crafted to the individual, my theory is the shape has to do with one's soul. Their preference."

My lips pulled further down. "So an explosive blob is *my* preference?"

He chuckled and his scythe faded back into oblivion. "I'd say your soul is lost and in need of direction."

That didn't make me feel better. Still, some clarity was better than none.

"Do reapers have souls? I feel yours."

I thought I caught him flinching. Hopefully, I hadn't been the rude one that time. "Yes, intelligence and a physical form become one's soul."

"Can you die, then?"

He sighed. "Death is just the transference of energy. When someone's body is beyond repair, reapers detach the soul and move it elsewhere. It's similar to what you do, except we don't gain anything from the souls. So, yes, I can go somewhere else. Or in the worst case, become trapped."

"Trapped?"

"A lifetime in prison sounds scary but it's nothing compared to an eternity. Immortals have to maintain order too, and when soul matter can't be destroyed, it has to be confined."

My jaw dropped an inch as a new fear awakened. There I'd been, fussing about mortal imprisonment. "They would lock you up *forever*? I thought Hell was the ultimate prison."

"Hell has many prisons." He lifted his arms like it was as casually as mentioning the weather. "Anyway, you should head to bed. It's late."

Sure, I'll just do that!

"Goodnight." I closed the door on the reaper's charming grin.

"Goodnight, Jess."

21

Something was wrong.

I awoke out of my room and staggered halfway down the stairs. Adrenaline brought me back to full consciousness and I tripped over my bare feet. The darkness surrounding me didn't help calm me down at all.

Sleepwalking? I'd never done that before. My dream hadn't been that exciting. I followed a voice that came from outside, but my body took the dream literally and I ended up leaving my bed.

The day following wasn't so hot either. I was getting sluggish already, even after Guy's help last night. We had to practice running in our new gear which was awkward at first. The boots were much heavier than my sneakers.

The video of me gathered mixed reviews. While people like Barrett were loud with praise, others took to judging in silence. Max's glares could burn through his sockets. Aiden and Mallory both wore smug expressions but never approached.

That unsettled me more.

After a warm-up, we separated for specialized combat. Yara removed herself from the field entirely. Not sure why. I had looked forward to seeing what she could do. That left Guy, Tori, and me in our group, but those two had their own system together. There weren't many ghosts to help Tori, so Guy filled in.

And since there were no demons, I had Zak again.

"You okay, Jess?" he asked. I could feel him observing my failing complexion. *He's going to offer his energy again,* I thought. *It wouldn't kill him so why did it still bother me?*

"I didn't sleep well," I said. *Almost fell down a flight of stairs, actually.*

Zak pressed his lips firmly together. "I know I said angels can't read minds but I can tell you're lying."

"I'm… feeling slow again."

He removed his hoodie and tossed it onto the grass. "More practice then!"

I groaned but not at his offer. It just felt like we'd made no progress in controlling the energy I consumed. My disappointment didn't last long, as getting to feel angelic power, especially Zak's, had become the highlight of my days.

Odd that I never craved Jarmiel's energy, though I assumed they'd be similar.

"It's all a mental game," Zak tapped the side of his head at me, "We all have to learn control. Not just demons. Tell your brain what to do and your body, your ability, will listen. Take my hand, but try not to *take* anything. Just for a moment."

The fact that his simple request felt *impossible* made me worry I might've been dumber than I thought. Weak minded. I tried self-talk at first, literally screaming into my headspace when I took Zak's hand. *STOP!*

My skin still buzzed. His warmth remained. However, I did manage to make the pull weaker. If I could turn it off completely, I'd feel invincible.

"Hey, that's an improvement!" Zak said.

"You felt that too?" I almost convinced myself it was nothing.

"Yup. Usually, your timidness is what makes your grasp weaker, but you did that all on your own. Maybe we should try going all out."

All out and kill him? "I'm fine with slow and steady," I said.

"Fine. Since you got a win today, I'll be nice. I just want you to practice dodging this time," Zak said, "Look alive."

I could dodge. I had to dodge him all the ti—

Zak swooped in before I could finish my train of thought. He was much faster than before. I didn't realize the dramatic difference from his holding back until now. His fist aimed for the center of my head. I jerked to the side so violently that I fell over.

"Not bad." He laughed. "I really went for it that time."

I guess he was ready to start actual training and not the fun kind. My chest hurt from my harsh gasp. "No shit."

"You're getting better," he noted, trying to sound encouraging. I think.

"Is she, Zakiel?"

I thought it was me who responded with that sarcastic tone but I never used his real name or spoke about myself in the third person. We both acknowledged the woman sparkling with glittering gems accenting her flesh.

"You know I love your surprise visits, Lisha, but I'm in the middle of something," Zak said.

"This little flirt-fest?" She pointed between us.

While my insides disintegrated, Zak made an effort to save face. "No need to be jealous, captain. What do you want?"

"My kids are bored," Lisha said, "They want to play with yours."

"Your kids are in their twenties," Zak countered.

Lisha muttered under her breath, "The wolves certainly whine like babies."

"And this has nothing to do with spying on my new recruit?"

Her gaze shifted to me and stayed. For sounding so serious about my training, suggesting we play games seemed ironic. Unless "games" meant something different around here.

"A curious video is floating around," she said, "Was that your doing?"

"*No*," I answered too quickly, "I don't even have access to a phone."

"Have you attempted to use these abilities again or is this fool holding you back?"

"Go easy," Zak said, "She's new to it."

Lisha's next words came out sharper than a blade. "I wasn't asking you. She can tell me herself."

I gulped. Better to answer her than let Zak get scolded some more. "I'm not sure how just yet."

Her gaze sent accusing daggers at Zak. "Really. She's not sure *how*, Zakiel?"

Great. I'd only made it worse. Zak slid his hand down his face, pulling his flesh nearest to his eyes. They reminded me of an old married couple having a quarrel. "Come on, Lish."

"I'm aware of your process, angel. It's lazy at best." Her brow pulsed once. "Are you waiting for her to use it by accident and kill us all first?"

I crumbled under the awkward tension until a noise that sounded like a chuckle escaped her nose. Zak moved his hands to his hips and after a few seconds, he too was laughing. The weird moment turned into two people having enjoyed something that I had missed. Still laughing, Lisha lifted a hand in surrender. "I apologize. I enjoy giving Zak shit when I can."

They're… teasing each other?

"You're good at it too," Zak said with an eye roll, "I want to make sure Jess is ready. You know what it's like using that kind of power. "

Lisha didn't argue. She looked between us with a silent understanding. "I'll let you handle it then until I can't stand to watch you pamper her any longer."

"So, you were spying."

"I never said I wasn't." Her hands clasped behind her back. I felt something unearthly coming from her, but it wasn't like any angel or demon I'd seen. "I like new blood and powerful allies. I'd hate to see her potential wasted while in your pitiful hands."

Zak feigned an injury to the chest, grasping at his heart. "Do all dragons have cruel tongues?"

I stood still. Stunned, more like.

Lisha was a *dragon*?

That would explain the scales and her exotic pupils. I should have known right away, and yet, but I never would have believed it anyway. Dragons were more ancient than even the race of elves or vampires. People still believed them to be gods, and no one has come forward to deny that idea yet.

I thought I would be more afraid but I was in awe. If Lisha had been here with EXO the whole time, why hadn't we had more news coverage on dragons? As far as I knew, dragons were either reclusive or dwindling in numbers. A dragon sighting was hardly heard of, even if they were the most fearsome of shifters.

"At ease, newbie." Lisha noticed my gaping mouth and chuckled. "Anyway. How about it, Zak? Game tomorrow. Mine against yours."

* * *

A *dragon*.

I paced my room, unable to sleep. Lisha was already cool but she was actually a legend. How long had she been with EXO? I hadn't been a resident in Volhold long but considering it was the most populated area buzzing with various crimes, I was surprised no reports of a dragon warrior were broadcast. Wouldn't that scare most criminals away?

Now I wished I had borrowed a book on dragons from Jarmiel.

It wasn't only Lisha's awesomeness that kept me up, but what she said about a "game" the next day. Zak said it was just more preparation for the peacekeeper exam, so, of course, I was curious.

Also, terrified. Holy fuck.

Zak also told me not to worry about magic, the dark matter, and to focus on my energy intake and strength. Weaken enemies and use their vitality to advance my own. I just wished we had practiced some more. It wasn't the actual exam, I kept telling myself. Just fun…

I flung myself over my mattress. The stone I used in my attempt to communicate with Naomi sat idly at my desk for days, now. I grabbed it and held it close to my chest.

"Aunty," I spoke into it like that would do anything, "I met a freaking dragon today. I haven't actually seen her shift but I'm pretty sure it's true. You would like her. She's cold and witty, like you."

I grinned but my eyes felt warm and wet. Naomi's absence left a lot of room for doubt to grow. She had to know more than she let on all those years but she chose to hide it. With her gone, I couldn't ask about it. "I'm still mad at you…"

But I really wish you were here.

When I shut my eyes, I could still feel a tear sliding down my cheek. The lights were off but from behind my eyelids, an orange light burned brighter and brighter. When I blinked, the stone I held was flickering.

I sat upright, frantically pushing my hair out of my face. "Naomi?"

"*Poor, Jessebel.*"

Not Naomi.

A lanky figure wearing a black hood faced me from across the room. I threw off my bedsheets and then froze. Just like before, slowly but surely my body stopped responding, like I was turning to stone. My heart stopped next when the man came toward me. Magic filled my lungs and made it harder to speak. "Wh-o… are y-you?"

His smile in the darkness was a crescent moon, except with rows of sharp teeth. I wanted to run. Wake up. Hide under the blankets. Anything. But I had to sit there and watch the nightmare happen to me.

"Come on. We've met before. Remember?" He asked with a jarring tilt of his head. His voice was coarse and distant, but shrill, like bats at the end of a dark cavern. Had I been right then?

The man I saw that night with the Ghoul *was* the same man EXO was after.

"Necrom…ancer?" I uttered.

"I give them negative points on creativity for that one. *You* can call me Clay."

The tightness was lifted from my airways as if he was allowing me to breathe. After a few recovering gasps, I used the bravest voice I could muster. "How do you know my name?"

He drew something from inside his coat pocket and my heart dropped. A knife. Not an ordinary kitchen knife either, but a wicked pitch black blade. The giggle that escaped him next made my whole body shudder. "I know a lot about you, *Jessebel Winters.*"

I was released from the paralysis.

As soon as I felt freedom in my fingers and toes, I ran for the door. What I collided with, however, was a blank wall. "No… No, no, no." I banged my hands on the walls, waiting for a knob to show up.

"No one can hear you."

I turned sharply to see Clay taking a spot on my bed. He crossed his legs over the footboard and twirled the pointed end of his knife into the wood. "What's wrong? Weren't you the one feeling lonely?" He made a clicking sound with his tongue. "You don't belong here, Jessebel."

The alarms should have gone off. If Clay were truly there, that is.

Was he real or was my subconscious trying to scare me? I could make out more of his details than in previous encounters.

Thick-soled boots, crudely crafted rings across every finger, and fair, almost silver, colored hair that spilled from beneath his hood.

Clay rose from his seat and I tightened my fists. The only exit left was the window, but I couldn't see any light. Just empty black. He took a step forward and the scent of his magic weighed down my knees. *Curse it all.* If I closed my eyes and opened them again, I'd have to wake up.

But when I opened them again, Clay was closer. He brought the knife up to the base of my throat. Magic now clogged my nose with burning charcoal. My eyes watered as I choked, "*What do you want?*"

Clay lowered his face to my ear. His words, cold against my lobe, made me shudder. "I guess you can say I'm a bit of a fanboy. It's such an *honor*… Princess."

"W—" I started to ask, but he brought a finger to my trembling lips. For whatever reason, he hadn't killed me. Yet. We were near one another but it wasn't energy that I felt from Clay. His spirit was clouded in a toxic fume. Did that mean he was a demon like me?

"I came to save you." Clay nodded toward my window which was still black. The window flew open and shook the walls. A magnetic force wrapped its large hand over my chest and dragged me toward its glass mouth.

No, no, no, no, no!

I took a huge breath but my lungs felt like they had been submerged in cold water. A scream finally broke free from my throat but it died when I saw that my surroundings had changed.

It was even darker than my room. And icy cold. I stood on trembling legs and beneath my feet felt crisp and damp. Was I standing on dirt? I looked down and sure enough, grass webbed between my toes. My sleepwalking had brought me outside.

What the hell…

Clay was gone but his sinister essence still hung around me like a looming cloud. The dorms were just behind me. Thankfully, I woke up before getting much farther. How had I arrived without anyone noticing?

Many of the lighted buildings were extinguished for the night. No moon in the sky either. The fence looping the track squeaked as a gust of wind blew by. I backed away toward the dorms, feeling something else out there with me, drawing near.

It was staring right at me.

The snapping of a twig made my stomach flip but I recognized the fierce, wolfish aura before he even spoke. "*Gods…*" I hissed, "Max?"

"What the hell are you doing out here?" Max scanned me once with his sapphire eyes. "You're not wearing shoes."

His face looked less pinched than normal and we'd both dressed poorly for the weather. Him in a black tank top with athletic shorts, and me in my pajamas. I bounced on my heels and flattened the dirt. "Yeah. Funny story. What are *you* doing out here?"

"Gym."

The gym? It wasn't even dawn. Or *late*. It was the witching hour. Max took being a morning person to a masochistic level. I guess you didn't get biceps like his from sleeping.

"Were you trying to run?" he asked.

"Run? Run where?" I hadn't even tempted myself with the idea and I definitely wouldn't have executed such a plan while wearing hardly anything. Judging from the glare on his face, I hadn't convinced him otherwise, though.

"Forget it," I said and stomped around him with my naked toes. It was humiliating enough standing there like a crazy person, I wasn't about to continue his detective work out in the cold.

He snatched me by the arm.

"What the fu—" But his other sweaty hand slammed over my lips before I could finish. He smelled like salt and metal with a hint of something sweet. Perfume. I had a feeling that late-night "gym" sessions were just code for hook-ups.

And he had his hands all over me. *Ew.*

Wait.

He's touching me.

Max's energy *roared.* Furious and blazing like the blue from his eyes. My eyes went wide. Even without me putting my hands on him, the flow of energy was like trying to block a tidal wave with twigs for a dam. My face, lips especially, burned from the heat of his palm. Training. I had to remember my training! *Block it out. You don't need it. It's all a mental game…*

I almost bit him but grumbled first in warning.

"Shut up," Max growled, but he didn't seem upset at me anymore. While desperately trying to communicate with my eyes, I watched his large ears twitch as he focused his gaze across the field. He could sense evil too.

Whatever waited for us outside distracted me just enough. My focus on Max's energy slipped and I felt the flow of life channeling faster through me. I didn't love the guy but I wasn't about to kill him.

With his attention elsewhere too, I planted my bare feet and gripped him by the arm. He only had a moment for a quick "huh?" before he came flying over my shoulder.

He was *heavy.* My back would be feeling that later.

Max lay in the grass, staring at me upside down. His blue eyes blinked feverishly before he got up and dusted himself off. "The fuck was that?"

"Don't grab girls from behind," I said, "You spooked me."

"*Spooked* you?"

The screaming of alarms ripped through the hushed night. Red and white interchangeable lights strobed from every building. The threat *was* real. Not a nightmare. I didn't see anything until Max's voicebox started rumbling. He turned his attention to the gates that shielded EXO's station from the city streets.

A figure blended with the shadows and slunk deeper out of sight. It felt like I'd fallen into a frozen lake. I knew someone would be there but hoped it had all been in my head. The voice from my dream cackled in the wind. Had *that* been in my mind?

The alarms continued to wail.

"What were you doing out here?" Max asked again.

Peacekeepers and purifiers exited from their respective buildings. Some were already in uniform while others kept to their sleep attire. The few that appeared combat-ready chased after our slippery visitor. Max, to my surprise, didn't budge.

Also standing still, but in the courtyard, was none other than Faris.

He looked directly at us with a blank expression. His lumpy blue robes wrapped around him like a self-proclaimed king. I wouldn't say it was satisfaction that crept up his face, but I was willing to bet he felt more confident in his prejudices against me. I finally answered Max while keeping my eye on Faris. "I don't know."

22

No one found anything.

Camera footage revealed the partial outline of our intruder but whoever he was never got close enough to trigger the alarm. When I overheard Jarmiel speaking to Zak about it, he said that the man could have had strong, magical properties that alerted the barriers prematurely.

Or it had all been a fluke.

"Jess?" Tori nudged my shoulder. "You okay?"

We sat together on the bus but it had just screeched to a stop. It was the first time I'd been allowed outside of EXO since my arrival. Zak and Jarmiel were present along with Lisha and both groups of peacekeeper trainees.

It was time for the games.

I could feel the heaviness from my eyelids. I'd been focusing on street signs, trying to figure out where we were but must've dozed off. In my defense, we were all frazzled by the alarm last night.

"Where are we?" I asked. Lisha mentioned the games yesterday, but we were somewhere in the mountains. The trees were dense with dark green, creating plenty of coverage. It was the perfect maze for supernaturals to play in.

"A forest outside of Gayle," Tori said, "Technically not in Volhold. It's close but far enough away."

I raised a brow.

She giggled as she explained. "Our games get a little intense. Can't be around too many people or buildings."

That brought me to an abrupt consciousness. What could we be doing that could endanger entire cities?

Lisha stood first, wearing a fitted tank top. It was the first time I'd seen her in something that wasn't her combat outfit, even though all of us had been required to. "Let's go. Everybody off," she said.

We filed outside and I avoided everyone who brushed against me. It wasn't to be rude, I swear. The spaces between my shoulders and elbows were bare, so each time someone else's exposed arm touched mine, I received a buzz. Shouldn't I have been taking advantage of that? No one would know unless I took too much and they fell over.

Zak and Lisha had us make a circle next to the entrance of the great forest. Whatever they had planned might get me killed, but my heart swelled being out in nature again. The earthy smell of trees and dirt mixed with the cool, crisp air did wonders for my fogged mind.

"We need a few volunteers to be our bad guys," Zak said, "Anyone?"

Mallory stepped forward. Half the group groaned, including myself.

"Mallory, great. Who else?" Zak pointed a finger at our lined-up faces until it stopped on Barrett. "Brave volunteers from my team. Nice."

Barrett jogged to his side wearing a large grin. At least it hadn't been Max. His furrowed expressions appeared less hateful and more pensive that morning. I didn't need him thinking about me too hard but after last night, I expected it.

Zak picked a couple more, as did Lisha. I didn't recognize most of them because they were from the other team. "That should be good," he said, "What I want the rest of you to do is to locate the hostage. Somewhere in this forest, our lovely damsel, Mr. Jarmiel, awaits his rescue."

Jarmiel, who stood beside Zak, blinked slowly and accepted his role in painful silence. Barrett snorted. A few of our new female comrades looked at Jarmiel with twinkling eyes. I could almost hear them saying *"I'll be your hero!"*

Cute.

"Everyone in red will be the criminals in your way," Zak continued, "Blue team, use your strengths and teamwork to bring back the hostage. The red team will attempt to either capture your team or the alternative… Don't worry, not *really*."

He made himself laugh. "Both sides have the option to subdue other players. You will all be handed targets to place on your chests and backs along with handcuffs. If someone hits your targets three times, you're out. If someone is able to get the handcuffs on you, you're out. Head back to the bus and wait for the games to end. Good luck!"

* * *

Gods help me.

The games had officially begun and there I was, squatting behind a tree while people mauled each other in the forest. I thought Lisha was cool but she might legitimately be crazy. Zak too. All of them.

The dragoness had a wicked gleam in her eye before letting the blue team begin their search. Only the colored sash around my waist distinguished who was hunting me and who wasn't. I gripped the fabric like it was my lifeline and didn't move from my hiding spot.

Zak reminded everyone that a verbal surrender was also an option but everyone seemed to favor the violent alternative. The new combat suits must have really increased morale.

Since most of us healed quickly I knew the blood stains on the ground and the crunching of bodies colliding together didn't mean anything fatal. Did it have to be so barbaric, though?

Everyone seemed to be enjoying it.

"*Psst.*"

"*Shit.*" I jumped, "Oh… Tori, hi."

She ducked her little blonde head and we watched someone getting dragged between two trees by their ankles.

"They're animals," I said.

"Yup," she snorted, "This is where they really let loose."

I felt a pair of phantom teeth against my neck in anticipation. Mallory was on the opposite team and I couldn't remember if Zak said biting was against the rules or not.

When I still made zero effort to move, Tori poked my ribs. "I know you're a little nervous but it gets better. It's also best if we keep moving. No pressure or anything, but if *I* found you, someone else sure can."

She was right. My scent probably saturated this poor tree already. It would be pathetic to be caught this way and without a fight.

There came a faint sound from the bushes directly behind us and without thinking, I threw myself forward. I caught myself in the dirt and looked back. A male voice grunted when he collided with the tree I'd been using.

Barrett's tall frame bounced back quickly. A smile of pure glee spread across his face. "Hello, ladies."

Tori disappeared from existence only to reappear behind Barrett. She leaped onto his shoulders and shielded his eyes with her tiny fingers. "Run Jess!"

"Not cool," Barrett said with a chuckle, "Wait, newbie! It's better if I'm the one who catches you, trust me."

Part of me wanted to let him get me but curse my minuscule ounce of pride. I forced my legs to run. My lungs were on fire as I ran. I knew the direction most of my team headed in, but that was about it.

The "teamwork" thing didn't play out smoothly. Without Barrett, Max was a lone wolf—pun intended—and left us all in the dust. Aiden couldn't be bothered. He was probably sleeping in a tree somewhere or handcuffed himself already.

I hadn't run into anyone else yet, but from the sound of it, I was nearing the creek. The view itself was serene; wildflowers and stones framed the moving water. I couldn't enjoy the view for long, not with the sounds of battle drawing near.

A jarring and enchanting melody tangled itself into madness. Someone sang without lyrics. The tones had random spikes in low to high notes that flowed eerily together. The world was spinning off its axis. Vertigo tripped me over with my own feet. Luckily, there was a big rock to catch me on the way down.

Yara.

I'd never heard a siren sing. Not unless it was filtered through an electronic device. It was a huge niche in the music industry, but this was war. The song ruined my ability to pinpoint where other sounds were coming from. She was on my team, so I doubted she was hunting me. I must have just been close enough to be in the range of her attack.

The singing slowed and a stoic figure crossed my path.

"Stay still." It was Darren, the more docile vampire sibling with reddish hair. His monotone voice sounded like it was coming from my left even though I was looking right at him. When I couldn't quite obey, still too dizzy, he pinned me to the nearest tree using one hand. I took a sharp breath but he glowered, signaling me to be silent.

The vegan was scary.

We waited. Darren must have sensed others nearby and kept us hidden. Yara did her job well to confuse anyone in earshot, even if that included us.

"That was close," Darren said, "Come on. We've already zeroed in on Jarmiel's location. Steady your nerves."

Easy for him to say. He sounded as hard and soulless as the rocks lying about. That last bit wasn't true, contrary to vampire myths. He had a soul. I felt the essence of a flame burning from his hand.

He let me wobble away from the tree and we set off in a new direction. "So. You're really a demon," Darren said.

That was sudden.

"Yeah," I said. The singing had stopped but we continued to speak in whispers. "Sorry, I didn't come with horns."

"Is that the story you're sticking with?"

He sounded annoyed like I'd patronized him. I'd been hiding most of my life, so his accusation tickled me. We stalked onward, careful with our footing. Leaf-lined paths guided us through the trees. At least we were getting closer to our goal instead of running blindly as I had been before.

"You think I'm hiding something?" I asked.

"Yes."

"Does that bother you?"

"If you didn't know I was a vampire, would you still be nervous?" Darren asked.

I frowned at the back of his head. "I'm not. The situation is just tense."

"Your heart is beating in my ears."

"Tune it out then."

He gave me another icy stare. I missed the days of living with Namoi when I didn't have to explain when my heart rate was slightly elevated.

"To be honest, I was raised to ignore what I am. All of this is like culture shock. I'm not trying to be secretive, I'm just—" My palms flexed like I was physically trying to grasp the words.

"Ignorant," Darren finished for me.

"Yeah."

What a ray of sunshine.

He stopped midstep, holding his foot an inch above the dirt. I stiffened too. His head turned to one side and he waited. But whatever it was, never came.

"That's not all, is it?" he said, mumbling through the tense air.

I groaned. "Why do you keep asking?"

Darren pivoted on his heel. His face dropped close to my throat and inhaled. The lack of personal space put me back into my nightmare with Clay. *Princess.* That was what he called me. Yet another annoying nickname I had to endure.

I heard the faint parting of Darren's lips and took a step back. Vegan or not, he still had fangs and they were much too close to my arteries. His amber eyes held mine while he spoke. "Because your blood—"

A giggle interrupted us from above.

The moon-kissed vampire, Mallory, dropped down from the forest's ceiling, landing softly on both feet. Darren crouched, arms slightly raised like he was preparing to tackle her.

"Even my baby brother is bothered. Your smell is only getting stronger by the day," she said, clearly having overheard us, "Do you really not know why?"

My smell again, really?

"Can we just get back to the stupid game?" I asked, "I promise to shower after."

Mallory tilted her head. Her dead gaze reminded me of a broken doll. "You want to know why you're so enamored by Zakiel? It's not just you. Angels draw all kinds of people to them. Some even go mad. Funny, right?"

Instead of her mocking tone, I heard genuine intrigue. Unfortunately, I was tired of his name coming out of her mouth whenever she spoke to me. "Do you like him or something? What does this have to do with your issue with me?"

"Jess, please. He's not *my* kind of man, but his blood? Every drop bathed in light…" Her eyes glazed over like she was lost in thought. "It's a sin to desire it, like the forbidden fruit."

I chuckled out of nervousness. "If you want to bite him, that's between you guys…" Knowing how nice Zak was, he would let her if he hadn't already. My own blood boiled at the thought of her teeth in his throat.

"I'm not only talking about Zakiel anymore."

There was no punch line. No creepy smile following her sentence.

"Me?" I asked. "You guys think I smell the same as Zak?"

I wasn't aware of my own scent like she was, but I had a hard time believing an angel's blood resembled my own. That would have to defy everything I am.

"She already said what she knows," Darren said, "Let it go."

Mallory's mischief was back and the crimson color in her eyes seemed to deepen. "Don't pretend you weren't about to say the same thing, brother. If she really doesn't know, we can always find out for ourselves."

She took a more predatory stance, mirroring her brother's. My heart dropped, remembering where we were. Alone, for one. I felt for the cuffs attached to my hip. Even if I managed to wrangle the vampire, I had a feeling Mallory wasn't going to play by the rules.

Mallory licked one of her fangs. "I'm not leaving here without a bite, Jess. Or is it *Cupcake* now?"

Yup. She was a bitch and she was coming for me. I had Darren by my side but I had watched Mallory during training for a while now. She surpassed us all.

But I didn't have to stand there and take it.

This was an opportunity to see if I had what it took as a peacekeeper, regardless of the outcome. Zak prepared me for swift attacks that I knew Mallory would throw at me. If I could touch her first, my increased strength might be able to overpower her.

The tricky part was getting close to those teeth.

A cold hand curled around my wrist and I looked up at Darren, confused. Mallory was closing in but he kept me from leaving. "She's crazy but she'll recognize your blood," he said.

What did that even mean? It didn't matter. Darren sided with his sister and her blood fetish. Two against one. I could just let Mallory take a tiny bite. If she really could perform a magical taste test and confirm I wasn't lying.

But I wasn't in a cooperative mood. What did it matter *if* I had weird blood? One drop wasn't going to satisfy her, anyway. "Look, maybe you're all freaking out because I could be related to the succubi," I said, "I hear they can be… alluring?"

Part of me wished Mallory just had a crush on me and it wasn't bloodlust. She thought about it with one sharp fingernail tugging on her bottom lip. "How interesting. Now I'm even more excited."

Both vampires shifted their focus to something else in the woods. While Darren wasn't suspecting, I wrenched him forward with me, smacking his face into the tree. My idea succeeded in getting him to release me. He didn't even try to stop me. Instead, he busied himself with his smashed nose.

I felt bad but he betrayed me first.

"Ouch." Darren licked the trickle of blood that hit his lips. His eyes deepened into a dark, golden brown. I sprinted toward the first opening I had, but a harsh kick sent me spinning on the ground. My body bounced over roots and rocks.

I grasped at the grass to pull myself back up, but damn, that hurt. The leathery blades turned brown in my hands. I'd shrugged this phenomenon off once before during training, but there it was again.

"At least you have some lady balls," Mallory said, grabbing me by the ankle. She dragged me across the bumpy earth before flipping me over. "It's no fun if you're a dead fish."

It looked like she was going to pounce on me, but I got my legs ready. As she came down just as I centered my boots on her stomach and used her momentum to throw her over me.

Twigs and leaves were tangled in my hair when I got back on my stomach. My strength surprised her as much as it did me. It felt like throwing a feather pillow off me.

She skidded to a stop like an agile little huntress. "I guess you have been paying attention during Zakiel's one-on-ones."

I sprang to my feet. Her leg came flying at me hard from the side and I brought my arms up just in time. My forearms shielded my head but the impact still flung me. I caught a tree with my arm and made a loop back around.

"Do you enjoy being Zak's pet?" Mallory asked, "We should teach you to play dead."

A flurry of punches aimed at my stomach. I couldn't catch them all. One of her tiny fists forced the air out of my lungs so hard, I thought I coughed them up. The hunger in her eyes gleamed. Technically, we'd hit each other's targets enough to both be out of the game.

As I suspected, Mallory had conveniently forgotten the rules.

More kicks. Every hit I deflected was like getting hit by a moving car. When I finally got a swing in, I missed, and her long nails came across my shoulder. They sliced my flesh open like little knives.

I clutched the open wound but I knew my smell was everywhere. While I hunched over, Mallory grabbed a handful of my hair and yanked. I gritted my teeth, already knowing what came next. Her pearly fangs glittered with hunger. The flawless beauty she paraded around as a mask slipped away and revealed the beast beneath. She hissed before diving in.

"*Gah!*"

I caught her by the throat before she could bite down. She choked as I closed my fingers tighter around her slender neck. She could chomp at me all she wanted but even if she succeeded, I wouldn't let her swallow a damn drop.

Mallory tried wrangling herself free, but I was already working on my next move. Her spirit energy level was somewhere between Zak's and Guy's; not as bright as Zak's but more fiery than Guy's. I squeezed her throat like I was draining an orange of its juices.

When I looked into her red eyes, I noticed they'd grown three sizes. I felt my muscles tightening already. She wrenched away that time but her freedom was short-lived. I brought my fist into her gut and the low grunt she made was seriously terrifying. And exhilarating.

After all the crap she'd put me through in training, I could finally make *her* scramble.

Mallory deflected more hits until one of my kicks landed under her chin, sending her body soaring into the creek. Even with my high from the fight, I cringed at her hard landing. Her white hair, now drenched, stuck to her face like webs.

When she rose from the water, the red from her eyes bled into the whites. She fumed, creating some monstrous, and somehow still feminine, growl before charging at me. Another body slammed into her from the side. Darren appeared so fast he only manifested as a blur. He stared his sister down while she made her huffy recovery.

"Go." Darren looked at me. He probably wanted to secure our team's overall victory and pretend he hadn't almost fed me to his sister.

Whatever.

As I ran, I felt the blood drying from my wound and on my hand. I hadn't seen a vampire act like that before. Her attitude went from standard Mallory to crazed. She could have licked her fingernails if she were that desperate for my blood.

I wanted to find Jarmiel before running into anyone else but without warning, an arm appeared from behind a tree and snatched me up like a hawk capturing a mouse. Someone lifted me onto a low-hanging branch, holding me to their chest.

Warm fingers silenced my screams.

"*Shh…*" A gravelly voice chuckled softly.

I forced my neck back and looked up into Aiden's dark and sexy glory. The veil of leaves above us deeply shadowed him. Had I fallen into a much worse situation? He grinned down at me and slowly removed his hand from my lips.

"Not the most stealthy of beasts are you, Cupcake?"

23

Aiden's long arms draped over me and secured me to our spot in the tree. He smelled faintly of herbs; sweet with a hint of spice. I never noticed before since I made efforts to avoid him. Ironically, it was a familiar and comforting aroma for me and reminded me a lot of home and Naomi.

We listened to birds whistling by and the occasional shouts from other players. It could have been tranquil if I wasn't so close. If Aiden was anything like his sister, he was going to get excited real soon. What did the vampire have planned, anyway?

His eyes darkened, just like his sister's had when I first bled. I took a sharp inhale, but then, I was guided forward and gently dropped back onto solid ground. Aiden slid down next and then walked off as if nothing happened.

"You're helping me?" I asked.

"What are teammates for?" He paused and lifted the ends of a blue cloth that sat on his hip. "Although, even if you had been perfectly silent, I would've found you."

He then pointed to the blood drying on my arm. The wound itself was clearing up, but the stained evidence remained. My hand made the perfect vampire lollipop after holding it earlier. I wished I could have washed off in the creek. "You can thank your lovely sister for that."

Aiden's grin exposed a single fang. "Maybe you should stay close. Never know what could be lurking out there."

"Besides you?"

"Besides me."

Aiden didn't appear interested in eating me, for the time being. Practicing caution, I followed behind him, keeping a few feet between us. He peered over his shoulder. "If you ask nicely, I'll stick around. I'm a gentleman like that."

Aiden had a talent for making everything sound condescending. I didn't want to admit that I could use his help so, like a proud coward, I said nothing. He never made it easy to be around him. I wasn't about to hold my breath at his generosity now.

"Can't have Zak's favorite pet getting hurt on my watch, "Aiden said, adding a pinch of petty sprinkles.

My jaw clenched as I spoke. "What's that supposed to mean?"

He flicked away a branch that hung near his head. "He obviously likes his new toy, or are you just used to being the center of attention?"

"Jealous?"

"Ooh. A spicy Cupcake."

Aiden didn't even look like he was participating in the game. I kept glancing around for anyone pursuing us but he blazed the trail without a care in the world.

"Don't make things weird with Zak," I said, "He's nice to everyone."

His harsh laugh gave me chills but also spiked my anger. "Don't give me that. His face makes your heart beat faster than a hummingbird. Huh… the same thing happens when you're with me. Does that mean you like me too?"

I stomped a little harder than necessary on the twig under my boot. Aiden took a break from his cocky saunter to let me see his amused face. "Am I getting under your skin?" he asked.

"You're all obsessed. It's gross," I said.

He could sense danger coming better than I could, but I took the lead and veered off in another direction. I needed him to stop looking so he wouldn't see my flushing skin.

"It's not like you can help it," Aiden called after me, "A succubus will drive anyone crazy."

I leered back at him. "You and your siblings, I swear… I love bread but I don't go around harassing my bread."

"You're comparing yourself to bread?"

"Is *Cupcake* better?"

His lips crept further up his face. "My sister's nutty but clever. She wasn't wrong, by the way."

Figures, he'd been listening the entire time.

"About what?"

"Something more than darkness lives inside you."

I watched him scan my arm and then my hand. It wouldn't even taste good now that it was dry, but what did I know? "I'm not pregnant if that's what you're getting at."

"Oh, I know."

I flinched, not loving the fact that he knew about *anything* that happened inside my body. A demon couldn't also have angel blood. First of all, the two would never mate. Even if they'd wanted to, I doubted they could. Oil and water don't mix. Light and dark would only create shadow.

"Forbidden Love is a tale as old as time. Who's to say an angel didn't fall for a demon? Isn't danger enticing?" he asked.

"You seriously think an angel got busy with a demon?"

"I'm open to the idea."

"Are you here to find out?" I asked, tasting the bitterness in my mouth. If I'd wanted an examination, I would've given Mallory a shot.

"Only if you're feeling curious. I don't bite without consent." His lashes fluttered with innocence I knew was absent.

We escaped the coverage of trees and reached a cliffside. The sun gave a warm welcome to our elevation. I had no idea where to go from there, and Aiden hadn't bothered to correct me. I'd brought us to a dead end.

The nearest tree became my post as I smashed my forehead against it.

"Guess this means we can talk for a while," Aiden said.

I lazily peered at him. He leaned against a tree next to mine, stretching his shoulders from all of his strenuous labor. I mumbled in response, half-hoping the game was over and Lisha and Zak would round us up soon.

"So, what's your deal?" Aiden asked.

"You'll have to be more specific," I said, "Right now, I'm anxious about being alone with you and your sister in the woods."

His red eyes glittered. "I'm talking about embracing your inner demon, not me. Unless you'd like to try that instead."

"I don't have to embrace it. And no."

"You're wrong there, Cupcake."

He waited for me to argue and then blew a stream of air up to reach his hairline. Like it was a choice? If it were, I would've chosen to be an elf or a fairy. A regular ol' human would've been great too. I could live and die without a bother.

But... I had enjoyed kicking the lights out of Mallory. I would never have been able to stand against her as a human. Remembering our fight got my heart pounding again.

"Just admit it. You think it's *bad*." Aiden's fangs teased his bottom lip. "You feel guilty about sucking souls. It must be exhausting living your life, starving to the point of passing out, and for what? Newsflash sweetheart, no one cares. You could be a selfless martyr with a heart of gold. Humans don't give a fuck. You're *still* a demon."

His words left a bruise. Could a true demon even experience guilt? Then, what feeling ate away at my heart whenever I needed to help myself?

Aiden relaxed his head against the bark and gazed at the sky. "Hey. Fuck 'em, right? There's no reason *we* shouldn't be friends."

"Fine. We're friends," I said, "Now, point us in the right direction so we can get the hell out of here."

His pretty face had a cunning air about it as he fanned his thick lashes. How could someone with such lovely aesthetics also inspire others to punch them? "You really want to go back? We're far enough away from the others. You could roll down this cliff and disappear."

"Disap—…" At first, I thought he'd threatened me, but then, I too looked out over the cliff. If I were careful, I could slide down without much trouble. Run and keep running. I could go home. Maybe not that, but I could search for my aunt. On my own.

I lifted my foot but brought it back down.

"Or we can keep playing their games like good puppets do," Aiden said with a sigh, "Let's *not* question Zakiel's intentions for they must be pure."

My patience was worn. I stormed off, like an elephant trampling my way back into the warzone. Why did Aiden make me so angry? Did his words actually have merit, and I wanted to ignore them? Had my admiration for Zak blinded me from concerns about EXO and the angels?

Aiden reappeared next to me, teasing my bloodied arm with the back of his finger. "If it were me, I'd want to know what was in my blood before some EXO scientist took a sample."

"So what if they happen to find something?" I said, "I'm already the worst-case scenario."

"If you say so."

I expected him to ditch me after that but he stuck by my side. The forest quieted before, I could hear the faint sounds of combat. I only broke our silence when I felt Aiden staring too long. "What now?"

"You're leaving a trail of breadcrumbs," he said.

"I have nothing to clean it with right now." My blood increased our chances of being caught. Not only that but if we found Jarmiel, I'd lead the sharks right to him.

I started rubbing my arm clean with some leaves from the forest floor and tossed them about. Aiden watched me with a hungry expression. The last time I used the same trick, I escaped Max the night of my arrest. Crafty and resourceful, but then…

We arrived at another cliff.

"You did this on purpose!" I pointed a finger at Aiden. The more pissed off with Aiden I became the braver I sounded. His teeth were perfectly straight, giving his canines a grand, white stage.

He raised his shoulders like an innocent bystander. "You were having so much fun playing the leader. I didn't want to interrupt."

I stopped myself from screaming profanities by covering my face with both hands. Even then, I could feel his smug face watching me suffer. We'd spent so much time trail-blazing that it sounded like everyone else had left us and gone home.

After dragging my fingers down my face, I worked the buckle around my forearm loose and removed the glove that came with my suit. Aiden's attention locked onto my exposed wrist. The only blood left was smudged on my fingertips and had turned a darker shade of maroon.

I lifted my hand to Aiden's chin. His eyes softened as if I were giving him a box of chocolates. "What's this?"

If I really thought about it, giving blood to EXO couldn't be much different than trusting Aiden. A vampire like Aiden had no agenda other than to serve himself but EXO could have reasons to keep something from me. I didn't believe Zak would do that, but he was one angel among many.

"Don't be creepy about it," I said, "If being *friends* means you'll get me out of here, then take some. Just tell me what you taste…"

How would he even know what angel blood tastes like, anyway?

Aiden snaked his fingers around my wrist. "You sure, Cupcake? It hurts but just for a second."

"I'm about to change my mind, so just do it," I closed my eyes. Two seconds ago I'd been motivated by curiosity to act impulsively but my arm shook the longer I anticipated his teeth. The deep laughter that followed did nothing to calm my nerves. Neither did his thumb making soft circles around the area I assumed he wanted to tear into.

I refused to look until I felt the softness of his lips above my veins. The view of his mouth coming over my flesh stirred a confusing sensation in my stomach.

And then, he pushed me.

I fell back into a soft bed of mud and moss. Had I really been fooled by such an amateur prank? Alarmed and infuriated, I laughed. "Wow, screw you—"

Then, I noticed his shoulder.

His composure melted away. Brows crunched. His lips popped over his fangs as he hissed. His pale fingers held the torn fabric on his arm like his limb would fall off otherwise.

"Aiden?" I got up slowly. "What's wrong?"

"Careful," he spat, but not at me. Something stuck out of the ground, right where I'd been standing. Aiden crouched low and examined the thin object. The dirt beneath vibrated from the energy buzzing in the metal. It appeared to have a sharp point but was too small to be considered a spear or even an arrow. The glow surrounding it was similar to Zak's sword but less radiant.

"What is that?" I asked.

"*Ah, ah.* Don't touch. Unless you wanna end up like me."

I drew back my creeping fingers. "It hit you. What did it do?"

"Purifiers love using these bolts. They're *blessed.* Just another word for burns-like-hell."

Blessed? Then, whoever shot it at us knew it could cause real harm. To prove my point, Aiden lifted his hand to reveal the wound. The flesh around his shoulder sizzled pink but the opened slit was clean. The bolt only grazed him but I could see that caused him a lot of pain.

"Can you sense someone out there?" I asked. He said the weapon belonged to a purifier and my mind immediately went to

Faris. We'd only had one encounter and that somehow warrant-
ed an assassination attempt.

Aiden shot into a standing position. His eyes narrowed at the
forest and I thought he might have seen the culprit from afar.
"I can't pick up a scent. They're with EXO for sure, or at least
trained to cloak themselves from supernaturals. Pissed off anyone lately, Cupcake?"

I thought about mentioning Faris but didn't want to be
responsible if his blood-drained corpse was discovered later.
Should he be proven innocent.

Aiden lifted his boot and stomped the bolt deeper into the
earth, making it sizzle. The opening in the ground expanded as
each particle fled from the light.

Something else bothered me, though.

Aiden was a vampire…

"You're not healing." I pointed to his wound.

"Rapid regeneration can't fix everything, and that wasn't
aimed at *me*."

The weight of his sacrifice finally set in. Angel magic. *Light*
magic. I started to say something again but froze. If blessed weapons worked against supernatural healing, and if the bolt had hit
me just right, that could've been the end for me.

"Don't get all sappy," he scoffed, "We couldn't have it going
through your sweet little heart now, could we? Let's move before
your stalker takes a second shot."

Everyone had already gotten back on the bus. Our team won.

Turns out, Max *can* handle everything on his own and teamwork be damned. While he wasn't the most gentle or courteous hero, Jarmiel looked pleased having been "rescued" and able to go home all the same.

I returned just in time to soil the victory with my almost-getting-killed thing. Zak pulled Aiden and me aside but everyone pressed their faces against the bus windows. Could it have been one of them? None of them were purifiers, though.

After the bolt had quit hissing at the ground, we wrapped it tight in Aiden's blue sash to bring with us, just to be safe. Zak fiddled with it. An unfamiliar tightening around his eyes took over and made me feel even worse.

"You didn't see anything?" he asked us.

"I see several people. Unless, you're certain none of them did it?" Aiden gave the bus a sly glance. He must revel in seeming mysterious. Normally his vague answer would've irritated me too, but in this case, I felt like I needed to defend him.

"He pushed me out of the way. The bolt nicked him instead," I said.

"Thanks. Aiden." Zak added the vampire's name with much effort. His eyes continued to drift away in thought. "Are you badly injured?"

"I'll survive. Captain." Aiden matched Zak's delivery all too well. I couldn't stop myself from cringing.

Zak took a deep breath before dismissing the awkwardness they'd created. "We'll figure this out. It won't happen again."

The stare he gave Aiden wasn't quite a glare, but maybe a challenge. "Hop on the bus. Jarmiel has some questions and Lisha can wrap your arm."

"Yes, sir," Aiden spoke through a bored sigh. I assumed that was the end of that, and followed after him.

"Not you." Zak stopped me but waited until we were the only ones left outside. His golden-brown eyes met mine and drooped, making him appear more puppy than man. "You're not in trouble, FYI. *I'm* in trouble. You almost got killed during a training exercise. Today was supposed to be fun."

The bolt rested in his hands like a haunting reminder. I hadn't been impaled or shot with anything before. Puncturing organs was a whole other level of pain that I wasn't eager to experiment with, even if I could heal quickly.

"I know it doesn't look like much, but anything containing high amounts of light energy is as deadly as it is lovely. I'm shocked no one noticed anything strange, unless—" he paused, "it really was one of them."

As he confessed his thoughts, I saw the hurt on his face as if the bolt had aimed for his chest instead. I didn't know Lisha's team very well, so I could've easily blamed one of them. That didn't feel right, either.

"So, what do we do, now?" I asked.

Zak stowed the bolt inside his belt loop and opened his arms to me. I took a step back. "Oh. I don't need *that* right now, but thank you."

"Huh? Oh. No, silly," he said, sounding lighter and more like himself, "We're flying."

Flying?

I pointed desperately over his shoulder. "But the bus is *right there.*"

Why did no one ever want to take the damn bus?

Zak made a face. "It's stuffy in there. Besides, we'll be safest in the air."

My heel hit the end of a root and I almost fell over trying to get away. I hadn't even been on an airplane before. There was no way I was about to fly around carelessly on a pair of someone else's wings! "How is a bus more dangerous than falling to death? Do you even have helmets?"

Zak quickly disguised his laughter as a coughing fit. Inappropriate, given the severity of our situation. "Would a helmet really save you if I dropped you?" I think Zak noticed my face turning green because he tossed his eyes upward. "I'm teasing. I haven't dropped anyone."

"Nope." I whipped around, ready to take my chances with the assassin in the forest. A wing made of light appeared in front of me and blocked my path. As soon as I felt Zak's arms crashing around me, I knew I was doomed. His wings pulsed and pulsed, making *whooshing* sounds as they carried us further up toward the clouds.

"Wait!" I grasped his forearms that cut across my stomach.

The wind pushed my head down. Individual trees turned into a sea of green and yellow. The velocity was so great that my legs felt like paper dancing in the wind. Same with my hair. My long, reddish-brown strands whipped at my cheeks.

Zak chuckled. "You okay?"

"Do I *look* okay?" We reached a level deemed high enough for Zak and our ascension slowed. I could see clouds getting close enough to touch. Amazing how much colder the air got while reaching for the sun.

"We're trying to be discreet here," he said, "Your screaming kinda ruins it."

I wanted to glare at him but I was too afraid to move. When Zak shifted a bit, I dug my fingers deeper into his skin. It was hard to focus on impending doom when I had an angel breathing on my neck.

"You can hide your face in my shoulder if you're scared?" Zak offered.

"I want to go back."

"Not an option right now."

My angry scoff was remixed with my chattering teeth. He assisted me in maneuvering around while I tried not to cry or vomit. Whichever happened first. Our new position had me facing him. My arms and legs wrapped around his body like a baby animal clinging to their mother. I had to be careful not to touch his wings, so my arms fit around his neck. If Zak's angelic body wasn't inhumanly strong, I probably would've decapitated him.

"How about now?" he asked, "Feeling better?"

I laughed maniacally into his shoulder to avoid swearing. "No."

"Are you really not going to look? That sucks because the view's not so bad." Zak tried to shake me but I burrowed even harder. "I promise you can close your eyes the rest of the way. Just one peek?"

"I'm starting to see why Jarmiel can't stand you."

Zak laughed harder than I'd ever heard before. His outburst startled me into ripping a small hole in his shirt with my nails. *Oops.* I refused to lift my head from the safety of his collar. No way I was going to open my eyes again. Who knew how high we were now? When would we run out of oxygen?

He moved his grip in order to cup my thighs. "There. I'm not letting go, 'kay?"

That was enough to bring my face up.

I got lost in the muddy diamonds blinking back at me, reflecting more sunlight in their depths. His gentle expression and the evening sky was like a cup of hot cider, heating me up inside. I thought I'd grown used to his shenanigans but there he was, making me melt. If only I were allowed to have feelings for him, then I'd become a puddle and rain down.

I dared myself to look over his shoulder and saw the mountains we'd left behind. As the sun dropped lower in the sky, the world was washed with a pink haze. A city soon hummed with bustling noises below. Building windows became an orange spectacle of dancing lights. I wished the night would come, only so I couldn't pinpoint exactly where my body would splat should I fall.

"I fly when I'm stressed," Zak said, "Making your problems look smaller is liberating, I think."

I glanced down and gulped.

Holy shit.

Still too high. I brought my legs higher around his torso, going full-on koala. He was my tree and like hell, I was letting go until he brought us back down. Was it shameful? Maybe. I was beyond caring.

"Think you can last twenty minutes?" Zak asked, "I'll drop us off and we can walk the rest of the way."

I nodded and returned my face to its hiding spot. He tipped forward and gravity beckoned me toward the earth. He continued speaking as we flew, probably to keep me at ease.

Eventually, I summoned the courage to ask more questions of my own. "Did you know something like this would happen?"

"I put more faith in my party than I should have, it seems," he said, "Have you had trouble with anyone?"

"There is one guy…" *Ew.* I was about to tattle on someone with no real evidence to frame him. But, Zak only asked if I had trouble with anyone, and I had. "A purifier. Faris? I met him the other day. Doesn't seem to like me very much."

All things considered, I was amazed he'd been the only one to approach me with that manner of hostility. I didn't want to blame him without proof but if we could start an investigation somewhere, it was better than nothing.

"Faris," Zak spoke his name with familiarity. "He's an excellent soldier but lacks basic people skills. Getting through a forest full of peacekeeper trainees, undetected, seems like him."

"How can someone who uses light not like people?"

"Good intentions aren't always *good* for everyone. A desire to be heroic can spark a light but will they be considered a hero to everyone? There has to be opposition before you can label someone a hero."

Could light matter be so unbiased as to feed even the delusionally self-righteous?

What a frightful thought.

Finally, we tilted further down and increased in speed before gradually coming to a stop. Zak's wings beat one last time, and my feet touched the ground. It was dramatic, I'll admit, but I fell to my knees and grasped the freshly mowed grass between my fingers.

Zak was unimpressed. "Oh, it wasn't that bad!"

I groaned before forcing myself back up. My stomach disagreed with this movement and threatened to purge, but the need to not be absolutely disgusting in front of Zak kept the bile down.

The angel was kind enough to let me lean on him while my legs returned to a solid form and not jello. He patted me on the back, like he was taking his drunk friend home. "You'll get used to it," he said but my wary expression had him laughing again, "What's with that face?"

* * *

I arrived home before anyone else.

Zak informed me to stay in the dorms. That was fine. I didn't want to see Mallory for a while anyway. What wasn't fine was having to wait for answers. Alone.

Before leaving me to my own devices, Zak mentioned Lisha having leads pointing to one or more purifiers. I wasn't sure if it was the relief I felt. Partly yes, because we were one step closer to finding them but I hadn't considered that there could be more than one.

My aunt warned me for years that something like this would happen. I hadn't been with EXO long and sure enough, someone already hated me enough to try killing me. That kind of hurt my feelings.

It was getting late and no one had returned yet. The emptiness in the building freaked me out. I wasn't actually alone. Zak left a few guards outside, but a girl couldn't help but feel paranoid.

I showered the grime and blood off my body, taking my sweet time and doing my best to put it all out of my mind. The snack stash in my room was running low. I should have asked Zak to fly by some burgers or something. He would have happily gone for it.

This sucks.

I licked peanut butter from a spoon and thumbed through a *non-demonic* book. Everyone else's day had been ruined too. Being held up for questioning wasn't one of my fondest memories, so I knew what they were in for.

I'd gotten so used to my solitude that the knock at my door puzzled me. They had to knock a second time to get me off my behind. "Gods…" I grumbled at myself and hurried to answer.

Guy towered over me in the doorway. When he noticed the peanut butter jar in my hand, he made a shallow snort. "Hey. You haven't been starving all night have you?"

"I haven't been allowed to leave, so kind of," I said.

"As your buddy, officially assigned this time," he added, "I can bring dinner back to your charming prison cell."

"Wow. More prison jokes?" I playfully shoved his shoulder. Were we close enough to do that now? I watched for his reaction but his eyes never left my hand. "I-In that case, you better bring back something good," I said.

"Or what?"

I wasn't prepared for his playful smirk. His head leaned into my room, making a physical challenge to his verbal one. My insides scrambled as my brain tried to process some witty retort. "I'll tell Tori you want to watch her favorite movies together."

His expression dropped.

"You wouldn't."

"The one with all the rich hotties consumed in their petty drama. What's it called? Oh yeah. 'Why I Hate My Life, vol. 2'." I nodded. "*So* good."

"You truly are a devil."

Guy backed off, but I caught a glimmer in his eye. "Give me ten minutes," he said, "Don't go anywhere. You know I'll always find you."

His last remark should have sent chills down my spine but my face felt hot. I put a stop to that before Guy returned, carrying three plastic bags full of something heavenly and delicious. He handed them to me like a delivery boy and turned to leave but I felt the urge to stop him. "Thank you. This is a lot, isn't it?"

"I didn't want to disappoint," he said.

"We can share if you want?"

What was I doing? Inviting Death into my room for dinner, that's what.

Was I nervous that he would say no or that he would say yes?

"You paid for it, you might as well have some," I said.

Guy's toothy smile made him appear bashful. "One bag is just dessert."

"My threat really got to you, huh? Then I definitely can't eat it all by myself." I allowed him back into the room. A draft followed him in, making my exposed arms shiver. I was in a tank top so I grabbed the sweater hanging off my bed and hoped that he wouldn't take offense.

We didn't have a table so I set the food on my desk. "Do reapers eat?"

"Yes," he said, and I heard him chuckle, "Well, I do."

"Do you *have* to eat, is my real question."

Guy had already gotten comfortable on my floor. His back rested against the bed while his legs stretched across the carpet. "While I'm here, I do. If I'm back home, eating is more of a hobby. The soul retains memories of your mortal life after you die; things like food and temperature. Senses in general. I think it's a comfort for some to eat and feel human. It is for me."

"What do you mean while you're here?"

"I won't be here forever," he said, "Not like this. Neither will you or anyone. I didn't mean much by it."

Since we didn't have chairs either, I joined him on the ground. My sweater kept me warm even though we were close to each other. I opened the bags and the pile of steamy, garlic noodles stunk up the room.

"Am I allowed to ask about the afterlife?" I asked and handed him a fork.

"You can ask and I'll decide to answer or not."

Cheeky bastard.

I twirled my fork into the noodles. "Fine. So your spirit passes on and you can pretend to enjoy food again? That's weird but cool, I guess. Being a spirit sounded boring but this helps."

"Boring?" he asked.

"Isn't it?"

Guy lifted his brow. "What exactly about Tori seems boring to you?"

"But she can't eat and she's a spirit?"

"If she crosses over, she can. The limitations between realms are difficult to explain." There it was again. His face hardened, or was he sad? It was hard to tell. Either way, his mind went somewhere else whenever Tori was brought up.

"Why won't she? Not that I'm in a rush, she's like my only friend." My attention was quickly pulled toward the contents of his mystery, dessert bag. "Who even bakes cakes this size?"

"It's a secret," Guy answered to one or both of those questions.

The single slice of chocolate divinity outshined any of my past birthday cakes in both presentation and flavor. I'd only stolen a taste of the frosting but the creamy, richness was fit for the gods. "*Mm…* Is this because you feel bad for me or did you *really* not want to watch Tori's movies?"

"I might've felt bad." Guy ran a hand through his thick hair. His eyes never left his shoes while he spoke. "To answer your question about Tori, though, she was born sick. I visited her in the hospital most of her life. They couldn't figure out what was wrong, just that her body wasn't going to allow her to do much more than sit like a vegetable. I pitied her too, I guess."

His voice fell and I thought he was getting emotional, but he took his fork and poked the container that had seasoned chicken. While I waited for him, I imagined the Tori I knew; young and full of life. Ironic that she lived the most in death.

"The day finally came. I told her many times I'd be the one to help her. She seemed fine at first, but then…" He let out a long, harsh breath. "She fought me. There was no life left, but her fear was painful to watch. She begged me not to. She wanted to 'live like other girls.' I'd wrangled many spirits before, but I was stupid and got attached. I kept her spirit tethered to mine, allowing her a mirage of life. Tori thinks she's happy but she needs to move on."

There was a pain in Guy's voice that he tried to cover up by sounding annoyed. I was at a loss for words. After a moment of staring down at my hands pressed in my lap, I said, "I didn't know. Is the situation permanent?"

"No, but she shuts down whenever I bring it up."

"I imagine that topic is difficult. And the bear?"

His lips twitched. "From the hospital gift store. I got it for her."

Her item of emotional value that her spirit gravitated to. It was the bear Guy bought her?

"She must care about you a lot," I said, feeling my heart break.

"I care about her too but not in that way."

Had he meant romantically? That hadn't been what I meant exactly but I couldn't imagine being trapped in time while someone I loved continued to move on. "Is that a reaper thing too? No attachments?" I asked.

"Not a rule, no. But it's complicated." He finally brought his head up and held my gaze. Why did it feel like he was addressing something else entirely? I thought he'd say more but he retreated to the previous topic. "It's also dangerous for her. Without a body, she's susceptible to demons or cultists in black market trading."

"Is that why you're keeping an eye on me?" I pushed down the hurt from that one with a bite of cake. It wasn't like he was blaming me specifically, but how did he really feel about me being a demon? If I fed on Tori's energy when she didn't even have a body, would she just disappear?

Guy had every right to worry for her.

"It's one reason," he said.

I focused on the carpet while battling my disappointment. "Why did you stop me? You could've easily let me go."

He leaned his head to one side and scrunched his brow. "I was doing my job."

"A job that isn't *really* yours. I don't think Death headquarters told you to."

"Zak asked me to secure you and I did… You're stabbing the box." Guy lifted my hand that had been murdering the noodle container. "Am I upsetting you?"

"Is there something else? I don't have any answers about myself and I keep hoping someone else does." I was practically begging him with my eyes. He was a reaper, the closest being to the World Soul. They knew the ins and outs of death and of Heaven and Hell.

Guy took his time leaving my hand and then cracked his knuckles. Not all at once, though. He took each finger, one by one. *Crack. Crack. Crack. Crack. Crack.* "There's a chance someone knows something," he said, "But *he* could get in trouble for telling you. Especially if he's wrong."

Was he seriously talking about himself in the third person? "I won't tell anyone."

"You should really go to Zak about this."

"I'm asking you."

His legs squirmed. He probably regretted dinner with me but I had to keep pressing. Aiden's poisonous words about EXO and the angels filled the spaces of doubt in my mind. I wanted to question everything. Zak too. I didn't love that.

Guy began with a heavy sigh, "There was a rumor once. Not even a rumor. Just whispers in the underworld. A being of both Hell's night and Heaven's light would be born from the World Soul."

I frowned, gave up on my noodles, and set the fork down. "The World Soul is a god. Why would it need to create something like that?"

He ran his tongue over the innermost section of his bottom lip. "To have something that defies nature. Destroys it, actually. Chaos."

"And that has something to do with me? That doesn't sound right…" I stopped. "The vampires think I smell like angel blood."

His head snapped up.

"Have any of them bitten you?" When I shook my head, Guy's expression relaxed. "It was premature of me to even bring it up. Can you promise not to do anything reckless for the time being and I'll promise to look into it for you?"

"Really?"

"Promise."

I crossed my arms just as he extended his hand. "You said you take promises very seriously."

"I do." He looked serious enough. Then again, he always looked serious. Guy kept his hand out. Waiting.

"Fine." I huffed but was secretly happy about it. We sealed our promise in his freezing cold hand. "So, like, hypothetically, if I was this chaos being you're afraid to talk about, what's the worst that could happen?"

"Just the end of the world."

25

The Necromancer perched at the end of my bed like a gargoyle.

A silver glow accompanied him from behind, illuminating his features in contouring shadows. The features themselves were handsome, unfitting of his gruesome crimes. If I only looked at his jawline or his nose, they were flawless, but if I took it all in, eyes, lips, cheekbones, and brows, it made for an eerie painting. Each seemed cosmetically enhanced like they shouldn't all belong on the same face together.

"Annoying isn't it?" he asked.

Clay had called for me a few times now. I ignored him. It was my dream after all. I gripped the blanket, unsure if I wanted to use it as a shield or throw it from me so I could run. The fear of sleepwalking again kept me from moving.

"*End of the world,*" he scoffed, unphased by my silence, "Who says shit like that and leaves?"

Clay let his arms hang in front of him, getting too close to where my feet were. Like a turtle hiding its head in its shell, I tucked my legs into my chest. "Is this your thing?" I asked "Creeping on girls while they sleep?"

I shouldn't have been surprised considering he messed with dead bodies.

His head fell to one side like a curious cat inspecting a rat. Ghostly white wisps poked out from beneath his hood. "You think it's all a dream?"

It *had* to be a dream. I put a lot of faith in that fact. The alarms would go off again if he were actually present.

But then, he made his move.

Clay sprang from his spot and landed above me on all fours. I brought my hands up in time to catch him by the shoulders, but not before releasing a shrill scream. Sharp teeth glittered from behind his sneer. "Couldn't help myself. You just look so pathetic under the sheets like this."

"*Fuck* you."

"Well, we're already here."

The menace plaguing cities with Ghouls was making jokes. I grabbed hold of him tighter and rolled us off the bed. My chest rose from taking ragged breaths as I stumbled toward the window. "Stay the hell away from me."

He was already back on his feet and still too close to feel comfortable. *Curse this room.* My dreams never allowed us to leave the box. I was stuck in there with him until it was over.

Nothing in his voice signified that he was bothered by my repulsion. "You're not really living up to your name. It's disappointing."

My weak stance and rumpled sleepwear did little to counter his insults. "*Princess* isn't a name. If you're that disappointed, go bother someone else."

Clay wrapped a dry hand, skin cracking at the knuckles, over his lips and chuckled into his palm. I didn't like any of it, but the way his orange eyes narrowed at me in the dark had to be the worst. "Sorry little demon. You're all that I'm after."

"I don't want you here. Just leave me alone!"

"So fussy. I told you, I'm a friend." The sinister grin spreading from behind his painted black fingernails said otherwise.

"Any friends I have wouldn't turn people into monsters."

Clay made a sharp pivot, showing me his back. The hand from his face dropped and he explored the deep pockets of his coat. I remembered the knife he had last time and my insides went cold. His neck turned unnaturally around and one of his eyes locked onto me. "What else would the dead be doing except feeding the maggots?" he asked.

"You're disgusting."

With a bone-chilling snap, the rest of his body jerked around to align with his neck. One quick stride and he was already in front of me. Before he could do anything else, I swung my fist at his jaw.

It never connected.

Black tendrils escaped from Clay's cloak. They flailed about at first, making a wet, hissing sound, until one wound itself around my wrist. My hand was bent back and I strangled myself on the scream stuck in my throat.

"*Shh…*" Clay brought his face nice and close, allowing me to count each of his many sharp teeth. His fingers pinched my chin so I couldn't look away. "Let me show you just how *special* you really are."

* * *

Sweat glued my face to the pillow. Tears? Drool? I felt like I'd been thrashed and beaten, even while I lay comfortably in bed.

I couldn't get the images to go away.

Clay manipulated the dream just before I woke up. My room had become fire and brimstone. The earth stretched for miles and was charred like an overdone steak. We stood over a field of dead faces, most I couldn't identify because they'd also been corrupted and burned by chaos. What was it, a vision? Another nightmare to torment me?

"This world needs a new start and you will be its creator," Clay's voice scratched in my ears. The worst was when I found Zak in the dream. His body had a gaping hole through his chest that continued to grow, sizzling his skin and clothes. He'd fallen to his knees, looking up at me with large, tear-filled crystals. "Jess…"

I couldn't bear it.

Before ripping myself away from the Clay and the horrors surrounding us, he left me with a final whisper. "See you soon, Jessebel."

See you soon.

It felt like a photograph taken in my brain and the images were permanent. Closing my eyes made it worse, so I stared at the wall, praying I'd never have to see Zak in that state. Ever. My chest felt swollen, sore, and distressed like pink around my eyes. *It was only a dream.*

I wished I could say that was all the weirdness from that night but when I woke up, a message was waiting for me. Written in a dark powdery substance was the word, "RUN."

A strong, herbal essence tickled my nose. I coughed. Empty jars were scattered on my desk. Someone had emptied all of Naomi's witchy seasonings to make the letters. Someone had actually been here.

They may have saved me from my dreams, though I didn't believe that had been their intention. Whoever had broken in was in a rush. The ends of each letter didn't quite connect. Had it been Clay? How would he have and why? I did want to "run." Run from *him*, that is.

That asshole ruined my sleep and now the floor.

A twinge of pain brought my attention to my hand. A pink ring wore itself like a bracelet around my wrist. The tenderness faded, removing my proof before my eyes; the only time rapid healing really sucked.

It was past time I warned someone about Clay.

No one had reported back about my house arrest yet. I hadn't heard anyone else arrive either, but the dreams were getting out of hand. If what I saw was any indication of what was to come or Clay's desires, someone needed to know. Or I was just crazy.

As soon as I opened my door, my breath caught in my throat. A nearly lifeless face stared blankly from across the hall. I clutched my chest like a proper damsel, or elderly woman, given a fright. "Guy, what are you doing?"

He had himself propped against the wall; messy hair curling past his ears. His scythe was also behind him for some reason, creating suspicion in me already. It didn't look like he'd gotten a wink of sleep but his clothes changed from last night from gray to grayer. His voice rumbled from exhaustion. "I didn't want to leave you unattended."

"Have you been here this whole time?" I asked.

Guy raised his slouching shoulders. Was that a yes? Was it cute or creepy if he'd actually camped out there all night?

I was still annoyed with how we'd parted ways last night; blue-balling me with minimal information, but there were bigger concerns. "Thanks for worrying, I guess."

It must have been how I said it because his gray eyes became pointed. "What happened?"

I thought about telling him. He was the one who brought up chaos and the end of the world. But I got stuck. What if I did tell someone and they decided I was too big a risk after all? Staying silent to protect myself didn't feel right either.

Gods...

What was I supposed to do?

Guy must have caught a glimpse of the new edition to my carpet because he stormed over to investigate. His face turned to stone and I thought his skin would crack. "You didn't do this."

"No," I confirmed.

"Who?" he asked.

"Would you believe me if I said it was The Necromancer?"

I didn't think Guy could glare any harder but I was sorely mistaken. "Is that a joke?"

It was too late to stop, now. I met his harsh stare. "I've seen him in dreams. I thought it was just in my head—"

"How long has this been going on?" His deep voice made my toes vibrate.

"A while."

"And you didn't say anything?" he asked.

"I wasn't sure if it was actually him, at first…"

Guy's mouth and eyes shut in unison, like he was preventing an explosion from coming out. When he spoke again, it was much slower. "We need to see Zak. Now."

He reached for my elbow but I stepped back into my room. Was he seriously going to drag me away like a child having a tantrum? "I can tell him myself," I said.

"Can you? You also kept quiet for this long."

There were times I really appreciated Guy. Many, in fact. I wasn't as experienced as he was. Not wise, either, or calm. I even enjoyed his dry sense of humor.

But not that. Not the accusing look in his eye. Hated that.

What if I'd just been a chore for him all along? Had I been stupid and desperate, hoping to be close to someone and blind to what really was?

"I didn't know if I was dreaming or losing my mind, but I wouldn't do anything to hurt Zak or anyone else here." My voice climbed in volume and his brows lifted in sync. Emotions were bubbling over again. It always had to be in that damned hallway and with Guy as my punching bag. "I'm not plotting *anything*. Maybe it's your job to make sure I don't screw up. I don't care. I need answers. Real ones. Not half-assed theories and rumors. If you can't do that then at least stop pretending you give a damn about me."

Guy paused in his tracks. His voice softened some. "That's not what I was getting at."

A low whistle alerted both of us to the end of the hall. I groaned. Aiden looked too lively that morning walking toward us with a carefree smile. "Good morning! What did I just walk in on?" he asked.

I knew he'd heard everything. Guy probably knew it too because neither of us humored his nonchalant entrance. His scythe was still in grabbing distance, whether Aiden could see it or not. I wouldn't have been shocked if Guy started swinging. Not with the hurricane he harbored behind in his eyes.

"Looks like she doesn't want your help, reaper," Aiden said, "Smart girl."

Guy kept a watchful eye on him as he lurked in my doorway. There was no explosive call to action or even concern on Aiden's face after spotting the message. It was like he'd walked into the kitchen and saw a stack of dirty dishes. "Now, who would do such a thing? Those pesky purifiers could've snuck up here undetected. You don't really think it was… *The Necromancer*?" Aiden shivered for us in the audience. "How scary."

"Do you have anything valuable to contribute?" Guy asked, sounding strained like he was balancing on his last nerve.

"Ouch. I thought we were all on the same team. Can't I show concern for my peers?" Aiden looked at me as if to see which of them I would agree with. "Your assassin isn't going to quit after one failed attempt, Cupcake. Whoever wrote your note probably cares more about your well-being than any angel. Or reaper."

Guy's fingers tightened and curled around his scythe. What exactly happened when a reaper was pissed? I didn't want to find out. Not without a morning coffee, at least.

Aiden on the other hand revealed his deep pleasure in taunting Guy with a twisted smile. "What? Worried she'll get smart and ditch you?"

"You can both go, actually." I couldn't wait another second. Too awkward. I left them both to stand in the hallway together. My ponytail swished back and forth from my quickening pace.

"Jess?" Guy called out to me.

"I'll take care of it myself."

I got on the elevator without looking back. Either of them could have caught up if they'd wanted to, but they didn't. Good.

The soft hum from the metal box calmed me down as it brought me to the bottom floor. Everything Aiden said was beginning to make sense, which was terrifying. Or was I allowing myself to be easily swayed by the vampire's cunning tongue?

Zak had done a lot for me, hadn't he?

I wasn't sure where I was heading at first. Zak's office? If he was even there, I had no idea. Then, I remembered EXO had purifiers prowling everywhere, and still no word on who my attempted murderer was.

It would've been nice to have Guy with me, after all … *Dammit*.

The elevator doors opened and I still had no plan. I didn't make it halfway through the main room when Barrett's massive shoulders created a blockade in my path. "Newbie! I'm supposed to tell you we have to walk in pairs now. Ya' know, buddy system and all that," he said, "You especially."

If it had been Aiden or Guy I might've been annoyed and pushed around him but Barrett was too chipper to snub like that. I was upset but that didn't mean I needed to carry an even bigger target on my back by parading around solo. "Right… You're right."

Barrett puffed out his chest, satisfied with his message. "Zak also said he'd stop by later. Want some breakfast while you wait? I made eggs."

He had. Barrett welcomed me over to the kitchen where he'd exceeded the max capacity for scrambled eggs in one pan. I aided him with his feast, sitting at the bar, but he could have handled the stack of fluffy protein himself. He ate faster than Zak with his pizza, and that said a lot.

"No training today so Max and I are heading to the gym. You in?" Barrett asked.

I grimaced. Gym time with Max sounded like the worst. On the other hand, I should have been training more, especially with people hunting me, and so close to home.

"Thanks, I'll think about it," I said, "Sorry you all had to stay up because of me."

Barrett dove into his second helping without skipping a beat. "Wasn't so bad. How are you holding up?"

"Alive."

"Is that all that's got you down?"

I sank deeper into the bar stool, thinking about who I'd abandoned upstairs. Barrett pulsed his brows, almost knowingly. "You're too good for Aiden anyway. I hope he hears me."

"You heard that?" I asked.

"Not all of it, but as soon as that guy opens his mouth, my ears perk up. Kinda waiting for him to do something stupid."

"I get that but if I hadn't bumped into Aiden yesterday, I'd probably be dead now," I said. It was bad enough having to be airlifted out of the forest in front of everyone. I appreciated Zak but I felt stuck in a cycle of being catered to. Aiden rescuing me made me indebted to him too, which I didn't love either.

Barrett paused to take a big gulp out of a glass of milk. "Does that upset you?"

"A little."

"Hey, c'mon. I'm a big dude and I rarely get anything done on my own," he said, "Maybe it's just pack mentality but around here, we're a team too. I keep trying to remind Max that."

"I guess I just—" I stopped when he leaned across the counter.

"You got a problem with a big man helping you?" he asked.

"N-No! I don't think so."

Barrett chuckled. "I'm messing with you. You'll save my ass and I'll save yours. Doesn't matter so long as we're all alive at the end of the day."

I smiled a "thank you" at him and finished the rest of my breakfast. Footsteps came from the stairs and my back tensed.

"Glad you didn't run off."

Guy's brow was still pinched but he maintained a mellow demeanor. I had the feeling there was no avoiding him a second time. He sat on the bar stool next to mine as if to answer my thoughts.

"What's up, Guy?" Barrett asked but then shot me the goofiest look as if we were sharing an inside joke. It was not subtle.

"Just enjoying my day off with an ungrateful demon," Guy said.

I choked on my eggs. Barrett did his best not to cringe which resulted in him coughing forcefully into his arm. "Sounds like a—*hm*, good morning," he said.

Guy swiveled in his seat to look at me head-on. "Were you unsatisfied last night? Is that why I'm being punished?"

My eyes widened and one corner of his lips curled. He was not holding back, not even for Barrett's sake.

"*Dinner* was fine," I said through my teeth. If that was clarification enough for Barrett that we hadn't been promiscuous, I couldn't tell.

Guy wasn't finished. He rested his hand on the counter and crossed into my personal space. "Just fine? Should we skip the cake next time?"

Barrett had been making a slow retreat out of the kitchen but came to a dead halt when he heard that. He leapt at the fridge, opened it, and shut it again. "Cake? No, wait. Gym first. Guy, you'd share with your friends, right? Buddy-ol pal."

"Sure. It's not like she wants it," Guy said.

"I never said that—" the whine in my voice was evident, even to me, "but fine. Whatever."

"You know he makes it himself?" Barrett lit up, probably at the prospect of a subject change. "Reapers have a sweet tooth and mad baking skills. Who knew?"

"You do?" My irritation subsided for a fraction of a second while I asked Guy. As soon as I saw the smug look on his face, I was back to being annoyed. "It was fine."

Guy rewarded my bluff with a staring contest. His lips pursed like he was holding back a laugh. "I seem to remember you salivating."

He had no right making those words sound suggestive with his rumbling tone. I needed to escape before I started blushing or sweating. When I rotated my chair to face the opposite way, he stopped the movement by gripping onto the cushion. With a sharp jerk, I was brought back around until we bumped knees.

Feeling flustered, I shooed him away to squeeze through the small space between us. "Some reaper you are, acting like a four-year-old."

"*I'm* the childish one? Who stormed off?"

Barrett finally caved. He rinsed the dishes, barely, and made to leave the scene. "Uh, Zak said he'd be here but maybe he got held up. Anyway, gotta run."

I heard him putting on his shoes and made to leave as well. "Hang on! I'm coming too."

"Not waiting for Zak?" Guy asked, appearing behind me in record time.

"I'm too anxious," I said. That was the truth. I wanted to be busy, doing *something*. Having petty battles with a reaper wasn't going to cut it. If anything, Guy made me feel more anxious.

"Let's go, then," he said. The cocky nature of his tone and the glint in his eyes was a shock to my system.

"I'm going with Barrett."

Barrett had already given me an apologetic smile and disappeared. I was left with Guy and his looming presence at my back.

"The wolf wasn't assigned to you," Guy said, "I was."

My heart skipped a beat. I blamed his low, melodic voice for confusing my thoughts and making me release a loud huff. "Right. Your job."

"That's right. Mine." He'd gotten much closer. The cold that came with him felt more like a soft brush of water than a harsh blizzard. I wasn't even sure why we were still going at each other.

Guy muttered under his breath. "I haven't forgotten our promise."

The stubborn fortress I'd built against him cracked a bit. Even if he had been cryptic and vague last night, he had offered to help me. "I'm sorry," I said, "I'm just sick of weird things happening to me."

"Don't apologize. If The Necromancer really is visiting you then you're in danger. I responded hastily with no regard for your feelings."

"A reasonable reaction," I sighed, "It's weird, though. I don't understand what he wants."

Cool fingers clasped around my hand. It seemed like such a simple thing, but not to me. His friendly touch of reassurance had my chest beating violently like my heart had forgotten how to work properly. "Whatever it is, it can't be good," he said, "I'm glad he hasn't hurt you already."

That last part wasn't entirely true. Clay had gotten bold and touchy, but I didn't go into those details. I looked into the glass fixtures of Guy's eyes, losing myself in a maze of gray. Our subject was serious but I felt completely calm.

"Why do you think he's coming to me?" I asked.

"I don't know. There's a chance he saw the video…" He stopped and the muscles in his jaw flexed.

"And what?"

Guy struggled with his next words. The peace I'd been enjoying turned to something more disturbed. "What has he said to you in these dreams, exactly?" he asked.

I searched my fogged memory bank for anything profound Clay had told me. "He told me his name was Clay, then called me Princess. I'm sure it's just some stupid nickname."

The overcast colors in his eyes turned dark, threatening a thunderstorm. At least we had a name, right? Maybe EXO could use that information to track him down more easily.

It was then that Barrett suddenly re-entered the room. "Forgot my towel. Oh?"

He smiled at us, still holding hands. "Did we make up?"

Guy dropped my hand and approached the door. "Take her
with you."

"I mean, sure," Barrett hesitated.

"Where are you going?" I asked, following after Guy. He
didn't respond which got me nervous. Wasn't he the one making
a huge stink about being assigned to me? Now he was rushing
out the doors with a phone in hand. I grabbed the back of his
shirt. "Hey! Don't just leave."

"I need to fulfill my promise, quicker than planned," he said,
"Go with Barrett and stay out of trouble. Please."

My fingers slipped away when his body turned into smoke.
Every particle of him faded until nothing remained. I still had my
hand raised to where his back had been.

He was allowed to make a dramatic exit but not me?

Barrett came to stand next to me and scratched his head.
"I'm not going to pretend to know what that was about. How
much can your demon-strength lift?"

26

I did my best to keep my mind in check while Barrett helped me learn the new machines. A new experience for me. I hadn't set foot in a real gym in my life. The yoga studio Naomi had in our spare room didn't include much in the way of weight training.

What the hell was up with Guy? I didn't even say that much, but it was enough to make him leave in a hurry. We were about to have an adult conversation and everything.

Barrett stood over me while I pushed a metal bar up at him. Admittedly, all my frustration was what helped the bar move. He had to remind me to breathe a couple of times. "Not bad," he said, "This is almost how much I lift."

"You're pretty strong." I breathed out. He gripped the metal with one hand and helped me finish the last rep.

"So are you. I flopped my first exam so Max is on my ass. Being stronger can make a life or death difference."

I remained flat on the bench even after he'd secured the bar in the placeholder above my head. "Zak said I should get stronger before using anything magical."

"Makes sense. People underestimate that kind of power and what it does to your body. My first wolf shift *sucked* because I didn't listen. Should've stretched more like my mom said, but I thought yoga was for losers. I do the *splits* now!"

We were in the same building they assigned our suits but all the training equipment had been returned. I didn't have Guy but Barrett was a good buffer from the other people at the gym. No one gave us dirty looks, and if they did, it didn't last long. He stood taller and broader than most, looking more threatening than I did.

No one would try killing me in front of so many witnesses. Hopefully.

Barrett had said we were there to meet up with Max but I hadn't seen him yet. Not until I wanted a drink and then I spotted him with his weights. His low and angry grunts might as well have been snarls.

I made the mistake of catching his eye. There was a moment of blood-pumping unease. Max didn't like me but he was no purifier. And besides, he had been too busy carrying the weight of our entire team by rescuing Jarmiel during the games.

He wasn't my man.

The wolf moved to a large mat in the back of the room where other trainees sparred like we would on a normal day. Max's presence made them scurry like a flock of spooked doves.

Geez. I hurried toward the fountains and was surprised to see Darren there. The vampire watched the water flow in an arch shape. Could he even drink it?

When he sensed me he swept brown strands from his face. "Oh. Hey."

"Hi." My reply sounded just as awkward as the tension around us. The last time I saw him, he had offered me to his sister. Mallory must have had other plans that day that didn't involve sweating at the gym. *Thank the gods.*

"About yesterday," he started, "I was out of line."

I hadn't expected an apology, although he didn't look torn up about it.

"Thanks, I guess," I said.

Darren rubbed the back of his neck, speaking to my toes instead of my face. "Listen. Aiden and Mallory are like… recovering addicts. I know I said she could help and that might be true but I was just trying to prevent another episode. I thought she'd calm down."

An addiction would explain the crazed look in her eye when she attacked me. Shouldn't Mallory have gone feral around Zak, then? She was the one getting tickled by our scent. I never noticed any such eagerness during training, though.

"Does she have episodes often?" I asked.

"Not lately." Darren's voice fell even softer. I'd always thought that an addiction to blood came with being a vampire. Before vampires came out, the ones with less self control fed violently, killing their targets. Did certain blood types give vampires a high, like catnip?

The Blaxill family history wasn't my place but I asked, "Is that normal for any vampire?"

"Depends on the blood," he said, ending on a solemn note, "Don't let my brother bite you…"

"Didn't plan on it. But why?" At least, I hadn't been tempted to until yesterday.

"Just don't."

Darren wandered off with a worn face. All three of the Blaxill kids were so strangely different that it was easy to forget they were related. I wondered then if what Darren's siblings went through impacted *his* particular diet.

Maybe he didn't want to end up like them.

I was finally about to enjoy my cool refreshment when something soft bumped into my heels. My eyes went to the bear hugging my ankles.

"Tori?" I doubted that she came to lift weights with her plushy arms.

Her girlish joy was missing from her voice. The buttons on her eyes morphed from their forever, round shape to reflect her concern. "What are you doing here?" she asked, "Guy's not with you?"

I did my best to take her seriously as her whispering became more urgent. "No, he took off mysteriously."

"Jess, you need to get out of here."

It was then I noticed a few heads from the weight machines turning in our direction. The group kept glancing at us but also down in the middle of their circle. Screens sat in their hands. Everyone had a phone or was looking over the shoulder of another. I could hear the sounds of the Ghoul attack from where I stood.

They were watching *my* video.

Again.

How had it not been taken down?

"Uh-oh…" Tori mumbled. Both of us jolted when we heard one voice roaring over the others. A pair of thick shoulders and fiery, blue eyes came charging at us.

No. Just me.

"Uh-oh," I said in agreement.

"What do we do?" Tori clung tighter to my calves.

"What're *you* scared of? You're made of cotton balls." When I turned, Max's iconic scowl had already reached critical levels. Whatever his anger was about, he came in hot. I nudged Tori away with my leg before she got trampled on.

"Hey, Max." I did my best to brace for his dominant impact. Everyone else closed in, making the situation a million times worse.

"What the hell are you up to, demon?" Max asked.

"I—" But he cut me off. He grabbed me by the arms and pulled me to his face. A puff of hot air assaulted my face. I should've been more scared, but I was too bewildered by the sensation of his grip.

It felt like my skin was on fire.

The time he'd caught me sleepwalking had been similar. He was hot to the touch, but what I experienced felt… *explosive*. Max had intense spirit energy, which suited him. My body responded immediately to the overflow of hot rage.

I wanted to devour it all.

The teeth he bore at me made a brief retreat. Could Max sense something strange happening with me too? Even stranger was my focus on his lips. I couldn't look away. It hurt when I dragged my eyeballs back up.

A different kind of pull called to me that felt as natural as breathing. Maybe it wasn't *him* that I found appealing. Just his energy. His scorching, wild fury…

Max snapped out of his trance but I remained in mine; stuck in his orbit.

"Is this a joke to you?" he asked.

I blinked. "What is?"

"Quit playing stupid." Max's grip would've broken the skin if I were human.

I used my strength to push him back, rescuing my poor arms. "Touch me again, you'll regret it."

Not a bluff.

Max laughed darkly. His pupils dilated. "Yeah? Have you been waiting for us to let our guard down before making your move?"

"*What* are you talking about?"

"Sure. Keep acting like a useless freak when you're capable of *that*." Max flung one arm toward the others with their phones. "What else are you hiding?"

Tori pushed her way through the sea of legs in her tiny, plush form. I still wasn't sure how her ghost form worked, but it seemed like she was stuck as a bear for now. Which meant very little help for me.

Barrett had a much easier time getting bodies to move. He plowed through the small crowd with his shoulders. His eyes were large and glossy as he stared between the two of us. "Max. Don't do this."

"You and me. On the mat." Max ignored him, not breaking eye contact.

A challenge. For some reason, the idea excited me. More than it should have. My pulse sounded like the drums of war, fueling my sudden itch for a brawl. "You have the wrong idea," I said.

"Show me then."

No one outwardly protested; fighting on the mat being socially more acceptable as opposed to an abrupt attack. He could beat the shit out of me now that it was a fair fight. I'd avoided sparring with him but I knew how he fought. No defense, only offense. Fast. Ruthless.

I followed behind him like we were walking the gallows. Barrett said if I ever beat him in a fight that he'd respect me. *If* I beat him. The outcome could get him off my back, but Max was already a peacekeeper with more training.

I outran him before… He wasn't invincible.

I felt an animalistic surge when Max chucked his black shirt away. *So much skin.* Too many vulnerable spots. He wasn't even trying to protect himself from me. My fingers twitched, like eager little knives ready to cut into his soul.

Gods… I silenced the outrageous urges in my head. How was I supposed to focus? Did I let my demon instincts get the better of me?

I could win, at the risk of killing him.

Max paced slowly in front of me, eyes scanning me and likely searching for a weak spot. He'd rescued Jarmiel on his own during the game, proving he was able to handle every peacekeeper and trainee who came his way. I was in for it.

His voice lowered and I shivered. "What was the other night? Are you and The Necromancer best pals?"

I was even less prepared for him that time. He sprang forward, feet never touching the ground until he reached me. A second later and I was pinned on the floor like a dead frog ready to be dissected. The impact was impressive; like he'd built up enough force to break through the ground. He trapped my wrists on either side of my head with his large hands.

"Max!" Barrett called his friend. Again, Max ignored him. His focus was on me, and potentially setting me on fire with his rage.

"I know it's all an act. Just admit it," Max said, and his canines extended. More of his harsh breathing blew the loose hair around my face. I could feel an intense heat radiating from his chest and from his palms. An irritated flush covered my skin like I'd baked in the sun for too long.

Dizzy with power, I spotted thick hairs sprouting from his arms. Was he about to shift?

"Yeah, I'm a demon but you *knew* that. So, what's your actual problem?" I asked.

His nails broke the surface of the mat, further securing us in place. I hissed, feeling the sharp points threatening my flesh too. Like many times before, I tried using my legs to save me, but when I kicked up, he slammed his knee down on my thigh. The force and strain on my leg almost had me in tears.

"Some random demon doesn't use magic like that," he said, "I'm sick of you getting overlooked because Zak's a pushover."

Barrett broke from the crowd and put a hand on Max's shoulder. "Seriously, Max. Let her go."

"Get *back*."

Even I retreated at his bark. Again, it didn't look like Barrett could oppose his friend. He bit his lip and dropped his arm. I was beginning to understand their relationship more. Mallory made mention of Max's alpha position before but since it was only him and Barrett, not a whole pack, I thought it'd been a joke. Max may actually be Barrett's alpha.

Damn werewolf hierarchy.

Max was back to demanding. "No more games. Show me what you really are."

He released my wrists. I could tell by the group's lack of effort in interfering that their curiosity was shared. As demon hunters, they had every right to want answers but I had a feeling nothing was going to satisfy Max.

The muscles in his arms flexed, pushing his veins to the surface. I heard joints popping. His ragged breaths came from somewhere deeper. More hair grew from areas that were normally smooth. With my back still on the mat, I used the brief moment of freedom to make my move. I had more power thanks to Max and rolled him off my legs. He was quick to recover and nearly had me pinned a second time.

I was able to catch his hands that time and I thought my fingerprints would melt off. It was like he had an endless supply of manic vitality, pumping and pumping through his veins. The longer I held him, the stronger I became. I pushed us into a standing position again.

His foot slid back.

With a growl, he twisted our arms to the side and caught me with his shoulder. I flew over his back. Tori cried out somewhere when my back hit the mat. No time for pain. I knew he'd be on me in a second. My swift turn over narrowly saved me from a slash of his claws.

"Quit running and fight me already!" he said. Draining him of energy didn't seem to slow him down at all. His anger served as his fuel as much as it had me.

I targeted Max's mouth again, and the pages from Jarmiel's books flipped aggressively in my mind. *The Kingdom of Lust…* *Succubi…* They were all part of me. I felt it now with my entire being. I imagined what a great incubus or succubus on a battle-field would've done. Using hellish wings to dive at him from the sky, tearing his flesh with whips soaked in hellfire. I didn't have either of those things. Never wanted them…

I wanted it all.

Now.

"Ignoring me?" Max scoffed at my silent pondering. His body had gotten hairier and claws sharper but something was possessing me as well; a different kind of monster.

"Why not?" My response caused him to go deathly quiet. "I've done *nothing* to you unless you're still butthurt about the night you failed to arrest me. Sorry about your ego, but get over it."

I struck first that time. Someone who only wanted to attack would leave their defenses wide open, and Max didn't disappoint. I spotted several target spots left exposed, ones Zak kindly pointed out to me during training. My fists flew to the first, reaching his stomach and then his chin.

His dazed face mirrored the surprise I felt, but quickly vanished behind new aggression. Max's massive arms made low *whooshing* sounds as they soared around my body, missing me every time by a hair. I punched him again in his stone-hard jaw, causing him to let up.

"We could've just talked but no, you'd rather act like an animal." I paused to catch my breath and delivered my next sentence with an icy punch that would make Mallory proud. "Come on, then. But we both know you're too slow."

Max's anger turned a shade of maniacal. He smiled. If bloodlust was a smell, it covered him and suffocated me. "Animal, huh?"

I wanted to take back everything I said but it was too late.

Shit.

The next sound from Max's core rumbled my bones. He'd be harder to touch once he fully transformed and was covered in fur. I blocked his next hit that had only been a distraction. My legs were swept out from under me and the full weight of his body crushed me into the padded floor. The rips in the fabric left from his claws scratched my face, as if preparing me for what I was about to look like.

Heat. Buzzing. His skin flooded mine with more of his internal wrath. I was drunk off it or in so much pain from being squashed that I was losing myself. As soon as I focused on the pain, I healed. Numbed.

I shut off the part of my brain that allowed common sense; succumbing to a dark and carnal drive. It should've frightened me how easily I was able to do so, but I felt nothing.

"Show. Me," he seethed, "Show them how twisted your soul really is."

He really wants to see? Fine.

Before Max could do anything else, I grabbed both sides of his head, using his big ears as handles. I had to be quick before he flung me off.

"The hell?" He grunted, but I shut him up with my own mouth. There was nothing romantic about it as I dove in for the kiss. There was heat and passion, sure. I tasted something truly delicious that compared to nothing I'd had before. It came from his potent fury. Flames danced on my tongue and sparked through my veins.

"Jess, stop!"

I tossed Max off me and he dropped like a rock. The connection was severed. At first, it annoyed me that someone interrupted my feeding. Who had gotten in my way? I could tell I'd almost gotten to the best part; like the tart, candied cherry hidden in a thick, chocolate shell.

Then, reality came rushing back.

I felt sick. *What have I done?*

"Everyone get out of the way!" Tori screeched and her bear slipped through the final obstacle of legs. Voices muttered in shock while others laughed at Max's defeat. I looked down at the werewolf at my feet.

He wasn't conscious yet but struggled to keep his head up. His eyes fluttered; weak and heavy like his breathing. My body's response to what I'd done was thrilled. *Rejuvenated.* I felt more like a machine than organic matter, running on electricity.

No. A lightning storm.

But inside, I fell apart like a castle made of sand.

"Are you okay?" Tori asked while gazing up at me. She had to see Max next to her. He groaned and coughed like he had the worst cold of his life. Shouldn't she be concerned about *him*? He was the one on the ground dying.

Dying.

Panic seized my chest. Something else happened to me at the same time. My heart felt like I'd injected it with a syringe full of caffeine. I didn't want it anymore or even craved it, but it kept coming.

Barrett approached us on the mat and crouched by his friend, slipping a hand under his neck to hold him up. *It's happening again.* I wiped my hands on my pant legs, trying to scrub murder from my skin. The murmuring grew louder along with a ringing in my head. I grasped the hairs closest to my ears and used them to muffle the noise.

Tori hopped onto Barrett's back to gain some height. "Everyone stay back," she said, "Give them some air."

She was right. Everyone needed to go.

They all needed to run.

"Jess?"

Run from me.

My eyes shot up. Guy came rushing forward. I didn't know where he came from but then, he had a knack for showing up at random. I drowned in my worry, but his face brought air to my lungs. Once he'd gotten close enough, he raised his hands as if calming a tiger.

"It's okay," he said, "He's going to be fine."

But all I saw was Peter, not Max, writhing there. I blocked the vision from my eyes by hiding behind my hands. That only

made my imagination worsen. Max threatened me first, but I'd
gone too far.

Barrett asked something. Guy shushed him but I hadn't heard
anyway. Everyone wanted to help Max, but the closer they got,
the more of their energy I could sense. No one touched me but I
could *feel* all of them.

"Stay away!" I urged. The hairs on my arms stood on end
like I rubbed a latex balloon. The sound of crinkling paper came
from somewhere inside my head. I could feel movement like ants
crawling around my eardrums.

"Jess, he's *fine*," Guy said, creeping forward regardless of my
warning. I couldn't see his truth, only the version that lived in
my head.

Monster. I'm a monster. He's dead.

And I enjoyed killing him…

I pressed myself further into the wall, desperate for them all
to go away.

My forehead broke into a sweat. I'd always taken minimal
energy from Zak or Guy, but now, I felt like I was a hot teapot
spilling over. Something was about to happen, something I wasn't
sure I could control.

And then, darkness sprang from my hands with a loud hiss.

The malevolent cloud walled me off from the others. My
fingernails blackened, and streaks of light reached my elbows.
Golden lights danced within an onyx galaxy. Popping sounds
bounced harsh echoes off the gym walls.

My skin split open at my bicep and I saw red. It burned and
bled while something else forced its way out. Dark matter wriggled free from my meaty vessel, lashing about in every direction.
I fell to my knees, hoping it would stop or aim low enough that
it wouldn't hit anyone.

I heard the same sickening pop of my flesh opening somewhere on my thigh. At the rate I was going, my body would explode
all over the walls. Through the less saturated sections of black, I

watched Guy drag Max away. He dodged another strike from the darkness and snatched Tori as well. "Jess, you have to stop, now!"

"I-I don't know how," I stated but it was a plea. The darkness had no leash. It continued to flail around like a wild beast. I pressed my fingers into the hard floor, wishing I could grip onto it for dear life and bury the next wave of attacks.

Like a call from heaven, Zak's voice rang out. "What's going on?"

I wanted to cry. *Zak.* He'd finally see the grave mistake he'd made in bringing me to EXO. I carefully lifted my head to see, but then, the angel was whipped by one of the erratic forms of matter. He shook his hand like it had actually hurt him.

"Everyone, *out*," he ordered. Lisha came with him. The dragoness unsheathed a pair of ebony wings from her shoulder blades. Her violet eyes observed my chaos, attentive and calculative like she was looking for an opening.

"Can you hear me in there, Jess?" Zak was emitting a glow that allowed me to see him more clearly. "Hey. Let's get this under control, yeah?"

He sounded like his usual self. As if I wasn't currently blowing up in front of him. I shook my head. "I'm trying…"

"You need to breathe." Lisha stepped in. "Big breaths for me. Count the seconds in your head. Do it with me, kid. One. Two…"

I didn't realize how bad my breathing was until I tried to count and it took several attempts to stop hyperventilating. It seemed to be helping. The matter drew into me, but the occasional spark of light still jumped at random.

Guy followed the cloud as it circled tighter around me.

"Guy, I *can't*—" I insisted but that didn't stop him.

"Reach for me."

Blood pooled around my knees from the openings created by the matter. Gravity felt like an anchor and the only thing keeping me from getting everyone swept up in the darkness. If I moved, I could get swept away.

Guy stood his ground while my cloud swirled threateningly around him. His hair blew free from his short ponytail and I saw a thin pink line appear on his cheek.

If he was going to endure…

I should too.

With trembling fingers, I found his hand. The cool dread of Death felt like ice over a fire; countering the hell thriving in my blood. Slowly but surely, my breathing slowed. The dark matter warped and retreated inward until it became one with my body again.

A single golden spark let me know it wasn't gone forever.

Guy caught my head as I fell. He lowered me down but kept his fingers between my hair and the cold floor. Everything felt heavy, including my eyelids. I got a quick glance at the sizzling, black markings along the walls before my eyes closed for good.

27

Not dead yet. Just asleep. *I think.*

I wasn't sure for how long, though. Wherever my body ended up, it was cozy. I vaguely remembered the sensation of being wrapped in someone's arms. The arms I felt now were an illusion; just a wool blanket.

When I shifted my position, the platform beneath me creaked.

A bed. Not mine from the dorms, though. Something about it felt wrong. Too stiff. My brows came together after I felt an awful headache split my brain open. "Ow…"

I groaned. Hot tears clouded my eyes. The memories of what I'd done came rushing back. Swirling blackness roared like an ocean in my skull. I was reminded of the pain from my body wanting to break apart. My muscles continued to ache but were back in their rightful places.

The vortex of clashing energies left me with uneasiness and awe. There was nothing uniform about it. It had been grander, more beautiful and terrible, than what I thought a demon's power should be.

Oh, gods… My stomach twisted in uncomfortable knots.

I kissed Max.

That woke me more than the headache. I sat upright in my mystery bed. A mix of fear and nausea washed over me. Max was a werewolf and stronger than humans. *Yeah. He's fine.* Guy even said so.

Max...

My involuntary shudder alerted me to the wires in my arm. Where the hell was I?

I had a monitor beside me, along with a tray and cup of water. The awkward gown I wore was more like an oversized t-shirt that didn't quite reach my knees. If I'd been taken to an infirmary of sorts, that would make the most sense, but I seemed to be the only patient in a very large room.

The machine beeped. Faster. Faster. I felt my insides squirm again, this time in awareness of my situation. There was only one door that appeared too dense and fortified to be a simple passageway. No windows either. The only window that let me see out of that room was a rectangle cut out of the white walls. I imagined the glass was just as difficult to break through.

Oh, GODS.

Had I been quarantined?

My breathing came out in pathetic whimpers. No, not my most impressive moment. But I was scared. Hurt. I felt betrayed, somehow. Were they keeping me there temporarily? Who had decided to put me there?

"Jess. Don't panic."

I gasped when a voice over a loud intercom introduced itself. It was Zak's voice. There was movement behind the glass barrier and I spotted the angel. His peacekeeper uniform hugged his body like a darkly clad executioner.

"What's going on?" I asked.

His sigh made the intercom go fuzzy. "Sorry for the shock. We haven't experienced your power like that before. We just want to make sure everything is under control."

The incident must've been worse than I thought, and I'd had pretty negative thoughts about it. At least it didn't sound like he wanted to keep me there forever. Could the walls truly stop something like light or dark matter from breaking through?

"It'll hold. For now," Zak said after catching my examination of the room, "I'm really sorry, Jess. I made promises and haven't been good at keeping them, but I'll make it up to you."

"It's okay…" What else was there to say, really? I was dangerous and they had to protect themselves. Hell, I thought I was going to accidentally destroy myself too. "No one got hurt, did they?" I asked.

"No one's dead. The gym might be closed for a while," he said, "You healed nicely. That's good."

"But someone was hurt?"

Zak paused. "Barrett, but he's already wrapped up and back at the dorms."

Not that I wanted *anyone* to have been a victim in the crossfire, but it just had to be Barrett? One of the only people, aside from Tori, who had been nice to me, no questions asked.

Zak placed a hand on the glass. "I should've been there sooner."

Someone I couldn't hear walked into the same room he was in. A peacekeeper. Zak responded to them with a head turn. He covered the mic he used to speak with me while answering the new person.

His beautiful eyes flickered with alarm.

"What's going on?" I asked, feeling useless in my hamster cage.

Zak spoke back into the mic. "I have to leave. He's on the move. We're going to catch him this time."

My heart gave me a jolt. I was supposed to tell him about Clay. About my dreams!

More peacekeepers beckoned silently to Zak. Their faces furrowed, not showing humor while waiting around. I tried leaving my bed but accidentally yanked the IV out of my vein. "W—*Ow.* Wait, Zak!"

It was a bad idea to start running while dizzy but I reached the glass without falling over. Zak ignored the voices behind him and gave me a sad smile. His eyes went straight to my arm. "Careful. You've been asleep a while. Clove's gonna be pissed you messed with your cords."

"He's been—" I stopped. "Wait, how long?"

"Days. Under Clove's watch."

Days? His eyes remained on me while his body fidgeted, responding to the peacekeepers stirring behind him. Telling him about my dreams would only waste more time. They were going to capture him right then. I would only slow him down.

Zak searched my face for the rest of my thoughts, but I let him go.

"It can wait," I said, "I can wait."

He gave me half a nod. "I'll come back. I promise."

Before I could say anything more, he set the mic on its desk and left. I was alone in my box. An hour went by, maybe two. I didn't expect Zak back for many hours but wasn't sure what to do in the meantime.

No one came. If they did, they were watching from somewhere I couldn't see. Something wasn't sitting well with me. A gnawing feeling in my gut kept telling me to be cautious. The isolated space hadn't helped.

Zak said he'd come back.

After what felt like half a day, I lay back on the bed since the only other option was the floor. Why hadn't Clove come by? It was like I'd been left there to rot. The longer it took to hear from another person, the worse my worries became.

Maybe they didn't know what to do with me and were too afraid to let me out.

How many other criminals with unruly powers had been held in the same box? I wondered what Zak and Jarmiel had talked about since the incident. Raguel likely had some choice words on the matter, if he was involved in any of those conversations. Which I knew he would've been.

I tried shutting my brain up. No use going crazy after *one* day of quarantine. I needed more willpower than that if I was ever going to control my power.

"Jess. Jess, it's me."

Spectacular.

Already hearing voices.

I rolled over and pretended not to have noticed anything. That worked for a whole second. My blanket lifted slightly before falling again. I must've broken a record on how quickly someone could go insane.

"Stop moping around and listen to me." The whispering voice practically screamed. That time I heard exactly who it was. Tori was completely invisible but her shrill tone was much clearer that time, as she yelled in my ear.

"Tori? How?"

"Shh." I could sense her aura moving about but saw nothing. Impressive, I thought. She hadn't come as herself or in her bear replacement. That meant she could travel in and out of walls freely like a true ghost.

"What are you doing here?" I pressed again.

"Make it look like you aren't talking to anyone. Their sensors pick up fluctuations of energy, but luckily, they'll just assume it's you. I hope." Tori let out a trembling breath. "We need to get you out of here! I'm still surprised you didn't leave after my message."

"Your message?" I used my best ventriloquist impression, which I'd never attempted before. When that flopped, I resorted to covering my lips with my hand instead.

"Yeah. In your room. I thought it'd at least spook you like in horror movies." she said.

It clicked.

"You seasoned my carpet?"

"I was going to tell you the other night but Guy stayed by your door all night. I thought he'd hear us talking. Having a room close to yours helped keep him off my scent, just barely."

"Why are you avoiding Guy?" I asked. If she had wanted to relay a message like that, why would she hide it from him?

There was a long pause. I couldn't see what face she made so I just sat there.

"I heard them talking. About you." Tori's softening voice haunted me. "You're not who you think you are."

"What does that mean?"

"I know you're part demon but it's more than that, it's—" she paused, making a questionable huffing sound mixed with a sob, "They think your father is a demon *lord*."

The words hit me like a punch in the gut. They played again and again, smacking the back wall of my brain until it finally cracked. Demon lords. Rulers of all kingdoms in Hell. Ultimately responsible for the suffering of humans, and even other demons.

I continued to stare at the air, pretending it was her face. "I don't understand."

"I don't either, but they aren't letting you out of here."

The world tilted on its axis. That couldn't be right. Or could it? What information did the angels find that I hadn't?

"Guy was almost certain I was something else," I said.

"You have to stay away from him," she said, "He was the one who told them. We need to *go*."

My head shifted back and forth on its own. If Guy had any thoughts of gutting my soul, why hadn't he? He brought me dinner. *Cake*, even. Had that been my last meal?

I recalled the chocolate frosting now with spite.

"We don't have tons of time," Tori's voice reminded me. "I spied on Faris while everyone was questioned. He's the *obvious* person to come after you. Anyway, he was talking to his friends, saying that the angels… well…"

I was impressed yet again by her ghostly sneaking about.

"Was it him?"

She hesitated. "Who shot the bolt? I don't know but probably. He claims Raguel wants you gone. It sounds ridiculous since Zak is so nice, but after what I heard Guy say I'm not sure of anything."

"Did Guy actually say my dad's a demon lord?" I asked, waiting for her to continue with a throbbing heart.

"He met with Zak, Jarmiel, Lisha, and Raguel. I was only able to hear Guy confirm what he discovered, and Raguel say, '*She doesn't leave this facility. We're putting a stop to this,* now,' before I got caught." Tori huffed and I imagined her pouting face. "Guy senses me too easily, but I don't think anyone suspected me."

Tori had a lot to say but spoke rapidly to condense the time. I replayed her message, desperately inventing scenarios in which I wasn't a demon lord's daughter. That they didn't need to "put an end" to me.

"Jess?" Tori sounded sad but I couldn't see what expression she made. "I know what I'm saying isn't nice but I'm really scared for you."

I was too. My aunt had been right about the angels. I'd let my guard down with Zak. Although, I also had a hard time believing Tori would suddenly oppose Guy. "Why are you helping me?"

"Well, *geez*. I thought we were friends."

Her palms must've smacked the bed because it shook from impact. "I think it's stupid for you to be killed for no reason. Even *angels* shouldn't have a say in that. You're healthy and you're kind. Sure, you scared the pants off everyone when you took the building down, but—"

"I did *what*?"

"It wasn't a big one, just the gym."

We both shut up when someone else appeared behind the glass. Tori hitched a breath and I suddenly felt her absence, like a warm body had been next to me the whole time.

She couldn't leave. Not after all she'd just said!

What was I supposed to do? I turned my attention to the new visitor. Clove walked in wearing her white lab coat and delicate wings pinched behind her back. Her straight frown didn't reveal if I was about to be executed or not.

"I apologize for not coming sooner," she said, using the same mic that Zak had, "I see you've taken the liberty of removing your IVs."

"Sorry." That sounded more curt than I intended.

Clove's lips parted like she had planned to continue promptly, but my response seemed to slow her down. "I realize this situation isn't ideal. You have to understand the position we're in."

"I'm not sure, actually. Am I being quarantined?" I'd only met her the one other time but I remembered her being direct. Unless she'd been instructed to stay secretive.

"This is for everyone's protection, including yours," Clove said, "Please, trust me on that."

"How long do I have to stay?" I asked.

"As long as it takes. Can you describe your current state? Any dizziness, anxiousness, or pain?"

I told her about the initial pain after waking up. Most of my symptoms, aside from a slight buzzing in my nerves, had gone. In fact, I felt *empty*, like a lemon peel trying to recover after being squeezed. That usually happened right before the headaches and blackouts.

"You need to eat," Clove said, and I don't think she meant a sandwich, "I wanted to wait until Zakiel returned but in the meantime, I can provide you with some protein."

Her behavior confused me. Why feed the animal before its slaughter? Unless she didn't know what the angels wanted me for either. "Can I ask you something?"

Clove's demeanor was an impenetrable fortress. She didn't blink but I did catch one of her antennas shivering. I thought she was going to evade my questions with a professional-sounding excuse.

Instead, she said, "Sure."

"What tests were you running while I was asleep?"

She took a moment to lift the glasses from her face and fold them up into her coat pocket. "This is unusual, even for me. Any information I have has been heavily restricted. I'm afraid we'll have to wait for Zakiel's return before speaking further."

"Why? It's *my* body." Wasn't there a patient and doctor confidentiality rule or something? Did Zak have a say in everything I did? I felt a fire in my chest and not the good kind.

Her eyes flickered with something other than complacency. A dark aura filled the room. The shadows from the corners crept closer to me. When I looked down at my hands, the backs of my fingernails had become purple.

I took several breaths. Nothing else was in there with me. Not even Tori.

I'm doing this.

"I understand your frustrations," Clove spoke more carefully, "but in order to figure out exactly what's going on we have to be patient, and not let our emotions get the better of us."

I would have silently agreed before but Tori's voice in my head kept telling me to run. Would Zak really let them kill me, or do the deed himself? Criminal executions were only performed by angels but those were rare and for the lowest of the low.

"This isn't right," I said.

She sighed and her slender shoulders bobbed. "I'll be back with a meal for you. Please, be patient with us, Jess."

I wasn't. Waiting around was worse the second time, but I kept myself in check so the darkness wouldn't act creepy again. I walked each corner of the walls so many times, I'd lost count. Where had Tori gone?

Really, I just needed clarification on whether I was awaiting my own death or not. It seemed unfair. Would I even be allowed to speak for myself? Even if my dad was somehow a demon lord, it wasn't like I knew about it or planned to act accordingly.

Which one, though…?

The Lord of Lust? Had Jarmiel been trying to tell me that all along with his haunted texts? Maybe he'd been trying to figure it out and hoped the answers would expose themselves if he let me search for them.

What if I truly was an unholy and dangerous thing? Was it right for me to fight back? I didn't want to die. That part of me was too selfish.

After roughly forty minutes, Clove hadn't returned, but a certain ghost had.

"Jess…"

Her voice was music to my ears. "Tori, thank the gods."

"Faris is coming," she said.

My body turned to stone. I don't know what I was expecting, but it wasn't that. "Faris? I thought Clove—"

"Yeah, I sort of locked her in her office and stole her keycard."

Before I could comprehend what she'd just said, the door to my room made a loud *clunk* as it unbolted itself. It propped open just an inch, tempting me to flee.

Tori manifested her girlish, physical body and waited for me on the other side. Her sparkly eyes dimmed as she waved to me in earnest. "Come on."

T ori and I made our way out of the infirmary. Any security cameras would have seen me already, so we had to move fast.

At my request, Tori remained invisible. It was my feeble attempt at saving her from getting in trouble. I stole a lab coat to wear over my hospital gown, but doubted I looked any less suspicious. "Faris is coming? Like right this second?"

"He is," she said.

"Does he have nothing better to do?"

"He's a die-hard purifier. Killing demons is the 'best' thing to do."

Tori breezed through walls, doors, and floors, making sure we weren't about to run into anyone on our way out. We decided against the elevators for now, since we had no control should anyone stop the ride or meet us on the way down. Unfortunately, that meant lots of stairs.

Inside, many of the lights were off but the sky outside was full of stars. It must have been late enough in the evening that the science crew wasn't wandering the halls. All seemed quiet outside as well. Too quiet.

Our passage to the stairwell and other locked exits were hardly an obstacle thanks to Tori's stolen keycard and scouting. The escape was going smoother than I'd anticipated but the big question remained: where could I go from here?

Not back home. Anyone with a brain would know to look there. Thanks to being secretive, Naomi and I didn't have friends who would take me in either. No relatives that I knew of, besides one of the rulers of Hell, apparently.

"I don't know," Tori admitted when I asked, "What about your aunt?"

What about her, indeed? My things were still in the dorms. Not that there was anything I couldn't replace. It wasn't like my communication stone had been able to reach my aunt, anyway. Clothes would've been helpful, though. If I ran out of EXO looking like a mental patient, I'd be captured in seconds.

Once we reached the third floor, all light that didn't come from the moon went out. The minimal sounds of electricity wiring the building settled into silence. Call me crazy, but a power outage seemed too coincidental.

Tori took shape and crouched by a window. Her small brows squeezed together. She gestured for me to lower my head before approaching. I brought my eyes up just enough to see what we were looking at.

Three men in purifier uniforms, adorned with white trimming, walked purposefully toward the building. The tallest one, with curly hair, and wide-set eyes, took the lead. I'd had only one encounter with the guy but I knew who he was right away.

"Faris…" I muttered.

He dragged an air of self-importance with him, along with his posse. I wanted to scoff. How ridiculous that he saw me as someone so deserving of death when he looked like a pompous flounder. But then, I remembered the holy weapon used in an attempt to kill me. I had to expect more from him.

"They shouldn't be able to wander the building freely," Tori mulled, "Then again, neither should we. I knew we were short-staffed tonight but now the power's out?"

"You can get around those guys, can't you?" I asked. It would be difficult for me, but evading a few purifiers should've been okay for her.

Her mouth made a line. "For the most part. They're trained to handle spirits, though. Even if mine isn't necessarily evil, they could trap me inside of a blessed item if we're not careful."

So, ghosts did have weaknesses.

"We need a better plan," I said.

Tori leaned against the wall and silently clicked her shoes together. "Okay. Um. Well, since no one's here, should we be able to walk out the gates?"

"What about this witch hunt Faris put together?"

"Just run really fast."

"You didn't think this through, huh?"

"Shut up." Tori puffed out her cheeks. "You're alive. *That's* my plan."

I smiled. Everything sucked but at least she cared.

"I really don't think Zak would sick Faris on you," she continued, "That coward is probably acting alone with the angels absent."

The truth was neither of us had enough information. All we knew was that purifiers were coming and there was no one to stop them. I could outrun Faris, or endure a fight or two if necessary, but I wanted to leave there without any casualties. EXO could call me a monster, but I wasn't about to prove them right.

I didn't want Faris to feel validated at my execution later.

"Come on," Tori said, "These stairs should take us to a back entrance."

"Wait." I stopped.

Someone was coming.

They turned the corner before either of us could hatch a plan. Two bodies appeared at the end of the hallway. We just saw Faris entering the building, so it couldn't have been him, but these two were also dressed in purifier suits.

Tori backed into me but hadn't vanished yet. "How did they…"

The purifiers stalked toward us with excitement in their eyes. *Gross.* Maybe I hadn't gotten to the thrill-seeking portion of training, but they looked too happy to have cornered some girls in the hallway.

"Come quietly, demon," one of them said, "We can put an end to this peacefully and without pain, unless you prefer the alternative, in which we will not hesitate to send you back to Hell in agony."

Was he being for real? It was like all purifiers spoke like they rehearsed for a play. Or perhaps that specific dialogue was reserved for special people like me.

"I don't see an official order on you," Tori countered, "You creeps have no grounds to touch her."

"The salvation of the world has a flexible set of rules."

We flinched in unison when the other drew a crossbow from behind his back. He whispered to the silver arrow until it illuminated the dark hallway. I looked around but the only way out was back the way we came.

"Get out of here, Tori," I said, hoping she would vanish, and then ran back toward the stairs. They would only take me up but staying in a narrow hallway with holy weapons sounded like instant death.

I heard the purifiers' heavy footsteps coming but I had the upper hand with speed, especially since I didn't have my own heavy suit dragging me down. Reaching the fourth floor again, I considered a new and more desperate plan. Jumping out a window? That would suck. Healing broken bones could take too much time, not to mention wear me out. I wasn't sure I had any energy to heal, anyway.

Or the elevator; a lot less dangerous than falling. So long as no one stopped me along the way.

I slowed my run to a fast walk and tried to stay quiet. They weren't supernaturals so I didn't have to worry about heightened hearing. The purifier's voices argued somewhere below about where to go next. Good.

The clock of a ranged weapon nearby alerted me in enough time to dodge. A bolt of light whizzed past my head and shattered a window.

Fudge!

Fuck.

Just how many of them were there?

"Here," I heard a female purifier shout, "She's making a run for it!"

I was, and I was about to pass the elevator but it opened at the same moment. It shouldn't have been working. Not without power. Another purifier emerged from the doors carrying a skinny blade with him. A faint light followed him out, almost like he had powered the thing himself.

He took one look at me and frowned. "Absurd that they make monsters so pretty. Your gods are truly cruel."

Pervert.

"Just get out of my way," I said.

That made him smirk, and his glowing blade swung forward anyway. I twirled out of range, bumping into the wall and pushing off of it to evade the next blow. With him facing away from me, I went for the back of his knees, bringing him crashing down.

"I said—*ah*!" I thought he would take longer to gather himself after face-planting, but he swept his weapon backward and sliced my palm open. My skin hissed like sizzling breakfast bacon.

"You must perish, *demon*," he said, "For the good of us all."

"*Ha.*" I felt acid on my tongue. "Screw you, then."

I didn't hold back that time. With a kick, my bare foot was still able to break his wrist midair before his blade came down again. He cried, but my fist to his gut cut him off. I lifted the bastard over my shoulder and threw him back where I knew the chick purifier would be coming next.

She found us just in time to catch his solid body with her face. The force made them collide with the wall. Breathing heavily, I checked to see if the elevator had any juice left. He must have powered it with light magic somehow. The doors opened after a click of the button and I stepped inside, keeping an eye on their motionless bodies.

What is wrong with you people?

Sure enough, he'd left an illuminated key in a slot below the buttons. Convenient for me. The ride down was quiet, but I knew what awaited outside. I hoped Tori was okay and no one captured her.

My hand hurt like a bitch.

I gritted my teeth, too afraid to examine the damage. I remembered Aiden's wound and how holy weapons didn't allow people like us to heal. At least it'd only been my hand. Could've been my head.

Had the angels used Faris as a means to dispose of me like some weirdly organized conspiracy? It sure seemed that way, seeing as no one was making an effort to stop any of them. No security. No guards. We literally just had a brawl in the hallway and nothing happened.

The elevator stopped just before reaching the bottom. *Shit.* I wedged my fingers between the doors and pried it open with great effort. Without a supply of spirit energy I grew weaker by the minute. I was able to create an opening large enough to fit through but by the end was seeing black spots.

I crawled out from the space and dropped on all fours. One purifier patrolled the lobby and I thanked the gods he hadn't noticed me. Were only purifiers out for my demise, or would peacekeepers be among them as well? My hand hadn't stopped bleeding. I was going to leave a blood trail again. Humans, purifiers, wouldn't be able to smell me, but a peacekeeper could.

All the more reason to get out of there. Fast.

I crept down another hallway, using the darkness as my shield. Tori mentioned a back entrance. Purifiers guarded outside. The one closest to my escape hadn't seen me yet but then, I could see out the window better than he could see in.

I could just rush the bastard. Before executing my plan, the purifier grunted. He hit the ground, out cold. A giant rock floated over his head where he'd been standing.

Tori!

I pushed against the door. Stuck.

"Didn't mean to hit him that hard… Still breathin', though!" Tori rematerialized and chucked the rock away like it was a snake. "Is it not opening?"

I shook my head. Turns out, it needed power too. If only we'd tricked the purifier into using his light and unlocking it for us before knocking him out.

I'd have to break it down.

Tori seemed to understand and waved her hands at me. "You'll be too loud. Let me try something."

She approached the door from the opposite side and felt the handle. I watched but then she did her usual ghost-like trick and was out of sight. A painful moment passed but then, the light above the handle turned green and the door popped open.

Tori's spirit burst out of the lock and she caught herself in the air. Her eyes were wide as she floated back down. "I actually haven't tried possessing other objects besides my bear before. That was crazy! Felt super weird, like my whole body turned to soup and fit in all the crevices."

She stopped but I cracked a smile. "Thanks, Tori."

We saved the chit-chat for later and cut across the courtyard. Faris's henchmen all seemed to be inside the building, making the outside empty and safe. Once we had a decent hiding spot behind some bushes, she pointed at my hand. "Are you okay?"

"It stings," I said. My breath came out in white puffs. The lab coat was too thin to give me much warmth.

"That's lucky actually," Tori said, "Faris has goons crawling all over the place. Who would've thought he was actually popular?"

I was about to comment when, across the way, something else caught my attention. "Tori, that's not..?"

She peered around to see what I was looking at. "Yeah. It's the gym, or was."

Just hours ago, the square structure had been perfectly intact. Now, half of it was in rubble. I noticed a dark outline of burn marks where the fissures began and tore through the walls.

I wet my lips. "I should keep going alone."

"What, why?"

"You have to be with Guy, don't you? If you follow me, he'll follow us. Plus…"

"What?" she basically snapped at me.

"I'm not sure it's safe. With me." I remembered my conversation with Guy. Tori was unprotected energy. Being close to her put her in danger; whatever danger meant to ghosts. Either way, I doubted she deserved it.

"But, it's not right." Tori balled her hands into fists. "We're EXO. We're supposed to do the *right* thing, so that's what I'm doing. Guy can… kick rocks!"

Her kindness sparked a small fire in my heart that had almost been extinguished after learning Guy wasn't on my side. But she was right. He did seem duty-minded and if I was in opposition of that, he'd come for me like he had before.

"We just need to—" Tori started. She was interrupted by something bizarre happening to her hands. They washed away like water spilling over a layer of sand. Tori lifted her arms up, but by that point, her shoulders had gone too. "No, no… *Dammit!*"

Her angry cursing had the same energy as a frazzled squirrel. I could see the frustration building behind her puffed cheeks. "Jess," she said, "I'm so sorry. I thought I had more time."

"What do you mean?" I asked, "What's happening?"

Tori's neck faded next and left her as a floating head.

"It's been over forty minutes and I don't have my teddy. I-I'll be fine! No time to explain but it's like taking a nap for ghosts. Once I'm asleep, Guy will notice. You have to run." She nodded aggressively, like she couldn't wait for my response, and answered herself. "You'll make it, right? Promise?"

I wasn't positive but not wanting to leave her more distressed than she already was, I nodded. Her face broke apart into twinkling starlight. I could have sworn I saw a tear fall across her ethereal cheek. A breeze blew the rest of her away into a spiritual reality I couldn't see.

Just like that, I was on my own.

I didn't know which was worse. Being totally alone...

Or realizing that I actually wasn't.

A silent presence remained after Tori's departure. The hairs on my neck prickled at the unknown danger creeping up behind me. *Shit.* I whipped around but caught my own fist before it reached its target; a shady figure with crimson eyes.

"Evening, Cupcake." Aiden stepped into the moonlight, revealing a devious grin. "What manner of naughtiness are you up to?"

His heavy jacket helped him blend in with the night. A plain white t-shirt bunched over the wide belt that held up his pants. Even with the excessive buckles, Aiden seemed like he could walk on air.

"What are you doing here?" I asked, wondering if I even needed to explain my situation, or if he saw it all.

"Me? I was just on my way out but got a little distracted." His sweetened tone was anything but as he leisurely scanned my body. Red eyes paused at the sight of blood. I took an automatic step back.

He curled his fingers, commanding me closer. "Why am I never allowed to help you?"

"I don't have time for this."

Aiden pursed his lips. "Because you're being hunted?"

When I glared, a wicked glint flashed across his eyes. Aiden took a step but I made a mad dash around him and toward the gates. There really wasn't enough time to figure him out; whose side he was on. Zak or Guy would return any second and Faris wasn't going to scour the building forever.

A dark shade cut across my path and forced me to stop. Aiden fanned his long arms out. "Easy. I'm not interested in handing you over to some purifiers."

I sized him up, trying to predict who would win in a scuffle. On a normal day of training, I would've thought me, but my head throbbed even considering an altercation. "And I trust you, why?"

"You really think I'm friends with Faris?" A fair question. His dark brows reached his equally dark hairline as he waited for me to challenge him.

"What do you want then?" I asked.

Aiden summoned me again with only one curved finger. "I have somewhere you can hide, and a car. It's not a bad plan, Cupcake. Better than running off in that slip of yours."

I wrapped my arms around my middle and squeezed the thin fabric that hung off my body like a bedsheet. He saved me once before. I appreciated my extended lifespan. His timing, however, felt too perfect. "What's your generosity going to cost me?"

"You know what I want," he said, "Make a pact with me."

"What the hell is that?"

The sound of restless purifiers made me dive back into hiding. We found the nearest wall while Aiden elaborated. "A blood pact. It's not a big deal, just an agreement between friends. My help for a bit of your blood."

No.

Absolutely not.

"Is this a one-time thing?" I asked in a mutter.

"That all depends on how much danger you plan to be in, and how much of my help you want. I could give you a nibble of my soul, perhaps?" The words rolled off his clever tongue. I gulped and the skin over my knuckles suddenly went dry, like a cracking earth that begged for rain.

It was as if his vampire senses knew I was in trouble. Aiden hummed an eerie tune. "Assuming I have one, I'm willing to share it. Let's seal the deal."

Fantastic. I looked down at my sorry state again. Just how desperately did I need him? Purifiers were already circling the exterior of the building. They'd find us if I didn't make a decision fast. "Any binding magic you're not telling me about? This isn't like a deal with a devil?"

"You tell me, demon *queen,*" he said, "Lady? What is it we call you now?"

My jaw snapped shut. "You heard all that?"

Of course he had. Nosy vampire. "Crazy enough, I prefer Cupcake," I added.

He slouched, playing into my stealth but with significantly less caution. "The pact's nothing you can't untangle yourself from. Demons are craftier than us vampires."

Funny. I wasn't feeling very crafty. Just in another shitty situation thanks to my lack of assets. With an exasperated breath, I lifted my injured hand but couldn't bring myself to make a verbal confirmation.

A pact with a vampire.

With *Aiden.*

"Positive?" Aiden asked but I knew he enjoyed the random power struggle by the arrogant look on his face.

"No. Just hurry."

He brought my hand to his lips and I watched his pearly fangs glitter with hunger. His tongue attacked first, following the line of blood. The wet muscle sparked tiny needles on my tender palm.

You'd think he was licking a spoonful of fudge chocolate with the way his eyes fluttered. *Yuck*.

"We can't be here all night," I reminded him while squirming in place but he hadn't heard me. When his grip tightened, I snapped. "Aiden!"

Aiden froze. Had he actually zoned out? A smile grew against my hand. He suctioned any remaining blood and saliva with a soft popping sound. *About damn time*. But he hadn't even bit me.

I wiped his spit off on my gown but noticed that the pain I had before subsided. "You used venom on me?"

"Just a drop." The dark purr that rumbled from his throat made me shudder. He folded his tongue back into his mouth and rubbed away any excess blood with his thumb. Did I *want* him to have enjoyed it? I think I would've been offended if he didn't.

His red eyes turned a dangerous shade darker, unless I just imagined it. "It won't heal entirely. Like I said, holy weapons are tricky," he said, sounding halfway normal again, "Come on. Let's have some fun."

"That's it?" I asked, looking back down at my hand. A blood pact sounded more ritualistic and scary.

In true Aiden fashion, he gave me a leer that couldn't be interpreted. "I'll let you know when it's time to pay up."

How the hell did I end up here? I asked myself many questions as I fit my body into the trunk of Aiden's car.

"Once we're in the clear, I'll let you out," he said with a smirk, "Relax. Yours isn't the first body I've had in my trunk."

"The fu—"

He closed me in.

I huffed. My mind flooded with the pending regrets. Had I been so desperate as to put my faith in a potential psychopath? What if he got hungry and pulled over? All that would be left to do is bury me in the woods. I should've brought my own shovel too.

If I stayed, though, I would have to face Faris. Either way, someone was getting hurt. My contract with Zak was about to be in flames. I groaned, feeling the sting of betrayal all over. If there had been time, I would've liked to hear Zak's side of the story. I wanted Tori to be wrong about everything; that I wasn't a demon lord's daughter on the run.

What exactly happens when you anger The Angel of Mercy?

I wouldn't see any of them again.

And that made me… sad?

It was always going to end this way, wasn't it? I was never going to stay with EXO forever. What a shitty goodbye, though. Everything felt so rushed. I wished I could've said something more to Tori for bothering to rescue me. She could have easily left me but had the heart to stay, even after learning who I was.

I still refused to believe it but pieces of a long, disoriented puzzle shifted together in my mind. *Chaos beings. Demon lords.* There had always been something beneath my surface; deadly and hungry. Not half demon. Half *lord*.

Had Guy left me to die after realizing the same thing? The image of his face made my chest throb like a freshly carved wound. I couldn't escape Death forever. Sooner or later, I'd meet him again, but a happy reunion seemed unlikely.

Even so, I wished we could've stayed friends longer.

The car shifted and I braced myself against the walls of my confinement. Before dumping me in the back, Aiden had me put on his jacket. Courteous, I guess. My fingers curled around the thick material that exceeded my arm's length. Its length reached my hips and smelled just like him; warm, leathery, and intoxicating. Had he wanted me to suffocate in the trunk?

We stopped. I heard voices outside, distinctly Aiden's charming the pants off of somebody. A guard or purifier, I couldn't be sure. I knew we were in the clear when the car lurched forward again.

Gone.

Just like that…

I *had* to figure out what to do next on the outside. If EXO caught us, I'd face the wrath of Heaven. But I had nowhere to go yet, except for wherever Aiden was taking us.

Aiden kept us on a steady path, not that I could see anything. The humming of the engine created a soothing white noise but the ceaseless rocking turned my stomach. I pressed my feet up to stop myself from jostling around.

After a while longer combating motion sickness, we slowed. The engine shut off and my aching hips rejoiced. The trunk lid lifted and I had to blink away the flashing neon outside.

"Ready, Cupcake?" Aiden waited happily for me like he'd just opened a birthday present.

"Just help me out of here."

Before Aiden could grab me, I jerked back. The incident with Max was still fresh in my mind. He cocked a brow when I slid the sleeves of his jacket up to swallow my hands. My precautions worked fine until he insisted on carrying me.

His hand curled beneath my legs, giving me a small buzz, before scooping me up. "Your highness," Aiden said while wearing a fang-filled grin.

"Thanks." I wiggled just enough to send the message that I wanted down. Why weren't his hands freezing? I'd thought most vampires were cold. Aiden was still a box full of mysteries. An even better reason I shouldn't have followed him blindly.

Once he set me down on my feet, Aiden opened the passenger side door. "I only have extra clothes of mine. Hope they're to your liking."

Anything should have been better than what I had on, but when he handed me a long shirt, I died inside. "No pants?"

"You can keep my jacket."

I already knew it wouldn't work. If I were short, *maybe*, but my legs would make a nice statement from beneath the dark material. At least it had thickness as opposed to the hospital gown I wore.

"Where are we?" I tucked loose strands of hair behind my ear, suddenly aware that I hadn't seen my reflection in a while. We parked on a busy street but it parted into three rows of buildings, all with their own brightly lit strips.

"Downtown Cosoco," Aiden said, "Never been?"

"It looks so different at night," I noted. Cosoco sat far west from Haverwick but Naomi and I had come before. They had a variety of special herbs we couldn't find close to home. During the day, downtown looked like any other mid-city, but the night made for a bright transformation.

Aiden appeared next to my shoulder. "Some things are meant to be enjoyed under the shadow of night. Like me."

I actually laughed. A *real* laugh. "Gods, you're cheesy."

He held my gaze until my snickering stopped. One of his pale hands reached out to take mine. "You should change before we head in. Use the car or hide behind that dumpster if you're shy."

"Okay but do I have to hold your hand while I do that?"

His tone became infantile, like he had to explain to me how school recess worked. "We need to go over some rules. First, the moment we walk through the doors, you're mine. Make it obvious to the other vampires and stay close to me."

"Your *what*, exactly?"

His request wouldn't matter since I planned on leaving, eventually. Once the excitement of my disappearance died down, I'd slip away. By then, Aiden might have a new conquest to fixate on.

"My date. *I'm* the vampire you're with," he said like it was so obvious.

"Okay, but why?"

"You walk in there looking alone and I guarantee you won't live to see tomorrow."

I gaped at him. "The hell kind of place is this?"

Had he seriously brought me to a vampire nightclub? I let out a heavy sigh.

This is on me. I knew better and came anyway.

"Hey." Aiden's dark and charming voice brought me back to the conversation. "You're safe with me. Everyone thinks you hate me, so who'd come looking for us together ?"

There was that.

I opted for the dumpster as my dressing room. Not graceful at all and kind of gross, but I managed to pull the shirt over my body in record time. The important bits had been covered but just barely.

Aiden's arm came from around the dumpster. Hanging from his fingers were a pair of black flats, branded with a curious logo on the heels.

"I wasn't done," I said, snatching the shoes.

"Sorry. Figured you didn't want to be barefoot over there."

Thoughtful. When I stepped out into view, Aiden had something red in his hands. The blood drained from my face. "Aiden…"

"They're clean," he said. The dangling lace taunted me but the breeze between my legs was just as humiliating. Aiden slowly lowered the underwear. "Unless you'd rather not?"

"Whose are they?"

"Untouched. We sell merch inside. Consider it a gift," he said.

"You sell *these* but not sweat pants?"

Aiden shrugged.

"Give it here," I said, retreating with my new underwear. My dignity slipped further away as I dragged the measly piece of red fabric past my thighs.

Aiden snorted at the apparent disapproval I wore with his ensemble. "I can go shopping later but our priority is getting you inside before anyone sees."

He tossed his jacket back over my shoulders and I slipped my arms through, appreciating any additional coverage. My old gown lay in a sad heap on the ground. Aiden pinched it by the neck and tossed it into the dumpster.

"Step back, Cupcake," he said while keeping his hand in the garbage container until a flame started. The intense heat pushed me back.

"What are you doing?" I asked, "You can't just set shit on fire!"

"Can't have wolves tracking your scent," he said.

"I think they can smell smoke too."

"But not *you*, anymore"

"Why do I get the feeling you've done this before?"

"Why don't you just trust me?" Aiden offered his hand and waited for me.

I adjusted my sleeves again. "Do you smoke?"

"Used to," he said and fit my covered hand comfortably in his, "Why?"

"The fire." I squinted at him. Who walked around with lighters in their pockets if they didn't actively use them? And yet, he chose not to explain or even confirm he had a lighter. I watched the fire continue to burn, wondering how else he'd started it unless he knew magic. "How did you—"

"Let's save the talking for later," he said.

We crossed the street and made our way down another dark alley. A dank staircase cloaked itself away, just behind it. Not sketchy at all.

I looked around us, almost like I hoped a better option would present itself. Aiden had a face girls would melt for but I couldn't ignore the little voice telling me to stay wary.

There was always running off alone.

No. Stick to the plan.

Recoup, wait, and then find my own way.

Another vampire stood at a tall doorway, ready to greet us. The muscle? He looked too spindly for the job, but then, supernaturals had their ways. He tilted his half-shaved head in our direction. With a bored roll of his wrist, he summoned us through. "Good to see you… and you."

His red eyes blinked slowly as he examined me. "Stay close to your date, love."

"Not a threat, right, Udi?" Aiden said more than asked.

"Not from me, boss."

Boss? Aiden was the boss of that guy? Did that mean Aiden owned the place?

That would explain his confidence in using it as a hideout.

Aiden seemed content with that response and waltzed inside with me in tow. Before shutting the door behind us, he turned to Udi once more. "Hey, no one's seen us."

"Sure, boss."

Past the entrance, the air thickened into smog. The smells consisted heavily of smoke, sweat, and rust. Lots of rust. It took my eyes a whole minute to adjust to the dark. I couldn't see anyone else's eye color but the alarming number of necking couples revealed the majority in attendance. *Vampires*. Vampires everywhere.

My willingness to be at Aiden's side increased the further we went. Low, changing beats vibrated beneath my feet. No lyrics. Just sounds. Humans wandered around, either doe-eyed or enthusiastic participants. The new laws discouraged blood-drinking in public but that didn't seem to apply.

Aiden's presence parted the sea of dancers so we could reach the bar. He commanded the room full of darklings. Even without touching anyone I could feel their energy seeping into my pores. It was all around; erupting from the heat of dancing bodies and sighs of delight that left their lips. Some harbored essence that stood out from the others, wafting my way. Tempting me.

I'm just another monster in the room.

"I should've bitten you." Aiden's statement dragged my attention away from my appetite. He kept a stoney expression when anyone came close. No one stopped us, but they weren't shy about their inspections.

"Hungry?" I scoffed, ignoring my own growing hunger pains. My stomach shriveled like a raisin. I'd have to feed too, and soon. Having so many humans around made my chest heavy with worry.

For them.

"Starved," he said, "But that's not all."

"Can it wait?"

"It'll keep other interested parties away. And there are many."

We sat at some bar stools when I felt a new kind of gaze; one of a different desire. They came from willing donors, hoping to gain Aiden's favor. Men and women. Their longing stares and exposed necklines gave me second-hand embarrassment.

I thought Aiden was the only vampire who lacked subtlety, but every red-eyed guest made their desires clear, scanning us faster than hummingbird wings. They sat like giant vultures at their seats or along the walls, probably waiting to see if I'd keel over.

The impatient ones approached other potential meals and most were rewarded with their target's wrists in their mouths. A few had a more sultry approach and received access to a neck. The gasps and breathy tunes made me blush. I hadn't expected the feedings to be so expressive… and loud.

"Come here often?" I asked, ignoring the vampire across who made a map of my throat.

Aiden answered by bringing my hand to his lips. Warmth traveled down my arm from tiny kisses on my knuckles. It wasn't much, but my energy tank ran empty so any little touch, my darkness gobbled up. "I invited you once, remember?" he asked, his purrs muffled, "It only took the threat of death to get you here."

I raised a brow at his romantic pursuit on my fingers. "Is *this* scaring the vampires away too?"

"It's for *you*. I figured you'd be snacky." His eyes shifted to the faces behind me. "If I bite you, you're off-limits to them. Tonight, that is."

He reached for the collar of his jacket that sat around my neck, tickling me. The fabric followed his touch and slid down my shoulders. Observers turned their heads or rolled their eyes, knowing very well what came next. My blood wouldn't be free for the taking.

I couldn't mask the tremor in my voice. "I-I heal pretty quickly so, I don't think that'll work. What would you be doing if I wasn't here?"

"You really want the answer to that?" His fingertips played with the hairs closest to my collarbone and gently brushed them to the side. He finally answered but his gaze stayed below my chin. "I would probably find some lucky soul to share the evening with. Club Eternal is accepting of many activities that some might consider to be indecent."

"Great," I said, "Why are we here again?"

"This place happens to be a haven for the unwanted, or extremely wanted, from time to time. You can relax." To prove his point, he pressed into my shoulder muscle that had reached my ears.

"Being hunted doesn't put me in high spirits," I said, not withholding the sass, "I also don't have a dazzling track record when it comes to parties."

"Shit happens, but you're free of those warped, angelic assholes. Cheers to you!"

It would've been terribly easy to give in to his antics. Flirty, confident, mysterious, and actually funny at times. Aiden showed his interest in me before but I'd blamed it on his boredom. I still needed to hear the real reason he'd helped me. The goodness of his heart wasn't sitting right with me.

"So, you bite me and everyone backs off?" I asked, "Like bug repellant?"

Aiden leaned in, giving me a front-row seat to his pretty, black lashes. Damned things put butterflies to shame. "It's rude to steal from someone's plate. Even monsters have some etiquette."

I turned my head to one side, unable to handle how close he'd gotten. "Just talk me through it. What does it mean to feed on someone?"

"Does it have to mean anything? We all eat to survive."

"It's just that it looks violent and erotic."

There was a perfect example of that sitting close to us. I watched a man getting drained by a dark-haired female, working his neck like a fat lollipop. He seemed to be in a state of bliss, not writhing in pain and agony. Unless he was about to pass out. Also likely.

"Humans naturally replenish their blood. It's a waste to kill them," Aiden said, all too casually, "The intimate approach has more to do with flavor. Frightened prey tastes bitter. Some like that. I prefer mine sweet."

His fingers danced around my collar again and heat burned beneath the surface of my skin. At least it sounded like murder was off the table. Also nice that vampires didn't like sharing. Humans wouldn't last two seconds being tag-teamed by blood vacuums.

"You kissed that wolf shifter," Aiden stated, "Tell me what you felt then?"

The longer I took to respond the more earnestly he waited, and his smile grew. His words continued to flow like a chocolate river. "When your lips touched, what was on your mind? I'm sure it wasn't *true love*. Not with that dog."

Fear. Hunger. Instinct.

"Nothing like that," I said, "Just…"

"—just the *need*?" Aiden grinned. "See. It's natural. You and I are the same, and what we do isn't a crime. We're just getting what we need."

I'd always known we were alike, I just wanted to ignore the fact. Why couldn't I be someone like Zak instead? Kind. Happy. He was able to appear to others with goofy humility even with all his great power. He'd made me believe I could push the boundaries of my birthright.

I can't.

Max hadn't seen it coming when I stole his energy, and neither had Peter. I couldn't control myself. At least Aiden had the decency to take me on a "date" first. Even if the location was spooky and bordered on blood prostitution. I think, out of the two of us, I was the worst monster.

"Maybe you're right," I muttered.

A velvety chuckle escaped his lips. "I was trying to give you a pep talk, not hurt your feelings."

He earned a snort that time. "You've helped me a few times now. I owe you."

"True."

Something hot grazed my neck. Aiden had dipped his head but stopped himself just above the flesh between my neck and shoulder. Out of instinct, I pushed his chest away just before his teeth could dig in.

"Wait!"

Impatience crowded his sensuous growl. He observed me from heavy-lidded eyes and my insides burned. What was wrong with me? I'd agreed to the dumb pact and been through worse than a vampire bite. Everyone at the bar drank with, or from, their dates, so our exchange would've been normal.

Aiden took a long inhale and secured my knee in his wide palm. "What if I help you out first?"

I froze when Aiden's thumb slid across my bottom lip.

Immediately, heat and tiny pin-pricks numbed that area. *Is he insane?* After we'd just talked about what happened with Max? Aiden had to see what I'd done to that gymnasium. Somehow, I hadn't gotten anyone killed, but the club had far more potential victims inside.

"Why would you want to do that?" I asked.

Aiden rolled his head back with a low groan. He stared for a long moment before laughing deeply. "*Ah…* You're too sweet. No wonder those bastards thought they could keep their demon pet."

I huffed at his insult. "Why are *you* still with EXO?"

"Maybe after today, I won't be," he said.

"I'm serious."

"Me too. I'm having too much fun playing deserters with you."

"Won't they suspect if we're both missing?" I asked, "Your sister will know."

He shook his head. "She doesn't want peacekeepers sticking their noses in here any more than I do."

"Then *why* are you both involved with them?"

"My hells, woman. *Fun* first." Aiden's last chuckle was dry and raspy. He flicked his hand toward the bartender who happily bounced over to us. She already wore a pair of fang holes around her neck like a badge of honor.

"From the bar, tonight?" she asked him, "That's unlike you."

"Not for me. Give her something sweet."

The barmaid feigned a smile when she was forced to notice me. I received no bubbly remarks and I could taste the sourness of her energy. She slammed my glass a little too hard while wearing the same strained expression. If I hadn't just watched her make the drink, I would've suspected it to be poisoned.

"Think she's jealous?" I asked.

"She knows what you're missing," Aiden said.

I inspected my drink. After I turned sixteen, my aunt started letting me have wine every Winter solstice. So, I'd had alcohol before, sort of. The concoction before me had a similar redness to it. Smelled fruity too.

Aiden nudged it closer to me. "Let's play a game. Every sip you take, I'll answer a question."

"Truthfully?" I brought the drink to my lips but he said nothing. The sugar mixed in helped with the burn. I coughed into my sleeve, earning more snickering from Aiden.

He gave me a small applause. "Look at you go. One question, then."

"You've had nothing good to say about EXO, Zak or anyone," I said, my voice turned raspy, "So, why become a peacekeeper?"

"Easy,' he said, "I'm not. Next."

"What? That answer is bullshit."

"You didn't ask for details."

I wanted to rip my hair out, or his. My next sip tasted worse.

"Fine, give me the *details*, then."

Aiden's glee dimmed by a fraction. "My old man wants his kids involved with the angels' grand plan for world peace by climbing EXO's ranks," he paused, "Dad wasn't always so high and mighty. I enjoyed him better then."

"What was he like?" I asked.

Aiden pointed at my drink.

Prick.

The glass hadn't been tall but it took forever to get through. When he looked satisfied with my pinched face he continued, "Before Roman was an angel-loving, ass-kisser, he saw a future for *us*. Survival of the fittest shifted after the war but instead of letting evolution run its course, we're encouraging humans to run the show again. Vampires are forced to keep their heads down but when angels vote themselves in to govern the humans, humans rejoice."

"Maybe because angels don't eat them," I said and Aiden grunted.

"Wanna know the real reason why Zak's nice to you?" he asked, "The answer's a lot darker than you think. Come on, *think!* He's seen as one of the strongest angels. Why?"

"He's an angel, he's…" I stopped. Why would an angel be kind? Kindness is in their nature, I thought. What else had Zak said to me about angels?

They thrived off love.

If angels only needed people to like them in order to be powerful, and everyone liked Zak…

He'd made himself invincible.

"Angels are like us too," Aiden spoke just loud enough to hear over the noise. "They feed off us every chance they get, but we're the only ones made to feel guilty for it. Especially you."

My next sip became a gulp.

"Me?"

"I know all about your secret lessons with Mr. Sunshine. Why do you think he insisted on it being *him*?"

"Because I can't easily kill him?"

Aiden blinked once. "He's getting you addicted to him, Cupcake. I'm sure an angel's soul is five-star dining. As a fellow consumer, I understand, but don't put him on some pedestal where he doesn't belong."

Zak wants me addicted to him?

The thought would've been absurd had the night's events not occurred. What would he benefit by doing that? My favor. My *adoration*?

My compliance.

My trust.

The second round of betraying feelings summoned a splitting headache. I pinched my forehead, like the pain could be popped like a pimple. Without the promise of Zak's spirit to fill me, I worried there would be no end.

"Why did you really bring me here, Aiden?" I asked, blinking away tears.

He took time to mull it over. "I'm curious."

"About what?"

Before telling me, he stole my hand again. The immediate relief to my head stopped me from taking it back. His energy was… strange. I couldn't pin down on feeling or another. Its pulsing sensation ebbed and flowed, making silent waves up my arm.

While I was stunned, he whisked us away toward the center of the room. Bodies packed in tight, sliding against their dance partners. Fear and unease begged me to go back where it was safe. No one showed concern, even as they wore their own blood like ruby necklaces. How could humans be so careless?

So many people…

Too many. Their auras bombarded me like a flock of birds. The ease of obtaining what I needed intrigued me enough to stay, but there wouldn't be much of a hideout left if I overindulged.

Aiden finally found the spot he wanted and spun me around. My back collided with his front. His hands curved around my hips, squeezing as if he could merge us together. He brought a dangerous whisper to my ear. "Dance with me."

I didn't want to admit he'd left me breathless. How could anyone sound so lethal and inviting at the same time?

Up against someone like Aiden, I felt brutally unprepared. I only ever danced alone. It wasn't until I saw everyone else humping each other that I gained a sliver of confidence. I could probably do better than that at least. Their form of dancing didn't seem to require much skill at all.

I made a breathy giggle at the absurdity of it all. *Madness. Pure madness.* My heart raced and I let my body loosen to better mold with Aiden's. His fingers scouted lower until they could feel skin. Just a tease. He didn't lift my shirt-dress or drag his hands down any further.

Bits of his energy still reached me. Aiden's confidence made me think he knew exactly what he was doing, and what his touches did for me. Max had felt like a ball of fire, but Aiden's soul was like lying in a bed of dark coals; smokey with a quiet, searing heat.

"Okay, we danced and it wasn't terrible," I said, focusing on my awful footwork and not his smoldering presence behind me. Aiden brought me around to face him, still keeping our bodies close. He took it a step further and looped two fingers around my wrist, guiding my arm up and around his shoulder.

"What's your next move, Cupcake?" he asked, caressing my inner forearm.

I wasn't sure what he was referring to at first. My gaze stayed glued to his jaw but I could feel him searching my face for a clue. What was my next move? The entire night had been one of chaos. My minimal amount of stability had been stolen from under me. Stopping, even for a moment, to let it sink in might've drowned me.

"I don't know," I said, "I need to find my aunt. She's out there somewhere and I need answers. So, I guess that'll be my first step."

"With a scary necromancer about? Sounds dangerous. Not for a princess of Hell, though?"

I dropped my head. "I can't even think about *that* right now."

"Is it true?"

"Probably." Although, I hadn't been able to ask Guy how he came to find out. I'd have to get Naomi to tell me.

Aiden pondered while he chewed his bottom lip with his fangs. "I could hunt her down for you."

"You'll hit a dead end." If I knew Naomi, then she hadn't left a trail behind, even for a vampire to sniff. It would be impossible for me to find her.

"You still doubt me." His smirk was the only thing I could see in the mood lighting. I felt his other hand find the middle of my back. We'd already slowed; just two creatures idle in the dance of blood. "Just so you know, drinking blood doesn't *have* to mean anything, but I am attracted to you," he said, "I want you to enjoy me as much as I'm going to enjoy you."

A lump formed in my throat. Warm fingers settled around my chin and he tilted my head to one side. My pulse pounded in my ears like a desperate cry but I did nothing. Aiden wasn't waiting for his payment any longer.

"Aiden—"

"Relax."

Relax. Sure!

His lips found my neck first, testing the terrain with harmless grazes. He paused at a spot around my collar and inhaled deeply. Pretty sure he'd taken a whiff of my artery.

It's just a little blood…

Then, why was I shaking?

He started making more meaningful motions with his mouth. The innocent, introductory traces of his lips turned into a messy massage. Embers from his soul hissed, cooking me from the inside. I thought I heard a sizzle when he wet my neck with his tongue.

A shiver shot through me. *So hot,* but it felt wrong, like I shouldn't have been experiencing that moment with him. Why? I wasn't in a relationship with anyone. *It doesn't have to mean anything…*

Maybe I did need to lighten up and just enjoy, like Aiden seemed to be doing.

He managed to lick his way through my icey fortress and thaw my nerves. Everything became a blur. There wasn't much to see anyway, as everyone tangled themselves in their own trysts. The dying voice that kept telling me to run faded away.

I didn't flinch when he pulled back, fangs at the ready. Not even when he angled his face to mine.

He isn't…?

He is.

The soft grip on my chin curled to the back of my head. Our lips touched and my thoughts turned to black. I questioned my sanity as I kissed him back. How troubling that I didn't hate it. Did I actually enjoy him, or was it the succubus talking?

Aiden pressed deeper into me. His movements, lips, and body moved slow and purposefully, much like his creeping vitality. The energy crawled under my skin, taking its delicious time recharging me. His fangs bumped against my teeth, reminding me of who I was dealing with; not a human and not someone who could die easily from my touch. He had his own dark and powerful side.

Comforting I suppose.

He gripped the back of my shirt. *His* shirt. My hand still rested behind his head. I hadn't been bold enough to hold him closer. Our intimate exchange acted as the catalyst to his potential demise but he glued himself to me with no restraint.

I wanted to become stronger. Less afraid. In control. No headaches, no nightmares, no necromancers, and no hiding in the shadows for the rest of my supernatural life. Aiden was a willing donor.

Why shouldn't I take advantage?

Something made my lips tingle, troubling me enough to lose the moment. Before, he'd tasted like mint and copper, but I was hit with something extremely sweet. All I could think of was his teeth.

Venom?

Before I had a moment to question it, Aiden broke the kiss and reared his head.

30

Fangs hurt like *hell*.

As soon as those suckers broke the skin I imagined two hot pokers eating me away. My agony was quickly washed away by a wave of sweet, numbing euphoria. Aiden's body greedily coiled around my slacked limbs until I couldn't breathe. Even then, I didn't care. *Couldn't* care. Even after listening to him swallow blood. A weak sigh left my chest. My eyes fluttered closed.

Aiden popped off my neck with an unearthly snarl. My head fell from the clouds, making a harsh landing back in Club Eternal. I felt for the holes that had already begun to close. Thank gods, I'd taken energy before losing blood. Although, the drunken stupor the bite left me in had me questioning everything. *Why can't I stand straight?*

Aiden held a hand over his face but I saw his widening eyes through his fingers. His shoulders quaked from harsh and choppy breaths. Was he having a bad reaction to my blood? I took a step back but vertigo sent me farther.

"Something's wrong," I said, "The roommmms ssspinnng…"

Aiden went still before his body gave a violent shake. His alert gaze found me through the small windows in his hand. I heard something like a grimace or growl. "It's just the venom," he uttered.

"*Just?*" I couldn't even glare correctly. The muscles in my face strained. Every movement took extra effort. Sickness pooled in my stomach. I'd solved my starving problem but my demon strength slept dormant behind an annoying wall of fog. Had Aiden given me any more venom, I would've turned to sludge.

This venom… is like a drug?

Drugged.

I'm drugged.

"Are you sure this is—" I stumbled into someone; another vampire. They assisted in standing me back up, but they clamped too hard around my bicep. I tried shaking them off before lazily demanding they do so.

Something hard caught my wrist.

With a swift, possessive snatch, Aiden had me back in his arms. His gentle touch had been replaced with iron, making him my shield as well as my shackle. The other vampire scuttled away, uninterested in provoking Aiden further.

"Aiden?" I peered up at him for a sign of his lost sanity. Even while half-delirious, I could feel a change stirring inside him. His rejuvenated pulse was a war drum. The veins hidden in his body reached for the surface. Having me close seemed to calm him, at least slightly.

"Let's go, Cupcake," he said and my feet lifted off the ground.

My question came out as a jumbled slur. *Where's he taking me now?* I wanted him to tell me but he didn't. He'd changed. Something had changed.

I'm not safe.

I'm not safe…

What I thought was a blink of an eye was actually several moments. Time meant nothing. I floated with Aiden's arms half carrying me away from the party. The ceiling became my only view as my head dropped back. Music played like a distant, haunting echo.

Everything turned red. The new room we entered was painted head to toe in it. I *dropped* onto something feathery. Almost as soft as clouds. Aiden's frame cast a shadow from a yellow lamplight nearby.

"Sorry. I had to bite harder to break your demon skin. But I didn't realize you were such a lightweight," he said.

I groaned, rubbing my hands over my face repeatedly. "What's happening to me?"

He caressed the side of my face and I smacked him away with a clumsy arm. My fingers were caught in their violent attempt by his much steadier hand. Stealing his energy would've been the best revenge but I was too upset to think straight.

"You… *drugged* me," I said.

He mumbled his next words into my knuckles before releasing them. "Don't be such a baby. It won't kill you."

"No one else is this messed up. Why am I?" I hadn't been bitten before but something about the aftermath felt intentional. The harder I fought to control my body again, the worse it got.

"During a more primitive time, venom was used to keep a vampire's prey docile during an attack," he said, pretty much confirming my thoughts. They sedated their food. Why hadn't I remembered that from Jarmiel's books?

My fingertips turned to ice. When I asked, my teeth chattered. "Are you trying to kill me or… I-I don't want to be a vampire."

I was able to focus on Aiden's face again; still handsome but altered. The laid-back persona had gone. Lust danced in his dilated pupils. "Didn't I say that'd be wasteful? It's smarter just to keep you. And I don't need you to be anything but what you are, demon princess."

"Gods…" I trembled but I couldn't differentiate the poison from fear. "You can't *keep* me, Aiden."

"Are you sure?" There was a sprinkle of his usual teasing but otherwise, his question sounded like a test. Could he actually keep me? I attempted to turn over and failed. Instead, I let out a roar mixed with a frustrated sob.

Aiden made a clicking sound with his tongue. "You're just making it worse."

"*Shut up.*" Something possessed me too. My voice darkened and scraped at my tonsils. The lights in the room flickered in response. "This better be a joke, Aiden Blaxill."

Aiden witnessed the scene with twinkling eyes. "It's not a joke. I promised to keep you safe and I will. For a long time."

Whether he'd meant it to or not, his promise sounded like a threat.

"Says the man who paralyzed me." I had a more colorful response but lost the desire to waste more of my strength. "This is kidnapping."

"You're surprisingly hostile after sharing such a pleasant moment together. I thought *both* parties were satisfied?" He asked with a raised brow. "If not, let me repent of my sins. I haven't had anyone complain about my kissing before."

Fuck this guy.

"Why sedate me? Worried I'd take off as soon as I knew how crazy you were?" I scoffed, "Well, you're right! When this wears off, I'm leaving."

"Where? Back to Zak?"

The icy tone in his voice revealed all I needed to know. One red eye twitched. My blood must have affected him. *Of course. He's an addict, remember?* Darren warned me.

Aiden then had the audacity to pat me on the shoulder. "You already chose to leave and it was the best thing you could've done for yourself. It's done." He turned to leave with a petty huff. "I'll have Udi get you some clothes. Maybe by then you'll have come back to your senses."

"You're leaving me here?" I meant to sit up but didn't make it far. The walls liquified and jiggled until the back of my head smacked the pillow again. "Aiden!"

But I watched him leave my side and heard a door shut. Gravity kept me pancaked to the soft surface I occupied. Horrible possibilities ran through my mind. What if Aiden's club was a front for blood trafficking?

Oh, gods. No. I had to calm down.

The faster my blood pumped the worse my vertigo became. I wanted Naomi. For the first time since our separation, I felt my inner child grasp for the security of my lost guardian. I would've given anything to hear my aunt berate me over getting into my stupid situation. As long as it meant she'd be there with me. She knew how to get out of anything. *What would you do, Aunty?*

Not wait around for Aiden to show up, that was for damn sure.

Was the reason he made me OD really because he thought I was going to bolt? All I told him was that I wanted to find my aunt. I was a demon princess, whatever that meant to him. His usual snacks would've been much easier to restrain and require less venom.

That's right. I wasn't the most skilled creature but I had inherited power. I could handle a pretty boy and his stupid vampire friends.

There were a lot of them, though.

My depleted blood moved steadier than before, filtering out the toxins. I almost threw up once from being able to feel *everything*. Time passed smoother after that. I wiggled my fingers and toes to hurry the process. Eventually, I could lift myself upright. *Now what?*

Aiden had dumped me off in some random room. The bed I sat on could hold three people, leaving me plenty of space on either side. I had to still be in the club or near. I could hear commotion through the thin walls.

At least he hadn't taken me to an underground dungeon.

I jumped at the sound of a door opening. A familiar face let himself in. He wore a vest and long sleeves buttoned at the wrist. The maroon tie matched his leery eyes. It was the doorman from before, Udi.

He stepped into the room with a silver tray in hand. I got to my feet but as soon as I did so, I fell over. "Whoopsie." Udi spoke a fraction more excitable than a robot. "Might want to stay in bed. You're a pint short."

Feeling spiteful, I used the bed to help myself stand. "Why are you here? Where are we?"

"Aftercare," he said, nodding at the glass sitting on his tray, "and one of the rooms upstairs. This one belongs to the boss."

The "boss's" room?

That meant Aiden's room. Aiden's *bed*.

I sprang from the sheets like a disgruntled cat. Gross. No doubt it was where he'd taken many of his "victims." And I'd been lying in it in recovery for who knew how long? The image of him and the bartender canoodling on the red comforter scarred fictional memories into my brain. *He better keep that thing clean!*

Udi offered his cup on the tray. "You should drink this. You'll feel better. It's just sugar."

"Right." I couldn't think of a reason why they'd poison me further but I still refused. Udi set the tray down on the bed. I spotted some clothing rolled into tubes next to a small plate of various treats.

"If you insist," he said, "I also have these."

"Is this how Aiden treats all his *dates*?" I asked. In his defense, it was more generous than some people provided for a lot worse.

"Just you. You healed fast." Udi's unblinking eyes looked expectant, as if waiting for his next command. His sights dropped from my face and I cupped my neck, hiding the proof that was no longer there. The holes already sealed themselves but left behind a tender, throbbing pain.

"Where is he now?" I asked.

Udi finally smiled but it only succeeded in making him creepier. "Aiden's dealing with a pest problem. I'm to deliver the goods and kill anyone who comes close to your room."

The words flowed so matter-of-fact that I almost missed it. Just who would he have to kill? *Why* would he have to kill them? I sized him up, wondering what sort of damage he could inflict on someone. "What kind of pests?"

"Nothing you need to worry about. Just rest. If you need anything, tap on the door. I'll leave the juice." Udi let me dress in private but I saw the shadow from his boots beneath the door.

So creepy…

My new clothes matched perfectly with my usual wardrobe, minus the cost. The tags printed how much Aiden spent in bold ink. The thin, olive and cream sweater contrasted nicely with the dark pants. He even guessed my shoe size correctly, slapping a bow on a pair of ankle boots. I shouldn't have accepted any of it but I had to decide between my pride or being forever indecent.

I wadded up the underwear with the club's logo, along with Aiden's shirt, and tossed them into a corner. If only I could burn them like he had with my hospital gown. The exertion from my strip made my legs wobble. I sat on the floor before dropping again.

Just a few minutes here… and then I could get back to escaping. I just had to dodge a club filled with Aiden's blood-sucking friends, his spooky guard dog in the penguin suit, and Aiden himself. After that, I'd be free. On my own. Alone.

Better than getting stashed in a cellar like a bottle of wine.

My eyes shut for a whole two seconds and the air in the room changed. Heavy steps thumped and stopped next to my feet. I looked up. "*Shit.*"

A dark silhouette of The Necromancer took shape in the room.

Clay flickered in and out like he had a bad connection. Was it new magic? Gods, not a teleportation spell! I dragged myself back with my elbows. I hadn't fallen asleep but then, how high were my chances of falling into a venom-induced coma?

He faded completely after that, like one of his many nightmares.

I waited for my heart to stop drumming before moving. Shouldn't Zak have captured him by now? If not, then Clay could be anywhere. Even at the club.

Bringing all of EXO straight to us.

Time to go.

Udi should've been waiting behind the door. When I checked, however, he'd gone. Was it too late? Did Zak know where we were? Which would be worse to find at Club Eternal, Clay or EXO?

Both.

Both would definitely be worse.

I poked my head out into the hall; nothing but long covered walls in velvet. A spiral staircase kept me from the noise below, although it hadn't sounded like a party anymore. The voices going back and forth had more bite than the vampires did.

That didn't take long… We'd already been discovered. I suppressed my startled breathing with my hand. Quiet. I needed a quick and silent route out of there. Using the textured walls for balance I looked around, exploring my options. There had to be a fire exit. I doubted vampires were above building safety standards. I turned around and sure enough, extra rooms lined the hall with one exit to the rooftop.

That could work.

"Going so soon?"

I heard someone's foot gliding over the carpeted floor just behind me. The vampire was neither Aiden nor Udi. He stalked the hall toward me with fangs at the ready. "I wanted to see what all the fuss was about."

"Back off," I said, trying to sound strong and not like a snack that hobbled away. So much for vampire dining etiquette. I was starting to think everything that came out of Aiden's mouth was bullshit.

"Not with a scent like *that*."

The vampire wasted no time in lunging at me. I couldn't dodge before his body collided with mine. He pinned us to the opposite wall ready to feast with dripping fangs. *Not more venom!* I brought my leg to his groin and launched him back. It knocked the wind out of me as much as it had him.

"Nice kick," he said through a struggling cough, "Thought you'd still be out of it."

His next attempt had my head smashing into the wall. Cold fingers covered my face. My legs had no room to move against his wide stance that time. His jaws closed around my neck.

Then, he was gone.

The weight of him was ripped away. My chest deflated only to sharply inhale again. A scythe buried itself deep into my attacker's back, hooking him like a fish. He gurgled and spat blood from his lips.

The skeletal mask of Death emerged from behind him. I felt his icy presence freezing me in place.

A reaper? Here?

Something else besides blood left the vampire's wound; a violet colored frost. With a cruel twist, the scythe encouraged more frost to exit his body.

"N-no… wait." He cried. "Please, no!"

"Begging?" the reaper asked and I swear I heard the gates of Hell with his chilling summons, "*Good*."

With a grunt, he catapulted the vampire across the hall, making a wet landing against the floor. The frosty matter made a desperate retreat back into his spine. I wanted to see what happened next but Death's messenger turned to me.

"Jess."

I pressed myself deeper into the wall as his scythe got closer. The wispy shadows draping over him fluttered to a halt. He shook his head and the illusionary skull blew away in a puff of smoke. "Jess, it's me."

Guy wore a look I hardly recognized. Lights shone through the many cracks of his crystal eyes, revealing a frazzled soul. A wintery aura followed him in stride, harsh and biting.

He came to retrieve me.

Just like before…

I ran in the only direction he wasn't blocking. Not an easy task, considering the room kept swaying under my feet. The last time Death captured me, all he had to do was tap my forehead. His touch was deadlier than mine.

A chariot of smoke blocked my path and he reappeared in front of me. When Guy came forward, I brought my hands up. "Don't!"

He stopped in his tracks. We had a moment to assess each other's body language; mine being that of a cornered animal and his, calm like a good shepherd. Clarity illuminated his darkened face.

"I'm not going to hurt you. Jess," he said, "I just helped you. I thought you were in trouble."

I heard the softness in his voice and paused. Reapers shouldn't have biased feelings but then again, he seemed loyal to Zak. Was he acting on orders again?

I opened my mouth but then, a chipper whistle sounded from down the hall. Aiden and Udi resurfaced from below. More vampires followed, scaling the spiral stairs like giant insects until they reached us.

"I thought reapers waited around for the trash," Aiden said, "As you can see, she's very much alive."

Guy ignored him and stared at me.

"Did he hurt you?"

I pressed my lips together. The fang marks were gone but I still wanted to hide. Guy breathed out his nose and finally gave Aiden his full attention. "Should I shorten your already short life, Blaxhill?"

Aiden wrinkled his nose at that. "Cool off. She's not some feeble tree branch."

Their tension made the room pulse. The vampire Guy sliced into earlier made his grueling recovery and got to his feet. His skin was paler than before.

He barely raised his head to meet Aiden and Ubi. "Boss…"

It sounded like the vampire was about to make a weak apology, but before he could utter a word, Udi drew a thin blade from his coat and cut his jaw clean off. I gasped but couldn't look away from the row of teeth bathing in a puddle on the carpet.

Hells…

Udi wiped the metal clean on a handkerchief until it glistened. Aiden watched with an apathetic gaze and kicked the bottom jaw bone away with his boot.

"I thought I'd made myself pretty clear, not to touch her," he said, "I admit I underestimated the effects of your blood, Cupcake. Even my dogs couldn't obey."

Another vampire hoisted the maimed one from the ground and dragged him off. The trail of blood only lasted a few drops. I was able to lift my gaze from the mess to find Aiden. No one else bat an eye, so it had to be something they were used to.

He had his subordinate's *face* cut off.

Guy's face, however, remained hard as stone. I'd almost read it as unimpressed.

"Now you've seen how he treats his *friends*," he said to me, "Are you sure you want to stay here?"

I felt for Guy's shirt and gripped it hard. No. I hadn't wanted to come that badly in the first place. And after getting drugged with vampire juices, I most definitely wasn't going to stay.

Aiden's eyes flicked to my every movement around Guy. "You weren't shy before. Go on. Tell the reaper you let me taste you."

If the fabric of souls could cringe, mine did.

What. An. ASSHOLE.

So, that's what I called him.

"Asshole."

Guy spoke through gritted teeth. "You could have killed her."

He'd glossed over how horribly awkward Aiden's insinuation had been and went straight for death. I wanted to thank him.

Aiden's eyebrows met. "What is it with you two? *I'm* keeping her safe. Besides, I wouldn't let rare blood go to waste."

I scoffed. Disgust crawled all over. He saw me as a prize. I kissed that big, evil mouth of his. Too bad it hadn't hurt him.

"Very noble of you," I said.

"It's not just about that, and you know it." He lowered his head and cast his eyes forward. "We had a connection. You felt it too."

I had. And I regretted ever noticing it.

Guy pressed into my side, as if to physically remind me that I had other options, like escaping. "Let's go. Before I do something stupid."

He left his demand sounding more like a question. It was then I knew everything was going to be different than before. Guy hadn't come to drag me off, although I could tell part of him wanted to for the sake of leaving the vampire pit faster.

I loosened my grip on his clothes in case we needed to run or fight. Gods, not a fight. My blood couldn't be worth that much. Our exit points were blocked by an army. Aiden's grin stretched even wider at my concerned scan of the room.

"No, no," his annoyingly charmed voice sang, "I promised to keep her safe from EXO. That includes you, reaper. What kind of gentleman would I be if I broke our pact?"

"What pact?" Guy asked, and his flat line caved into a frown.

"I traded him my blood for a place to hide," I muttered, "but I'm calling a veto."

"Jess, what has he told you? Why are you running from EXO?"

My eyes dropped to the floor. Was he acting oblivious on purpose so he could pull the same stunt Aiden had? That didn't seem like Guy at all.

"He didn't," I said, "Tori told me what the angels said. She told me everything."

He paused but not for very long. We were still surrounded after all.

"Tori had it wrong. Faris, sure, he's shit, but Zak wasn't involved. He never was."

"I know everything, Guy," I repeated, "*All* of it."

It took him a fraction of a second for that to click. "I told you I was looking for answers, but those answers didn't change anything for Zak. Hell, he wasn't even shocked. So no, he wasn't about to turn on you."

He wasn't?

I knew the vampires around us were getting restless but I didn't care. Zak hadn't been surprised or even upset? Wouldn't an angel have a visceral reaction to the announcement of a demon lord's offspring?

Guy also ignored our company. "I'm sorry that I didn't get to you before someone else did."

Aiden kept a shameless smile as I shot him an accusing stare. I couldn't prove it, but something told me he'd known all along that Zak wasn't a threat to me. He'd made everything work in his favor.

"Hey, it's not like I lied about anything," Aiden said, "Where was he when the purifiers came? Maybe the angel doesn't want you dead, but they sure did. The reaper's own ghost-pet told you to leave him in the dust."

The lights in Guy's eyes dimmed until they returned to normal again. Still, he only spoke to me. "It's true. I wasn't there but not for the reasons you think."

Aiden's barking laugh made us both flinch.

"We all know how this ends. EXO doesn't want a *demon*, princess or otherwise. But I do." His red eyes became hooded beneath his lashes. The hoard of vampires glowered intently beside him, turning the hall into a dim cavern with glowing orbs.

He stepped forward, "Cupcake—"

"Just stop."

I finally snapped. The many red eyes shifted to the shadow that grew around me.

No-no-no.

Don't blow up the building!

I willed the darkness back, which felt a lot like trying to shove the overflowing sock drawer closed while holding my breath. Except that my body was the drawer and my insides were the socks.

I caught Guy leaning in, but his hand didn't quite reach my shoulder. Was he waiting for permission? I'd wanted to scare the vampires a little, but not at the expense of our lives. With a quick nod, I signaled his help.

His cool fingers descended, but since I wore a sweater, they rested where the seam met my skin. The drawer shut. My shadow dissipated.

Aiden curled his tongue at my display.

"*Jess.* It was Faris this time, it'll be someone else tomorrow."

He got as close as he could without being in slashing distance of Guy's scythe. I could tell the temptation was strong by the way Guy's knuckles turned bone-white around the staff.

I heard a foreign sincerity that seemed to pain Aiden to speak. "Stay with me."

His gaze was neither menacing nor kind. I had a feeling that depending on my answer that could change. But how could I? He'd already lied to me. Comfortably, I might add. He was a vampire, and should have heard Faris coming for me well before we ran into each other. If that was true, Aiden had let it all happen. *Let* me get scared.

I should have listened to my gut, and now my gut wanted to follow Guy out of that hell hole.

"You blew that chance the second you drugged me," I said.

Aiden resembled marble. He didn't lash out but I sensed his fuming energy bubbling over. His honeyed words remained behind his tightly pressed lips. I almost felt bad but reminded myself what he did. We might've had a lot in common, but that didn't mean I had to be okay with his choices.

"You know what she is, don't you?" Aiden shifted his gaze to Guy.

Guy didn't agree or rebuttal his accusations. Hadn't we established the demon princess thing already?

When Guy still refrained from answering, Aiden went back to me. "They'll destroy you."

"That won't happen."

We both looked at Guy. The hand that kept my darkness in check slid down my arm and across my front.

"Chaos falls under *my* jurisdiction," he said, "It doesn't matter what the angel's want now."

Aiden's face strained to remain emotionless, like he'd been torn between cursing or rolling his eyes. I held my breath until I felt my lungs collapse. Gods, how much more of this could we take? I welcomed a fight at that point just to quit suffering from anticipation.

"You're really flighty, aren't you? Jumping into another man's arms so quickly." Aiden spoke with some resolve and, to our surprise, stepped aside. "Go, then. Run back to your angels. I won't be so quick to rescue you a second time."

Guy took the invitation before he even finished. He gave Aiden a deadened stare as we passed. The indifference struck cold. When I slowed our pace with my baby giraffe legs, Guy swooped an arm under my knees and lifted me over his shoulder.

"Just until we get outside," he assured me. Yup. Death's lackey carried me through a hall of vampires. It would've been terrifying had I not been dying from the embarrassment.

We had to puzzle our way through the vampires. Some refused to move at all, hissing as we bumped their shoulders. Why hadn't Guy teleported us through? I'd seen him do it many times.

As soon as we were down the steps I looked behind us to see Aiden's sights on the back of Guy's head. He followed us at a much slower pace; a hunter creeping on his prey.

"I take back what I said, Cupcake," my nickname left his lips with the pettiness of an ex lover, "I think I will see you again."

Unlike a good predator, he let us go.

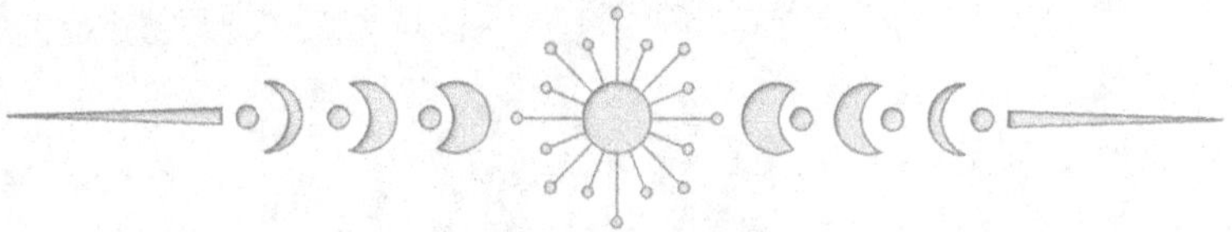

Aiden seemed to respect my wishes, but I held my breath and glanced back every few seconds.

Guy set me down, as promised. He vanished his scythe but hadn't slowed his pace. We emerged from the alley and onto the busy streets of neon. Cars roared by. The intensity of light and sound made my senses crumple like a wad of paper.

"Guy, can we talk, please?" I asked while squinting.

He halted and I slammed my face into his back. I hadn't expected him to listen to me with such enthusiasm. "I don't understand," he said, "Why him?"

"I didn't know what else to do." Blaring horns from the street drowned my pitiful response. When Guy turned to face me, the fury in his eyes froze the next words in my throat.

"He took advantage of the situation."

"Yeah, well…" I paused to catch my falling forehead in my palm, "I know that now."

His breath released with more aggression than was natural. "He did a number on you too. You're lucky you didn't turn."

It was my turn to have frustrations bubbling over. "I was left in a locked room with demon-killing fanatics on the other side. I didn't know *who* to trust or *where* to go! Tori had just told me I was the spawn of a demon lord so my options weren't looking optimistic."

Another long exhale escaped from his barely parted lips. "Zak's been busting his ass to protect you, even from his own colleagues. Risking a hell of a lot more than just his position with EXO. The *only* reason he's gotten away with opposing angels is because he's an angel himself. Do you understand? And now, while he's busy hunting a mass murderer, he has to worry about finding you too."

I dropped my head like a child getting scolded. Guy cursed under his breath.

"Are you crying?" he asked.

"It's just t-the s-stupid venom."

A loud sob broke free of my chest. My emotional meter overflowed; aided by guilt, blood loss, and stress from the evening. I couldn't see Guy clearly through my blurred vision, but I felt his hand on the back of my head.

He pulled me into his shoulder. I felt secure in his harbor, smothered by his smokey scent. Not at all how I imagined Death to smell, honestly. I favored the burning musk over rotting flesh and decay.

"I failed as a buddy," Guy said, "I'm sorry."

I made an awful snort; tears mixed with a laugh.

"You found me, didn't you?"

"I guess I did."

His coolness invited me in further until I brought my arms around him. After a minute longer, Guy signaled that the moment ended by patting me on the head. When I pulled back, his eyes stopped at the knitting of my sweater near my neck. I'd forgotten to take the tag off.

He gripped the slip of paper with a cold fist and yanked, making it pop clean off.

"If you even think about shedding another tear over your vampire boyfriend, I will arrest you, after I arrest him," he said, "For public indecency. And idiocy."

Wow. He killed the mood fast.

"Are you really upset that he bought me clothes?" I asked, "You should've seen what I had on before."

I turned myself out of his not-at-all, passive-aggressive embrace. On the bright side, I'd finished crying.

"I'm not upset. He's just irritating," Guy said and dropped the tag like it was lathered in poison. "Come on. We're taking the bus."

"The bus?"

I halted, both physically and mentally. A reaper was opting for public transportation? Were we *finally* going to choose the most sane option; no broomsticks wormholes or flying with angel wings?

"What?" he asked.

"Nothing... I was expecting a van with bars for windows."

Guy deadpanned, either at my comment or because he was frustrated with himself. "I left in a hurry and didn't plan a way back."

"You were that worried?"

He held in his reply to let pedestrians walk by. When we were in the clear, the words flew from his lips. "Unconscious bodies were scattered around Clove's lab. You, Faris, and Aiden have been missing for a day and a half. Tori, once I got her to wake up, was a crying mess. Zak's in crisis mode which means Jarmiel is unbearable. You'd just told me about your dreams with The Necromancer, who *hasn't* been caught yet *and* showed up at EXO the same time you disappeared. We're still looking for him while his monsters are terrorizing every city. Yeah. I was *worried.*"

I didn't look away, but his delivery made my heart thrum faster.

"I'm sorry."

"Get your sorry ass on the bus."

Guy didn't say a word at the stop or after we found our seats. Granted, he seemed busy sending a flurry of texts on his phone. Our mood was dampened with awkwardness. It didn't help that the venom made me queasy and our ride smelled like armpits.

Guy crossed his arms. I knew his personality could be cold but we'd dropped to freezing temperatures. *Brrr.*

"Tell me everything," he said, "Start from the lab."

I told him the tale of Tori and I escaping the purifiers, and then Aiden's sudden emergence. Guy listened but faced forward the entire time, burning holes in the back of another's chair. His shoulders raised during Aiden's participation in the story.

"Tori," Guy mumbled, "She didn't hear everything Zak and Raguel said. As your *buddy*, they questioned my absence during the gym incident. I didn't say anything about your dreams, since you asked me not to, but Raguel formed his own conclusions from the night The Necromancer approached EXO's gates. Things have changed since taking you in."

"You really didn't tell them?" I asked.

Guy gave me a look but not an answer. Did this have to do with what he told Aiden about being part of his "jurisdiction?" I'd been dying to ask about that too, but hearing we had it wrong about Zak brought about so many emotions.

He hadn't changed his mind about me.

The skin around my eyes tightened from the urge to cry but I'd already dried out. "So Raguel freaked out and gave Tori the wrong impression," I said, "How did you find out who my dad was?"

"The fact that The Necromancer has taken an interest in you confirmed my suspicions. I just had to do some… digging."

"Digging?"

"It might have involved communicating with a knowledge demon."

"A *knowledge* demon? Doesn't sound sketchy at all."

Guy cracked his icy exterior with a smirk. "Not all demons thrive from deception and violence. You're a perfect example."

"I technically thrive from others' suffering, whether I enjoy it or not."

I chewed the inside of my cheek, bitter at the thought. Guy, again, said nothing, but I could feel his aura getting warmer, like the dawn rising over a snowy peak. "You think The Necromancer knows and that's why he's harassing me?" I asked, changing topics. "Am I still a chaos-thing?"

Guy looked around us before dropping his head closer to my ear. Rumbling whispers confirmed the truth, "The conflict you feel hasn't been for nothing. You're both a being of darkness and light. Conflict and chaos *is* you."

I opened my mouth to speak but he shook his head. "We should wait. We don't know who's listening."

"But how is that possible?" I asked anyway, "And what makes that so different from a human? They're exposed to both elements too."

"Humans are born empty. Pure. Even upon their death. Even after a hundred years, the measure of light and dark they accumulated is miniscule. Could they be like you? Yes, maybe after a thousand years of conflict. The only way someone like you can exist here is if the World Soul allows it and if that's true, then… you're mine to protect."

I heard every word and yet, only the last bit burned in my mind.

Mine to protect.

I swallowed a lump in my throat. "You have to protect chaotic beings?"

"Death has a duty to keep order in the mortal realm. Keeping order doesn't always mean heroic acts of good deeds," Guy said, "Natural disasters, while tragic, serve a purpose. A living chaos vessel serves a purpose as well, though I don't even know what that may be."

"So, you're keeping me alive to make sure I succeed in doing horrible things?" My rise turned some heads in the bus, so I quieted back down. "*No*. What? *No*, Guy."

"They're only horrible to those with limited understanding. I told you why I came to Zak. For Tori. But there was something else too. You're who I've been waiting for, all this time."

His hands flexed as he spoke. "Even before I knew, I felt the strange urge to shadow you; make sure nothing happened to you. I couldn't help it, like it was second nature. *My* second nature. I thought I was going mad."

Death needed to protect me?

No. Protect a disaster.

Guy cupped a hand over his lips and stared out the window. His finger tapped impatiently against his cheek. "I can't promise we can rely on the angels forever, but we can trust Zak. For now, EXO is still the safest place."

"Why don't you trust them?" I asked, "Aiden mentioned something similar."

I knew why *I* struggled to trust angels. Call it my "second nature."

"Remember, dark matter isn't inherently evil? The same can be said for light matter. Just because angels have the best of intentions doesn't mean you fit the equation. If anything…" He stopped himself maybe because of how distressed my face had become.

"No. Tell me," I begged, "I need to know."

"I don't like Aiden, but he's right. Some angels might see you as a threat. The only beings of your kind in living history have been to serve one purpose. Destroy something the World Soul doesn't like."

"What does the World Soul dislike?"

"Whatever is in opposition to balance."

I knew he didn't want to keep talking about it so openly, but my brain was exploding with information. Had Naomi known about this?

"I don't want to destroy anything, though."

"Not *now*," Guy responded to my concerns with eerie assurance, "As for The Necromancer's interests, he must have seen or learned of your power. The more who know, the hairier things will get."

"I'm pretty sure I saw Clay that night before the peacekeepers showed up." I groaned at the revelation and lingering lethargy. "Gods. How long is venom supposed to last in your body, anyway?"

"It takes a day to replenish a small amount of blood. For you, maybe half that, but I don't know exactly when you were bitten or how much venom he used."

"I feel stupid." I laughed at myself. Aiden hadn't cloaked his intentions so well that I couldn't spot misfortune coming. And I hadn't hated all of it. I even found myself liking him, just a little.

"Don't. You were in a tough spot and I made you feel shitty for it," Guy mumbled at the end. Back in silence, we sat in our cramped seats with smudged windows obscuring our view. I shifted around so that our thighs wouldn't touch as much, but nothing seemed to help.

"Thank you," I said.

"For what?"

"Showing up, I guess. How did you know where I was?"

"I said I'd always find you." He wiggled his shoulders forward so he could reach into his coat without bumping me. I recognized the purple animal toy right away. The toy seemed lifeless, however, and not inhabited by a teenage spirit.

"She's resting. Probably won't wake for several hours," he said, "After some tough love and a lot of crying, she told me you left. Since Aiden hadn't joined the manhunt, I asked Mallory where he could be."

"Mallory?"

Aiden would be disappointed to hear his own sister ratted him out.

"She probably just wants to get me in trouble," I threw in.

"You don't need her help for that."

His eyes rolled and then steadied as his thoughts drifted. "We should get you some liquids to help with the venom. If our routes are blocked by the search, it might be a while before we reach Volhold. Think you can make it?"

"I think so."

"Does your neck hurt?"

The memories made my face flush at an alarming rate; Aiden all over me. Hands on my body. Mouth devouring mine. He probably thought I was such an easy target.

"No. Does Aiden rule the vampire roost or something?" I asked, wanting to avoid my shame, "Everyone looked like they wanted to kill you."

Guy stuffed Tori back into her hiding spot. "The living fear Death. It's an inescapable fate, but necessary to the whole cosmic, spiritual system in place. When vampires were created, the guardians of the World Soul decided to cut their life to half that of a human's. If not for that, vampires would disrupt the balance. They exist like immortals; strong, powerful, never experiencing illness. Godlike, really, but it's short-lived. So yeah, I'm sure they'd delight in killing me. But I think tonight's animosity had more to do with me stealing Aiden's dinner."

I gave him the side-eye. "I forget that you're funny."

The bus rolled to a stop. Guy got up so I did too.

"Can you not teleport with another person?" I asked once we were back on the streets. We hadn't been able to take the bus all the way home. Pity.

"Not anyone living, no," he said and pointed to the convenience store down the road. The open sign flashed red, but hardly anyone was inside. I hugged myself as we walked, protecting my arms from the whistling wind that blew by.

What would happen to Aiden, anyway? Guy didn't mention what he'd report back to Zak. After what he did to his subordinate,

I couldn't believe Guy hadn't arrested him on the spot. Hell, I wasn't sure what punishment awaited *me*, a deserter.

As upset as I was about the whole thing, I couldn't bring myself to truly and passionately hate Aiden. It sounded like he wanted to live as humans did, not micromanaged or condemned. He wasn't the first supernatural to bring up injustice and wouldn't be the last.

It would be nice to live that freely.

Our eventful evening took a comedic turn as I watched Guy purchase our late-night snacks. A juice box was presented to me as well as a cookie the size of a frisbee. I grabbed both items, looking either diabetic or pregnant. "I'm starting to think you want to plump me up for the vampires."

"A simple 'thank you' would do just fine."

"*Thanks.*" I eyed the cookie with great concern and peeled away the protective plastic, but Guy followed my fingers with his own. He struck the baked saucer with his open mouth and stole a chocolatey portion from the top.

"Gods." I balked.

"There," he spoke with crumbs still on his lip, "Less cookie for you to complain about."

"Yeah but now your germs are on it."

"Just eat it."

I smiled. At least we had a walk to look forward to, and I wouldn't be sitting with a giant cookie in my guts.

In all the times Guy and I walked together, he'd usually keep his hands in his pockets and look bored of the world around him. That hadn't been the case that evening. The way he made eye contact with everyone we crossed made me think we were being followed.

"Where is Zak now?" I asked.

"We thought we had The Necromancer cornered, but it was only his Ghouls. Several locations called for Ghoul activity, giving us the go-around. I think he's baiting us."

"A distraction?"

"Yes. Unfortunately, many people are hurt."

"I see…" If it were possible, I would have felt even more stupid. All I'd done was drag us out in the open for The Necromancer to find. "You said Clay came to EXO. What happened to Faris?"

"A Ghoul attacked the gates shortly after the security system rebooted. He didn't stay long, I'm assuming because you were already gone."

I gulped. Just what was Clay's plan? Why terrorize people, for the hell of it?

"Faris will be dealt with after we find him," Guy continued, "Tori's mix-up might've been a good thing, actually. You would've been surprised by Faris *and* The Necromancer."

We slowed as we reached an elevated platform that brought us to a metal track and busy public terminal. Everything had an updated appearance, including the train with its chrome sheen. We were getting close to Volhold once again. Was I relieved or scared to go back?

"We need tickets." Guy's enthusiasm dropped another octave. A booth and lounge were already filled with people off to the right. The line to get tickets backed up next to the train. Voices sounded urgent. Impatient.

I sucked down the rest of my juice box. "That's a lot of humans…"

"Everyone's trying to get home. I'm sure the news is covering the attacks," Guy noted with his sharp eyes still scouting about. The sugar overload from the snacks on my empty, poisoned stomach made it gurgle.

Oh no…

"What is it?" Guy asked after I'd stopped dead in my tracks.

"I'm gonna be sick," I said.

"What?" At first, he held out his hands, almost like he was going to catch the vomit himself. How sweet. And totally ridiculous.

I shoved him aside and dove head-first into the nearest trash can. Everything came up. Likely my ghost as well. I did Guy's job for him. As much as I blamed his selection of snacks for my disgusting demise, the regurgitated juice helped lessen the vile taste in my mouth.

Guy let me finish before tapping me on the back. "There's a restroom."

He pointed across the way to the blue, public restroom signs. A few people inched away from us, but for the most part we hadn't been noticed. Still, that went right on my list of most humiliating moments.

After ensuring I was done puking my guts out, I hurried to the facilities. Guy's presence felt close behind but he didn't follow me inside. Once I was alone, I took the nearest open stall and hung myself over the toilet. Nothing elegant about it. I fully expected to hurl again but the longer I stood in preparation, the less nausea crawled up my throat.

I waited thirty more seconds just in case. Nothing. Thank gods. The sugar helped after all. I knew Guy was going to tease me, and I had the rest of the way home to look forward to it.

When I turned to leave the still empty toilet bowl, an odd sight caught my eye.

A woman's black heels planted just outside my stall. There was nothing odd about that specifically, but the lack of distance they'd left from my door didn't feel natural. If I pushed it out even an inch, I'd bump her nose.

"Excuse me," I said, but I got no response. The other stalls hadn't looked occupied when I came in. Surely, she wasn't waiting to use mine? Just to check, I crouched to spy on each adjacent stall. No one. Empty.

When I looked forward again, the feet had gone. She must've realized my toilet was in use and skipped to the next. When I pushed the door out, I saw a woman in the same heels washing her hands at the sink.

She works fast.

I ignored her and found my own sink two down from hers. First order of business was cleaning my mouth out and banishing the sour aftertaste of my sickness for good. Once I was satisfied, I splashed my face with cool water and dabbed myself off with a paper towel.

When I checked myself in the mirror, I frowned. *Yuck.* My skin tone looked a shade of blue under the horrid lighting. Very corpse-esque. But that wasn't what caused me to flinch.

The reflection of the woman with heels and personal space issues stared right at me. Smiling. Her hands remained under the running water. The longer she watched with unblinking eyes, the more I questioned if she were a mannequin and not a person.

I shut off my water and waited for her to say something. It was like she'd gotten stuck in time. Or drugs. City-life must occupy a whole new level of weirdness I hadn't gotten accustomed to yet. Either way, it creeped me out, so I made for the exit.

Locked.

Even if someone wanted it locked, it locked on *my* side. From what I could see, nothing should have prevented me from leaving. I tugged again, and then pushed, just to cover all the bases.

I felt something over my shoulder and looked.

"*Shit!*" I hissed. "Okay, lady. What do you want?"

The smiling woman swayed directly behind me. For a while, she did nothing. Her stuck expression fueled the weariness growing inside me. Not only that, but she *reeked* like raw and turned meat.

"Hello, Jessebel." The words escaped her lips, but the only voice I heard belonged to my recurring nightmares.

"Clay?"

What was I supposed to do next? Punch her?

I hadn't noticed her eyes before. Too distracted by her teeth. They had a ghostly white coating. A dull light flickered from her pupils, like a dying candle deep in her soul.

"I've been looking for you," he said, still using the woman as a puppet, "I had everything planned but you'd already gotten yourself out of the angel's grasp. Nicely done."

The woman raised a hand and captured the ends of my hair that had fallen over my shoulder. There was no doubt in my mind it was really him. I could smell his disturbed magic with every word she uttered.

I pushed her away. Too hard. Her frail human body hit the back wall. A wave of regret washed over me as I saw her expression change to one of pain. She trembled on the tiled floor.

"*Ah…* it hurts."

I almost—*almost*—came to her aid but then, her smile returned, followed by a scratchy laugh. Her neck popped and twisted upward to see my disgusted reaction better.

"Help me, Jessebel," Clay's voice mocked.

More frightful thoughts seized me. Was I just dreaming? Had I actually been rescued by Guy or would I wake up in Aiden's room?

Reality and dreams blended as one. I put more effort into the door that time and it opened without resistance. The noise of the station roared with voices and trains screeching to their stops.

It has to be real.

I struggled to keep up with my beating heart.

"Guy…" I breathed his name.

Someone's loud boots sounded on my left. I looked up at the stranger wearing all black. My body stiffened. Dark energy filled the cramped space between us. The brightness from the overhead lights dimmed and shuddered.

Clay's sickening energy harbored within another human puppet. I recognized it right away this time. The unknown man draped a thick arm over my shoulders. Chills prickled the flesh beneath my clothes.

"Stop it," I said.

"Stop what?" Clay's voice asked.

I shook his arm off. "Whatever it is you're doing. Shouldn't you be busy with peacekeepers?"

"They're the busy ones at the moment," he said, sounding proud of himself.

"Stay out of my head."

"I've no idea what you mean. I'm very much awake. Just like you."

Ice flooded my veins. Just how many more puppets did he have wandering around the station? I made a quick look around, hoping to find Guy. He wouldn't have left me, not after all the "I must protect you" crap he said!

The stranger hosting Clay's voice chuckled. "You look nervous."

I ran in the opposite direction, and he didn't stop me. Someone else walked in my path and muttered to me as I dodged them. "Don't run far, little demon."

I whipped around, ready to grab the next possessed person and shake them back to life. Instead, I saw *him.*

Clay's slender figure filled out with the help of his heavy-duty coat. How could no one else notice him? I could feel his ominous threat from where I stood. He rested his head against a metal pole with a satisfied grin and a gleam in his corrupted eyes.

More bodies shuffled into me, anxious to reach their train. Clay slipped into the crowd, blending in like a shark underwater.

"Hells…"

I whipped around and found the *other* hooded man of Death.

Guy's cold hand clasped around mine. "What're you doing? Trains move quickly here. We need to go."

"Guy, wait."

He directed us through a pair of sliding doors to the silver train. I still hadn't gotten used to touching someone so freely. No restraint or worries. But I couldn't think about that yet. I kept an eye out for Clay, waiting for him to pop up again.

"Guy, something's not right," I said, "I think—"

The train moved before everyone could find seats. We grabbed onto the handrails that dangled in the aisle, but momentum lurched us in the opposite direction. Guy caught me with his chest, his smoke and frost tickling my nose.

I eagerly righted myself. "I saw Clay. He was here at the station. He was, like, using people to talk for him. I don't know how many."

Guy lifted his eyes from my face and gazed over my head. He'd heard me but something else held his focus. Buildings stretched outside the windows like taffy made of blended lights. I felt a new chill crawl down my spine. The taste of charcoal coated my tongue. A dull ringing drowned in my ears.

Getting on the train had been a mistake.

I'd just turned around, assuming it was Clay emitting the dark magic that filled the car, but something came crashing down on the roof.

Glass shattered. The impact shook the train, causing several passengers to shriek, fall, and point at the deep crater dipping from the roof. Guy kept a hard grip on my shoulder. Shards from the windows fell from my sweater like hail.

We crouched in unison, as the ceiling caved-in above us. The ripping of metal pierced our eardrums. People had already left their seats in an effort to get farther away while a few hadn't moved at all.

It was then I caught another awful whiff. The same as the woman in the restroom. Nothing looked physically amiss, but when I bumped into the passenger next to me in the aisle, I felt an echo; an internal and spiritual one that someone like me would notice. He lacked *any* life essence.

He's… hollow?

"Guy." I grabbed him by the sleeve.

He followed my thoughts exactly. "He's undead."

At that, the standing corpse chuckled. Guy glowered and pulled me closer to him. The man still didn't move, but we heard Clay's voice escape his lips. "Buckle up, buttercup."

Whatever landed on top of us finally broke through, revealing a black sky through a huge slit down the middle. The lights shut off. Walls rattled. An elderly couple shouted *"earthquake!"* and escalated everyone's fear. People stumbled over each other in a panicked frenzy to get nowhere. All except the frozen few.

My mouth went dry as I counted how many soulless, immobile bodies I could see.

Three… Six…

The train jerked again.

We'd been hit a second time but from below. Our car rocked, tilting over the rails with the view of a long fall to the street below. I lost my hold on Guy, slamming my head into a metal pole.

My pulse throbbed from my newly bruised skull. I wrapped my arms around one of the headrests to stop myself from moving. The train broke in two, detaching our car from the half with an engine and slowing us down.

One giant fist molded from several hands burst through the door, crushing passengers in the aisle and flooding us with its stench.

A Ghoul.

With its sudden attack and our already lessening speed, it wasn't long before we came to an uncomfortable stop. Its wide body brought the split end of our car up like a pyramid and passengers tumbled back. I grasped my seat even tighter, only able to catch one older woman falling past me by the collar of her sweater.

She dangled there with horror in her eyes.

"Hang on," I said.

Where is Guy?

The car came crashing back down and bounced us back into the aisle, right in front of the monster. Instead of three heads like the one before, it had one. Its jaw sat unhinged with a string of drool dripping down. Two mountains made entirely from twisted limbs compressed the neck.

"Good gods." The woman I still held onto quivered beside me. "Devils… *Devils!*"

Screams ping-ponged off the destroyed tin walls. I lifted the woman with a bit too much strength, startling her further. But it was too late. We'd started to tip.

Airborne. For a terrible few moments, we floated inside the car. I wished for the strength to stop our fall, but how could I catch a train? Even if I'd wanted to try, I was a victim trapped inside like the rest of them. All those screams. All those faces…

The remaining two cars behind us held our weight, barely. A man and woman fell straight through the aisle. One got chomped by the Ghoul, removing his arm clean off. The woman splattered on the streets.

Adrenaline sparked a tiny flame of bravery inside me. I willed myself across to the other seat, creating a net with my body to catch any other fallers.

I stopped two. The man almost broke my arm with his weight and gazed at me in shock. Yeah, I'm pretty shocked too, I wanted to say. His female companion clawed at my back and wailed but luckily had the sense to move to the seats to hide behind.

Another body went over my head.

Gods…

Help us.

One second later, and our connection to the other cars snapped. We were going to hit the street in a nose-dive. Hard.

I watched the Ghoul smack its bloodied lips at us, undisturbed by the crash that awaited. What could I do? Guy could teleport, but he couldn't teleport the living. And we were all alive for the next few seconds.

Gods. Gods.

I couldn't think! All I could see was doom.

The older woman I'd helped earlier couldn't hold herself in her seat. She prayed loudly as her feeble fingers pinched the chair's fabric, which ultimately betrayed her. I watched her close her eyes as she fell.

I dropped down after her. Once I felt her hand, I held it tight. Her bones were like blades of straw and her spirit even softer. Fear but also acceptance welcomed me when her eyes opened again.

Guy blew in from the windows like a gray hurricane, returning just in time to help us mortal souls. He looped one arm around my middle while the other hooked his scythe in the ceiling's metal cavity. That allowed me to use all my strength to hold the woman I'd saved.

"Saved," considering we were all about to be pancakes.

What was the point of EXO, or my power, if we couldn't perform some miracle? But then, I was no angel. All I could do was destroy.

"Let go," I told Guy.

"*What?*"

I almost thought he wouldn't. His arm had been compressing my ribs. At the last second, for whatever reason, he decided to trust me.

The Ghoul's several disorganized eyeballs observed my final descent. I did my best to throw the woman behind me before commanding my chaos forward. The aggressive matter escaped from my chest, shredding my sweater like tissue paper. One powerful blast sparkled gold; brighter than I'd ever seen. The woman howled behind me, surely confused and terrified.

I felt the force of it push us back just as we hit the street. The Ghoul crunched, and so had the walls of our car. However, as I'd hoped and with all the luck in the world, our fall lost some of its gravity from my chaos.

The plan was to use the monster and my power to cushion the fall. Sure, passengers, including myself, flew around like rag dolls, but we made it. The car groaned before finally settling.

Had I actually done it? How many were still alive?

I felt a searing heat in the center of my chest. Light trickled back into the glowing hole I found at the base of my neck. *Ow.*

Also, curious. I heard sobs and exclaims of surprise. The passengers' jumbled energy felt like electricity tickling my brain through my ears.

Everything ached. I tried shifting around and froze, feeling a sharp pain in my leg. A jagged edge of debris found a sweet spot to pierce just above my knee. *Great.* Just what I fucking needed. To be impaled.

Okay. That was an exaggeration, but ripping it out still sucked. I'd watched the bad-ass heroes do it in movies and somehow walk away afterward, but it took three excruciating attempts to get it free and after that, I didn't want to move ever again.

I waited for my healing to close the bleeding wound before sitting up. The world turned upside down. My head had been laying on the ceiling and the shattered windows faced the gravel outside.

Glass cracked beneath me. My hand felt like I'd taken an iron rod to my knuckles. I gasped, remembering I'd had the older woman with me. Her hand looked worse than mine, bent and broken, but her fingers stayed gently clasped around me. She was laying too still, like a heap of clothing and not an actual person. Cuts carved at her face, but she wore a misplaced smile on her lips.

I nudged her and squeaked. "Ma'am?"

My gaze went to our joined hands and my stomach sank. How long had I been touching her, *exactly*? I felt my heart lodge in my throat. New tears threatened to fall. Her wrinkled skin already turned a shade paler.

From her hand, I felt Death.

My second attempt to reach her sounded weaker than the last. I tore my hand out of hers. It didn't matter. I was too late. Had I killed her in all my effort to do the exact opposite?

Why had she died with such a peaceful smile?

"Ma'am!"

Nothing.

As I examined her body, I couldn't help but hate the itching sensation of my skin and muscles sewing themselves back together. I probably had her soul to thank for that.

Guy's shadow fell over my head. His silhouette grew until it appeared like a monster with wings. When I finished healing, I cracked my neck with a loud pop. The obvious rejuvenation had me fuming on the inside like an angry tea kettle. Just a torn sweater and a few bloodstains? *What bullshit.* I couldn't use the excuse that humans were weaker forever.

Murder is murder.

"Her body was old. She wasn't going to survive," Guy said, and then added, "That's what she wants you to know."

My head shot upward. His eyes glowed once again, and I caught the sight of a light purple wisp dancing around his shoulder.

"You already—?" I didn't have the guts to finish. He reaped her soul and she even spoke to him? Reapers really were efficient. She hadn't suffered long, at least.

I went back to looking at the tarnished car, avoiding Guy and the woman's lifelessness. What was her name? Should I find her family and report to them personally? Did she have a family?

"Jess," Guy spoke but I kept my face lowered, "She wasn't going to survive no matter what you did."

No matter what *I* did. Right. Zak could've saved her, though. He could've flown everyone away; performed a *real* miracle.

My self loathing blinded me from what caused the crash in the first place. A hand, or maybe several, wrapped around my thigh, sending ice down my legs. The remaining corpses of the Ghoul acted as one but broke into several moving body parts, crawling toward us like cockroaches.

Guy sliced through the corrupted flesh that captured my leg. Inky blood splattered the floor. Clouds emerged from Guy's back and shielded me from the animated gore. His shadow moved, fluid and lethal, through the smokey barrier. A dance of Death's macabre.

"Gather yourself and get the hell out of here," he said, "I'll find you again."

Guy continued their battle outside the car. A streetlight was knocked over. Parked vehicles dented. Pedestrians that had been closeby screeched, and rightfully so. He seemed mindful of the people around us, keeping the Ghoul and himself at a distance, but Guy made Death an art.

Every cut he delivered splattered tar-like paint over the city; his canvas. I could almost hear music directing his steps and blows, an effortless dance filled with purpose. His merciless, otherworldly blade struck cold like the blizzard stirring behind his gaze.

And there I sat. Still wallowing.

Get up. I didn't think it would be such a difficult task but my chest felt heavy and kept me planted. Maybe my guilt would root me to that spot for eternity. Maybe that would be okay. Did I deserve anything less?

Get UP!

Then, I remembered the second Ghoul. What if it fell as well? I located the remaining survivors from the train, half hanging from their seats or passed out in the wreckage. Some were stunned or injured. All except one.

My mouth went dry. The lone passenger stood tall in the mess but with one glaring problem. His head lay flat on his shoulder, detached almost completely from his neck. I heard a woman scream, probably having just noticed the nearly headless man as well.

He smiled at me.

"Clay…" I barely mouthed his name when his neck jerked back into place. His dark hood flipped back over his head like the snap of a lid. He hadn't lifted a finger.

Another shriek pierced my ears and I realized that he'd made his move. Like a ghostly shade, his arm cut violently through the air at each and every passenger. An awful gasp left every pair of parted lips.

"Clay, stop!" A glint in the darkness caught my eye. I knew exactly what was happening, but more fell to his blade before I could even blink. Every cut felt like an invisible knife deep into my own chest.

My mounting failures crushed me, creating my grave in the earth. I used my body to cover the dead woman in front of me because it was all I could think to do.

He stabbed them…

He stabbed them all.

Clay's grin exposed a row of sharpened teeth. He twirled his black blade between his hands, before clapping them together in a slow, mocking rhythm.

"Jessebel. In the flesh."

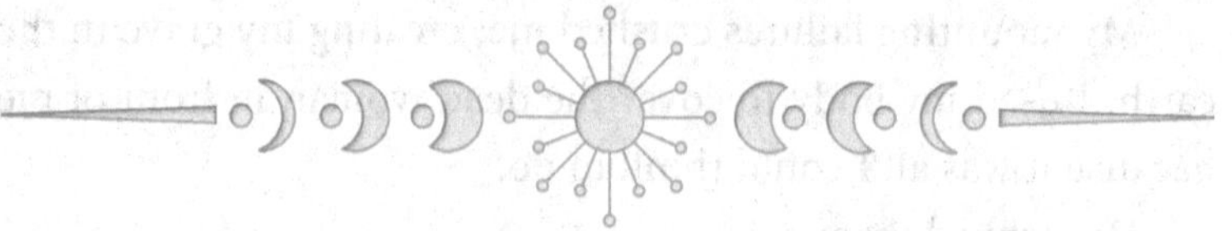

T he car became a coffin filled with hollowed figures.

Like an organism of one mind, Clay's victims all turned at the same time. Fresh blood still leaked from their bodies. Their eyes glowed like haunting white orbs.

Clay had made an army before I could even pick myself up off the floor.

I sat on my knees, trembling like a frightened kitten and not a great demon of Hell. He had no regard for the lives on that train. I knew from the moment I smelled his dark magic that he was perfectly capable, but seeing his evil firsthand? That was a brutal slap of reality.

"Wishing you were asleep now, princess?" His snicker came out quiet and creeping, like skittering rats. He took confident strides toward me, and survival kicked in, rattling me from my gloom.

I was trapped in a metal box with a psycho.

Get your ass off the ground and run!

A tickle, so delicate I almost missed it, trailed up my arm like the back of someone's finger. I looked down at dust particles, at least, that was what I thought, until I saw the same sheen of soulful violet. As soon as the ethereal specks settled on my skin, a spark warmed my insides.

The old woman had been dead for a few minutes, but that had been *her*. What was left of her. Her soul barely grazed me, but it had been enough. I brought my hand forward as if to push Clay back. Nothing happened at first, but then a small burst of dark matter left my palm.

The surge charred the seats closest to me and created a small shock wave. Clay dove out of the way, avoiding it entirely. I squeezed the dead woman's shoulder one last time, thanking her from beyond the grave, and then ran.

A dam broke from behind me.

The undead followed through the wreckage with impressive speed. Hundreds of voices carried above us from the lucky cars that hadn't fallen from the tracks. We'd crashed on an intersection with bystanders flashing their phones and narrating the scene from the safety of the sidewalk. Especially Guy and the Ghoul.

"*Go!*" The roar split my throat. "You're not safe here."

The Ghoul still hadn't relented, even in its state of dangling body parts. Whatever magic fueled the beast disregarded pain. It caught Guy with a heavy, backhanded smack that rolled him across the gravel. He lifted his head and revealed pinkened skin on his scalp.

The sound of nails scratching rudely alerted me to my own peril. Zombies climbed out of the train. A shredded piece of metal on the ground threatened to cut my ankle open. Not a bad choice of weapon.

Except *not*. I didn't want to kill the people I'd just tried to save. They were already dead, but I couldn't stomach the idea of hurting them again. Some demon I was. I just watched as they got closer, mindless and clumsy while I clutched the metal piece.

The earth shook. Something landed close to me. I lost my footing but forced my head around to see the new threat. As

I feared, the second Ghoul had arrived; dropping down from somewhere, unseen.

I hastily backpedaled, paying no heed to the zombies. My weapon felt extra tiny in my hand. The Ghoul's height and width surpassed the first. Hundreds of fingers created the bumpy texture to its massive arms. Its torso almost appeared clothed except the cloth was made out of the many faces of the dead. Their jaws hung open, and the eyes shifted in no clear direction. *Holy shit.*

Distracted by the terror before me, I fell right into Clay's trap.

With a rough tug, a long, black sleeve wrapped across my chest and secured me against my captor. The edge of his jagged blade pressed into my neck. His hood served as the only divider between us, warding off his hot breath. "Calm down, Jessebel. A little cut is all it takes."

With the warning loud and clear, he released his grip to fight the sharp metal out of my hand. It hit the ground, taking my hopes with it. The remaining zombies formed a half moon, using the Ghoul to close us in a circle.

Clay dragged the knife past my chin and up to my face. I saw my tense reflection in the black metal. And Clay's. His blood-orange eyes crinkled above his massive grin. While his skin resembled stretched plaster, he still looked younger than I expected for a mass murderer.

I felt for his arm holding the blade and tried ripping it away. The coolness of his skin sparked hope in me. I could sap him of his vitality. He'd realize it too late!

Instead of a soul, I found something more twisted than the smile on his face.

Unlike anything I'd encountered, Clay's body hosted something sinister, and the blackened roots ran deep. I felt them coiling around his muscles and poisoning his veins. And as soon as I sensed it, *it* sensed *me.*

Whatever malicious entity he inhabited responded to my touch. A thousand needles pricked my palm and dragged up my arm. A harsh gasp scraped the back of my throat. Shaken to the core, I retreated higher up his arm where the sleeve covered him.

What was I supposed to do with *that*?

If Clay had any idea what I'd tried to do, he didn't reveal it. Instead, he carried on like we'd met for brunch. "I planned this moment quite differently but couldn't shake these assholes off you. No one should bother us now."

Recalling how Guy had fallen, my heart sank even lower.

"What've you done?" I asked, looking at his mindless army.

"Them?" His dry chuckle made my skin crawl. "I gave them greater purpose! Humans aren't relevant anymore, just parasites surviving only by the coddling of angels. It really *bugs* me, you know?"

The laughter darkened. Despite his feeble appearance, his strength doubled in the mere seconds we stood there. He brought me to my toes while his arm crushed my collarbone.

"What do you want?" I spoke through my teeth and kept my eyes locked on his weapon. The metal had dents from torture under its crafter's hammer. Something inside the blade *squirmed*, like a malignant worm stuck in a tube.

He let up just a bit so I could touch the ground again. "I've been anxious since that night. I knew I had to step up my game if some random girl could interfere with my Ghoul. But you're not random, are you? A lost demon. Abandoned, just like me."

I shuddered at the thought of being anything close to what he was. "I wasn't abandoned…"

Clay swayed, swinging me along with his movements. "Sure. That's why you have no teacher. No family. Just an obsessed, ex-cultist who snatched you from your unholy cradle."

"My aunt wouldn't go near a cult," I countered, "And she definitely wouldn't steal kids."

"You've been with her all your life and I know more about that witch than you do?" he asked with a wet scoff, "I hope you aren't actually this stupid."

The longer he took keeping that knife at my face, the less sanity I had left. His chin landed hard on my shoulder. He didn't quite have the putrid stench of the dead, but that could just be the smokiness of his magic acting as a neutralizer. "Have you noticed how people are around you? Are they too nice when they shouldn't be? Or maybe, they get violent."

I said nothing and waited.

"A demon's lure can be so unpredictable. You manipulate these insects without even trying. You can never trust them. You can never *love* them. And they'll certainly never accept you." Clay's delight left his wicked tongue like a children's song. His words carved an opening in my chest so wide, it amazed me that I didn't bleed out. *No. He's evil.* Evil people lie. He was just trying to get under my skin.

"The only thing you can expect from them is their hate and their need to control you," he added, "but it's you who controls them. If you have someone to show you how."

I couldn't stop shaking. *Evil people lie. Evil people lie.*

I *did* love. I loved Naomi. I loved… Well, I grew attached to my new friends. And I knew those feelings were similar. If something happened to Zak, Tori, Guy, Jarmiel—really any of them—I would feel sad, just as I would if Naomi were hurt. That couldn't just be explained away.

Clay continued humming in my ear, "I've seen your loneliness, deep inside your dreams. Power separates us from the weak, naturally. But it doesn't have to be that way. We're more alike than you realize."

I did my best to sound firm, but the tremor in my voice gave me away. "I don't need *you*."

His spidery fingers left my shoulder and curved around my chin.

"No need to act so righteous, little demon. No one's coming that you need to impress. It's just us, two demons that the world, and even Hell, turned its backs on."

I shivered.

"I brought you a gift." He forced my sights back up at the Ghoul. I gasped as it shifted, snapping bones and creating a cavity in its chest. Bile burned my throat once more. A more put-together body was spat out from the unholy mess.

Faris slid across gravel, scraping up his back. The ink-like bindings constraining him reached his neck and across his mouth, splitting the edges of his lips. His long face looked dark purple, either from bruising or suffocation.

"How did—" I stopped. Stunned.

"He followed you here. Unluckily for him, I followed him too." Clay beamed like he expected me to praise him next. Faris already knew where to look. His wide-set eyes glowered for a moment until panic took over. He dropped in front of us; a lamb to the slaughter. All he could do was wriggle but doing so made him choke on his gag.

"What should we do with him?" Clay asked, waving his knife in front of us. Faris shriveled like a burning leaf. I shook my head but Clay's nails pressed deeply into my tender jaw.

"What?" he snapped, "He's the one who wants you dead. *Punish* the worm. It's your right."

He waited for an answer. And was he wrong? What right did Faris have to *my* life? He knew of my existence for all of a few days and decided it was enough to kill me. Sent his friends to murder me while I slept in Clove's lab.

Worm.

Looking at his pathetic shape now, he really was a cowardly worm.

Gods. I shook Clay's words out of my head with a sharp jerk. My blood raced with something other than fear. Sympathizing was idiotic, but killing Faris wouldn't give me triumph either.

"You'd spare this human trash?" Clay grumbled. His forceful huff hit my face, but then, he smoothed his rough thumb over my cheek; a bit tender and awkward considering the situation. After a long pause, his hand fell away from my face entirely. "Mistress says I should be patient with you."

Clay pointed his knife at the ground and granted me a foot of space. I turned it into four. Who was this "Mistress" and what authority did she have over him? He seemed like a loose cannon until that point.

I faced him. "You still haven't told me why you're doing this?"

Sleeplessness outlined his eyes in deep purple rings, reminding me of Guy. His pitiful tone mocked any real emotion. "They didn't tell you about Mommy and Daddy. If they did—" He stopped himself with a nervous hiccup. "*Oh.* I wish I could've seen the angels squirm. Did you finally figure it out, *Princess*?"

"I… I don't care," I said.

"Liar." Clay captured my attention with his gaze, orange shifting to red and then black. My muscles itched to strike him, especially when he started closing the gap between us again. He grasped both of my arms, the knife sandwiched between his palm and my bicep.

"Your old man lost track of his little hellspawn, and now, you'll be hunted by assholes like me. Forever," his voice trembled, along with the rest of him, "Heaven and Hell are just brats fighting over their toys. *We* can break the cycle. Never answering to any gods. Never dying."

His mania was too much. I twisted away but his hold tightened. My sleeves guarded his vile spirit from me, but I wasn't eager to feel it again. "I'll take that into consideration," I lied, "You can let go now."

"Are you even listening? What've I said that makes you think you can just *go*?"

He graced me with another troubling sneer as his forehead met mine. "We were made to be gods. We'll burn Terra to the ground and sit you on a pretty throne of ashes. Doesn't that sound fun?"

"Not really," I said, still trying to hold any semblance of power in our situation, but inside I was screaming "*get the hell off me, you're insane!*"

"Come with me." Clay's voice cracking startled the hell out of me. His menacing act seconds ago digressed into an awkward plea. Before he could continue, he was ripped from my sight by a silver hook across his entire belly. The blade whistled in the wind and threw Clay into his line of zombies.

Guy took his place beside me, breathing heavily. Sweat and blood pooled from his brow. Black ooze splattered across his shirt and smelled like putrid rot. "You okay?" he asked, his voice husky.

I couldn't tear my eyes away from the blood. "You're not."

He brushed away my concerns and locked eyes with mine. "Shit. Another one?"

The Ghoul paused, going eerily quiet before releasing a terrible roar. Guy cursed a god I didn't recognize, at least three times, and then swung his scythe.

Even with a cluster of bodies to cut through, he was able to remove the main head in one foul slice. It had several more but the abomination staggered. I had some Ghoul blood of my own decorating my clothes. *Poor* Faris, still curled up, got rained on by the stench.

I'll admit, I forgot he was down there.

Clay rolled his crumpled body from the ground, face pinched. He glared at the gray smoke that started curling at Guy's feet. I saw it too, and followed the ethereal trail up to see a face made of bone instead of flesh.

"You're under arrest if that needs to be said." Guy's naked jaw moved for the words to easily flow, even without the use of lips. The blood from his brow trickled down and disappeared into his gaping eyeholes.

"Careful, reaper." Clay's eyes burned with hate-filled passion. "Death can't take me now."

"Sounds like you can take a beating." Guy brought his scythe forward, crusted over and dripping with new blood.

Triggered, Clay leaped forward and made furious slashes of his own.

I retreated from their fight and my heel bumped against Faris. He prepared an accusing stare. The balls on him, having the audacity to scowl while completely helpless. If I wasn't concerned about Guy, I would've given him a nice kick.

Harsh intent emanated behind Clay's weapon. The brutal motions only seemed to brush the vapor-like substance existing on Guy's person. An opening presented itself, and Guy hooked his scythe into Clay's ribcage.

I clutched my own chest, feeling the pain from where I stood. The same black liquid as the Ghoul trickled down the staff. He stole back his scythe, splitting Clay down the middle.

"*Fuck*. That hurt." Clay sputtered, wobbled for a moment, but then started to laugh. The hue around his eyes deepened to a striking eggplant. "And you ruined my coat."

"You weren't lying about not dying," Guy drew close to me again; drenched in vile blood and made of bones. Somehow, those aspects about him made me feel safer. "How long do you want to play this game? Until you're in cubes?"

"Quit getting in the way…" Clay hissed and his struggling laughter became more aggravated, "You and your god had your time. It's mine now. Mistress gave me the power to do whatever I want. *Take* whatever I want. And, I intend to."

His face suddenly brightened as he pointed his knife at me. The Ghoul that Guy had just decapitated rumbled from its core. Its oozing opening from the neck stopped and, with horror, I saw why.

The new zombies sacrificed themselves to the single mass. One by one, they pressed against the Ghoul only to be swallowed up. I winced and gagged at the crunch of each bone and popping of bursting skin. The Ghoul rearranged its human puzzle pieces to create a new, monstrous shape. Eight arms. Eight legs. Eight sets of jaws.

Shit.

Clay hadn't made a verbal order but the Ghoul seemed to answer its master's distress with an angry screech. The arachnid figure bulldozed into us and I went flying into someone's car, breaking their window with the back of my head.

Stars. Growls. More stars.

I groaned. My natural stitching tugged at the gash in my scalp. Too slow. I was running out of juice. Another mortal injury and—

The Ghoul's crashing feet coming toward me. One of the eight hands crafted rose above my lying frame, but Guy brought his bloodied weapon down hard on the wrist. The fleshy mess hit the ground and the magic gluing all the pieces together came undone, leaving a pile of carnage.

"Gods!" I sat up and flung a severed arm off my thighs.

"Sorry." Guy said halfheartedly before returning his attention to the Ghoul. "Grab Faris and get out of here. Wait for Zak."

With that, Guy herded the Ghoul back with more blows. Would he really be okay? It looked like he took less damage while in his bony form, however that worked. Still, I'd rather help him than help Faris.

Ugh. Faris. The temptation to let the purifier fend for himself tickled at my conscience, but he could hardly do that. He squirmed in a heap on the ground. The Ghoul had him barreling over like a useless log, but he was otherwise alive.

It would be easier if I untied him.

Or *used* him…

His soul pulsed, polluted with his anger toward me. Taunting me. I hovered over him, earning a violent jerk. When I lifted him by the tight restraints across his chest, fear flashed across his face. He felt dense, but I managed to get him over my shoulder.

His was the only potent source of energy I could sense nearby, now that the survivors from the train were Ghoul guts, but I pushed the idea of draining his vitality out of my head. I couldn't count on him surviving my touch in his current condition. The last thing I wanted was more death on my hands, even his.

When he made a gruff sound from beneath his gag, I snapped. "Complain and I'll drop you."

Faris shut right up. With a sharp turn, I took us toward the open street. More people had fled. Thank the gods. My energy was on fumes and the need to devour Faris's soul gnawed even harder. It would be easy. I already had him in my hands…

We didn't make it far before Clay swooped in with the same, unreal speed he showed before. He flipped his blade out, ready to make a killing blow. I gritted my teeth, unsure if I should drop Faris or throw him. In a panic, I did both.

Free of Faris, I knocked Clay's hand away just in time. My pride dwindled when I realized he hadn't been aiming for me at all. He swung at me next with the butt of his blade. I ducked before it could bash the side of my head.

My heart strained to pump any faster. I longed to train with Zak again. At least then I knew I wouldn't get stabbed, but the speed of their attacks were almost similar. I just imagined my angel instead of the devil.

With a roar, I caught Clay's next swipe in my hands, clamping onto his arm for dear life. Our strength matched in that moment, which meant neither of us were moving. Clay's glowing gaze spotted Faris by our feet. His smile turned cold.

"Remember that I asked nicely first, Jessebel," he said, "But I'm not leaving empty handed."

I waited a second too long. Clay twisted us together until I was pulled into his shoulder and he drove me into the ground. He looked down on me and planted his feet on either side of my hips.

"I expected *some* resistance, but this is getting annoying." He bent down and wrapped a cold and calloused hand over the lower half of my face. Just then, Faris—*freaking* Faris—wiggled toward us. Muffled words spewed from his gag. I couldn't be sure, but I think his intent was to distract Clay. And it worked.

For the split second he took Clay's focus off me, I launched myself upward, fist raised. The *thud* from my punch hitting his groin let me know I'd hit my target well. Clay lurched. His face twisted until I thought he'd pop. I grabbed him by his torn coat collar, pulled him down, and with one foot thrusting into his ribs, sent him flying behind me.

It took every ounce of willpower not to give up and lay there, but Faris was already bumping against my leg. My labored breathing made the hairs framing my face dance. I got myself up and readied to haul Faris away again. When I stopped, Faris's brow flattened.

I gripped at his ropes. "I can't do this on my own. Can your issues wait until this is all over?"

He blinked, unable to give me a verbal answer. I wanted Faris to nod at least, but he granted nothing of promise. If Guy couldn't kill the undead, maybe Faris's light magic could.

Or he'd kill me, but I decided it was a risk worth taking.

The material refused to give way. It required something more than my bare hands, but I couldn't explode so close to Faris, if I even had the energy to. But no time for trial and error. I closed my eyes and searched my own soul for anything I could use.

Please. Help me.

Cold darkness swam behind my eyelids, but eventually, a tiny spark answered my pleas. It warmed the tiniest spot in my core, searching for a way to ignite itself. I called to it, using my emotions as kindling. *Don't blow him up. Don't blow him up. Don't blow him up.*

The rope popped.

I watched the material get eaten away by a fast acting, multicolored flame. Faris released a garbled breath like he'd been holding that in for the last twenty minutes. He cast the remaining binds off and sat in silence with me.

My senses took over; hair standing on end. Even with my back turned, I painted the outline of Clay down to his stance and position. I turned and caught Clay's knife inches from Faris's neck. I'd gotten too close to the sharp end that time.

He added to the pressure and kept me down in my compromising position. I shifted my sights around him to see Guy. The Ghoul hadn't given him time to breathe. Even the chunks he cut down would come back to life and swarm him.

Clay hissed through his tightly clamped shark-mouth, "Forget the reaper. *LOOK at me!*"

Shadows took shape around him, giving him several extra arms like a Kraken. I counted them, dread pooling in my stomach as I remembered something similar from my dreams.

The tendrils pancaked me into the rough asphalt, pounding the air out of my lungs. If he'd struck any harder, my bones would've shattered. A new split in my lip forced me to taste my own blood. My brain felt that one too.

A white light made a blazing trail in the air, piercing one of the tentacles. Clay left my body and fell back several steps. His hellborn, octopus growth flailed on his back in equal distress.

Faris crawled close to where I sat but didn't dare touch me. Smart. He glanced at me once before turning his attention back to Clay. "I have one left," he said and reached into his shirt to reveal a single, unlit bolt.

The bolt was brought to his lips, and he whispered words I couldn't hear. It responded to the secret and burned brightly. "His weapon controls the creature." Each word Faris spoke to me sounded like it pained him to do so. "Makes him powerful too. It won't break easily."

He pointed to where the knife had fallen. My chest tightened. That was an opportunity if I ever saw one.

"If you can't destroy it, get it somewhere he can't reach." Faris huffed before standing himself up. I'd wanted to hate him some more, but a molecule of respect bloomed as I watched him hobble headfirst into danger. All he had was his short bolt and one, good-working leg to carry him on.

Clay would absolutely kill him. Easy.

Even worse, I realized then that if I couldn't destroy the blade, then he'd die for nothing.

It wasn't an answer of *if*. I had to destroy it. My feet carried me toward the tiny source of evil. I dropped into a slide, ready to feel the hilt hit my fingertips, but something caught my ankles and dragged me back.

Clay had managed to remove the bolt and still had six or more shadow whips to use. Each tentacle tangled around me and cut off my circulation while the spare choked Faris until he turned blue.

Failed. Again.

The one at my throat spiraled up my head, stealing my breath. Unimaginable pressure swelled in my skull. Clay dangled me in front of him. His expression remained void of remorse as I suffocated.

I heard Guy's voice somewhere in the madness. Too far. It killed me so much that I couldn't see him. I didn't know if a servant of Death could die. My heart ached at the thought. It would've been nice having a familiar face guide my soul to my end.

"I don't get it." Clay's voice softened from his spitting wrath before. "I offered to show you real power, *real* freedom. This is the last time you can leave with me. Willingly."

Things weren't looking good for me. Even worse for Faris. Clay hadn't offered a bargain of any kind, and I doubted he would. I noticed the feeling of needles again from his corrupted soul.

The tendrils… His soul.

He wore it like a coat and was strangling me with the sleeves. His soul. Right there! Just out in the open. Touching my skin.

My resolve wavered. I didn't want to feel more of his corruption. Two seconds with his blackened soul had been enough. Absorbing it could have deadly consequences. But so could doing nothing.

My nails found the coils nearest my wrist, and I dug in deep. I fully expected hell but underestimated it at the same time.

Pain. Anguish. Rage.

Horror.

A boulder sat on my chest. Screams of the damned and tormented lived in my ears. Something sharp clawed at my skull. My stomach. Dissecting me. Sweat fell from my brow in beads, but it was worse than any fever. I let his energy in until I couldn't anymore.

When my eyes snapped back open, everything silenced. Felt no pain. Heard no sound. Heat poured out of my eyes. Something new lived in my bones. The malicious energy fractured my skeleton and begged to be released.

Clay wore a bewildered scowl. He had just opened his mouth when the chaos broke free of my body. My power trembled the earth. Shook buildings. The golden stars that usually accompanied my darkness were overshadowed. Clay's malignant arms *burst*. Each one, sparking at the ends, like a string of fireworks. He tumbled over himself to avoid getting scorched as well.

My arm snapped loud and quick, falling limp at my side. I prayed that relief would follow once I released the buzzing beneath my skin. Destroying his shadow tentacles alone cost me my left side.

Clay's eyes rattled in their sockets as he scanned the ground.

His knife. It needed to be destroyed, but Clay's energy burned its way to my organs. Just a few feet away, I saw the glint from Clay's weapon. Like a woman possessed, I willed the dark matter through me and channeled my intentions at the necromancy weapon. Every last cell of that abomination I wanted ablaze.

The demonic materials screeched at my touch. Clay's voice rang like a desperate cry but sounded miles away. It didn't matter. He'd never make it. There was a chance I wouldn't either.

I'm sorry I never found you… Auntie.

I secured my fingers around the hilt.

I unleashed everything I had; expelling the malice and freeing my soul.

But the damage was done. Pain became as familiar as breathing. There was no end to it. Fissures appeared beneath my feet from earthly tremors. Heat like fire left every cell of my body. I couldn't stop what I'd started. The world swallowed me whole.

I blinked dirt from my eyes. The whispers and tearing of my insides had gone still. I dared not imagine myself in pieces, even if it could be the truth. Remnants of my chaos cloud twinkled into oblivion; a phantom of its former glory. The clothes I'd gotten from Aiden? Burned. Wounds? Open. Bleeding.

My hands were empty. Clay's knife had gone without a trace.

Funny. I didn't feel anything. With the blade broken, my worries seemed to wash away. Was this Death? His face appeared to me, like I'd summoned him with my mind. I could recognize Guy's skeleton, or maybe it was that he wore his silly gray hoodie. My face couldn't move but I imagined giving him a smile.

I'm happy it's you. I wanted to say.

Tiny shapes, like pixels, reconstructed his human face. He looked terrible and beautiful at the same time. And so sad. I wished I could feel the coolness of his hand behind my head, but only noticed myself being lifted toward him.

Why was a reaper so sad?

The dark brows below his forehead kept shifting. Wavering breaths left his parted lips. I still couldn't feel him. What was he waiting for? I was already gone, wasn't I? My soul was his to take. I waited behind the prison of my eyes, watching as he refused to break me out with his scythe.

His eyes that always looked like they'd captured a storm flickered with lightning. Guy smoothed the hair from my eyes and held my face like a precious object.

And then, the kiss of Death.

I couldn't see much after he closed the small space between our noses. His eyelids scrunched closed before relaxing, like he'd fallen asleep.

My spirit gave a jolt. I could feel something, like I was reconnecting with the nerves in my body. It was my lips. They were cold. Cold and soft. No, wait. *His* lips were cold and soft. I only felt them because they were on mine.

There was something tender in his delivery. No possessive force. No race to satiate hunger. It was as if he wanted that kiss to be just for me. A sweet parting gift—

Crack.

Air expanded my lungs and pushed my broken ribs. I smelled blood. Tasted blood. Tears wet my face as I screamed. Guy kept a steady hand behind my head while I writhed. "Hang in there, Jess."

No! I wanted peace from before. Why had it left me to suffer? More cries rang in the air, but I noticed my volume fading. Every broken bone found its home. The sense of gravity returned, making everything feel heavier than I remembered. I felt *alive* again. And it sucked.

"Why?" I glared up at my reaper. Was I actually upset he'd saved me? No, but at the same time, I felt robbed of something. Maybe I didn't want the responsibility of harboring chaos anymore. Not once in all my life had I ever wanted to die, though.

Death's door had been that seductive.

Guy slumped over into a pile of dust and broken rock, looking notably more pale and drowsy than normal. I made a note of each vertebrae as I sat up. My hands shook uncontrollably but I crawled toward Guy anyway. "Guy. What've you done?"

"You're talking again," he said, gruffly before laying completely flat on his back. His eyes closed and I felt a pang in my chest. There was no way he could die. He *was* Death!

I grabbed him by the shoulders and shook him. "*Guy.*"

His tired face pulled down into a frown but he still hadn't opened his eyes. "Let me rest, woman," he mumbled out of his pouting lips. I hadn't noticed their fullness as much before.

"Not if resting means leaving me—*here*," I added quickly, feeling a blush prickle and spread across my cheeks, "You brought me back to life. Take some responsibility."

"You have the strangest way of showing appreciation." Guy's lip twitched. "I am sorry I kissed you without permission."

Kind of him to be considerate, however, that was the least of our worries. We were in a crater about the size of a small pool. I attempted to sit up and winced. Yup, still sore. My muscles were still tying themselves together, thread by thread. We'd only gotten a few feet deep but it looked like a mountain from where I sat.

"Did I do this?" I asked.

Guy grunted. He hadn't shown signs of discomfort other than exhaustion, so maybe he was fine. We both looked like survivors of an explosion. My blood mixed with Ghoul blood covered every inch of his clothes.

"Then the necromancy weapon?" I already knew it had disintegrated from my power, but I had to be sure. Guy coughed once, cleared his throat, and nodded.

"Faris?" My priorities thought of him last. When the dust in the air settled, I spotted something inside the crater with us.

It was no purifier.

The being before me appeared disfigured and quite large. It kept its head faced toward the earth. Pale hair cascaded over its brow. Pointed ears with several piercings jetted out from the dirtied strands. Remains of a black cloak lie in pieces beneath it.

"Clay?" I said stupidly. At the mention of his name, Guy finally stirred.

Clay muttered into the beaten dirt. His massive hands crossed over his chest and cupped both shoulders. My eyes traveled down his exposed back, counting every rib. His new figure had thicker bones but the meat, skin, and organs were vacuum sealed. How was he even holding himself up?

He lifted his face. Ridges covered his leathery skin; long scars took up so much of his backside that I thought it was a mere discoloration of the skin. His front wasn't much better. A rather brutal and jagged scar started from his brow, fell over his eyelid. It was Clay, but not the one I recognized.

All eerie smiles had gone; only dry, snarling lips and pointed teeth remained. His eyes, once bright orange, dimmed to a light chestnut.

"Clay…" but I swallowed my words.

"Don't." Clay's sharp gaze froze me further. "Don't *fucking* pity me."

Before, he had looked more human. The marks of abuse carved into his empty shell painted a sad story. Had a glamor spell cosmetically altered him before? Everything around us had gone quiet too; not a single zombie or Ghoul. Destroying the knife must have worked, and stopped *all* of his magic.

Clay popped his bulky shoulders, sounding like a roll of bubble wrap. He stood three heads taller than before and my stomach dropped into my pelvic bowl. A faint but cruel grin appeared on his sunken face. "Now, I'm really pissed, Jessebel."

With great effort, I flipped onto my stomach, reaching for Guy to clamber us out of that hole, but Clay snatched me by the ankle. Guy's bloodshot eyes were wide, awake but barely. I got even more nervous when I didn't see his scythe appear. He lunged toward Clay but received a devastating backhand. The reaper dropped back into the dirt.

I didn't even have time to scream before Clay dragged me back to him and closed a hand around my throat. He didn't squeeze but kept an uncomfortable grip and lifted me closer to his height. "Why'd you have to do that, huh? You know what that weapon cost me?"

I wriggled his grip, knowing damn well it wouldn't help. There was no malice to steal anymore. He was practically hollow. To my horror, crumbs of living shadow started collecting themselves from the rubble. They crawled up his legs, forming one dark mass that umbrellaed over us.

After all that, I'd done absolutely nothing at all.

"Yes… That's true…" Clay said as if answering his own thoughts. The way his eyes lit up again, returning to their unnatural orange made my whole body shrink. "I expected too much too soon. You can't possibly know real suffering. Just look at you. Soft. Pretty… Can't even leave a mark."

His spare hand gently traced the side of my face. I thrashed, feeling his nail, now sharp and claw-like, pierce below my cheekbone. Seconds of intense itching later and the slit sewed itself up.

"No one hates your face." Clay's own face deadened, lost in some trance he put himself under. "You're… sheltered. It's not your fault."

His demeanor changed. A smile split his already dry lips. I couldn't see them but I heard someone saying the same words as Clay, like he was an echo. A woman; her haunting, cunning voice traveled like the wind, passing too quickly. Had it come from the shadow?

My heart just about burst when I heard more movement outside of our hole. Clay's head snapped in that direction as well, and a bright light blinded us for a second time.

Clay fell, dodging a second holy bolt. His weight almost crushed me, but he caught himself and caged his arms above me. The missed fire lodged into the earth, hissing and spitting.

Faris sat on his knees at the edge of the crater. The shock of his failure made the skin around his face tighten. Clay spotted the purifier and glowered. "You aren't dead yet?"

Faris could've easily aimed that bolt at me. He wouldn't have missed either, with me being slow and injured. Before Clay could move, I grasped his arm still pinned above my head..

"Clay…" My dry voice reached his ears and he turned his neck. No more. I couldn't handle watching anyone else die by his hand. "You came here for *me*."

He arched his brow. I achieved one thing at least; getting his attention. Pretty sure I hadn't passed out yet purely out of spite, but I wavered as he leaned in closer.

"You are kind of stupid," he said, and I couldn't tell if his exhale was out of disappointment or the opposite. The dark matter on his back morphed and the tentacle shapes returned, but instead of being attached to Clay, they became their own entity.

A feminine, hourglass image matched the voice I'd heard earlier. Most of her had been made up of shadow, save for the single emerald eye in the middle of her blank face.

"*All children must learn.*" She sounded softer than a witch's lullaby but every nerve and muscle in my body recognized her corrupted energy, like a trauma response. Clay's magic came from her. I recognized the scent of her toxin.

The shadow woman draped her many arms over Clay's shoulders, each one waving slowly like we were under water. "*She is infantile, compared to me,*" she said, "*Do not be dismayed, for she does not yet see.*"

"Who the hell are you?" I squeaked out.

There was no mouth on the she-devil. Her whispers entered my mind instead. *"The Queen of Desire. Mother of the Deprived. Forge to the Dark Materials. Goddess of Malice."*

Well, fuck.

She presented herself like a goddess worth knowing, but I had my doubts. Especially to leech off Clay. In a weird and creepy way, she seemed to comfort Clay. Almost like a guardian.

"So much of your father." Her daydreamy comment made my guts twist into knots. The pressure from her presence made the back of my head throb.

I released a shuddering breath. "My father really is—"

"*Asmodai.*"

The pit widened in my stomach. I'd heard that name; *seen* it in Jarmiel's books, to be exact. My mind went blank. I already knew the truth, but hearing his name…

I cursed and banged my head back into the crater once. Clay and that woman were still above me but I didn't care. Avidus, The Kingdom of Lust and its ruler, The Demon Lord, Asmodai. My *dad*.

Had Naomi known the entire time exactly who my father was? *Is that why she never came back for me?* Every small memory of my aunt and our life together played like a film reel that caught fire. How had no one else known about me until now?

No. Someone had.

I lifted my gaze back at Clay. Strands of his dull hair seemed to reach for my face. The shadow woman remained close but did nothing to interfere. I pegged her as the evil puppeteer pulling the strings but she showed too much patience.

For a moment, there was peace behind his fierce eyes. "That's right. You can't hide anymore. The angels can't offer you anything. That reaper even less."

A life of hell. Darkness eating me alive? Could I really deny that it had been the most powerful I'd ever felt? His energy, while disturbing beyond imagining, had worked like a tool in my hand. I'd almost been able to bend the chaos to my will.

Just as I felt the seeds of hell sprout in my heart, a star burned brightly behind Clay's head. I mouthed the angel's name it belonged to. *Zak*.

Zak appeared from above like a champion of white flame, escorting heaven's fury. His sharpened, crystal gaze pierced through Clay and his mistress, finding me. At the same time, the wings of a much stonier angel flew over our heads. Jarmiel carried a white gold pistol that cast an ethereal glow. He aimed high at the one-eyed shadow lady.

"*Vileth*." Jarmiel addressed her with an authoritative ring.

She released a hiss that could have been conjured by an entire pit of snakes. Her tendrils beat rapidly, showing little concern for me or her pupil. I heard the gun go off, followed by a stream of brilliant light. Vialeth's shrieks shattered the night.

Clay's anger returned with a vengeance. His hand closed around my skull. I was hauled up into his chest, facing out to see the mayhem. His hunched posture encased me like a cocoon while his hand continued to crush my face.

"Fucking angels…" he spat, "Don't get any closer."

I pushed away from his scarred body but to no avail. Zak landed before us, casting a blinding light and searing the tips of my hair. Angels used to scare me but I just about peed myself at the righteous fury that scorched his entire being.

"Clayton." Zak's voice altered as if he held an amplifier. "Let her go."

Was that Clay's formal name? Had Zak finally figured out his real identity? But the way he said his name with such familiarity…

No. They knew each other.

Clay released a hoarse cackle. "*Me*? You're the ones keeping her."

He dragged us a few steps back and out of the crater. Carrying me around was nothing. I felt like a doll in his grasp. Zak pursued, taking careful steps, assessing Clay's outline, as if looking for an opening.

"It doesn't have to be like this," Zak said, his crystal eyes meeting mine.

"You angels and your false heroism make me sick…" Clay brought us even further, and I noticed Guy wasn't in the crater anymore either. "I'm going to end you all."

Another gunshot and burst of light hit just below my vision. Clay fell to his knees, giving me a chance to pull away. I looked up, expecting Jarmiel to descend on us. Instead, a purple blob wrapped itself around Clay's face.

"Let her go, you ugly creep!" Tori's shrill voice cried as she blinded him with her stuffing.

She really knew how to make an entrance.

A skeleton with black wings dove in next, like a vulture ready to pick a carcass. The scythe he carried cut through the air, missing me completely, but I heard it meet Clay's neck. Smoke whipped around us, flinging Tori away. I caught her with one hand while the controlled storm knocked Clay completely over.

Clutching Tori, the smoke cradled around us both, and reeled us into Death's cold embrace. I froze, face to face with the meatless figure until it revealed Guy to me once more. He kept one arm around my waist, scythe in the other.

A much deeper voice than anything Guy had unearthed before left his lips. "You won't touch her again."

Clay slumped. Jarmiel's bullet had made it clean through his leg but the hole kept sizzling. The gash Guy made left a wide opening from his ear down to his chest, adding more line work to his already tortured flesh. When he moved, I thought his head would roll clean off.

I brought my hands around Guy's shoulders for support, ignoring the gore coating *his* chest. Clay's pointed teeth ground together as he watched, hatred boiling behind his eyes. Even with his vocal cords *surely* destroyed, it didn't stop him from sputtering, "What threats do *you* have, reaper?"

"Stand down!" Jarmiel boomed from behind.

The angel's fight came to us. Vileth's shadow roamed the earth, clawing and tumbling over itself to reach where we stood. With Jarmiel closing in as well, Zak acted fast. He wielded his flashy sword made entirely out of light, sparkling with brilliant ferocity. It ate away Vileth's inky malice, like watching the sun rise before night was through.

Cries that could only be born of Hell ripped through the tentacled monster's throat. She'd taken another bullet from Jarmiel. Zak's sword carved into her mass, creating waves of heat that even reached Guy, Tori, and me.

The battle seemed over, but I felt Clay's gaze on us. On me. He did nothing to help Vialeth. He had to surrender. It was over but I continued to hold my breath. Part of me hoped he would give up and avoid the agony his mistress faced at the hands of the angels. Who had he been before to receive those scars?

I wanted to pity him but his past couldn't justify everything he'd done; all the lives he'd stolen. Whatever happened to him next, he'd asked for it.

Another cry, and Vileth's form reduced to a whirling vortex. She kept Clay protected inside her torrent. He stared at me a moment longer before turning his attention to the angels.

I couldn't tell what happened next.

With the gesture of his middle finger, he disappeared completely into Vileth's darkness. After she enveloped him, she shrank into a tiny sphere. A silver glow pulsed once before the ball swallowed itself up.

"*Clayton!*" Zak's eyes burned as brightly as his sword. He plunged the weapon down where they once were and pierced the ground. His efforts failed. They were gone.

If angels swore, it would have been an excellent time. Zak bit his lip so hard I thought he'd chew it clean off. Jarmiel landed beside his partner, wings switching off like a light. He shared in his partner's disappointed silence by placing a hand on Zak's shoulder.

Guy loosened his tight hold around me. In response, I leaned into him. I wasn't ready to stand on my own just yet. His voice rumbled like a dark summons in my ear. "Sorry, I took so long."

I flattened my forehead against his chest. Tori's teddy bear did the same to me, although I could feel her fidgeting in a desperate need to unleash every thought and feeling she had. Guy hadn't asked me to stop, so we stood like that for a long while.

Zak arrived, just like Guy said. It was over.

Clay was gone.

34

T he streets looked like a truck carrying bodies crashed and spilled everywhere.

I knew they'd been dead well before all this, but the sight burned into my brain. One peek at the unbound Ghoul was enough to make me consider adding more disgusting fluids to Guy's shirt.

Ambulances arrived along with more peacekeepers and law enforcement to examine the damage. Two more angels arrived that I hadn't seen before. Even their reverent demeanor was challenged. Guy got a medic to look at him while I sat alone in the back of a peacekeeper car. Human medicine couldn't do better than my natural healing could and, thanks to Guy, I was almost completely whole.

I reached for my lips, trying to remember what he'd felt like. But everything was numb. I thought I should cry at least or excitedly retell the events when asked, but I didn't say a word. My eyes dried out as I counted the tiny stitch marks in the gray interior without blinking. I kept one of the ambulance's spare blankets draped over my shoulders to hide my tattered clothing.

On a maybe positive note; Faris survived.

The peacekeepers and purifiers who'd followed Zak and Jarmiel arrested him. He sat in the back of an ambulance, also silent from what I could tell.

"Winters?" Jarmiel came around to the vehicle again. The door hung open so he could check on me periodically. His perfect, smooth features scrunched but otherwise he kept a professional tone. "Jess. I don't want to rush you, but we should talk."

I nodded. The conversation I dreaded had inevitably come. What would they do now? EXO couldn't allow demon royalty in their ranks. At least, that seemed damnable to me.

Zak made himself known by clapping his friend on the back. "Let me handle this, buddy. We all know you're not so great with sensitivity."

The air got warmer, along with the space around my heart. I barely glanced up at his bright and cheery face. Jarmiel muttered incoherently. I thought he would argue, but he left to assist the others.

I let my eyes shift to Guy with his medical team, getting some quick patchwork done on his forehead. It looked like they had to cut him out of his shirt too; no loss there. He gave me a gentle raise of his lips. Thanks to him being terribly difficult to read, I didn't know if that was a "goodbye" smile, a "you're screwed" smile, or a "don't worry about it" smile.

"Jess." Zak's voice made me jump. I forced myself to meet his twinkling eyes. The dawn crept its way up around us, still shrouded by the tall buildings. He raised one hand and opened his palm to me. "Go on. Gods know you're seconds away from keeling over. What a night, huh?"

I let out a sharp breath. He offered his life to me, as he had many times. I wanted to scream; shake him by his shoulders and demand to know what his problem was.

"You knew what I was," I said.

Zak's hand retreated an inch. "Not hungry?" When all I did was glare, he added, "I wasn't positive. But I had an idea."

"When?"

"Soon as I met you."

I squinted at him through a sheen of tears. "Why didn't you say anything? Why *recruit* me? The hell is wrong with you?"

He didn't flinch at my rudeness. "I told you I wasn't a perfect angel. It's true. I used my authority and position to bring you to EXO. I wanted to be sure my hunch was correct."

"Did you know Clayton too?" I remembered the way he'd cried his name.

His handsome features never tarnished, even as he frowned. "I knew him when we were younger. I'd wanted to help him too, back then. I didn't realize he was The Necromancer until recently. I thought he died." Hurt pooled in the crystal lake of his eyes. "Maybe he did, in a way."

"Who is he?" I asked.

"Someone a bit like you with even worse luck. I guess it's not surprising he reached out to you. He's always been the lonely sort."

"He's a demon."

"A changeling demon, yes. They switch places with human infants. It's a rare occurrence and even rarer if the changeling survives. Neither of the children can consent to it, obviously, so, it's traumatic for all parties."

I nodded. "What now?"

"Now?" He huffed, either impressed or offended by my sharp tongue. "Now, I ask for your forgiveness."

My chest had already puffed out, ready to release more of my angst, but his words popped me like a balloon. "I'm sorry?"

"No. I'm sorry." He got on one knee just outside the car and my jaw dropped. I was torn between being appalled and embarrassed. His head dipped into a bow, like a dutiful knight. "Jess—" he began.

"What are you doing?" I asked.

"Proposing. Obviously."

Heat consumed my face until I felt my heartbeat in my cheeks. Zak widened his glorious smile. "I am being a little serious. I'm proposing new changes to our contract since the old one is void. Ya' know, since you ran away."

"Right…"

He rolled his neck and shoulders and cleared his throat. "I want to offer you another chance with EXO but you can also walk away. Right now."

I opened my mouth but half a vowel came out. We all needed a meal and a nap before having these serious conversations. Neither of us was in our right mind.

"You were approached by Clayton with a similar offer, right?" Zak said, grimacing a bit, "I'm delighted you turned him down, but truthfully, you have little reason to trust me either. When I offered to bring you to EXO, you knew you were given the illusion of choice. Not very *angelic* of me, I think you said. And you were right. I still want to figure this out together and I believe we can, but if you want to find your own way, you can."

"The other angels won't let you do that," I said, knowing better.

He shrugged and his wavy hair bounced. "I'll give you a nice head start before chasing you."

"Why?"

"Redemption, maybe? My intentions are good but never perfect." His lips thinned into a sad smile. "Although, I would miss you terribly if you left. So would a certain ghost and her pet reaper."

I snorted. The illusion of choice, indeed! Especially with him pouting like that, who could turn him down?

Zak looked out toward Guy's ambulance and paused a moment before chuckling. "I have a feeling he's loyal to *you* now."

"Loyal to me?"

I looked back and caught the cold stare Guy gave Zak.

That was weird.

"Where's Tori?" I asked. The battle replayed in my head and I couldn't imagine her stuffed animal making it out unscathed.

"She's good. Her little teddy lost an eye but we'll stitch it back up."

Thank the gods. My harsh exhale tussled the hair framing my face. "I was happy when Guy told me it was a misunderstanding. I didn't think I'd see any of you again. Not in the best circumstances, anyway."

"*This* counts as the best circumstance?"

Zak gave the scene of carnage around us a scrutinizing look over. It was awful but as always, he somehow made the situation lighter. He baited me until I laughed but too much giggling triggered my sore ribs. "Remind me again why you're not in an ambulance?"

"They have plenty of people to worry about who can't heal themselves," I said and coughed before mentioning that Guy had kissed me back to life earlier.

"Jess. You are the weirdest demon I've ever met."

* * *

We crammed together in the same car. We were going home.

Yeah, I chose to go back. I never wanted to leave in the first place. As I sat there between Guy and Zak while Jarmiel had the passenger seat, I wondered if it was the right thing. I still didn't know what my presence would bring to EXO. My friends.

Zak moved his legs a *lot*, and kept the window rolled down. Normally, he would've flown away at the option of driving, like fleeing the plague. I knew he stayed for me because he kept my hand in his, even after I told him I healed. Every bounce of his knees, I felt. Really annoying and kind of adorable.

His energy worked like soothing drops of oil on my rusted bones. My body was fine. My spirit—I wasn't so sure. Zak made conversation with Jarmiel and the driver; occasionally answered a call or text. News about our evening and Clay's escape traveled fast. We had no idea where they disappeared to, though Jarmiel suspected the Hell realm. Jarmiel mentioned something about portals but I didn't have the brain capacity to take that in or ask yet.

Guy fell asleep with his arms crossed over his bare chest. A blanket also covered his shoulders, leaving his chest bare. The breeze from Zak's window pushed his soft, mousy-colored hair. I couldn't blame him for needing the rest, but then, I heard him stirring. The dark circles made his waking eyes shine.

I slipped my hand out of Zak's.

"How's your head?" I asked.

Guy mumbled. "Better than my arm. Being alive can suck."

"That's so weird for you to say."

"I know."

"Do reapers not heal?" Almost all manner of supernaturals could to an extent.

"I'm in a different state of being right now, so it's… slower," he said, "What about you?"

"I think the venom trip is over," I offered.

"Thank gods for that."

"Tori?" I inquired. Her purple bear rested on the floor of the car between his feet, still unresponsive, but her eye had been replaced with a new button.

"We'll see how she feels about my craftsmanship." There was a pleasant silence between us until Guy noticed Zak hanging halfway out the window like a dog. "So, he really talked you into staying, huh?"

I glanced over at Zak, speaking to somebody on his phone while the wind whipped at his face. The recipient sounded annoyed; I could tell by how many jokes Zak made to purposely aggravate them.

"Not sure how he managed it." I smiled. "He made a funny comment about you."

"Hm?" He questioned with a lazy grunt.

"He said you were 'loyal' to me."

He resumed resting with his head leaning back against the seat that time. I watched his eyes close again with his lips stuck in a soft smile. No answer, but he also didn't deny it.

The sun lit one half of his face. A contrast shadow brought attention to the very faint mark of his cleft chin. I felt strange, one for creepily observing him while he tried to nap, but also because of the tingling in my chest.

I wanted to tell him how grateful I was that he came to find me. He did what my aunt didn't. Couldn't? I didn't think anyone would care that much if I disappeared.

Guy popped one eye open in my direction. "I go where you go."

I slumped back into my seat. Where there was chaos, surely there was Death. Maybe that was all he meant by it.

Grim. Very grim.

But I couldn't sit. Couldn't wallow. Learning what I could about my lineage and my power was the best thing I could do. Not just for me but for everyone else too.

Something fuzzy moved out of the corner of my eye along with a sleepy moaning. Tori's voice mumbled from the bear's stitched lips. "Where are we… Jess?"

She scrambled up Guy's pant leg and was in my lap in seconds. "I'm so sorry I let you go with that creepy vampire! What about Faris? Where is that sneaky, no-good, fancy-haired, bastard? And why is my left button lower than my right?"

Guy snorted and gave me an apologetic stare from over her purple head.

35

The only people who really knew everything that went down were Guy, Faris, and myself.

So, naturally, all three of us, along with Jarmiel and Zak, sat in Zak's office with Raguel. The morning rays made Raguel's white hair blinding, quickly countered by his demeanor which did not shine. He rested his elbows on the desk so he could hide his lips behind clasped hands.

"Raguel, if I may—" Zak spoke up first.

"No." His blinking slowed as he addressed Jarmiel instead. "And Aiden Blaxill?"

"Still missing," Jarmiel said.

A brief wave of anger shot through me, dulled by curiosity. Aiden was missing? Surely, he was off enjoying himself in the city. It did seem strange that he returned to EXO so recently, only to leave again.

"Pity. I had questions for him," Raguel said, "That was his final strike but we should locate him all the same. Now, I want to hear from you three… Where to even begin."

He turned his big head like a rotating fan to meet all our faces. "Faris Caldwell. You attempted to murder Jessebel Winters on two accounts. Went so far as to gather others in your cause. The purifiers who stayed behind have been captured and questioned but several disappeared. Prison makes the most sense to me."

Faris sat three chairs over beside Jarmiel with cuffs around both wrists. His head hung low. He made no attempt to defend himself or his actions.

"However," Raguel added, "You revealed that The Necromancer had been visiting your mind, inserting dreams and manipulations that had made you fearful of Miss Winters. Is that correct?"

I gripped my armrest. Clay failed to mention *that* part of his grand plan. The whole time I thought I'd been alone with my hauntings but he was riling up the purifiers for a witch hunt. The brilliance of it made my blood boil.

Faris lifted his eyes to meet his superior. "Sir. While he encouraged my actions, my feelings about the matter remain unchanged."

"Explain." Raguel's majestic tone had an edge that time.

Guy had been sitting stiffly since we arrived but at that, he dropped his folded arms. His fingers curled into themselves as he rotated his shoulders. The sharp look in his eyes said that he was *very* engaged in what the purifier had to say next.

Faris went pale. He held on tight to his answer but eventually said, "You know what she is. She may not be cruel but that doesn't change anything."

It was like hearing my own thoughts and insecurities come from someone else's mouth. The worst was the silence in the room that followed after like they all agreed on some level.

"What exactly did The Necromancer reveal to you in these dreams?" Raguel asked.

"Cataclysm."

I shifted uncomfortably in my seat while Faris continued. "If she were an imp or any lesser demon, I wouldn't question the angel's judgment, but she's not. Chaos won't bring peace."

Raguel gave him a solemn nod. "You openly admit your doubt in our judgment. Fear is only natural but to wish death on another also *won't* bring peace. A versed purifier such as yourself must know this."

More thoughtful silence.

"Yes… " Faris finally uttered.

"You will sit in a holding cell until the council is ready to pass final judgment," Raguel said, and two peacekeepers let themselves into the room. They waited for Faris to stand on his own. He didn't resist or spare a complaint before leaving with them.

I'd sleep better knowing my assassins weren't sharing a dorm next to mine, but mostly, I remained confused. He didn't even apologize. After saving his ass, he'd left with his convictions still intact. He must truly hate me.

It was down to the five of us. Six, if you included Tori, fast asleep again.

Raguel returned the conversation to his angels, "We've identified The Necromancer?"

"Clayton Cassidy," Jarmiel replied but there was hesitation in his voice as he waited for Zak to speak first. "He seems to have survived or postponed his initial death."

"You were suspicious from the start," Raguel addressed Zak that time, "I doubt the outcome would've changed had you known sooner. He is beyond saving, Zakiel."

"You all knew him?" I shut my mouth after interrupting. Luckily, Raguel didn't appear bothered.

"The Cassidys lived in a small pocket just outside of Volhold," he said, "Well known to their neighbors, active in church, and very social until their first child was born. They claimed their son passed at birth. After that, they became recluses. Neighbors reported glimpses of the boy wandering in their home, never with his parents or brought outside. We were asked to look into the matter but it took a plucky young angel to really verify the rumors."

Everyone's head turned to Zak at once.

"I was younger in earth years then, but Jarmiel and I were still friends," Zak explained, "We found a maid who'd quit working for the Cassidys. The family had bought her silence. Apparently, Mrs. Cassidy had a healthy son but, overnight, he became malnourished and grew pointed ears and teeth. They had no idea that their son had actually been taken and replaced with a changeling. They're rare half-demons, usually born with defects and get sick easily."

I knew the story could only get darker the deeper we went. "What happens to the other baby when they're swapped?"

"We don't really know," Zak said, his frown deepening, "Some believe a demon mother keeps them. Not that they would survive in Hell."

Hell hosted all manner of evil, but imagining tiny babies being taken and then expected to survive in alien circumstances crushed my heart. Not only that, but abandoning the changeling child to do the same.

Hadn't Clay said something similar happened to me? His story about Naomi "adopting" me differed slightly from the one I'd been told all my life. Naomi said I was abandoned by witches, but Clay made it sound like I'd been kidnapped too.

Who were these witches that had me in the first place, or did they ever really exist?

"What happened to Clay then?" I asked.

"The family never introduced us to Clay but we saw him. *I* had, for sure. Spoke to him once through a basement window. There were clear signs of abuse, not just on his body but his spirit. We had a plan to approach the family but when the day finally came, everyone was dead." Zak paused. "We believe Clay's mother killed herself, but it was clear Mr. Cassidy attacked Clay, and Clay retaliated. Not a pretty sight."

"There was a burial for the family. Clay was taken to be examined and later cremated," Jarmiel added in a reverent tone,

"An investigation is pending to confirm that his demise never occurred. We also searched the Ghoul corpses and were able to identify *both* Mr. and Mrs. Cassidy."

I let out a soft gasp. Clay survived and dug up his parents? So much cruelty and haphazard crafting went into the Ghoul's design. He made them into the monsters he thought they were, bringing them to life with his hate.

I noticed Raguel watching me with peculiar interest.

"You feel conflicted," he said.

Something bumped against my knee. Guy was nudging me with his elbow. He hunched over, arms resting on his thighs. The miniscule touch helped comfort me, even a little.

"I know what he did is unforgivable," I started carefully.

"Harming a child is also damnable."

Was I crazy or did I see pride in Raguel's gaze? Never thought I'd see a pleased expression from him. "Having a compassionate heart is a show of pure kindness, something Faris could benefit from" he said, "Even so, don't blind yourself to the danger Clayton presents now."

I nodded, still disturbed in my thoughts. At least he didn't seem angry.

When Raguel asked about Clayton's dark companion, Jarmiel answered with a twitch of his neck. "Vileth has latched herself to the boy."

"I see." The white-crowned angel let out a drawn sigh. "The council is impatiently waiting for a full report. Vileth making a move is no small act from Hell. However, I'm certain they'll expect more on *this* one as well."

His big finger aimed at me. "We've been able to do things your way for the time being, Zakiel, but the council wants to know how Clayton's hell-blade was destroyed without an angel present."

Zak's grin widened and I actually felt the anxiety flickering in my body, wondering what crap he'd pull next. "I told you, she's a special case."

I turned to Guy, who had been silent the entire time. He seemed to be in his own world, eyes wide, taking in Zak's words and imploding with some internal crisis.

Same, though.

Raguel cracked a smile too, but I couldn't tell if it was out of joy or frustration. "We will look into the matter further, with or without your help. If Uriah comes for her, I can't stop him."

Zak's grin was strained. "We'll deal with that if the time comes."

Raguel altered course again. "Mr. Shepherd. Miss Winters, will you recount the night's events, and whatever else you believe could help with this case?"

Guy and I took turns retelling the events that led to us finding Clay; the purifiers in Clove's lab, the vampires, and the train station. I still had a gallery of questions and concerns of my own, but at least I knew the angels weren't going to kill me. For now.

"You two were on your own against a demon lord," he said, "Vileth rules the sinful Kingdom of Envy. It sounds like she only visited in spirit. Still, no lord should be able to trespass here. She and Clayton escaped but thanks to you, they lost a powerful weapon of dark matter. EXO appreciates your efforts."

"Thank you, sir," Guy said.

I copied him, but didn't know if we really deserved the praise or not.

* * *

We were dismissed shortly after, not entirely free of our duties but Raguel mentioned something about how we "mirrored the undead." I couldn't see myself, but if my eye bags were anything like Guy's then we were in bad shape.

Jarmiel and Zak followed us through the courtyard outside. Outside was quiet, odd since it had been midday. I wasn't entirely sure where we were headed. No one said.

"Your angel weapon is a pistol?" I asked Jarmiel, who lifted his brows at my sudden question.

"Yes," he said.

"Not as cool as a sword, right?" Zak interjected.

I hummed, pretending to consider the matter deeply. "I think a pistol makes more sense than a sword, actually."

Jarmiel held his head a little higher while visibly Zak mourned his betrayal with a solid pout. "What are you talking about? It's way prettier than a gun, for one. It's an extension of your arm, doesn't run out of ammunition—"

"Technically it does since it's made of light," Jarmiel countered.

"Let's all remember which of us almost sent you to jail, Jess."

"Very mature." Jarmiel clicked his tongue as his phone rang. "I don't want to take this."

"They always call you, and you're the least pleasant of us two," Zak said.

"Seems I'm not the *least* pleasant when it comes to you and I."

The angel took his call, but before walking off, looked over his shoulder at us. "It's good to see you alive, Jess."

I wanted to say something back. Thank him, maybe? But he spoke into his phone again and I lost my chance.

Guy gave a half-hearted chuckle. "You two were made for each other. Like an old, married couple."

The reaper yawned and glared at the bright sunlight. Come to think of it, I don't think either of us had slept in over a day. The energy Zak gave me kept my eyes open like a strong, morning coffee. I'd crash and burn soon.

"Neither of you need a trip to Clove's?" Zak's shifted over both of our faces. "I like tough soldiers but don't be negligent."

Oh, no.

Clove. The last thing I remembered about the doctor was Tori locking her in a closet.

I cringed. "I guess I should apologize to Clove."

Guy raised a brow. "What did you do?"

"Nothing horrible," I said and looked at the ground, "Just trapped her in a closet."

"Right… I'm taking a nap." Guy dragged himself and Tori's bear toward the dorms. I knew I could head there too; back to my room. The home I'd adopted into my heart and hadn't realized yet. I stood in place a little longer, listening to the breeze with Zak who also hadn't moved.

"So, your ambitions for a 'new dawn' haven't changed?" I asked.

"Not at all," Zak said, with gusto, "Now I have a princess on my team."

"We're a weird team," I said.

"Demon. Chaos. Princess. Peacekeeper. *Jess*. Maybe you're a bit of everything, or something between? Whatever you wanna be, I don't think we need to take *chaos* so literally." When I gave him a look he dished one right back. "Hey, sassy. In order to make new and beautiful things grow, sometimes old things have to be destroyed. I'm just saying, let's stay positive."

"Still sounds crazy," I said but I liked that ideology better.

The daylight brought so much peace, I could hardly believe the night before happened at all. We had the courtyard to ourselves; every simple flower held more vibrancy than I remembered. I didn't mind staying frozen there in time for as long as time allowed.

"You were sad earlier," Zak said, "Want to talk about it?"

I'd forgotten that I'd been in a room full of super-attuned angels.

"I know Clay's not a good person," I said, "I just had a weak moment."

"Weak?" He repeated, letting his jaw fall open. "Weak, she says! Like you didn't sacrifice yourself to stop a demon and his magic knife."

Warm embarrassment flooded my cheeks. "Guy told you?"

"Just a performance review, Jess. Don't get so embarrassed. Although, some caution in the future would be appreciated. A little less *dying*, and I think you'll pass with flying colors."

I snorted. "That easy, huh?"

"Yup. And look, about Clayton. If he'd had better circumstances, I'm sure his future could've turned out differently. But hurting others is his choice. We can all choose something different for ourselves."

I bit my tongue, not wanting to announce how alike Clay and I could've been; his story being the darker side of the coin. Both half-demons who grew up in hiding. I battled with resentment toward my aunt, the woman who was more ghost than guardian at that point. But Naomi never hurt me. Secrets and all, she'd been loving. We celebrated every holiday together. She taught me how to read and write, baked my favorite treats, and gave me plenty of work to keep me involved in our hidden world together. We laughed at absurd television and gossiped about our grumpy neighbors.

She changed her entire life to have me in it. It could've turned out so much worse.

Clay was proof of that.

"Hey, you." Zak snapped his fingers in my face. "Still with me? Not regretting your decision, already?"

To that, I leered. "I swear we've had this conversation before."

"You must make me anxious. I keep needing reassurance." He grinned all over again before shooing me off. "Go on. You deserve a nap too."

*　*　*

I reached the dormitory doors and stopped. Why was it so hard to walk through? I'd just faced a demon lord, but potential awkwardness with my roommates sounded worse somehow. After a few controlled breaths, I pushed myself through.

As soon as I looked up, I saw *everyone*.

Several realizations came at me in an instant, like how I'd kissed Max to near death. His blond head aimed readily in my direction all the way from the couch. They probably heard me coming, and heard me pausing outside for forever.

"Newbie!" Barrett sprang from his spot next to Max. He planted his feet inches away from mine and scanned both sides of my head. I probably smelled terrible but he didn't mention it that time. "And just what the hell were you thinking, huh?" he asked.

"I, well—" I stammered, unsure of which offense he was referring to. Blowing up the gym? Running away? Being drugged in a vampire nightclub? Destroying a whole intersection? Actually *dying*.

"Back for more?" Max scoffed but didn't sound as pissed as he looked. It may have been the first time he'd spoken to me without growling.

"What he *means* is, you're pretty cool and we'll keep you around," Barrett said with a wide smile and thick canines, "Hope you're ready for training because I call dibs on being partners."

"Really?" I asked.

"Anyone who can squash a necromancer is cool in my book."

A new white line decorated his throat like a necklace, beginning at his ear and ending somewhere below the collar of his shirt. I'd almost forgotten, but Zak told me Barrett was in the line of fire when my chaos magic went wild.

"Barrett, I'm so sorry." I pointed toward his scar. Had he been human, he'd probably be dead. His thick, shifter neck saved him that time. "Actually I'm sorry to all of you…"

"What, *this*?" Barrett asked, pride enhancing his stance, "Thanks but I'm fine. Makes me look tough."

Yara stood off in the kitchen boiling her tea. She wore a cunning grin but otherwise acted like I hadn't run away and had the craziest night of my life. "Water's hot if you want some, killer," she said.

"Thanks." I didn't know what to do with myself. The whole reunion went much differently in my head. Darren and Mallory's attendance bewildered me the most. Where did they stand with Aiden's actions, if they even knew about them? It didn't seem like they'd been waiting long; both just lurking in the corner.

Mallory looked me up and down from behind her curtain of white hair. "I see you're alive."

"Yeah. Sorry about—"

What was I sorry about? *I* didn't make Aiden disappear. Still, if I had a brother, I guess I'd be worried.

She gave me a dead-eyed stare. "You know, Jessebel is a harlot's name."

My mouth gaped open like a fish. She didn't expand on that either. Whatever she'd needed off her chest or to accomplish, apparently that had been enough. Mallory turned on her heel and made for the elevator.

"Thanks for that," I mumbled as the doors slid shut.

There was the cold welcome I was expecting. Darren had apparently been satisfied with the verification of my arrival as well. "See you," he said, also taking his leave but up the stairs.

"What's she talking about?" Barrett asked, "Anyway, we should hit the gym again. Oh. We'll have to wait for that but we can use the track—"

"Let the girl rest, Barrett," Yara sang, "Gods know she needs it."

His shoulders slumped. "Fine, I was just excited to hear what happened."

"We'll talk soon," I said, "I just really need to change… and shower."

He grimaced. That he seemed to agree with. After a few goodbyes, I was free to return to my room where my bed called to me. Opting for luxury and laziness, I waited for the elevator to get me.

Everything was just as I left it; sadly that included Tori's message in the carpet that made everything smell like a pantry. I dropped a towel over the mess to be vacuumed later. The only thing out of place was the small box pillowed in the middle of my duvet.

There was nothing on it, save for EXO's logo of a wing. No name or card. I lifted it with skepticism at first, wondering who left it and why. It appeared opened and taped shut again; also suspicious. The seal was simple enough to tear. Inside, I found a silver container branded with another wing and circle.

A company gift? I continued my exploration of the weird box and found a black screen shaped similarly to the phones I'd seen everyone else use.

They trusted me with a phone now!

My grin reflected back at me from the glass. It came with set-up instructions, my own EXO profile verification codes, and a… *bank account*. Wildly curious, I started up the phone and did exactly what I was shown to do. It took a minute but eventually, I was able to create a login. My eyes widened.

I had money.

Ding!

And a new text message, apparently.

A random number lit up the screen with a tiny green envelope. I let my finger hover over the icon and read my new message. The person's name had already been added to my contacts.

Guy -

Tori is very apologetic about the carpet

Hope you're settled in

My smile grew.

Cute.

Not sure how he had my number already unless he was the one who left the phone. It wasn't so different from using my old phone so I quickly typed a reply, only to realize I was recording audio instead, which definitely contained me giggling.

"Oh, shit?" I tried stopping the red glowing button and pressed send instead. "*Shit.*"

Guy -

Need some help later?

"You…" I growled and carefully tapped the screen that time.

Yes.

Guy replied with the image of an upward thumb. I could almost picture his smug face but I was too happy to be mad for long. My fingers hovered over the keys, wanting to type out a proper "thank you" for all he'd done for me, but maybe "proper" couldn't be done over text.

Something else was hidden in the box. I nearly missed it. My old phone. The one I thought I'd lost at Peter's. Its thick brick shape dated itself next to my much newer device from EXO.

A note was stuck to it: Don't do anything stupid.

I crumpled it up and turned the phone over. A large crack went across the screen from when I threw it at Peter's wall. How many minutes did I have left on that thing? It turned on with half battery life; half more than when I'd lost it.

The first thing I hunted for were messages from Naomi. I gave the device a minute to catch up. The dinging was out of control, updating the many texts and calls I received in my absence.

Not *one* was from her.

Not a damn thing.

I did my best to ignore the sting. She couldn't have sent me *something*? Anything. A text from a different phone, even. I would've settled for a magical carrier pigeon, but no. All of my messages and calls had been from… *Peter.*

My heart stopped. I felt my tongue becoming dry like sandpaper. Peter had been trying to reach me the whole time. Were the messages written with hate, demanding some sort of justice for what I'd done? Although, if Zak told him or his family about my placement in EXO, that might've satisfied them enough.

The texts played on my curious soul; the same curiosity that brought me to his room in the first place. I held my thumb over the power button until the screen went dark.

"I'm glad you're alive," I said to him, and to no one, before sitting on the floor.

It was for the best. I doubted I'd ever see Peter again, anyway. Having his messages stare me in the face sucked, but the guilt didn't sink its claws in as deeply as before.

I knew what else was on that phone. Photos of life with Naomi. It would be like looking at a life I didn't recognize anymore. Our pretend life that she'd seemingly given up on. All things that would hold me back and answer nothing.

Dragging my dirtied sleeve across my cheek, I picked myself back up. The rock I used to contact Naomi, and failed, still sat collecting dust on my desk. I took it, along with the old phone, and placed them both in the drawer.

It shut with a defining thud. I couldn't wait around and hope any longer. She'd find me one day, or I'd find her. Maybe there was more to her absence, or the explanation was simple, and she wasn't coming back. Until I knew, I had to keep moving forward.

Heaven knows what Hell had in store for me next.

THE END

ACKNOWLEDGEMENTS

First of all, thank YOU for taking the time to read *Mercy and Malice,* the first in the *Chaos Between* series! I'm sure every author has said it before, but it's been a wild ride and I would not have gotten here without all the love and support in the world!

My loyal writing group, Melissa, Ashley, Zach, and Kayla. Saturday morning meetups have not only been a delightful respite, but they've really kept me focused. Not including the many hours we spend mostly chatting and drinking Starbucks, which are also delightful. You all inspire me and I'm proud everyday of how much we've accomplished, together and individually.

A special shout out to my editors, Meghan and Melissa. The whole terrifying process of ripping my manuscript to shreds and piecing it together into something prettier was less painful because of you. You really saw what I was trying to create and were willing to listen to my millions of questions. Not only your craft, but your patience and tolerance are both deserving of an award.

John, Rhonda, Alexandra, Katherine, and Jake have assisted my family in creative endeavors more times than I can count. This book is no exception. I appreciate the work you've been willing to do to make this all possible!

To the busy-bodies who are always working on their next writing project and various life adventures, Darla and Lara, thank you for taking the time to read my manuscript over and over… and OVER again. You've delivered solid feedback in my hours of need, not to mention read the same chapters as many times as I have.

My lovely, lovely family. I've always been able to look to you for support.

Mom and Dad, thank you for nurturing my creativity all these years, even if I like vampires and live in fantasyland half the time. Because of your endless support, I feel like I have the confidence to create and pursue my goals. I'd also like to thank you for your special appreciation (maybe avoidance) in all the gore and language in this book. Much love.

To my super-cool, totally excellent, goofy-goober brothers, James and Dylan, thanks for a childhood full of imagination and pure silliness. It inspired me. For sure.

More awesome mentions: my sister in-laws, grandparents, crazy grandma Tina, cousins, aunts, uncles (yes, we have a BIG family), and close friends. I want to say thank you for loving me and my fascination for fiction.

Penelope. My joy and my light. You were a newborn so you don't remember, but I got the bulk of my writing done with you asleep next to me. Having you is an inspiration. You create so much magic. You are magic.

And to my husband, Blake. My person. My artist. If you hadn't talked me out of several imposter syndrome meltdowns, then I probably wouldn't have made it here with this book in my hands. Thank you for caring about my dreams even when I felt like giving up on them.

Love you all!

RUIN & REDEMPTION

This *again?* A dark ring of sweat on my pillow gave away the damning evidence of my gods-awful sleep. The back of my throat burned in an effort to swallow.

Nightmares.

More nightmares.

Except, these I couldn't remember.

Three months had passed since my encounter with Clay. He hadn't shown his face again, not even in the form of dreams. Aside from trauma sweats, the only thing I could remember from them—or remember feeling, rather—was compression on my chest; the same hopeless sensation I'd felt when I couldn't save a single person on that train car.

Something *wriggled* behind my eyes.

It slithered about, twitching like a distressed muscle. Not as painful as my starvation headaches, but equally disconcerting. And then, it silenced. My tongue sanded the roof of my mouth. I needed a drink, or a shower. With great effort, I threw my legs over my bed and waddled into the hallway, bouncing off of door frames in my clumsiness.

Once I made it to the bathroom, I splashed my face in the sink and spat out the gumminess that coated my teeth. The cold water shocked my senses back to life—too quickly. My fingers trembled against the porcelain sink. After a deep breath, I looked up at the mirror and froze.

Gods…

My *eyes.*

Black. So black, I should've been blind but I could see clearly. Glowing copper streaks highlighted my irises, glittering like wicked embers. A dark vein rose to the surface of my forehead and began sliding across like the tail of a serpent…

ABOUT THE AUTHOR

aylor is a subjectively superior sentence seamstress. She prefers the world of fiction; enjoying magic and whimsy to beautify reality. Really, she's a huge dork, loves her nerdy husband, video games, movies, and of course, reading!

A great deal of her time is spent with her adorable family, at a beach or a coffee shop, typing away to expel the stories dancing around in her head.

For more book-related fun, visit Taylor at taylorgoode.com